PIVOT POINT

CLIVE HALLAM

authorHOUSE®

AuthorHouse™ UK
1663 Liberty Drive
Bloomington, IN 47403 USA
www.authorhouse.co.uk
Phone: 0800.197.4150

Published by AuthorHouse 04/11/2019

ISBN: 978-1-7283-8052-0 (sc)
ISBN: 978-1-7283-8053-7 (hc)
ISBN: 978-1-7283-8051-3 (e)

Print information available on the last page.

*Any people depicted in stock imagery provided by Getty Images are models,
and such images are being used for illustrative purposes only.
Certain stock imagery © Getty Images.*

This book is printed on acid-free paper.

To Jak

Pivot Point is a work of fiction, written at a time of immense change and contention in geopolitics and culture. Questions surrounding the states of Israel and Palestine and their place in the world sit at the centre of this story. Opinions expressed by the characters herein are theirs alone and do not reflect those of the author. Many places in the world are used in this book, in an entirely fictitious way. Any resemblance to actual events, political views, or persons, living or dead is completely coincidental.

Those who do not remember the past are doomed to repeat it.

—Jorge Santayana, 1863–1952

Prologue

It was a clean shot, middle of the forehead, about an inch up from the bridge of the nose.

A crack. Another hole formed, slightly to the right, causing them to morph into one large ragged rent.

The third ringing shot hit the target centre mass, bursting the heart, confirming death. Nodding contentedly the shooter placed his gun, a Glock 17, on the counter of the shooting range. Not a chance in the real world.

'Not bad.'

The man looked across at the face that had appeared around the cubicle divider. He would never admit it, but he enjoyed his partner's rather parsimonious attitude to his abilities. 'Are you going to have a go?'

'Watch and learn,' came the reply.

Three flat barks—fast, loud, and harsh—signifying a heavier weapon. He knew the other preferred the Beretta 9mm; the damage it inflicted on the paper target drew testament to its stopping power.

'Those were okay.'

A light, disembodied laugh reverberated in the still air. 'Let's have a closer look, shall we?'

The two targets travelled towards them on the pulleys and stopped just beyond the shelf. The man took in both. His colleague's bullets made a perfect triangle of overlapped holes, dead centre of the target. 'Lucky shots,' he observed.

'Poor loser more like,' retorted the other. 'Anyway, I think you owe me a drink, Mr Logan. After all, I won best of three here, and I wouldn't want to embarrass you further.'

'Who says I'm embarrassed?'

'Your lack of ebullience, my dear.'

Steve Logan safetied his weapon, holstered it, dropped his ear defenders to the counter, and walked round the dividing wall. 'I am not lacking any enthusiasm, Ms Murtagh, merely ensuring that this one victory doesn't go to your head.'

'Oh sure.' Brooke Murtagh mocked him. 'You still owe me a drink though.'

'Come on then. Hand in your weapon, and I'll take you down The Dog and Duck.'

'God, you so know how to treat a lady,' she breathed back at him.

He pulled her close. 'Of course I do. A pint of IPA, with pie and peas is on the cards for you, my dear.' His lips brushed hers, the slight tearing of the skin as they parted sending a thrill through him.

Her deep green eyes glinted with the Irish ferocity that was her birthright, her mouth flashed a smile. 'Just the one pint? Afraid I'll beat you at drinking too?'

The laugh was good-humoured. 'No. One pint because I have a very important meeting in the morning, and if we start drinking tonight, I shall be late and, thus, in very serious trouble.'

Murtagh smacked his backside. 'Okay, old man. Let's go for pint, pie, and peas. If you're very lucky, we might have an early night.'

Logan flashed his security ID at reception as he walked through the lobby of Vauxhall Cross. 'Morning, Jimmy. How are you today?'

Jimmy raised a wearied eyebrow and returned the smile. 'Not bad, sir. We have a heightened security status today, sir.'

'Oh yeah? What is it this time? Somebody stolen the boss's Jag?'

'The usual, sir,' Jimmy replied, ignoring the officer's flippancy. 'With all the talk in Washington 'bout peace in the Middle East, there has been increased communications traffic among Islamic Brotherhood, Al Qaeda, Palestinian groups. You name 'em, they're making noises. The Israelis are sounding off about the Iranians and their "nuclear" programme,'—he jabbed the air between them forcefully—'as if we haven't heard enough about that. They're threatening air strikes.' Jimmy's bulk heaved in mock disillusionment. 'I wish they'd all give it a rest.'

Logan shrugged. 'People are always talking, Jimmy. It's not a crime ... yet.' He crossed the foyer, eschewing the lift and climbing the stairs two at a time to the third floor. There he made his way to his boss's office. Amanda Galbraith waved him in as he made to knock on the glass door.

'Morning, boss, what gives?' He slid into the chair opposite, an easy unconscious movement.

'The Jerusalem Accord.' When he raised an eyebrow in inquiry, she continued. 'Negotiations are going well between the Palestinians and Israelis, but we expect a backlash from extremist groups.'

'Jimmy on the foyer was saying things were heating up.' Catching Galbraith's disapproving look he moved on quickly. 'Which side?'

Galbraith arched an eyebrow. 'Which do you think? Hamas and Hezbollah are already ramping up the rhetoric; Iran is "helping". IS and Al Qaeda are threatening to suicide bomb Haifa, and Lebanon is stuck in the middle. Meanwhile, Israeli hardliners are blaming Iran for everything. We expect something to happen soon.'

Logan mulled over Galbraith's words. The US secretary of state's relentless diplomacy was being hailed across the world as a landmark event. Yet dissension of John Kemble's work was inevitable—on both sides. 'So ...?'

'We start watching and listening. If something does take off, we want to be on top of it.'

'What do you want me to do?'

'Be ready.'

'Well?'

'Hmm?' Logan stared at his idev, scrolling the news items, only half aware of Brooke's question. The cushion landed expertly in his lap. He looked up sharply. 'Sorry. love,' he replied, chucking the cushion to one side. 'I wasn't all there.'

'You don't say?'

The smile was sheepish. 'What's up?'

Murtagh bit back the exasperation. 'How did it go this morning?'

'Oh that.' Logan shrugged. 'Not much to say really. Galbraith just talking stuff we already know. The Middle East is in a state, and something might happen any time.'

'And what are we supposed to do?' Murtagh glimpsed the momentary indecision in his stare.

'That's it. We're just supposed to sit and wait.'

'And we're going to do?'

Logan grinned. 'What we do best—some digging.'

'Are we ready to roll?' The reporter checked his earpiece as the cameraman nodded in affirmation. Nervous energy rippled the reporter's skin as he readied for the first live report of his career. With his foot tapping the sandy ground, he tried to block out the *crack, crack, crack* of light weapons that seemed to close on him with each breath.

The splayed fingers of the cameraman counted inexorably to transmission. In his ear, the anchor was cueing him in.

'We go over to our correspondent in Gaza, Dan Gardner. Dan, give us just a flavour of what is happening there at this time.'

'Good morning, Andy. Yes, it's a fluid situation here, with Hamas committed to securing the Strip on two fronts. To the east, over my left shoulder, Israeli defence forces have been massing on the border, threatening to cross from the direction of Sa'ad with huge numbers of tanks and troops. Israel cites concerns over Hamas's apparent inability to check IS. Away to our south-west, IS continues to consolidate in the settlement of Nuseirat. Hamas are desperate to neutralise that threat before the IDF decide enough is enough and do the job for them.'

'Tensions must be running deep there at the moment, Dan?'

'Very much so, Andy. The city of Gaza itself has almost become a Hamas enclave, suffering air strikes from Israel and suicide bombings from IS.'

'So what happens now? Surely Hamas can't fight on both fronts. Isn't there a sense that IS only have to hold out for Israel to defeat Hamas and then the Strip belongs to them?'

'In fact, Andy, some observers believe that to be the sole plan of IS. Their activity has been to harry Hamas, worry them, and inflict enough damage for the Israelis to defeat them once and for all. Hamas's survival depends on whether their cousins, Fatah, will come to their aid.'

'And what of the current round of talks brokered by the United States between the Israelis and the Palestinians? What is the chance that could improve the situation in Gaza?'

'US Secretary of State John Kemble will be hoping he can negotiate a sustainable deal that will give Hamas a breather. Since IS have lost so much ground in northern Iraq and eastern Syria, they're eager to move in on Hamas territory and wind up Israel enough to start an all out conflict. If they can do that they hope to generate more support for themselves and transfer the focus of their caliphate. The US is desperate to stop that from happening.'

'What prospects are there for peace in the Middle East, Dan, with this toxic mix?'

'That's the question testing everyone right now. Israel is disinclined to give Hamas anything other than rope to hang itself with, making the same mistake others have regarding IS. They believe they have the answer to the Islamic State group, feeling their experience with suicide bombers prepares them for the ferocity. They are still geared for conventional warfare.'

'And what of Iran?'

'Iran continues to skirt around the borders of this particular issue. The Iranians are fundamentally opposed to Fatah, Hamas, and IS, all Sunni Muslim factions. However, the actions in Gaza give the government in Tehran the opportunity to work behind the scenes against Israel. There are reports, as yet unsubstantiated, that Iran is rearming Hezbollah in Lebanon while The Iranian Navy has been conducting manoeuvres in the north of the Red Sea.

'Turmoil fogs the area at the moment. Everyone is hoping the US administration will be able to bring the parties together for a peace that transcends history and cultural differences. The alternative is a bloodbath, as Israel, Hamas, IS, and Iran all vie for power over the region.'

'Dan, thanks for that report. That was Dan Gardner for BBC World News in the Gaza Strip.'

2

The flight from Heathrow finally touched down at Ben Gurion Airport twelve minutes late. Logan stretched his legs and shuddered as the pilot taxied to the hardstanding. A yawn escaped his tired lips.

'It's a hard journey, isn't it?' His flight companion was an old woman who was lined beyond belief but had humour in her eyes.

He smiled back. 'Yes. Yes, it is. It's the hanging about at Istanbul that does it for me.'

'Me too,' she assured him. 'Still, home now. What are you doing here?'

'Business.'

'Not a good time for business out here,' opined the old lady as she rose to get her bags from the overhead locker.

He reached up and handed her bag down to her.

She thanked him.

'What makes you think that?'

'Oh, you know, all this hoo-hah with the accord thing.' The woman bustled into the corridor and headed to the exit, Logan in train. 'Nothing good will come of making a deal with the Palestinians. You mark my words.'

The following day, Logan reflected on the woman's words while in a café in downtown Tel Aviv. Watching the news being played out on the TV, he couldn't help but feel she had hit the mark with her observation.

Whatever the channel, the same message played, albeit in a spectrum of tones. It ranged from a hand-wringing liberal to hawkish right-wing Likud supporters. Malbert was fighting a lonely battle over the Jerusalem Accord.

He sipped his coffee while ruminating on the situation. *I need some background on this,* he decided, *something to contextualise all the hyperbole.*

The British consulate was situated at the confluence of Arlozorov Street and Ha-Yarkon Street. From a third-floor office, Logan looked out over the marina, where yachts swayed in the warm breeze while heading in from the Mediterranean. It was a beautiful day with a bright sky of the deepest blue—simple and clear. If only humanity were so uncomplicated.

He turned as the room's door opened with a flourish. The person who entered was young, fresh, and overly enthusiastic. Not what he was expecting. Should he have been expecting something?

'Hi. You must be Steve Logan.'

'Hello. You are?'

'Penny Lane, cultural officer.' She sat down at the table, placing files on its surface.

The officer watched each flex, movement, and tic.

Lane regarded Logan in return. He recognised her look—the unrequited desire to be a field officer, although turned down perhaps by her superior. He'd have to tread carefully.

'Thanks for seeing me, Penny.'

'No problem.' Frost. 'What is it you want?'

'Jerusalem Accord. What's the feeling on the ground?'

Lane shrugged. 'Did you go out on the streets when you got here?' After he nodded, she continued. 'People are fearful in the main, worried that anything Malbert signs will denude Israel of its hard-fought security, of its decades of fighting its neighbours and ruling over the Palestinians with an iron fist.'

You don't like being here, Logan thought while silence filled the small room.

Lane coughed, and a little colour rose in the high cheekbones. When it was clear Logan wasn't going to respond, Lane coughed again, flashed another frosty glare at the officer, and continued. 'So they're vocalising their fears. Everyone is running scared of the Palestinian question. What will happen if they gain political status on the international stage? After that, there is concern over the settlements. If the Palestinians build a power base, will that give the Arabs, Syria, and Iran the ammunition to bring down the State of Israel?'

'You make them sound paranoid.'

Lane considered the view out the window before responding. 'You think?' The sarcasm washed over him. 'Israel is a very paranoid state and for good reason—good and bad.'

His head dipped in acknowledgement. 'What's the response?'

'I-I don't understand.'

'What does Israel do about it?'

Lane mused a moment and then said, 'The elections are in the next week. Malbert is on borrowed time. Olmet is more hawkish and will probably try to duck out of the accord—unsuccessfully I'll add. The United States will not allow it, and Israel will *reluctantly* follow through.'

'Okay. What about the Palestinians?'

'Al-Umari is a poster boy for both the West Bank and Gaza Strip. Everything he touches at the moment turns to gold. They love him.'

'All of them?'

Lane allowed a smile for the first of time. 'No, not all of them,' she conceded. 'Qureshi doesn't like al-Umari—'

'Qureshi?'

'Sorry. Qureshi is a key Palestinian leader. He lives in Jerusalem and is very belligerent towards both Israel and what he sees as the soft approach of al-Umari and the authority.'

'Hmm. Your analysis.'

'Analysis?'

'Yes. What do you think will happen?' Logan indicated the files before her. 'You've already compiled evidence, but you're unsure how your boss will take all this extracurricular activity.'

Lane blushed, her fingers caressing the files. 'There are rumours of some conspiracy, but that's all they are.' She shrugged. 'You know what conspiracy theories are.'

He smiled. 'Yes, the product of lazy minds.' It was the moment that brought down her barrier.

'Logan, this is the Middle East. Everybody hates everybody else. They're all looking for a chance to beat the other. Israel is seeking to maintain its position and keep Arabs in what some Israelis consider to be their place. There are many political, religious, and cultural views that, brought together, would create the perfect storm.'

'That's a cold assessment.'

Lane shrugged. 'You live here long enough, you get cold.'

'So,' he continued after a moment's silence, 'what would you suggest?'

The shrug again. 'Passive surveillance? Tell the Americans? I don't know. I thought that was your remit.'

Logan smiled. 'Very good.' He paused and pointed to the files. 'May I?'

Lane looked from them to him a couple of times before pushing them in his direction. 'Fill your boots.'

Galbraith closed the last file and then pushed them slightly across her desk, her fingers drumming them. She asked Logan, 'What are your thoughts?'

'The girl's an asset. You need to bring her on board.'

'That's great, but what about the Israeli situation?'

'I think Lane has delivered a good assessment, given what is known.'

'Which is?'

'Israel is always going to try to protect its arse.'

'Nothing new there, but where does the conspiracy Lane talks of play into this?'

He shrugged. 'Not sure … yet. This isn't actionable intelligence, is it.'

Rhetorical question, Galbraith's nod the merest of affirmations.

'So. We watch and listen, wait till there's something to tell Washington.'

'Well, that was a waste of time and money,' Galbraith rebuked caustically.

Logan flushed.

She gathered the files, before sighing and pushing them towards the bin. Pausing, she caught the look of alarm in her officer's face and stopped. 'Okay, I'll consider them further, but you need to drop this for now and get on with the day-to-day.'

'What about those?'

'You're right. Lane has done a good job with them. They still mean absolutely nothing. Israel is doing what it always does, and the Palestinians are getting what they always get. So we leave the US to get this accord thing out of the way, and we can get on with other stuff.'

Logan let the words sink in, said nothing.

'Now, what about Ukraine?'

'Hmm.'

Galbraith arched a brow. 'What?'

'Is this latest UK policy? Leave things to the Americans and look the other way?'

His boss paused. 'Why are you getting antsy about this? The Americans are leading on the Middle East, always have. And we provide the specialist support.'

'Why don't we keep Lane on this, get us the background so we know when to move.'

Galbraith regarded her officer. 'You like her.'

He shrugged.

'Okay, we'll keep her looking. Do we know what for?'

'No. But Penny will.'

Galbraith smiled. 'Okay, let's get *Penny* on the case right away.'

3

The photograph lay on the stained dark wood café table, its surface shining in the rays of the late morning autumn sun. To the casual observer, it looked like any typical family picture: a contented woman, glowing in the presence of her two children, who grinned at the camera's eye, perhaps beyond—at the photographer. Its colours were faded from too much exposure, as if this was the only reality of their existence.

Lifting the picture to better appreciate the focus of his affection, the man confirmed to himself they were the only thing that mattered in all he did. He stared wistfully at the busy street beyond the café. People strolled along, couples, families, laughing and enjoying the last rays of warmth before winter settled over Geneva, but Johannes Olsen could only remember his children from afar and wonder how it had all gone wrong.

Another sip of coffee, a bite of the consolation pastry he'd purchased, hollow comfort when judged against the loss of a family. Once upon a time, life had seemed so idyllic. An Israeli wife, beautiful and brilliant and someone he'd felt honoured to have won the affection of. They had met when he was new at the CERN and she an aspiring and inspiring scientific journalist. Suddenly, almost, he remained in Geneva, and she was nearly two thousand miles away—with their children, Greta and Benjamin, building a new life on the West Bank. Self-pity welled, not for the first time in the last few months. When did it end, this feeling of disconnectedness, being adrift? He didn't understand – it had all been so easy, early on, when passion and love had been on tap. Constantly. And then, it had crumbled, dissipating in a haze of silences, odd looks, and exasperation. There had never been anything overt, a glance, shake of the head when he had been irritable with one of the kids—or both—comments when parents were coming over.

Olsen bit back the sigh that threatened tears and glanced at his watch. Another hour of Saturday morning filled with regret and boredom, instead of ballet lessons or football in the park. He wondered what they were doing now, in Tel Etz, the settlement they had been whisked to. Two years had passed, without him touching, smelling, or feeling them in all that time. His only connection was through relatives, upset at how Judith had handled the split, informing him of their growing up. There were newer pictures of them now, Greta beaming with pride for getting a prize in ballet, Benjamin growing tall and strong and helping his grandpa move logs on the farm. But it was this weary, weathered photograph that was the anchor—this was from before. He could pretend, while he drank coffee alone in this Swiss café, that things hadn't moved on.

If he saw them now, what would he say? He realised he didn't know, and maybe it wouldn't matter. They were his kids, and he would always be a father to them. And even though they didn't know him anymore, that bond couldn't be broken. The cup touched his lips before he realised he'd lifted it. The liquid inside was cold, and he grimaced before swallowing it.

'Can I help?'

Olsen started, glancing round at the intrusion. A young blonde woman with a tan that spoke of another land stood smiling at him.

He shook his head nodded mutely. 'No, thanks.' Fumbling in a pocket, he dropped some small change on the table. 'Thanks,' he mumbled again as he swept up the photo.

'No problem.' Her smile remained fixed in the way all waitresses' smiles did, Olsen figured, when the tip was too small. No matter, it was all he had. He pushed through the doors and made his way into the muted warmth of a September day in Geneva. What would it be like to be in Israel now? he wondered as he wandered along the street.

Bleached bones shone gold in the early morning sky, their shape providing the best available cover for his watch, as the operator lay in the remains of some large animal. The arching ribs snagged the corner of his vision as he scoped the far mountains and the plain in between.

Deliberately, the watcher zoned out the glare of the sun-whitened ribs and the haze of the desert heat. Fortunately, the body was long dead and stripped of muscle, cartilage, fur—anything useful in fact. Just the one vestige of life remained on its sandy deathbed.

Behind him lay the last line of mountains before the Jordan, the river that had steadfastly maintained its timeless journey to the Gulf of Aqaba and the Red Sea, while religious, cultural, and political upheaval had raged along and across its banks. Before him, the focus of his attention, was a sandy desert bounded by stark arid mountains. In the middle distance, shrouded by the haze, stood a collection of structures and buildings that could have been a small town but were the Dimona nuclear research facility—alleged centre of Israel's nuclear weapons production at one time.

Ranger Conway had been in the area for about a fortnight, having made a HALO drop from a Globemaster out of Incirlik, Turkey. Altitude had been necessary in order that the aircraft flew far enough north not to alert the trigger-happy Israeli defence forces that jealously protected airspace over the facility. He had glided in, using a batsuit until he was low over the hills to the north of the site, and then, using his parachute, had put down out of sight. Once he had stashed his means of ingress, Conway had started observing. Traffic in and out was high, considering the place was supposed to have been mothballed in the nineties. *Guess business was being resumed*, had been his first ironic thought; it wasn't his job to figure why that might be the case, though he could guess. John Kemble, US secretary of state, was advertising, very publicly, that he was close to the prime minister of Israel and Palestine's president signing a historic agreement, effectively ending several millennia of conflict. It would be easy to find any number of hardliners, on either side of the political divide, willing to mess up Kemble's hard work. If anybody had the means to inflict maximum damage, it was the Israelis.

Surveillance over the following twelve days had served only to resolve his initial feeling into a full-blown assessment, coloured with a certain amount of genuine concern. More and more movement, military and civilian, had travelled down the single road to the plant. Much had been construction traffic; other vehicles had pulled secure containment for what could only be nuclear material. Someone was reactivating the facility; something was brewing.

Conway continued to regard the site through his powerful binoculars as he considered events. Enough speculation—he was due to report tomorrow. Today, he needed to get over the border into Jordan to arrange his extract. Carefully, he eased his body out of the carcass to check the time, careful about exposing his position.

Sitting in the dirt in the lee of the small rise, the ranger methodically checked over his equipment, ensuring everything was correctly stowed. He pulled his idev from his wrist and shook it out; the information device sprang into shape and assumed a hard oblong, on which he began typing. Conway loved the new devices, made from graphene, a substance that could be made to assume just about any shape, surface or device, with the right amount of programming. His report was nearly complete, but there was plenty of time to submit it once he was safe. He allowed himself the luxury of a bite to eat before heading for his extraction point. He pulled back his *shemagh*, which he had tied round his head as camouflage—after all, nobody would see him here—and unwrapped a ration bar.

The bar was at his lips as the bullet scythed through his forehead, forcing his head against the rock behind in a way that would never hurt him. Another projectile followed it.

As he scrambled over the loose rock to the dead man, the Israeli operator scanned continuously for any backup. Even though he'd been told the man was alone, it paid to be alert. The American was dead for sure, and, satisfied, the Israeli began stripping down the corpse of any identification and checking his gear off. That the body was also an operator was evidenced by the calibre of equipment the Israeli tallied—a Heckler and Koch 416 assault rifle, an MK 23 sidearm from the same company, and a Gerber multitool, among others confirmed his suspicions. These he stowed away; good weapons were always useful to have at hand. He piled everything else for disposal.

Eventually satisfied, the man stood, looked up to the skies, and sighed. It was shit that it had come to this, but even the spies of Allies could not be allowed to report what was happening at Dimona. The man would be disappeared, a tragic accident in the depths of the Negev Desert.

He tapped a code on the idev around his wrist. 'Ready for extraction.' He listened. 'Understood.'

Cutting the communication, he lifted the large pack, with all the American's kit, and shouldered it before moving off down the track to his rendezvous point. The corpse would be left there—after all, the wildlife needed to eat, and that was the best, most complete way of removing the evidence.

The drone pilot watched the story unfolding on her screen and felt sick through to her stomach. Her finger had caressed the trigger since she'd seen the Israeli move into position, but her orders had been very clear—Ranger Conway was expendable.

In a small office at the Dimona site, an air force lieutenant also watched the scene unfold on the screen before her. Her high-altitude spy drone relayed pictures real-time, as it had for the last eight days, as soon as the man's presence had been picked up. His MO had nearly always been the same—bad tactics on his part. They had been able to easily work out his likely behaviour.

The lieutenant activated her table screen and, swiping the dialler app, tapped in a number. A quiet voice infiltrated her ear, acknowledging the call.

'Situation resolved.'

'Any response from our friends?'

'Negative.'

'Excellent. Well done. Maintain your watch.'

The lieutenant acknowledged the order and ended the call. She looked at the desert, tranquil once more. How much longer would that be the case?

'This shit will be the death of us, of everything we've fought for since '48.' The old man spat in the dirt as he took in the city, sprawled over the landscape before them. His companion remained silent; after all, what could he say? It was the truth.

The city of the Dome of the Rock—the dichotomy of Arab and Jewish culture and heritage—lay before them, shining in the dawn, divided between two cultures and separated by millennia of prejudice and divine intervention. The heritage of birthrights, brought to one point of geography and time. The quiet extended across the hills, until even the birds seemed expectant.

'Is it a good idea for us to be giving away so much ground Moshe? Do you believe we are doing the right thing to give them'—the old man waved a hand dismissively at the hills behind them—'so much rope with which to hang us? Well?'

The last word was barbed, demanding a response, and Moshe steeled himself against the flinch he felt in his belly. Moshe wasn't his name, just as David wasn't his companion's name, a device to protect reality from prying ears. Such tactics had changed their relationship, once close; it was a necessary evil to ensure ultimate success. 'It is the way of the world, David. We must bend sometimes. The cedar that doesn't, breaks and dies. So we flex and remain patient. Our time will come.'

David, his beady eyes set in too much flesh, peered at the younger, fitter man, appraising his colleague, perhaps for faults, and then hawked and spat more phlegm in the dirt. He had come to trust the younger man's observations implicitly and enjoy their philosophical debates. But now was not a moment for such deliberations. David felt a need for action, which he knew must be tempered. 'Maybe. It's just my frustration. But, Moshe, we must be ready to strike when the time is right, when the cost to them will be so high they will not be able to repay us.'

Moshe nodded. 'That time will be upon us soon enough.' Sometimes he hated the way he had to placate the other who, despite that, he considered a friend. 'We must prepare as we always have—in the shadows, away from the eyes of those who would stop us.'

David nodded, taking in his beloved city. His gaze rested briefly on the golden dome, symbol of struggle and hatred to him; it was all about hate, cultivated for thousands of years, ensuring neither would surrender to the other. He, as with so many before him, sought a final solution (the irony of those words was not lost on him), one to settle the conflict that had shaped both civilisations. 'So what of those preparations? How go they?'

Moshe withdrew an idev mini from his pocket and held the screen before him. It blinked to life and in a moment, he had a file on the information device's screen. He passed it to David. 'These complete "The Seven".'

David glanced briefly at the names before him and looked over. 'They are all onside?'

Moshe considered the question for question's sake. 'All understand what this venture is about. They realise the opportunities and the risks and what failure could mean for all of them.'

The older man grunted. 'So many say they understand, until the reality breaks, like a storm tide, on them.'

Moshe quelled the sigh threatening his lips. 'It is always so, David. And yet, where else do we start?' His companion seemed lost in thought, as was his way, and Moshe stood patiently waiting.

'At the beginning. Always at the beginning.' The breeze carried the older man's soft exhortation away from Moshe and over the unknowing city. What did it seek? Peace? It would search a long time … unless.

Moshe remained patient.

'Organise a meeting.'

Moshe nodded.

'I want to address them. It is time to put thought into action.'

'I'll sort it. When do you want to meet?'

'The day after tomorrow. That meddler Kemble is set to announce his "accord".' David punctuated the hot afternoon air with fat fingers. 'We must change before it is thrust upon us. Now is the time for us to shape our destiny. Nothing must stand in our way.'

'It won't. They are aware of what is at stake.'

David grunted. 'So, they should be, if they wish to continue to see this great nation stand firm against its enemies, old and new.' His fists clenched spasmodically with the anger he felt. 'I cannot believe their betrayal of us, after all we have done for them!'

The other nodded. 'It grates, but they're responding to other voices. We have never been truly loved in all the world. Why should that change today? Only we can alter that, David, only we.'

David caught the expression in the other's eyes and grimaced; they were kindred spirits. 'You are right, Moshe, as always. Continue with your plans. I need to get on. After all, I have an election campaign to win.' The laughter tumbled from his lips like a torrent as he saw the look on Moshe's face. 'However this turns out for you and me, we both win, my friend, if we stick to our plan.' He beckoned the other to him. and they embraced, kissing each other's cheeks. 'Shalom, my brother. God is with us.'

Moshe watched David walk to his car, climb in and drive off, speeding down the dusty track to the black tarmac that headed into the city. Only then did he reach for his mobile. He pressed a speed dial number and let it ring twice, cancelled the call, and waited for a moment before redialling.

A voice answered almost immediately. 'Hello.'

'Inform the others a meeting is called. They're all to be ready.'

'Very well. When is it to be?'

'Day after tomorrow.'

'I'll advise them.'

The line went dead. Moshe expertly dissembled the cheap mobile, crushing the SIM card; poured lighter fluid over the components; and set them on fire. He watched the blue flames crackling across the bent surfaces, before grinding them in the dirt. Another batch of mobiles would be needed; such actions kept them all secure.

Moshe regarded the view David had lingered over for so long. Everything came back to this one city, this one pivot in the history of two cultures that, over the years, had pulled in other civilisations in the same way quicksand pulled in the unsuspecting. He and David had planned long and meticulously, as was the Israeli way, for this moment. So many points in history were converging on this time, this place. And both knew something would change the destiny of this area of the world for all time. It was a matter of whether it would be Israel who took control or other forces.

Who would be victorious? He shook his head; in the coming battle, he feared no one would be.

Illinois Senator John Harrington Kemble regarded the report open on his idev, idly swiping the device's screen to read another page of his crowning glory. The 'Jerusalem Accord', as he increasingly referred to it as, would be the defining moment of this administration for sure, and he would forever be known as the architect of the Israeli-Palestinian peace, which had eluded all Western diplomats for decades.

Kemble was a career politician who'd lucked into a Democratic nomination several years ago, having helped his predecessor overturn a fraud investigation that could have run into million dollars. Thanks to that intervention, Kemble had developed a friendship, running campaigns, lobbying, attending balls, doing deals, shaking a million hands, before being handed the reins only a few short years before.

Patiently he'd built his reputation as a negotiator and communicator, listening first, doing second. In that way, he'd helped bring about sweeping changes in health care, budget reduction, and administration. Now he was confidante to the president of the United States of America, performing the role of secretary of state in a way that was astounding to everyone who figured he was a tyro despite his age. A smile played on his lips, and he ran a hand through his thick grey hair, luxuriating in his self-absorption.

The knock on his office door made him start. Straightening his tie by reflex, he acknowledged the intrusion. His secretary popped her head round the edge of the door and smiled. 'Your car is waiting, Senator.'

'Thank you, Sarah. Tell the driver I'll be out in five.'

Sarah Anderson dipped her head in acknowledgement and disappeared, while Kemble allowed the memory of the previous night to play over. Sarah had proved a most agreeable partner at the President's Ball, afterwards gracing his bed at the hotel quite passionately. In fact, her fervour had impressed him, seemingly borne not just from a desire to be 'the senator's fuck'. There were no qualms at playing away from home; he and his wife had worked out an agreement years ago, so that their relationship was mutually beneficial, politically and commercially. What they each did privately was up to them.

Buttoning his waistcoat, Kemble shrugged into his suit jacket, before considering himself in the office mirror. *Not bad for your age, fella*, he told the image and grinned. At fifty-two Kemble prided himself on his build and appearance, though he noted his joints were a little stiffer than ten years back—ah well, it happened to the best. He picked up his idev, flipped over the cover, and walked from the office. One thing he didn't miss was lugging a large briefcase around to every meeting. Everything he wanted and needed was held on the information device he carried in his hand, and what was better, he could sync with any device in range, sending or retrieving communications, documents, whatever he wanted, without waiting.

That had been the saving grace for these peace talks. There had been no chance for the parties to change their minds while documents were drawn up or drafted; a secretary was on hand to receive his notes and put them into an order instantly available to everybody in the room. Nowhere-to-hide diplomacy he liked to call it.

He settled into the back of the Lincoln town car, his secretary opposite. The driver signalled the Secret Service detachment in the Suburban ahead they were ready to go. Both cars accelerated away from the senator's house, a modest mansion near Capitol Hill, ownership dictated by precedent. They made their way onto Constitution Avenue NE and the journey to Camp David some sixty-two miles away. He might have taken a helicopter ride, but at this time of day, it was often more difficult getting to the airport and then transiting to the facility. Since the expenditure clamp down, use of Marine Corps helicopters was severely limited.

Fortunately, his schedule was fairly lax today; any preparation could be carried out in the car on the way up. Tomorrow morning, he would be meeting with Ehud Malbert and Jamal al-Umari, Israeli and Palestinian leaders respectively, to develop the detail of the plan. Nobody had ever tried anything quite as adventurous as this, whereby the Israeli government rolled back its settlement plan, brought down the walls, and left Gaza and the West Bank. In return, the Palestinians had agreed to recognise the State of Israel in its entirety, including its right to exist. That was the historic nature of this accord—two foes embracing the opportunity to become regional partners. No one had truly envisaged such a time, and Kemble knew that he would be forever lauded should he pull this coup off.

Ever looking for political advantage, he had handed the publicising of the accord to President Carlisle. It was expected the signing of the agreement would take place in three months' time, in Washington, as part of her State of the Union address in the new year. A departure from the norm, it would hail Carlisle's diplomacy and crown a series of successes over her term. And he was part of that glory. The year after was election year—his election year.

A hand closed over his, and he realised he had been drumming out a rhythm on the leather seat. Sarah regarded him, concern and something else in her deep brown eyes.

'Anxious?'

He smiled. 'A little perhaps. More pre-match nerves I guess. It's going to be a success—just how big is all.'

Sarah's face glowed. 'I'm sure it will be a fantastic success, my darling. All the effort and work you've put into this—how could it be otherwise? I'm so proud of you.'

Kemble kept the smile fixed on his face as he received her plaudits. Inwardly, he recoiled. There was no need for another woman to fill his life with inane babble and needs. Mentally, he'd already signed the transfer for Sarah Anderson to a new post—anywhere, except to remain in his office.

Set in the wooded hills of Catoctin Mountain Park, an hour and a half north-north-west of Washington, Camp David had pedigree in delivering world-changing accords. John Kemble was only too aware of this as he stepped into the Laurel Lodge's conference room. Used by Carter in 1978 to broker the historic peace agreement between Egypt and Israel, Naval Support Facility Thurmont had been a firm favourite with numerous incumbents since Roosevelt converted it to a presidential retreat in 1942.

It had seen many of the world's greatest leaders grace its lodges and enjoy its wide vista of mountain views.

A dark mahogany conference table, around which stood eighteen high-backed leather office chairs, dominated the room. The surfaces of all the furniture gleamed and smelled of newly applied polish. Before each chair was a tumbler with the presidential seal engraved on it, a leather executive blotter, leaves of white jotting paper, and a silver Waterman Carene rollerball pen. Carafes of water were lined up dead centre of the table. The only concession to modernity, a large interactive screen flanked by low sideboards, stared blankly from one of the dark panelled wall.

The room was empty, but in half an hour, Kemble would be presiding over the final meeting before he presented the two Middle East leaders, and the all-important agreement, to the president. As he considered the room, awareness of the burden of history that came with sealing the deal at Camp David overcame him. The ghosts of Menachem Begin and Anwar al-Sadat, statesmen whose signatures had heralded an unlikely peace between Israel and Egypt, loomed large in his thoughts.

Now Ehud Malbert and Jamal al-Umari were to be encouraged to end nearly 150 years of terrorism and armed conflict between their people. A smile played briefly across his lips at the thought of that—and his place as chief architect. Kemble sat and sank into a brief meditation as he waited for the delegates.

His reverie was broken as two men filed into the conference room. Following was Sarah Anderson. She looked alluring in a pristine white shirt, two buttons open at the neck to reveal her neck and the beginning of cleavage. A charcoal pencil skirt, sheer stockings appearing from its hem, with black patent heels, finished the look. She smiled with those deep red lips, whose touch he remembered so well.

Those lips would be missed; so too the feel of her body and the warmth of her laughter.

Opposite him. Israeli Prime Minister Malbert sank his heavy frame into the leather upholstery. Malbert was a big man with small eyes that seemed to seek the sunlight vainly from the folds of flesh that surrounded them. His pudgy fingers slid across his forehead, stripping the skin of a fine patina of perspiration and wiping it on a large white kerchief. He nodded to Kemble, who returned the gesture with a smile.

The man who sat to Malbert's left couldn't have been more different. Al-Umari was younger by perhaps fifteen years, and a good-looking man, despite the pockmarking on the olive skin. Thick jet-black hair crowned smouldering looks, which always seemed to wear a cynical smile, but there was honesty in the eyes—something Kemble thought was sometimes absent from the Israeli's.

As the remaining delegates and Kemble's team filed in and took their places, Kemble exchanged pleasantries with the two. An air of affability cloaked the developing meeting, lending serenity to the underlying sense of expectancy and occasion. The US secretary couldn't contain his enthusiasm for what would be the penultimate act of his brokerage—agreeing on the status of Jerusalem.

Coffee was administered to the delegates as they settled into place.

Kemble tapped the screen of his idev, coughed, and addressed the assembly. 'President al-Umari, Prime Minister Malbert, ladies and gentlemen, thank you for attending here today, the last day of these talks on the future of your respective countries. I thank you, Prime Minister Malbert. I know it's been a busy forty-eight hours for you because of the elections in your country, and you're tired after your flight.'

The Israeli smiled. 'Such efforts are necessary, Secretary, to ensure the safety and mutual growth of our two countries. I trust we can show the world that we are now ready to live in peace.'

Beside him, al-Umari nodded slowly in agreement.

Kemble acknowledged the Israeli's words. 'Then let us carry on to the final issue that separates your two great people—Jerusalem. It is a symbol of the history and struggle of both your peoples, reaching back into the past. Dominated by foreign powers and passed between races, Jerusalem holds a record of both your struggles and is claimed equally.'

Both leaders assented silently.

It was Malbert who spoke first. 'It is well known that we Jews'—he was aware that this was the first time he'd used that nomenclature in these negotiations; he had been very careful to leave it till now, to maximise its impact—'lay the most extensive claim, going back in history, to the city of Jerusalem. It holds a significant, no, a holy place in our culture, our past, and our minds. And any Jew would die rather than lose Jerusalem to another.'

Kemble kept his council as the stark words of Malbert carried around the room, but he was keenly aware of al-Umari stiffening with each word that fell, controlled and pointed, from the lips of the Israeli.

'Yet, progress must be made, and now is a time of peace and reconciliation between our two people. I have placed my political career on the line to support and complete this accord between Jew and Palestinian. Jerusalem will not stand in the way. I am ready, on behalf of the nation of Israel, to negotiate the future of our city for the benefit of all.'

Kemble sat back alone in the deck chair on the veranda of the lodge, wrapped against the late autumn chill. He drew slowly on a cigar, savouring the smoke that reached down and warmed his insides. A smile drew slowly across his face, and he resisted the laugh that threatened to rise from his lips.

It was done. The Jerusalem Accord, as a document, was concluded. All it required now was the signature of the two leaders, and he could bask in the triumph of the greatest feat of political engineering the twenty-first century had ever known.

Jamal al-Umari couldn't quite believe what had happened. Even though he ran over the words of the Israeli prime minister again and again, he still dared not hope that he'd finally gotten the country his people had always desired, safe passage between the West Bank and Gaza, and equal governing of the city of Jerusalem. More, Palestine would have the mayorship of the new city for the first two years after the signing of the accord, with the Jews playing second fiddle.

The smile played over his dark features—this was good. He reached for the official phone and tapped out a number on the simple device allowed them by US security. He waited. The time was late back home, but maybe Faisal would be awake, waiting for the call.

'Hello.'

'Faisal, it is Jamal.'

'As salamu, brother.' Faisal Hamid, Umari's prime minister waited expectantly on the other end of the line.

'Wa alaikum salam. I have news.'

A tired little grunt from the other. 'I expect you have, ringing at this time of the morning!'

Al-Umari laughed. 'Apologies, my friend, but I could not wait to share it with you.'

'Well, hurry and tell me! Less of this small talk. What have the Jews done this time?'

When al-Umari had finished, Faisal drew his breath sharply through his teeth. 'Really? They gave all that?'

Jamal al-Umari nodded, before realising his friend couldn't see him. 'Yes,' he exclaimed enthusiastically. 'Can you believe it? For the first time in over a century, we will not have to fight for our people's right to live, to land … to anything. It is a great day for the Palestinian people, my brother, and we shall celebrate as a people on my return.'

Faisal drank in his president's enthusiasm as the other waxed lyrical about the magnanimous nature of the Israeli. Yet, as al-Umari finished the call, Faisal Hamid couldn't help but allow centuries of history to feed his doubt.

In his room further down the corridor, Ehud Malbert was making a call, this time on his own device, smuggled in his diplomatic bag, confounding the tight American security around the conference.

Now he was through to his personal aide, the call scrambled to prevent any snooper from eavesdropping. It was a Jewish thing—suspicion of the world. After all, there was much reason to mistrust it.

On the other end of the line, Schmuel Netayev was congratulating his prime minister on a well-executed negotiation. Malbert thanked him and outlined the nature of the final agreement. As the prime minister reached the part concerning Jerusalem, Netayev paused pointedly.

'That will be contentious, Prime Minister.'

'Don't I know it, Netayev. But it had to be done.'

'It could damage your election prospects. You know how the population feels about Jerusalem.'

Malbert was only too well aware. The polls and the press for the last seven months had sung a song of accusation loudly, as preparations, plans, and then negotiations had slowly but resolutely come to this point today. 'We cannot fight every battle. The world expects us to give some ground. This is not the same as the West Bank and Gaza. When people learn they will lose their homes and businesses, then they will truly end my career.' Malbert sighed. 'But it is a price worth paying to have Palestine say they recognise Israel. How long have we wanted that, eh?'

'I agree, Ehud, but people will not see that. They don't care what the Palestinians think. They are prepared to fight.'

'A moment ago, you were congratulating me.'

'And I still do. I just caution that we need to prepare.'

'I know, I know. Allow me a moment to take in this success,' he chided his aide.

'Certainly, Prime Minister. When will you be returning?'

Malbert hesitated a second. 'Tomorrow I will be back. We can meet the day after though. I need to rest.'

'Of course; it was a gruelling schedule.'

'If only you knew, Schmuel. I'll get the accord sent ahead for you to look through. It will be signed next year when the president addresses the Union. I need to sell it to the people of my country before then.'

'I'll work on that for our meeting and try to be imaginative.'

The two shared a short laugh.

'Okay, my friend, I must go sleep and let you get some also.'

Nine and a half thousand kilometres away, Netayev pondered the words of his boss and shook his head. No good could come of this he feared as he rolled over in his bed and contemplated the sleep that wouldn't return.

From:	Operative 27768-9A1
To:	Director, NSA
Date:	Wednesday, 12 October 2017, 17:43:37
Subject:	Pre-report update

SIGINT Exercise: India-Papa 957 – Approved Comms Surveillance

The following is for information only. Full report to follow under separate, physical cover.

Data retrieval from Papa: Non-threatening exchange with aide. Communication via AC device.

Advise: One communication of duration fifteen minutes and twenty-three seconds to position in Ramallah, West Bank.

Data retrieval from India: Not possible. AC device not activated. Target used own device, possibly from DB as no check run on contents. Two communications. Comm 1: Duration, twenty-one minutes and six seconds; position, Tel Aviv. Comm 2: Duration, four minutes and thirty-four seconds; position, Jerusalem.

Message ends.

From:	Director, NSA
To:	Director, NI
Date:	Wednesday, 12 October 2017, 18:12:53
Subject:	Pre-report update

Sir,

Report from NSA ref SIGINT Exercise: India-Papa 957 – Approved Comms Surveillance

We may have an issue, Bill.

Chas.

A dmiral Bill Foreman, director of National Intelligence, read the cryptic message from Charles Eissenegger, the new director of the National Security Agency. Such things always unsettled him, and in this respect, what he held in his hand was no different to many he'd received. It was unfortunate it concerned something for which the administration wanted no such 'issue'.

His hand strayed to his balding head, scratching methodically, not that it proved effective—the itch was much deeper-seated than that. So the Israelis were concealing something. Of course, that was supposition. The Israelis were naturally suspicious; it might just be to do with their security obsession. By comparison, the Palestinians had pretty much everything they'd only ever dreamed of. He instinctively believed al-Umari would end the armed struggle in return for a secure place to live and recognition of his people by the world. The Israelis had so much more to lose in this accord, and Foreman was surprised it had been so easy for Kemble to get them to agree to his proposals.

It didn't hurt to be prepared.

Foreman tapped his reply on the screen: 'Agreed, Chas. Call a meeting of the intelligence chiefs for tomorrow.'

7

It was an intentionally cool dark room. Situated within the shell of an innocuous house in a Tel Aviv suburb, it was isolated from the structure by dampers, while within its walls was a web of anti-surveillance devices to prevent snooping—a Faraday cage. Two hermetically sealed doors were let into either end of the eighteen-foot-by-ten-foot room.

Seven chairs ringed the heavy glass and metal table, six already occupied. Moshe sat to the right of the head of the table. His idev, which he was syncing with the screens set into the tabletop, commanded his attention, but he was aware of the small, whispered conversations that breathed through the conditioned atmosphere, imbuing it with life. People were seeking answers.

The door to his left opened, and a bulky figure entered, settling awkwardly into the remaining chair. Given the lighting, and the distance of that seat from the others, it was impossible to identify the figure that had just entered—by design. It suited the room's occupants.

'Welcome, everybody.'

The acoustics were also adjusted to disguise their voices. Nothing had been left to chance to secure identities. Even their names were aliases in each other's company. In this way, Moshe figured, they had about the best security to ensure that, if one fell, the others could continue. Certainty, though, was an ever-changing state, and there were contingencies that he and David, the one who sat at the head of the table, had worked up, should any one of 'The Seven' seek, or chance, to compromise their plans.

Seven was a sound Jewish concept, expressing completion and perfection. David and Moshe had discussed long and hard the composition

28

and naming of their cabal and this was right. In a foreign country, David knew Israel was having to sell its soul, that Malbert had been destined to do so, even though it hurt him and would cost his premiership. That was, ultimately, unacceptable.

Such things were a problem for Israelis; as a culture and a nation, they had been forged in battle and adversity. This time was no different. Since 1967, Israel had been determined to stay ahead of the opposition. Arab, communist, Palestinian—all had come to crush the Jew; all had been repulsed. This would be no different.

And here in this room were the people who would change the destiny of 'the accord'.

Those individuals now turned to him, paying homage in the subdued lighting. They were specially picked, and David had the utmost confidence in Moshe's selection. He took a moment to look down the list on his idev and nodded. If any team could save the soul of Israel, it was these people. He glanced at each as he briefly read the highlights.

Next to Moshe was General Avram Topol. Topol was a member of the Planning Directorate of the Israeli Defence Force—tasked with strategic planning and the build-up of military forces. Someone of Topol's stature was absolutely essential to the success of this endeavour. Topol was a heavyset man; age and good living having slackened his stature. However, his intelligence shone as sharp as ever from the honey brown eyes.

To Topol's right sat a striking young woman, deep wide-set green eyes dominating even features, bounded by lustrous black hair that fell to her shoulders. David knew her to be Natalie Epstein, a right-wing freelance journalist who blogged, day and night, her objection to everything not Israeli. Her pet hatred though, was the threatened dismantling of the West Bank settlements, which Malbert was offering to al-Umari and the United States as part of the accord. Epstein railed against the 'Jerusalem Discord' as she named it, continually warning her audience of a war to end all wars in the Middle East.

Three more sat along the other side of the table. First was Avi Perez, another hardliner. In his mid-forties, Perez had taken over his father's shipping company, after spending time learning his trade in the manner that had been the family way since the fifties—grafting from the shop floor. He was a fit man, whose ascetic features embraced ill-humour and a haughtiness that spoke of his feeling of superiority. *One to watch*, thought David. Avi Perez was set resolutely against any agreement that would damage the security of Israel.

The second was Miranda Klein, an air force major general who couldn't have been less like the fashionista Epstein sitting opposite her. Deeply lined olive skin and closely cropped black hair, which strangely added to her sexuality, spoke of a life on the front line. Klein had been a pilot, flying F-16s during the intifada and more recent Syrian troubles. She was exactly the type of operations person David knew was needed to ensure victory.

The final piece of the jigsaw was the industrialist Benjamin Kompert, a solid name for a solid man. There was something soft in his appearance, but Kompert was ruthless underneath the limp exterior. Born and raised in the United States of America, Kompert had been an industrial designer who rose through the ranks of Boeing's military arm, working on F-15s for export, AH-64 Apaches, and UAV technology, before moving to Israel and joining the country's aircraft industry, developing unmanned aerial vehicles. It was for that wealth of knowledge he had been recruited to this project.

With those five and Moshe as his lieutenant, David had no doubt that his cabal would see victory. It was just a matter of how that would be shaped.

They waited expectantly for their leader to speak. When he did, it was with a delivery carefully judged to shock. He'd worked on what to say for the last few days; he wanted his chosen group to build a wrath the world would quake before.

'Yesterday, the final words were put to an accord, which, when signed, will bring destruction to the struggle our people have borne since 1948. No more will we have the security of controlling the West Bank and the Gaza Strip. No longer will we be able to settle as we think fit within the lands God gave us. Instead, we will broker and barter for space with the Palestinian. A treachery has been wrought by those we believed friends, to bring about accolades and Nobel Peace Prizes for leaders who know nothing of our struggle, our nation.

'The biggest treachery? The decision, thrust upon us, to share the city of Jerusalem and for the Palestinians to lead when the peace is signed. To rub our very noses in it, the document has been dubbed "The Jerusalem Accord".'

A murmur rippled around the table. But before any could speak, David raised a hand to indicate quiet. 'Yes, we are to be emasculated in the desert by our one-time American friends, who intend to sacrifice us for wider friendships, new partners.' He carried on, detailing what he knew of the accord—agreements to pull down the wall built to segregate Jew from Palestinian; to halt all new settlements on the West Bank and to reduce the current number by half; to provide free, safe passage across Israel between Gaza and the West Bank. Each proposal brought a gasp. 'And finally, that greatest of treacheries.' He punctured the air with spittle.

A silence surrounded The Seven.

'Yes, share our capital, because it is theirs also. Apparently, the Palestinians are as much citizens of Jerusalem as are we. But this is not just about the Palestinians. We know the strength behind them. We know the nation that funds and arms the Palestinian. We will show them and the world—Israel will bow before no one.

'It's time to explore our options. Moshe.'

A glance, and his lieutenant nodded. 'People, on your screens are some options being considered by David and me. We need a response that will send a message across the Arab world.'

'And beyond,' David said, reinforcing his point.

'Indeed. Moshe hid his irritation quickly. He flicked a finger over the screen of his idev, and in response, the others saw a list appear before them.

Option 1:	Forced expulsion of Palestinians from the West Bank area and Gaza Strip and strengthening of the Arab-Israeli borders.
Option 2:	An eradication programme to exterminate the Palestinians and full mobilisation of the Israeli defence forces to ensure any transgression or military action along the borders are fully repulsed.
Option 3:	Assassination of al-Umari and his council and the imposition of martial law in Gaza and the West Bank.

Option 4:	Option 3, accompanied by strikes against Syria and Lebanon, which both provide support to the Palestinian cause.
Option 5:	Stage the assassination of Prime Minister Malbert, to make it look like a Hamas or Hezbollah action; break off the accord.
Option 6:	Do nothing.

An uncomfortable silence descended across the table, broken by Perez. 'I understand where you're coming from with these, but there are serious connotations involved in any of these. For me, perhaps option three is the least offensive. But one and two evoke memories of our own suffering, never mind the total mobilisation of the forces of Israel, which will not necessarily share our view of circumstances. However, it is more the thought of forced expulsion or extermination that makes me sick to the stomach.

'As far as staging an assassination, that obviously cannot be a serious contender. And with regards to option six, well I'm sure you didn't call us here just to say don't do anything at all.'

'You are free to go, if you have no stomach for this endeavour.' David ground out the words, not because Perez opposed his options, but because he needed to know where the man stood.

Perez looked resolutely at the leader of The Seven. 'I want to resolve this situation as much as any here. You asked us to join you, not because we would slavishly follow your every word, but because we would offer strength, intellect, and imagination in showing the world what Israel is about. Following the pattern of the Germans in the thirties and forties will afford us nothing but opprobrium and vilification from the world. Whatever we do must be seen as a response to a real threat to our security and survival.'

David concealed his smile. Perez was good. 'So, what do we do?'

'As I said, option three is the easiest, though it would have the least impact on the world stage. Four, perhaps, but it doesn't take account of Iran.'

David glanced at Moshe and nodded. Perez's perception was spot on. Iran remained the real issue. A naked and vociferous supporter of

Hezbollah, Iran would seek to maintain some form of struggle against the nation of Israel, despite the agreements signed by al-Umari. They would leave him for the dogs, the poor sod.

'What does anybody else think?'

A cough emanated from Topol, who presaged his words with a wave towards the screen and then the shipping magnate. 'Perez is right. To expel or eradicate all the Palestinians in Gaza and the West Bank would be a logistical nightmare, bordering on the impossible, even with the complete support of the Israeli Defence Forces and the general population. As I think you well know, it is a completely unworkable scenario.'

He paused, perhaps, thought David, seeking the support of others. As he expected, the others merely waited while they figured which way Topol was going and whether he would be dismissed out of hand. 'That is your opinion. Do you have any other views?'

Topol nodded, unbowed by the lack of support from his fellow conspirators. 'Again, I agree with Perez about the others, so what I'm thinking is this—what is option seven?'

'What makes you think there's an option seven?'

Topol grunted and waved at the people around the table before regarding David with a look akin to disgust and amusement. Moshe tensed and slipped his right hand to his knee. In a holster strapped under the desk was a Glock 19. The move was not lost on Topol.

'It's okay, Moshe. You do not have to reach for your gun. I am not here to disrupt anything. But any course of action must be supportable and achievable and must pre-empt any action by an enemy. And, make no mistake, whatever course of action we follow, save for option six, we are going to make enemies.

'That being the case,' he continued, 'there has to be a plan that isn't tabled here—a plan, that, if we agree to it, will have such a devastating effect on our enemies, present and future, that they will not wish to oppose us.'

David laughed, a deep, passionate sound. 'Your reputation as an incisive, observant man doesn't do you justice. Moshe, relax please and present the last option.'

Moshe tapped the screen of his idev again, and another option appeared before the gathered assembly.

Topol offered only one brief response upon reading it. 'Fuck!'

8

F oreman strode purposefully into his office at the Pentagon; nodded at Jenny, his secretary; grabbed coffee from the pot; and pushed open the door to his inner sanctum. As he sat, he surveyed the two others patiently awaiting his arrival. He had just made his way here from his regular morning briefing with the president. He liked his time with Angela Carlisle, a president whose skill and determination had been borne out of adversity and battle. She appreciated clear information and simple, effective responses but had been worried by Foreman's, admittedly limited, briefing about the Israeli-Palestinian situation. Foreman had been honest with her.

'It might be nothing, Madam President,' he had admitted. 'There is precious little information, and the report, to be tabled by the NSA later, may not shed any more light than we have now.'

Carlisle had considered his words. She looked older than her years, her light brown hair silvered by events. He wondered sometimes how she had coped with the aftermath of the Faulkner situation. It was something she never mentioned, but he imagined it could've been real easy just to slip away into the shadows and deal privately, silently with the impact of having a huge target drawn on your back by a home-grown terrorist.

'Admiral, I have found that what appears to be nothing can often take on alarming proportions if left. While Charles's work needs completing, I want to know if anything could happen that might derail the secretary of state's accord. You know it's to be signed at my State of the Union address.'

'Yes, ma'am.'

'In that case, Bill, do whatever it takes to make sure that either the train stays on the rails, or we park it safely somewhere it won't affect us if it blows up.'

Foreman had suppressed the smile that threatened a response to her candour and made his way to the Pentagon for this meeting. He hoped the director had something more to go with his slightly cryptic correspondence of yesterday evening. Since then, Foreman had not heard from him.

Eissenegger's lanky frame dwarfed the person next to him.

After acknowledging the NSA director, Foreman turned his attention to the other. 'Director Markham, good to see you.'

Sarah Markham nodded but resolutely failed to return the smile Foreman flashed her. So, all the stories were true; Sarah Markham was a hard bitch. He was going to enjoy working with her, he decided ironically.

'Shall we get to business, Admiral?'

'Bill,' he replied and noted, with a little satisfaction, her response. She'd be attractive, if she just relaxed a bit. 'I like to keep the formalities minimal here. Okay, Chas,' he turned to the NSA director before Markham could reply. 'What have you got?'

Chas looked a little crestfallen, not a good start figured Foreman, as the director reached in his briefcase and pulled a manila folder from it, positioning it on the desk before Foreman. The admiral was disappointed to see it was a very thin file.

The others waited silently as Foreman worked through the short number of pages contained beneath the bland surface. When he finished, he looked at Eissenegger. 'It's not much, Chas.' He tried to keep his tone neutral, but it was difficult.

Eissenegger shrugged, his face impassive. 'There is very little to say, just rumours.'

Foreman turned to Markham. 'Have you read through this yet?'

'It's thin.' Markham responded laconically. 'It needs following up.'

Foreman raised a bushy eyebrow in reply. When nothing was forthcoming, he encouraged the CIA director. 'Expand please, Sarah.'

Markham was aware of two things—her status as a tyro and her reputation. Although she had been pivotal in the situation that had resulted in the United States' first female president, her promotion to director of the CIA had remained a surprise to many. It had come about when her predecessor had chosen to stand down, rather than be pushed for his lack of oversight on home-grown terrorists—especially ones previously in the employ of the organisation. They saw her as somebody without the pedigree to succeed. She was just someone who acted like a man to prove that she was better; such was the rumour mill.

She knew she had to change people's opinion. But she was acutely aware she couldn't rush—or take too long in—her decision making. This fine line walking was not new to her, just several magnitudes of severity above what she was used to. When Markham spoke, she bore these things in mind. 'Two things might have a bearing on this report.' She indicated the folder. 'First, we've been monitoring activity, along with Charles's agency'—she refused to use his nickname—'in Israel itself. There are snippets I'm sure the director has passed to you previously, which intimate a group, or groups, opposed to the accord.'

Foreman nodded. 'I've read through them. We figured they were the usual rumblings of discontent and bravado in the face of the inevitable.'

Markham regarded the National Intelligence director, while attempting to keep her incredulity under control. Perhaps her next words would change matters. 'Ordinarily I would agree. However, three weeks ago, a ranger was inserted into Israel on a covert observation mission in the south of the country.'

Yes, that did the trick, she thought as Foreman struggled unsuccessfully to hide his surprise. 'The ranger was observing activity at a remote facility in the Negev—'

'Dimona!' The interruption was involuntary, and Foreman apologised.

'Yes, Israel's nuclear research facility.'

'Isn't it mothballed, since the nineties?'

'Not anymore, sir.' Sarah Markham shook her head slowly, in the way you did with people who were a little hard of hearing. 'The ranger reported significant traffic to and from the site with construction work and increased security around the area.'

'Where is this ranger? Can we debrief him on what he observed?'

'I'm afraid not. He went dark this week, just prior to his extraction.' It was all she offered.

You didn't have to be a genius to work out what that meant, thought Foreman. 'Was nothing done to find him? Didn't you have any oversight on his activity?'

For the briefest of moments, Markham appeared uncomfortable, a moment not lost on Foreman. He felt a little satisfaction but also foreboding at the instance.

'We … lost sight of him. It's a difficult area to surveil. The Israelis closely guard the facility and its surrounding environment. We only confirmed he was missing when he failed to rendezvous at the extraction point within the appointed time.'

There was more, much more, but for now Foreman merely grunted his displeasure. 'So what conclusions did you arrive at, Sarah, for this renewed activity?'

Markham glanced at Eissenegger. 'Both Director Eissenegger and I are of the opinion that the Israelis are resurrecting the site for some'—pause—'currently undetermined task.'

'No shit.' Though he felt angry and impotent, Foreman kept his delivery deadpan. 'Well, shall we assume they're reopening their nuclear weapons research programme,' he paused, 'just for the sake of argument?'

Markham coloured. Being chastised publicly by her boss placed her in unfamiliar territory. Quickly, she regained composure. 'It was on our radar.'

'Good! I'm glad.' Foreman rose and turned to look out of his window, seeing nothing. He needed a moment to digest what he'd been told. Scrambled Israeli communications from Camp David, Dimona reopened, and a missing ranger—all pointed to a situation he'd rather not have contemplated.

'Okay, it would seem we have a potential situation on our hands.' He dispensed with niceties in his anger. 'I want all the information both of you have from this ranger expedition. Meanwhile, put maximum effort into finding out what the Israelis are up to. And don't forget the Palestinians. I have a real bad feeling about all this.'

9

The weather was mild for late October as Steve Logan climbed the steps to the foyer of Vauxhall Cross and entered the imposing ziggurat structure that was the home of Britain's Secret Intelligence Service, better known as MI6. Late morning sunlight warmed his neck and then was lost as he entered the overheated interior. As with all government buildings, just the mention of winter sent the thermostat several degrees higher, reaching what he alone deemed uncomfortable.

Passing security, he walked to his station, purchasing a black coffee from the restaurant on the way. Hanging his messenger bag over the back of his chair, he retrieved his idev and placed it on the desk, which was devoid of obstructions, to sync with the SIS mainframe. Logan liked clear space at which to think and plan. His mail and messages came thick and fast, and he smiled as he figured the obstructions had just moved online. His mind wandered to Murtagh and their recent break.

Reluctant to admit it, Logan had needed Brooke's company after the Faulkner case, to come to terms with the loss of so many people and to help him look forward. That she had done that, and more, was evidenced by her move to England and a switch to the CIA, which had only been too glad to take on an officer of her calibre and intelligence.

He still had a shitload of emails to get through.

As he turned his attention to the detritus of communications, his idev chimed. Glancing at the screen, he saw it was his boss, Galbraith.

'Hello.'

'Logan. You have a good break?'

He smiled sourly at his boss. 'Right up to the moment I synced to the 'frame and saw my emails.'

'Do what I do.'

'What's that?'

Galbraith smiled, something of a rarity for her. 'Every email I get while I'm off is deleted as soon as it hits my inbox. If something is really important, they'll contact me.'

Logan nodded. He saw the sense in that. 'It's really important then?'

'What?'

'The reason for your call.'

'Touché. Yes, I'm afraid it is. Can you spare me a moment?'

'Boss. Why did you ask me up?'

Tapping her idev, Galbraith caused a document to appear on the desk before the officer. 'Take a look.' She waited as Logan scanned it. 'My counterpart at Langley is concerned, as is the director of national intelligence, that the current negotiations concerning "the accord" are in danger.'

'Because of a scrambled Israeli phone call?'

'Not just that. Read on,' Galbraith encouraged him.

He flipped the page; his eyes widened momentarily as he continued. He sat back and regarded his superior.

'You're taking this seriously then.' It was a statement rather than a question.

Galbraith nodded.

'Bill Foreman is taking it seriously enough to have written a preliminary report to Secretary of State John Kemble, outlining the intelligence communities' concerns.'

'I'm sure that is going to go down well,' observed the officer.

'Like a fart at a funeral.' Galbraith wasn't often given to such colourful language, emphasising the gravity of the situation. 'Foreman has already apprised the president of the situation, potential or otherwise.'

'What do GCHQ say?'

'They provided a briefing for when the DNI rang me.' She sighed. 'He doesn't hold out much hope of Kemble backing down. The perception is this threatens the secretary's career. I can't argue with his assessment of that. Fortunately, Carlisle is more bothered about making the same mistake as previous administrations and ignoring the signs.'

Logan nodded. He remembered President Angela Carlisle as a considered incumbent, one given to asking the right questions at the right time and not afraid to stop something or someone if it was the correct decision to make. He'd quickly assessed her as a potentially great leader. It seemed a new situation was about to test that theory. And what of the other matter? 'Nothing has been heard from this ranger?'

'He's been silent for a couple of weeks or so.'

'Still under cover?'

'No. He was meant to be extracted about the time he went dark.'

'So. You're thinking eliminated.'

'At least neutralised. But Langley is being quite coy about the circumstances of his disappearance.'

'And he was surveilling Dimona?'

'Correct.'

Logan allowed the information to run through his mind, working permutations, considering options. There were few, to be fair, he decided. A US ranger was dropped into Israel to spy on an allegedly defunct nuclear facility, at a time when the administration was supposed to be helping Israel bury the hatchet on a centuries-old conflict. What did they suspect?

Galbraith considered his question. 'At first it was unrelated. NSA had noticed that there was activity and they wanted it checked out.' She went on to outline the HALO insertion and subsequent surveillance of the facility. The ranger had communicated his information in super-high burst transmissions up until the day of his disappearance. It was believed Mossad had intercepted the transmission bursts, which had enabled them to pinpoint the man and position an asset to despatch him.

'So you're saying the Israelis took him out?'

Galbraith nodded. 'We agree with the CIA; this is the most likely outcome.'

'Didn't they have overwatch?' The look on her face told him all he needed to know. 'They intentionally sacrificed the guy so the Israelis would believe they had kept their secret safe.' He paused. 'What is coming from Lane?'

'Our Tel Aviv office also picked up the communications. Lane'—Galbraith cursed under her breath—'has picked up other conversations she's convinced are part of a code.'

'You think?'

'That we don't have time to wonder about secret codes. Any work we run on this now could be picked up by Mossad and compromise US investigations.'

'This is an active CIA-NSA investigation?'

Galbraith offered neither confirmation nor denial.

Logan let out a short sharp whistle.

Galbraith allowed herself a nod of the head.

'Our involvement?'

By way of reply, Galbraith sent another document to the screen in the desk before him.

He read it in silence and then looked hard at his boss. 'You've agreed to this?' Galbraith nodded.

Logan looked again at the orders shining from the desk's surface. They were interesting, to say the least; vague; brief; and, perhaps, hopeful. He waved a hand at them. 'They don't exactly give me much to go on.'

Galbraith smiled, a smile borne of experience with her most effective officer. 'I'm sure you will find a way to make it all more meaningful.'

Logan nodded thoughtfully. 'Okay. I'd best get started.'

Galbraith considered him for a moment. 'To reiterate, this is a US-UK operation. You'll be using assets from the US too.'

He thought about what she'd said for a moment. 'Of course, I have just the ones in mind,' he opined as he swiped the document to the internal comms link on the desk and typed in his ident, sending the document on its way. 'If that's everything?'

Galbraith dipped her head briefly in response.

'In which case, I have some work to do. Good day, chief.'

'Have a good day, Logan. Let me know your progress.'

'As always.' And with that, he was gone.

'How are we supposed to deliver this?' General Topol stared at the screen and then at his proposed leader. Suddenly 'doing nothing' seemed a sensible strategy.

An uncomfortable silence descended on the room. Topol had sensed the mood; the others were fascinated yet reviled by the idea presented to them by Moshe as the solution—both to the 'Jerusalem Accord' and the Arab question, a conundrum that had puzzled and vexed the Jews since time immemorial. Uneasiness pulsed like a monster in the air, and Moshe slid the Glock from its holster.

David coughed. It was clear he was in danger of losing The Seven if he didn't quickly counter Topol's remonstrations. Truth be told, he'd expected somebody to object, so the general's question offered him some room for manoeuvre. He glanced at Moshe. It was enough; the other slid the gun back in place. 'You didn't ask why?'

Topol waved a big hand at the proposal. 'There are so many questions. It's difficult to know where to start. I'm presuming you are serious.'

David nodded. 'Yes, indeed. How else are we to counter this threat?'

The army officer grunted. What was proposed offered a solution of sorts, but it was reminiscent of the bad old days, when Israel tried to silence its enemies *before* they did anything. Topol felt foreboding settle on his shoulder. He had to admit, though, it was daring—a typical Israeli response to something yet to transpire. But who were the targets? The Palestinians were too close to consider seriously; fallout on Israel would draw censure and vilification from all sides, including internally. 'It depends what threat you are referring to.'

'I must agree with my colleague. This represents a serious escalation of conditions.' Air Force General Klein's voice cut the air with concern.

Dissent was increasing. Time to explain. 'You are both right. And for the sake of everyone here, I will expand.'

Expectancy filled the enclosed space, and David felt briefly intimidated by the gaze of so many people—it was a curious feeling.

'People, we all know that the accord—which will, in just a few short weeks, be signed in Washington—represents an emasculation of everything Israel stands for. Malbert cannot be faulted for his work in trying to deliver the very best for this country in the glare of the world's lights. He knows, I'm sure, that this cannot work—that it will signal the end, not only of his career as a politician, a leader, but also of Israel as we know it.

'Consequently, we must help our brother set us on a path to rescue, rejuvenate, and reinvigorate Israel and make her a regional power worthy of respect. Malbert has given us the weeks necessary to deliver the first blow against our ancient enemies.'

'That's all very well, David, but a nuclear weapon?' Topol stroked his face wearily. 'We have always denied their existence, and America has always enabled that smokescreen to remain in place. You are insisting we deploy such a weapon against our enemies? The fallout will not only be radioactive.'

'I agree, but think—what other weapon will send such a clear message to our foes and command such respect from other countries?'

'But against the Palestinians?' Topol maintained a healthy air of scepticism.

'Not Palestine.'

The air became electric with possibilities as David corrected the general. He allowed the speculation to run through the place, watching for the first person to question.

'If not Palestine then who?' Kompert's fingers drummed a steady light rhythm on the countertop as he awaited the reply.

'Iran.'

More murmuring.

'And Syria.'

In the instant that followed, the audience was his. The old foes, hated more by Israel than almost any other country, were often a clarion call, a rally point for the emotional investment by the Jew. Iran was viewed implacably as their foe, still calling for the armed struggle against the Zionist aggressors. Meanwhile, beyond the Golan Heights, the government of Muslim Brotherhood, tightened its alliance with Tehran, used the same rhetoric, and thereby signed its own death warrant in David and Moshe's eyes. Now to infuse the other five with the same zeal.

'For decades, these two have snapped at our heels, fed our enemies at home, and displayed open animosity to our right to existence. If this accord is to become a living, breathing reality, it is because the world has listened to the voices of these two in particular. No one cares about the Palestinians, what they're doing, what they want. This is merely Tehran and Damascus ensuring Israel is emasculated.

'Well, I, for one, will not stand by and see that happen. I would protect Palestinians' rights in this country where that does not disadvantage the Jew. What I will not countenance is an agreement, a situation, where our enemies gain from our weakening.'

'I agree, David. These two are the real threat behind the accord. Palestinians work for me, in positions of great responsibility. We have followed an open policy on employment for many years now.' Avi Perez puffed out his chest. 'But I'll not bow to the Iranians or Syrians telling me how to run my business or live in my country.'

'Well said, but I would say this treaty threatens the very security of this country, by allowing the Palestinians freedom to go where they please. They are still the enemy, whatever the words of al-Umari. They will always find sustenance from the Iranians and Syrians. We must stop that first and then deal with them.'

David looked at the others. 'Does anyone disagree?'

Silence greeted his question.

'Do we need a vote?'

'It would be appropriate to record whether we are in accord, though I use that word with a sense of irony,' advised Kompert.

David seemed a little irked by the comment but acquiesced. 'Very well. All those in favour of option seven, please raise a hand.' He counted six hands in the dark atmosphere. 'Unanimous then.'

'I return to my original question. How?' Topol raised an eyebrow for emphasis.

'It remains a good question, colleague, and we shall consider it now. Moshe, if you please.'

Moshe flicked a third document to their screens.

Option Seven

Objective
To neutralise the strategic threat to Israel and the practical support to the Palestinian Authority represented by the regimes currently in power in Iran and Syria.

Method
A nuclear device delivered against strategic targets within both countries. Such a device will need to be designed and constructed in Israel and deployed by elements of the Israeli Defence Forces.

Type

Consideration should be given to an area denial weapon, which will:
- Occupy the regimes in supporting their affected populations, logistically, medically, and rebuilding infrastructure
- Ensure the ramifications of a counterstrike are prohibitive
- Prevent retaliation from other regional factions

Area denial will require a weapon from which the fallout lingers for a specified time, preventing expedited entry to the affected area, thus imposing a two-part support plan—first, assisting resettlement and logistical care of displaced and sick populations and, second, entering the bombed area and starting the process of decontamination and rebuilding. The preferred weapon therefore is a 'salted' nuclear device. Salting places a non-fissionable jacket of a specific isotope around the second-stage fusion fuel. Upon detonation, the jacket captures the escaping fusion neutrons and creates a radioactive isotope with an enhanced fallout hazard envelope.

Salting Isotopes

This plan considers the following isotopes as appropriate salting subjects:
- Tantalum (Ta-182)—half-life = 115 days
- Zinc (Zn-65)—half-life = 244 days

For this operation, gold isotope has not been considered, as its half-life is less than three days. However, it may be a potent testing option.

Topol was silent, but David caught the flicked glance at his military counterpart, Klein, who briefly inclined her head.

'All very good in principle,' offered the old general, 'but two things. You must get the raw material for the jacket, and you have to involve people at Dimona who may not share our views. You need a scientist who will do it because he or she shares our goal or who will not question why Israel is producing such a weapon.'

'You are correct. With regard to your first point, that is why we have the services of our industrialist colleague. His contacts will enable us to import the material we need for the making of the isotopes.'

'And our colleague's second point?' Epstein queried David.

'That is already being considered, as we speak.'

'Expand.'

David ignored the imperative in the tone but did reply to the army general. 'We have a team grooming a prospective candidate right now. Hopefully, they will be working on our device in a few days' time.

'Enough of that for now. There is no dissension?' David's gaze swept the room; no one moved, and no one spoke. 'Good! Then you must know this. As of this moment, you are committed to this approach. You are committed to a course of action that will see you vilified by the world, should it ever find out who you are. You will, most likely, be indicted for war crimes and mass genocide. Has this not always been the fate of Israel? To be sanctioned and despised by the world. Your fate will be no worse than that of any of our forebears.

'However, it is precisely to offer some protection that Moshe and I have devised The Seven. Outside of these walls, it is all we will be to the world. From now on, wherever we engage in work as the group, we will be known not by who we are but by special identities. Moshe has given this much thought and deliberation. And as we are known to you as "David" and "Moshe", you will be known as other great leaders from our country's past.'

David paused as he consulted his screen, looking back at the five before him. 'General Topol, You will be known as "Ariel", after Israel's greatest modern leader and strategist, Ariel Sharon. You will follow him in those shoes. Natalie, you become "Golda". Moshe is not without a sense of irony in giving you the name of the one who put in place the Wrath of God in 1972 and who certainly didn't share your passion for fashion.'

A trickle of laughter sounded in the room.

'Mr Perez, you will be known as "Yitzhak"; General Klein, "Uzi"; and Mr Kompert, your cover is "Shimon".

'All of you remember these names. them to your deepest memories, as you will use only them in your communication with each other from now on, even here. Moshe has programmed phones with all the contact details on them. However, do not rely on these. After each call, you must destroy them. Another burner phone will be provided you after each call. Irksome but necessary for our security and survival.' David stopped as Moshe caught his eye. 'Yes?'

'Just to reinforce,' Moshe said, turning to the others, 'all communication must be by these cheap phones or paper. Outside of this room, no other devices or systems are to be used to pass information between us. Technology can be tapped, traced, and infiltrated. When you write something, use a fountain pen lightly, on a hard surface, so you leave minimal imprints. And when you receive a letter, commit its content to memory, and then burn it. That way, tracing will be difficult for security services.'

'Thank you, Moshe. Well, you all have your phones. It is time to part and await the next stage. Moshe will be in contact soon with details, but do not fret if you are not contacted for a while. We have picked you for your specific skills, and these may not be needed immediately.

'Take your time leaving here. Our guards will give you all specific instructions for leaving the building. Thank you.'

With a speed that belied his bulk, David rose and was gone, leaving Moshe to administer the final matters.

Silence descended on the five recruits as they absorbed just what it was they were getting into.

10

The man, framed by the ornate window, stared beyond the pavement tables on Place du Cirque, his eyes failing to register the busy Geneva traffic hurrying by or the people walking and enjoying the weekend sun. Periodically, he would sip from his coffee, which the observer opposite figured must have been cold, before continuing his reverie.

'Any news?'

The onlooker glanced sideways. A wiry young man with thick black hair, wearing sunglasses and licking an ice pop, sat on the wall next to him. A curious half-smile occupied the even features, suddenly making them lopsided. Danny turned a page of his newspaper, an eye still on the coffee drinker over the road. 'Nothing. Just the same vacant shit every time.'

Binyamin sucked noisily on the ice pop and regarded his colleague. 'You know, you have to respect the man's position.'

'Is that so?' Danny regarded his colleague coolly. 'Please, share your insight.'

'Yes. I mean, his wife only left him two years ago. You expect him to be over her yet? Damn! You've seen her photo, haven't you?'

Danny Levine nodded.

'Would you be over that?'

Levine shook his head in despair.

Binyamin Rabin's big brown eyes adopted a forlorn expression, and he gesticulated with the lollipop. 'I would pine for her, forever.'

Levine shook his head slowly. Sometimes Binyamin could be … a retard. 'Concentrate on the matter in hand. It's your turn to look after our lovesick friend. Just don't fall asleep on the job.'

His relief grinned. 'No danger. I've always wondered what a nuclear physicist does on his days off. You finished with the paper?'

Danny Levine passed the broadsheet to him. 'It's like our friend there,' he said as he stood, 'nothing in it. We may have to find somebody else.'

Johannes Olsen pulled on the coffee and grimaced as the cold liquid slid down his throat. Late Saturday morning and here he was again, wasting his time, drinking coffee, and moping over his wife. *Get a grip, Jo. Life is walking past you on the pavement, and you need to either join the stream or …*

Or what?

The emotion surged, raw, in his belly, remembering her last words. "You are never here, Jo, never with the kids. Always, you are experimenting at that fucking laboratory. You're married to your job, and we're just filling the gaps!"

With that, she'd disappeared from his life; kids too. Perhaps he could have done more, maybe followed, searched for them, demanded he be given access to the children. Truth was, he was out of his depth, incapable of understanding the mechanics.

He was a fish out of water.

And yet, he couldn't live without her. Judith's face occupied every moment he wasn't thinking of his job, often when he was. What had his position gotten him? One of the premier nuclear physicists of his time. Not enough to keep the woman he loved.

'Another?'

Olsen looked up at the young waitress. All smiles and wide-eyed expectation, with no idea about loss. He shook his head, pulled five euros from his wallet, and placed them on the table.

'Thank you.' He rose and walked from the café, heavy in thought so that he failed to notice the young man who dropped his ice pop stick in a bin and slowly walked in his train.

Rabin slouched along, shadowing the scientist, hands in deep in pockets, and seemingly aimless—a young man with nothing on his mind. Mossad trained its operatives well in the art of blending in, but he was alert to the other members of his team. Should Olsen grab a taxi, his driver would quickly appear.

'Hey! Wait!'

The two figures had not journeyed far when Olsen was brought to a halt. It was the waitress from the café. She was holding something in her hand. Rabin nodded his approval as he walked by. Sharon was only young, but she was good at deception, misdirection, and gaining trust.

'You dropped your wallet.'

He hadn't; Binyamin knew that much. It was one of the young Mossad agent's skills—sleight of hand; Olsen would never have known.

Automatically, the scientist patted his jacket; checked pockets, as if he couldn't believe his eyes. But, no, the wallet was still waving in front of him like a flag of negligence. He reached out tentatively. 'Thanks.'

Sharon smiled her smile. 'No problems. I didn't want you to wonder what had happened to it.'

Olsen opened it and pulled a note from it. 'Here, for coming after me.' He bent his tall frame over the girl; it wasn't a threat, more awkwardness.

Sharon shook her head vigorously. 'No. I can't. It was the natural thing to do.'

'Well.' Olsen shrugged. 'Thanks anyway.' He made to walk away.

Rabin stopped to watch a bird in the cemetery, wondered when Sharon would make the play.

'You come here quite a lot.'

Olsen turned again and regarded the diminutive blonde quizzically; a frown troubled his thin face. 'Yes. What of it?'

'I'm sorry. I was just being nosey. You seem to be lonely.'

The frown dropped, and a cold expression took over the eyes. 'I'm not after a relationship or … sex,' he concluded forcefully, as if to ensure there was no ambiguity to his reply.

You're losing him, Rabin silently admonished his colleague from the shade of the cemetery wall.

'No!' The indignation was real, and Olsen took a step back. 'That wasn't what I meant at all. You just looked lonely, and I thought if you wanted, while you're in the café, I can always take lunch, and we can chat. I'm from out of country, and you look like you work here.'

He nodded slowly, unsure.

'Good! I'm here on work experience, and I need somebody to try my French and Italian on. You do speak them?' The hope was plaintive.

Olsen considered his new friend for a moment. 'I know French, some. I work at the laboratory outside town.' When she looked quizzical, he explained, 'I work for CERN, the research establishment.'

Sharon's eyes widened. 'Is that the place that has the new Very Large Hadron Collider everyone is talking about?'

Olsen nodded.

'Wow!'

'So, I don't need to know too much French. My German is better.'

'It's just that I thought, with your accent …'

Olsen smiled; she had him. 'No, that's just from working in Switzerland for the last three years. You pick up the inflection. I'm from Norway originally.'

Sharon didn't even miss a heartbeat. 'Really? I'm from Israel.'

Make or break, thought the agent.

It appeared for a moment that Johannes Olsen baulked at the statement, but it was delivered so easily, off the cuff, that Rabin knew he was pulled in. Here was a girl from the land of his wife, someone with whom he could connect. This was too good an opportunity to miss. Even so, there was a slight hesitation, the kind that means, *This is too good to be true.* 'O-okay.'

'I thought we could talk over my lunch hour, and I could learn a bit more, perhaps even some German? It can't hurt to know German.'

'Okay.'

More conviction this time, the other agent noted. Good; she was in.

'I'll be here next Saturday, so we can …'

Sharon smiled, a big beautiful come-get-me smile, and Johannes Olsen smiled back. 'I look forward to it,' she accepted the unspoken invitation greedily.

Olsen shook the proffered hand awkwardly before turning and walking away.

Sharon turned, saw Rabin, and winked, before disappearing into the café.

'Here she is! Wonder Woman!'

Rabin, Levine, and other members of the Mossad team were seated at the kitchen table in the safe house as Sharon Horowitz returned from work. She bowed to all in turn, who clapped long and vigorously.

'That was a masterful piece of work you pulled there with our Norwegian friend, Miss Horowitz. You ever thought of becoming an agent for Mossad?'

Sharon, pouring a glass of wine at the countertop, showed Rabin the finger without stopping, turned, and pulled on the deep ruby red claret before speaking. 'Yes, and I thought, would I want to show up guys like you? You know what the answer was?'

Rabin flicked up an eyebrow enquiringly.

'Yes!'

Laughter rippled round the room at the expense of the young man, who smiled back. 'Got me there. Seriously though, I thought you might lose him at one point, but then the master stroke—"I'm from Israel". Pure genius.'

'That's because I am!' Not a trace of irony emanated from the young woman's lips.

'Okay, let's not get carried away. That was the easy part. Now you must win him over, and quick. We need to be able to get him into Israel as soon as possible. Moshe will expect no less.'

The others turned to Levine, looking serious. As team leader, he knew the difficult task in any mission was not the first contact, fraught with danger and failure as it was. What demanded greater skill was winning over the target and getting him or her to either divulge information or do what you wanted of him or her.

Horowitz knew he was right. The newest member of the team, Sharon's was a critical role; she had to get Johannes Olsen to play her game. That would rely on things beyond her control.

'Don't worry about my ability to get Mr Olsen to do what I want. You must be ready to have the evidence I need to convince him the cause is just.'

The mood turned sombre in the room as everyone felt the pressure emanating from her words.

Levine nodded slowly. 'It'll be ready by Saturday. Now! Let's eat! I'm starving, and it's been a fantastically successful day.'

Later that evening, Danny Levine was on the roof of the house, satellite phone in hand. He was listening intently to the monologue from the other end.

When it finished, he coughed. 'I agree with you, and I told her the next phase was critical … Yes, I think she's capable … Sharon is right, though, her work relies on the information, the publicity being available by Saturday. Is that achievable?'

He took in the words of the other and nodded to himself. 'In which case, I believe we have our man.'

11

Gunfire rent the blue vault above Ramallah as President Jamal al-Umari's motorcade struggled through the crowded streets of the Palestinian capital. His Fatah guards maintained a steady jog alongside his black armoured Mercedes Benz S-Class, AK-47s held across chests, ready to bring to bear. There was little to fear here, though. The faces of the men and women in the crowds mirrored the joy he felt in his heart at the historic deal he was bringing home for his people.

Faisal Hamid watched his president soak up the adulation of his people and smiled, despite the foreboding he harboured in his own heart. It was a good day for the authority and for Palestinians. At last, a country they could call their own, despite Israelis on three sides and Hamas but a stone's throw away, in Gaza. Maybe now they would stop fighting their own people and join for the common good. He smiled sourly and grunted—fat chance.

'What's funny?'

Hamid glanced sideways. 'Nothing, Jamal. Just wondering if our friends in Gaza will be as enthusiastic as we are for this deal.'

Al-Umari considered the question as his hand continued to wave to the throngs cheering widely. He took in the raucous chatter of the AK-47s and the sharper report of semi-automatic pistols piercing the chanting of his name—"Umari, Umari, Umari!" It was a chatter that reminded him of the fragility of his tenure over the Palestinians. While Gaza remained isolated and ruled by Hamas, he could not know true peace. 'I think they will not appreciate it the way we do, my friend.'

Do we? Hamid asked silently. 'I'm sure they won't, Jamal. They are forever shouting, "War!"'

54

'War solves nothing. But is the easiest thing to start.' Al-Umari paused. 'Faisal, I want to thank you for supporting me in all this process, even though I know it was not what you believed in.'

Hamid dipped his head, thankful that al-Umari understood and acknowledged the dilemma he'd carried through so much of their time together in power. Once of Hamas, Hamid had come in from the cold as he liked to term it, following his penchant for Cold War thrillers, to work for the good of all Palestinians. Jamal al-Umari had promised something he had not seen in any other politician before—not a victorious struggle against oppressors, not big claims of political power, merely honesty and determination to carry the fight through diplomacy, whatever the personal cost. Who couldn't be swayed by that?

And now, he was on the brink of a Nobel Peace Prize. Would al-Umari be Palestine's Nelson Mandela?

Al-Umari waited for his men to give the all-clear before stepping from the car and greeting the crowds in Al-Manara Square. The noise, once softened by the triple glazed windows of the car, pulsed through his clothes and seemed to flex his skin, pounding like drums, throbbing to the beat of his heart. He soaked it in as he sauntered around, under the gaze of the stone lions, which stared impassively at the gathering.

Soon he would have to get down to the business of choosing a candidate for mayor of Jerusalem and going to Gaza. For now, he wanted to luxuriate in the praise and adulation of Ramallah, his town, his home.

The burning sensation to his ear, a sudden pain, caused him to retch, followed by the crack of a gun somewhere close by. Women screaming; sudden shouting of his guards; more gunfire, this time away from him; arms grabbing; his feet scrabbling across the tarmac; a trickle of liquid down his neck—*shit; I'm hit!*

Then he was in the car, door slamming shut, and the driver, horn blaring, was thrusting the big vehicle through the crowds, next veering down a road at speed, seemingly going anywhere, just away from the gunman.

Hamid closed the door behind him as he entered al-Umari's personal quarters in the presidential building on the outskirts of Ramallah. His friend and president looked ashen as a doctor tended the wound to his ear. Apparently, it was only a flesh wound; even so it had been a mighty scare, especially given the conversation concerning Hamas only a few minutes before. Suddenly, in the aftermath of the euphoric celebrations, al-Umari looked a forlorn figure, lost in the betrayal of his own people.

Sitting at the table, Hamid stared at his leader, incongruously bandaged about the head. And yet it was such a symbol of the life of the Palestinian. A bullet. Meant to kill? Meant to maim? Who knew, though likely to be the former. This area of the world was not known for its patience or acceptance of what it perceived as treachery.

'Was I stupid?'

He sounded like a child who'd just slipped from a tree. Hamid shook his head. 'No, no. Not at all. You have just done the single most adventurous and courageous thing in our people's history. Not everyone was going to like it.'

'I'm not sure I expected this response so quickly.' Al-Umari bit his lip—that little child again.

'Well, you got it, a proper welcome home, if you want to think that way. But remember this—there were a hundred thousand others, cheering and waving and congratulating you on making the biggest difference this country has known since the British gave it to the Jews. You are their hero. Know it.'

Al-Umari nodded his head slowly, and gradually, a smile creased his features. Leaping to his feet, the suddenness making him wince and his doctor jump, the president grabbed hold of his prime minister and hugged him close.

He looked into Hamid's eyes. 'You are right. One bullet cannot stop me. We have much planning to do. First thing is to make sure nobody can get close enough for that again. Then we have to ready for the elections.'

'What will you do about the mayoral elections?' Peter Halfin, head of Mossad, directed his words to the room's other occupant, though his eyes concentrated on the screen in front of him. Halfin was proud of his multitasking abilities. Unlike most people he knew, he could devote time on one thing and accomplish another. Like rubbing your belly and patting your head, it depended which you began first.

The silence caused him to look up; the other was busy consulting his idev, a worried frown creasing the brow.

'Mr Prime Minister?'

Ehud Malbert stirred from his concentration. 'Y-yes?'

'Is everything okay?'

By way of reply, Malbert dropped his device on the table and swiped the article he'd been reading to Halfin's screen. The Mossad chief read the words:

> AP—Breaking news: Gunfire cuts short President al-Umari's triumphant return to Ramallah from Camp David. First reports suggest al-Umari hit by at least one shot. One Hamas gunman reported killed by presidential guard.

'So, it starts,' was all Halfin said.

Malbert grunted. 'And people wonder why we hesitate,' Malbert responded fatalistically.

Halfin shrugged. 'There is little we can do about this. Umari has to fight his own battles; we have our own. You must convince people all the harder after this that giving up settlements and sharing Jerusalem is viable.'

Malbert rubbed his face with a big hand, as if it would scour away the news. 'What of other matters?'

The Mossad chief took the cue Malbert was not in the mood for talking about the elections. 'It will be close, may not be to our design, but that is the way of things these days seemingly.'

Malbert snorted. 'It'll be worse before it's better. You know what to do.' Statement, not question.

Halfin nodded.

'Good. Get to it.'

Halfin's eyes followed the despondent prime minister as he left the room. Then he pulled a small mobile from his pocket.

It was the perfect night as Benjamin and Rebekah relaxed on the roof of their brand-new house, staring at the stars, drinking wine, and relaxing into the Sabbath. They'd secured the last plot in the settlement despite some fierce opposition, but it was perfect for them. It mattered nothing that it was only a matter of miles from Ramallah. The army would protect them; of that Benjamin had no doubt as he lay back on his recliner sipping a glass of chilled Chenin.

'What's going on behind those gorgeous brown eyes of yours?'

He glanced over at his beautiful woman and reached for the trailing hand, brushing the skin. It always shocked him when he touched her; he couldn't believe his good fortune. 'Just thinking how lucky we are, I am, to be here right now.'

When she laughed, it was the sound of fast mountain water running over pebbles, or so Benjamin dreamed.

'You are lucky.' Rebekah's laugh was slow and easy, knowing.

He grinned at her. 'More wine?' He lifted the bottle.

She mouthed, *Yes*.

It was empty. 'Just a minute, baby.' He rose.

It took four bullets, in quick succession to blow him into the reclining body of his young partner. Afterwards, she would tell of no warning, no sound, just the vision of her lover falling backwards, replayed over and over in her mind as the fountains of blood spilled from his already dead body.

The killers made their way, silently, methodically, through the tiny settlement, firing indiscriminately into houses, at people enjoying the last warmth of the day before the Sabbath. One family of twenty, celebrating a birthday, were all massacred in the deadly attack.

In a final act of terror, the silent killers set charges and demolished the synagogue. The local rabbi was murdered in the explosion.

'I can only denounce this act of needless violence in the most extreme and unequivocal terms possible, and I thank those leaders of the world who have condemned the atrocities carried out against Israel and its people. It is my firm hope that this will not derail the accord, which both President al-Umari and I have worked hard to forge at Camp David.

'That is all I have to say at this time, until I have spoken to my experts.'

'What are we to do?'

Not for the first time in the last thirty-six hours, al-Umari looked lost. Hamid didn't blame him. After all, the events had been harrowing and, perhaps, unexpected. Their ferocity and speed, so soon after his return to Ramallah, were troublesome in the extreme. 'Be robust. Offer your support to Malbert but refute any idea that this has anything to do with us.'

'What about Hamas?'

Hamid shrugged. 'I can't tell you one way or the other; I can only say it wasn't us. You have to convince the Israelis it wasn't Fatah or the PNA, Jamal.'

Al-Umari bent his head over the desk and ran a hand through his thick hair. He felt old, weathered, like an old cedar left to fall and wither in the desert. 'You think they'll believe me?'

Hamid looked through the window—a perfect day for such evil. The sun shone down on a city celebrating the victory of its leader, and even then, someone was sabotaging the deal. 'You have to make them believe, Jamal. It's your job.' He sounded less than convincing. But he knew that, if anybody could do that, it was Jamal al-Umari.

'Last night, fifty-six people were murdered and over a hundred seriously injured in a Palestinian attack on the West Bank settlement of Tel Etz when gunmen rampaged through the little town, finally bombing the synagogue and killing the local rabbi, Daniel Levi.

'This is Channel Five, and I'm Natalie Epstein asking, why are we talking with the Palestinians and believing al-Umari when he says he is working towards peace? Last night's brutal attack was something we all thought had been put behind us. And yet, we finish today mourning the death of good Israelis who thought they had, at last, won the right to live where they chose.

'The question is this: What will Prime Minister Malbert's answer to this atrocity be? I'm joined tonight by professor in politics at the Tel Aviv University Ariel Shimon and political columnist Simon Kerowitz.

'Simon, you first, if I may. How does Ehud Malbert respond to this atrocious attack on the integrity of Israel?'

The satellite phone went dead, and Danny Levine surveyed the group. A big smile creased his features.

'It seems we have a cause for Mr Olsen.'

‘Shit.’

The word fell unprompted from his lips as he read the headline in *The Times*. He swiped the article, loading the main piece from the paper's Tel Aviv correspondent.

'What gives?'

Logan turned. Murtagh regarded him over her coffee mug. Sunlight streamed through the window of their houseboat moored on the Thames at Ealing, catching her tumble of raven hair, glinting off her eyes, and kissing the high cheekbones.

Stop it. 'What gives? Palestinians have attacked a settlement on the West Bank.'

'Really?'

'It's what it says here.'

'And you believe "*The Times*" implicitly?' Her fingers spiked the air with parody quote marks.

Logan shrugged.

'Somebody attacked a settlement, killed fifty-six people, and injured nearly a hundred others. It would seem to be—'

'An open-and-shut case. Yes, that's right.' Murtagh mocked him.

'I'm just saying—'

'What?'

'We should look into it.'

Murtagh sighed. 'You got that right. Check your phone. I think you'll find your boss has the same idea. Bang goes a relaxing Saturday.'

'Toast?'

Brooke Murtagh laughed. 'I would love toast, "Mr Bond", and then we'll go get the bad guys, huh? Make mine peanut butter and jelly.'

More humour tumbled from her lips as she caught the grimace on Logan's face.

Logan tapped on the situation room's glass wall. Galbraith beckoned Murtagh and him, and they entered, taking places at the large glass oval table dominating the room. Others already occupied it, some he knew, one or two unfamiliar. Des Farrow and Eddie Powell were there, now part of the senior team, as was Helen Reed, recruited from the British Army, post-Washington as a full-time tactician. The other two he knew vaguely.

Galbraith saved him any embarrassment. 'Steve, Brooke, let me introduce Phil Okri and Sally Nugent. Phil is one of our latest intelligence delivery officers, just in from GCHQ, while Sally is our new project support officer.' She turned to the new team members. 'This is Steve Logan, senior field officer, and Brooke Murtagh, our CIA liaison officer.'

There were nods of greeting all round before Galbraith called order. 'Okay, people, we have a potential situation developing in the Middle East.' She indicated the six screens, dominating two walls of the situation room. Four streamed bulletins from main news programmes—BBC, Sky, Al Jazeera, and CNN. One of the remaining screens displayed high-altitude thermal image video, which Logan took to be the settlement that had been attacked. Even as the thought crossed his mind, he could see specks of light moving towards the hot blocks and then spikes of light as weapons were discharged, punctuated by a huge explosion; it repeated.

Galbraith continued. 'First indications are this may be a Hamas attack on the settlement of Tel Etz, perhaps to cause maximum damage to Jamal al-Umar.' A picture flickered on the previously empty screen, showing the Palestinian president.

'How does this tie in with what we spoke about the other day?'

'What's that?' Farrow cleaned his specs on his jumper; Logan noted with humour the older Yorkshireman's sartorial choices hadn't changed any.

'Steve is referring to the NSA concerns over communications between Malbert and Israel shortly before his return to Israel.'

'Oh, right.'

'Short answer, we don't know, other than it is probably going to raise a response from the Israelis.'

'Can they afford to retaliate? Won't that just fall into the hands of Hamas?'

'It's something we can't rule out, Eddie. Just as al-Umari doesn't speak for every Palestinian, neither does Malbert speak for all Israelis.'

'Was there any advance notice of the attack?'

'No, Des. Hamas was particularly quiet preceding it. That might just be because they had little time to react to the news release from Camp David the day before.'

'When did they attack?'

'Late last night, just as people were readying for Sabbath.'

Logan mulled the information over. This was an unwanted diversion. Or maybe this was the main attraction, though he doubted that. But why now, after so little notice? And so little publicity afterwards? Received knowledge suggested Hamas would have made some sort of statement prior to launching an attack, even if just to say they were against any kind of deal and that there would be repercussions. Hamas wasn't shy at coming forward, especially if it meant embarrassing the Palestine National Authority in Ramallah.

However, there had been nothing from them, other than an abortive attempt against the life of al-Umari, by a confirmed Hamas member acting as a lone wolf.

So who? Hezbollah was an option. They still held the avowed goal of ridding the area of the Jewish state and still got funding from an increasingly more autocratic Iran. They'd been quieter, ever since Iran had reached its nuclear deal with the UN a few years back. It was unlikely the leadership would sanction anything not receiving the full support of Tehran now.

'Steve, you seem preoccupied. Perhaps you could advise us as to your reverie.' Galbraith appeared a little vexed at the silence surrounding her senior officer.

'Apologies. I was just trying to think who might have something to gain from this attack.'

'And?'

He shrugged. 'It doesn't make a lot of sense for the main antagonists to be involved; ultimately, they have too much to lose.'

'Could it be al Qaeda?'

Logan turned to Murtagh, and his shoulders rose and fell once more. 'It might be. They're backed by the Muslim Brotherhood government of Syria, which has been increasingly polemic about Israel. But where's the statement? There's nothing other than the media speculation and Israeli and world condemnation.'

'What are you suggesting?' Eddie Powell waited expectantly.

'I don't know,' he confessed. 'All we can do now is maintain surveillance. We need to seek out every bit of signals, electronic and human intelligence that might throw some light on this.'

Powell gave a short cynical laugh. 'Easier said than done. You know how we're restricted since the Mass Surveillance and Information Gathering Act was passed a couple of years back.'

A grimace. 'I hear what you're saying, Eddie. But this is after the fact, not before. We're not seeking to pre-empt anything. This has already happened—I'm interested in who and why. Anything we can pull up is good.'

'What if we find nothing?'

'That's equally important, Philip,' Logan told the latest member of the team. 'If there's a hole in the traffic around this, then we need to know.'

The young man dipped his head in acknowledgement and glanced at Powell for encouragement, who nodded. 'I can get on that,' he confirmed. 'I'll ring in some of my contacts back at the "Doughnut",' he added, using the slang for GCHQ's Gloucestershire-based headquarters.

'Wait till we get clearance to continue,' Galbraith advised, curbing Okri's enthusiasm. 'Okay, team, that's one aspect of the situation. However, the FCO also want us to look at the prospect of backlash within Israel itself, for which Steve already has a brief. He'll be working with Brooke to resolve this.'

'What's their main concern?'

'Not everybody in Israel is for this accord. Political newscaster and blogger Natalie Epstein speaks for a growing number of hardliners in the country, questioning the authority of Malbert to speak for the country so close to a general election.'

'She also had quite a bit to say about the attack on Tel Etz.'

'That's right, Brooke; she did, which isn't a crime in itself. However, her outspoken views are cause for concern because they offer a barometer to public opinion. If Malbert should lose the election, where does that potentially leave the peace process?' Galbraith looked justifiably concerned.

'We all know what happened after the Oslo Accord. Greater violence and misunderstanding on both sides. This is a region steeped in mistrust, going back to biblical times. By comparison, people have been trying to find peace here in just the last few minutes.'

'I understand that, Steve.' Murtagh frowned. 'What concerns me is that we're using a political blogger as a gauge of political intent.'

'Agreed, which is why we need that intelligence as soon as Philip can get it for us.'

Galbraith raised a hand. 'Let's get the paperwork done before we expose the service and Philip to the possibilities of legal action.'

'Meanwhile, more people could die.'

Galbraith was visibly stung by Logan's response. 'In which case, you had best get your plans in place to get hold of intelligence by more traditional methods.'

'They're advancing,' he retorted, taken aback by the rebuke. But it was his own fault, he figured.

'Good! In which case, when you have them, we'll meet again, and Sally can sort the details out.'

Back home, Murtagh stared at Logan from over her coffee. After the silence threatened to become embarrassing, she placed the mug on the table. 'So, want to tell me what that last bit was all about?'

'What do you mean?'

'Oh, come on, Steve! I haven't known you long, but long enough to see that Galbraith hit a chord somewhere in that big manly chest of yours.'

Even when she was being implicitly insulting, he found it hard not to smile at the brash American he'd fallen for.

She grinned as he fell to her ploy once more.

He shrugged expansively. 'I don't know.' After a short pause, he added 'Probably that everyone is so frightened about gathering information these days. So we must do the "paperwork",' he punctured the air ironically with his fingers.

'Yeah, sorry about that. That's our fault,' responded Murtagh, referring to the revelations and leaks about government-sanctioned NSA activity from the 2000s and Edward Snowden's leaks in 2013. 'Once you start prying, it's difficult to know where to stop.'

He laughed a short sharp bark of cynicism. 'Hey, our lot were just as bad. And don't get me wrong; it was right to curb it. But now we can't start any surveillance without having to get forms signed in triplicate and people wanting to know your inside leg measurement and shoe size.'

Murtagh sipped her coffee and consulted the image of her boyfriend. She loved his passion for the job, his professionalism but … 'Sometimes, Steve, you can talk such shit.'

'Hey!'

She laughed. 'That's why I love you, honey. Your conviction shines through—whether you're right or wrong.'

Logan paused. 'That's what worries me about this whole situation. If the Israelis and Palestinians are the same, where will their convictions lead them?'

'What about your new girlfriend in Tel Aviv?'

He cast a sidelong glance at Murtagh.

She was smiling at his discomfort. 'Well?'

'She's not my girlfriend; she's just very good at her job.'

'Defensive.'

'Not defensive at all!'

'Ooh, shouty! Mr Logan has something to hide, maybe?'

'No-o!'

Murtagh walked over to him, her fingers working the buttons on her blouse. She smiled wickedly, dropped slowly into his lap. Her lips brushed his cheek, and he felt the warmth of her breasts pressed against his chest.

'Can't have competition, Mr Logan. Lane has work to do, and I have mine.' Her hands closed round his head and drew him towards her mouth.

13

'**Y**ou're sure you know what you're doing?'

Sharon Horowitz resisted the urge to sigh as Danny Levine stared earnestly at her. She knew the senior field officer wanted only to ensure a mistakes-free mission—or, at least, that they'd be minimised. So instead she merely nodded once.

'Good. Olsen must suspect nothing.'

'I think she gets it, okay?'

Levine looked up sharply at the interruption, glowering at Rabin, who sat impassively sucking on one of his ubiquitous ice pops. 'Just saying.'

'It's okay Ben,' she responded using her partner's preferred soubriquet. 'And I'll be fine, Danny, honestly. After all, I'm just chatting up a guy in a café.'

Levine made to retort and caught himself. What good would going over it again do, save actually make the girl nervous? 'Okay. Just—'

'What?' Horowitz asked, with barely concealed exasperation.

'Just stay focussed.'

Horowitz made to speak, closed her mouth, regarded her superior, shook her head, and rose. 'I'm going to bed. I have an early start in the morning.' With that, she took herself off.

'Well done.'

'What do you mean by that?' Levine looked at his lieutenant.

Rabin licked a drip of bright orange liquid that threatened the integrity of his white T-shirt and considered his boss. 'What I said. Sometimes you can be a bit of a dick, Danny. Sharon has it covered. You know that. She kept Olsen onside the other day without any encouragement from us, and she'll keep the guy sweet, tell him the news when she's ready. Keeping on about how to do it will only serve to make her nervous and increase any doubts she might have.'

'We don't have time to wait while she decides the best way to turn him.'

'Maybe, maybe not. Rushing her, when she knows what she's doing, will only make things worse. Leave her be.'

Levine grunted.

'You know I'm right.'

'What did he say?'

'Move over,' Rabin said to Horowitz as he climbed on the bed.

'Well? Stop it!' she demanded as Rabin slid a hand over her breast. 'Not till you tell me what he said.'

Rabin pulled back and looked at his colleague. 'He thinks I protect you because I sleep with you.'

'That's not what I asked, but it's a fair assumption. What else?'

'Nothing. I said what I needed to, and he said we don't have time to wait for you to do your job.'

'How long does he think I'm going to take?' Her tone was incredulous as she quizzed Rabin.

'He worries. The accord will be signed soon, and he wants us to have done all we can to ensure things are as Israel expects.'

Horowitz considered this point. 'And are they?'

Rabin shrugged. 'I don't know.'

'Well, you don't need to keep standing up for me, like a macho man. I'm quite capable of doing that for myself.'

'Okay, I just thought—'

'Don't.'

'Oh. Does that mean we're not—'

'There you go, thinking again.' Horowitz giggled as she reached beneath the covers. 'Clearly, not with your head,' she remarked, her voice heavy with emotion.

Levine placed the satellite phone back on his bedside table and considered the content of the last call. In the next bedroom, he could hear Rabin and Horowitz making love in their usual energetically imaginative way. It was a distraction he disliked and the source for most of his concern about the young woman. With the news from his controller back home, it made the operation even more dangerous.

Part of him wanted to ditch one or the other, but both were indispensable to plans now that he knew they would have to complete the conversion on their own. His controller had been quite clear. They couldn't use normal methods of communication; this evening's call was the last until Olsen was theirs and they were back in Tel Aviv. If they were caught, the Israeli government would disavow them. That wouldn't be difficult, Levine decided sourly, given the fact that most of the government had no idea they were in Geneva.

How did he feel about that? Excited, he decided, and angry. This was a mission to save the State of Israel, so a little more spine from back home wouldn't have gone amiss. Then again, it gave him a chance to run things without interference from the powers that be—an enviable situation indeed.

No, it was far from perfect but, provided the two animals in the other room could work efficiently in the field, success should be assured.

Provided, he thought again as he was entertained by the sound of them both climaxing against the adjoining wall.

Halfin perused the report again and sighed. Placing his idev on a table, he went to his cabinet, grabbed a bottle of scotch, and downed the two fingers he poured without thinking. The next two fingers went with him to his leather 'thinking' chair on the other side of the room. He sank into the pliant and worn comfortable cushions and considered what he'd read.

It had made good reading, and he was happy with the decision he'd made on the back of it. These were difficult times, what with everyone watching everybody else, waiting for an advantage. Sometimes that gain could be found by the expedience of free rein. What would his colleagues think of his decision? Did it matter? Time would tell.

Once they had their orders, Mossad agents were adept and experienced at working on their own and reaching decisions acceptable to the state. Sometimes, like in the latter days of Operation 'Wrath of God', the desire to extract justice had overridden common sense; on his watch this hadn't been an issue. Operations were not planned as vendettas but as devices to secure Israel as needed. This latest was no different.

Halfin sipped on the whisky, wondering what the new day would bring in the latest chapter of the Israeli-Palestinian question. Whatever it was, he was sure that both cultures were on a long road of pain and change, which neither side would enjoy before the end.

It was dark, and the sleeper felt something had disturbed him. Raising himself, ensuring he didn't disturb his wife, he powered up the mobile and checked. A message awaited him; he marvelled at how he'd instinctively known. He read the first line and decided to get up. Before that, he reached over and kissed his wife, Rebekah, lightly on the forehead. They had been married forty-three years, built a family numbering in the tens, and ran a farm near Jaffa- it was where he and she would retire.

Retire—what a thought, seemingly as far away as ever, unless this worked. So what was the text? He padded down to the lounge of his official home, poured himself a brandy and opened the text. Slowly he read the contents, sipping the amber liquid. When he read the last words, he nodded slowly, satisfied with them.

His fingers worked carefully over the keys of the burner, pausing to read the message. He clicked the send button.

'Who are you texting at this time, darling?'

David started and turned. Rebekah stood in the doorway, the smile on her lips banishing the concern that had immediately crossed his mind.

'Just one of my advisors. They had a question for tomorrow's meeting. I couldn't sleep.'

David pressed the power button as Rebekah came over, put her arms round her husband, and kissed his head. 'This job will be the death of you. I wish you'd really consider retiring. You've given yourself to this country all your life. It's time for others to take up the struggle.'

David drained his brandy and placed a hand over his wife's. 'You are right, my dear. But there are times when the country must come first.'

'You keep saying that.' Her voice was tetchy. Or was that just his imagination? 'You have given even more than normal over the last few weeks, and with this election—'

'Israel comes first. I feel bound to ensure its future. The election is important.' He patted the hand. 'Now, let's get back to bed. I have a busy day tomorrow.'

'I am not stopping any celebrations for the sake of a fucking Jew settlement!'

'It would be expedient, Mohammed. After all, it could look as if we were capitalising on the death of those Jews. President al-Umari—'

'Can fuck himself. And fuck expediency,' Mohammed Qureshi spat the words at his aide, Youssef Ganem, who saw no need to hurry to argue the point.

Qureshi was a big man, in height and girth, and, in his youth, had been a frontline Hamas soldier. Ganem thought his stance on pragmatism in this matter was somewhat ironic, given his public denouncement of Hamas ideals, to appease al-Umari and ultimately win the position of Jerusalem mayor. The young man could only wonder at the longer play in Qureshi's head.

Seeing he was unlikely to engender an opposing response from his aide, Qureshi crashed out of his office and onto the veranda, which looked out at his favourite view, the Dome of the Rock and, to its right, the al-Aqsa Mosque. Beyond, the Mount of Olives could be seen, shimmering slightly in the late morning warmth.

This was his time! There was no way he was going to rein back from celebrating the victory over the Jews that the Jerusalem accord represented to his people—not the mewling of al-Umari and not the death of some Jews, unlawfully on Palestinian land. Whoever had killed them had done Palestine a good service.

He knew, though, it wasn't Hamas. His contact from Gaza had contacted him earlier that very morning expressing surprise at the events. Palestinians were a lot of things—stupid wasn't one of them. No, this was the work of somebody else, a troublemaker. Maybe whoever it was would surface and claim responsibility. Perhaps a darker purpose would maintain the silence. Who knew?

All Qureshi knew was he'd promised the West Bank a celebration if al-Umari came back from America with an agreement for a Palestinian mayor of the city.

And that's exactly what was going to happen.

Kemble read the papers with something approaching foreboding. The news of the attack was now old news, his new aide, Kathryn, calling him in the middle of the night to say what had happened. It was the quiet, save the meandering rumour-mongers in the press, that gave rise to his unease. By now, there should have been some sort of message coming out of the West Bank or Gaza, claiming responsibility, though he couldn't, for the life of him, understand why the Palestinians would have done something so crazy.

Maybe that was it. Yes, that was it. They'd realised that it was a catastrophic mistake and consequently were keeping quiet. It was Hamas, had to be Hamas. Hezbollah would be on a short lease because of the Iranians, who wanted to deny America any adverse propaganda.

The phone icon shone on his desk; Kemble swiped it with a finger.

'Senator, the president for you.'

Shit. A pause as he pulled his head into the right space. 'Thank you, Kathryn. Put her through. Good morning, Madam President.'

'I'm glad you can manage to call it good, John. I'm struggling right now.'

'I understand, Madam President.'

'Good. Can you explain it to me?' He couldn't, but before he could form words, Angela Carlisle carried on. 'Is this something you saw on the scope, John? Because this is a game changer. An Israeli settlement devastated on the eve of the conclusion of your talks. I can't even begin to think of the consequences.'

'Ma'am, I think we have to take a moment before we come to any conclusion. One thing I do know; it had nothing to do with President al-Umari. That man wants peace, and he will do anything to prosecute a settlement with the Israelis.'

'You are most certainly right, John. However, Mr al-Umari isn't the only influential Arab in the area. We know what Hamas and Hezbollah are like, and this bears the hallmark of one or the other, even if they refuse to take responsibility. What I don't want is an Israeli response of any kind. I will be speaking with Prime Minister Malbert today. But you have to do the groundwork on this one, John. This is your baby. Don't let me down.'

14

'The silence is eerie.' Murtagh shivered as she spoke.

Logan glanced up from his perusal of his device. 'Hmm?'

'I said—'

'I heard, just wondered what you meant?'

Murtagh shook her head. 'Israel? Settlement? Death and destruction?'

'Yeah, you're right. It's odd … in a way. Come and look at this.'

'Glad, you think it's "odd", Steve. That your tactical eval?'

The smile was wry. Sometimes she could be a little too New Yorker in her sarcasm. 'Just come and look at this?'

Murtagh walked round the desk and stared over his shoulder at what was on his idev. 'Is this a social media?'

Logan nodded. 'Yeah, Eddie put me onto it earlier. He said we might be interested.'

'Okay. What's the topic?'

'Tel Etz.'

'And? ' Sometimes he could be so obtuse.

'It's an Arab site, and most of the discussion is about the attack. Nobody is claiming responsibility, and there's a lot of talk about the possible types of weapons used.'

'Go on.'

'People are saying that cartridges found on the site are five point five-six, not seven point six-two.'

Murtagh paused. 'That would mean not Kalashnikovs.'

'Exactly, and if it was a terrorist attack, what is the most likely weapon they'd be using?'

'Damn!'

'Also, there's a thought the attack was launched with a suppressed weapon. That's unconfirmed,' he added as he saw the expression on Murtagh's face.

'But that means—'

'Nothing at the moment,' he cautioned, seeing the thought behind the eyes. 'However, we need to tell Galbraith, and C.'

'Of course.' Pause. 'I should be telling Langley. If what we're actually seeing here is correct, I think we can kiss the accord goodbye.'

'Let's hope not.'

Sir David Masters could have been a city banker, with his three-piece suit, crisp white shirt, cufflinks, and Liberty print tie. He wasn't. Masters answered to Her Majesty's Government as 'Chief', or 'C', head of Secret Intelligence Service. At this moment, instead of being at his club, as was his usual Sunday midday ritual, he had called a meeting in response to Logan's cryptic call to Galbraith. Sir David held his idev in one hand, his eyes devouring the words in the full yet succinct report.

'This is a grave analysis. Do you realise the consequences of what you're saying?' He spoke softly, an urbane tone cultivated at Eton, not given to remonstration or incredulity, but Logan could tell he was deeply concerned.

'I do, sir. That's why we requested a discussion with you first.'

Sir David looked across at Murtagh. 'You concur?'

The CIA officer regarded her words before speaking. 'I agree it's something that is disturbing. We don't intend to scare, but the evidence is stacked against this being Hamas or Hezbollah, unless they've started receiving different munitions. Surveillance from one of our satellites suggests this might be the work of … operators.'

'You paused. What made you hesitate?'

'Like Ste— Logan, I'm wary about jumping to conclusions.'

Though Sir David noted her quick self-correction, he chose to ignore it and turned to Galbraith, who sat quietly next to him. 'What is your analysis?'

Galbraith shot a look at her senior officer, which seemed to accuse him of being the puppy that had peed in the corner at the party. After what seemed an interminably long pause, she spoke. 'Logan isn't used to hyperbole. So, if he thinks this is not terrorist, it probably isn't. That gives us a much bigger problem, especially regarding the accord, as it implies an inside job, or subterfuge on the part of the Israelis.'

Sir David sat silently, hands resting on the desk, almost appearing to be in a trance. When he spoke, it was with measured force. 'Very good. I think we are in accord ourselves. I need to see the PM. Amanda, if you haven't already started, we need a team on this right away. Logan, Miss Murtagh, thank you for your work on this. I'm sure we have much for you to be getting on with.'

The meeting was over. It was time to get on.

Galbraith settled in her high-back leather chair and regarded her officer. 'We need you in country as soon as possible, Steve, before things really kick off.'

Logan took a long hard look at his boss. She was right. Unfortunately, his Israeli ran to greeting someone and asking for a beer, neither of which was going to be much good in maintaining cover. He wasn't sure about Brooke's but supposed hers was as limited. Another way would have to be found. However, he'd known that when he'd first received the assignment, as he'd known they'd have to go in at some point if things took a turn for the worse.

'I've been working on a cover for us. We need access to someone who can speak Arabic and Hebrew reasonably fluently. If we can get that, we can enter the country as a current affairs team from one of the papers here or in the States.'

'You have somebody in mind, I gather.'

Logan gave a short laugh. 'Yes, I have.'

'Who would that be?'

'John Black.' When Galbraith made to remonstrate he raised a hand to quiet her. 'John was a reporter for a small paper in Alabama before he joined the navy. Only for a year or so, but when he joined up he worked on one of the US Navy internal media outputs for a while. I think that puts him in a strong position. Oh, and the fact that he's a SEAL, with tours in Iraq and Afghanistan.'

'I'm sure. But won't that have to be cleared with his superiors?'

'I've taken the liberty of talking with people. Since President Carlisle has requested Secretary Kemble do some groundwork on the situation, I thought it expedient to be ahead of the game. John is ready to go.'

Galbraith raised an eyebrow. 'I'm sure he is. But again, what about his superiors?'

What about them? Good question. Black had said leave it with him, which had given the British officer a sleepless night, until he received the call back.

"We're good to go?" the big American had informed him in his slow Southern way.

"Was there any trouble?"

Black had laughed wryly. 'The usual, Steve. "This is above your pay grade. What do you know about the situation? Where did you get your intel?"' Black had then regaled Logan with how he'd just dropped the SIS officer's name into the conversation. "You are still a bit of a hero over here, Steve. After that, it was a matter of packing my bag."

'There's not a problem with his superiors. He's heading into Mildenhall day after tomorrow.'

Galbraith made to say something, thought better of it, and constrained herself to a dismissive, 'You know what you're doing. I'll leave you to it.'

As they walked back to their stations, Murtagh offered her insight. 'You perhaps should have told Galbraith about John before today.'

Logan snatched a glance at her. 'Maybe.' He paused. 'No, you're right. I should have. Too late now though. And we need to get a drive up to Mildenhall for tomorrow morning.'

Murtagh stopped him. 'I thought you said day after tomorrow, Steve?'

He smiled. 'So I did.'

The retaliation for Tel Etz, when it came, was more savage and brutal than anyone had expected, and from a completely unexpected quarter. Al-Bireh was waking up to the first day of work after the Sabbath. It was rush hour in the centre of the city of some 179,000 people when a young Israeli stopped his car, slowly and deliberately got out, and opened fire indiscriminately with what was later identified as a defence force-issued

Galil rifle. The man managed to kill sixteen men, women and children and injure another twenty before being shot by Palestinian police. They'd managed to only wound him, but the man shot himself with a semi-automatic to prevent capture.

The mayor of Al-Bireh shut down the city within an hour of the atrocity and called for all men and woman between the age of eighteen and thirty to report to their local police stations, where they would be sworn in to defend the city. In nearby Ramallah, President al-Umari appealed for calm. But in Gaza, his opposite number from Hamas urged all Palestinians to rise up against the Jewish oppressor.

In Tel Aviv, Ehud Malbert remained ominously quiet.

Meanwhile, Natalie Epstein blogged on the latest activity: "Another Child of Israel gives himself in the defence of this great nation. When will the government take heed and do the right thing? Malbert, forget the accord. Give Israel the defence it deserves. Take my vote for the accord. Does it work for Israel? Yes or No."

Her vote got over 90,000 hits in the first four hours of it being on the web. Verdict? A solid 70 per cent voted no.

At the same time, Malbert's popularity rating plummeted from a low 29 per cent to 13.

There was only one way all this was going.

Al-Umari was locked in his office, his security having decided it best for now. Hamid busily fielded calls from world politicians, reporters, and various guerrilla groups who all had a view on what should be done.

The president could hear his aide's patient voice explaining to each caller that, 'No, President al-Umari is not available for comment at this time.' 'Yes, he has expressed his condolences to the mayor of Al-Bireh. He will be visiting in due course.' 'Naturally he abhors this expression of violence, he also understands it in the context of Tel Etz, and he advocates peace and calm across the area.' 'No, this doesn't mean he will be backing out of the Jerusalem Accord.'

Al-Umari walked as far from the door to his aide's office as possible and sat in a chair, attempting to block out the searching, chattering voices reflected in Hamid's responses. His closed hands resting on his knees, al-Umari tried to figure how it was that things were spiralling so quickly out of control. Who had anything to gain from this sort of conflict? He could have wept. On the eve of a historic agreement, which gave Palestinians their own state, their own lives, people were acting as they ever had—singularly, isolated, focusing on hatred. There was only one thing he could do to change this situation.

He rose and strode across the marbled floor of his office, immediately noticing its incongruity with his people's struggle. That would change. At his desk, he picked up the receiver of the telephone and pressed a speed dial.

'Hello?'

'Ehud?'

'Yes. Is that Jamal?'

'It is. We need to talk.'

'Carry on.'

Al-Umari bit his lip. 'Not on the phone. We need to meet face-to-face.'

A silence extended into his office from the other end of the phone, until the Palestinian thought the other was gone.

'You think it will help?' The voice seemed at once scornful and full of suspicion, and al-Umari doubted his choice of ringing.

It was too late now. He had to carry on. 'Our people didn't raid Tel Etz.'

'Nobody said you did, Jamal. It could've been Hamas or Hezbollah. One thing is sure; Israel will finish it.'

His stomach lurched as he registered the fatefulness in Malbert's voice. 'You must do something to stop them!' The urging sounded more like pleading.

A weariness came through the line from Tel Aviv. 'I have no more sway over my people. The election will show me to be impotent. I did what I could my friend. All that exists for me now is the cold comfort of retirement.'

The emptiness of his stomach spread like a cancer, eating his enthusiasm, his dreams until al-Umari thought he might faint as Malbert's words resounded round his mind. If that was the case, then there would be bloodshed, and the accord was dead.

He couldn't let that happen.

15

Monday mornings off were a luxury Johannes Olsen treasured, this week being no different. After a breakfast of sausage, eggs, tomatoes, and mushrooms, washed down with a strong black coffee, he had picked up his camera and headed out into the city. It was nice to be doing something other than research. After all, wasn't science what had brought loneliness into his world?

He banished that thought. Things were as they were, but perhaps now he had a little reason to be happier. His thoughts went back to a previous visit to the café on Place du Cirque. The young Israeli woman had been something else and, though he was determined there would be no sex. (And who was he kidding anyway? As if she'd want sex with him!) It was nice for a young woman to be so open and seek his help. It was some relief to the aching he felt.

Olsen walked out of his apartment into the bright October day that held Geneva in its grasp. On the corner of his street, he entered the shop and picked up a packet of gum and some lens wipes. As he was leaving, his eyes caught the headlines on the local paper, and his breath left him as if he'd been hit in the stomach. The photograph on the front showed a scene of massacre, and the headline made him reach out for support. After a moment, he headed for the door, still reading the paper.

'Monsieur, vous n'avez pas payé.'

Olsen turned, in a dream. 'Pardon?'

'Votre journal. Vous n'avez payé.'

Olsen looked at the newspaper and at the shop owner, who shrugged and pointed at the paper. After a few seconds, the Norwegian walked back to the counter, as if in a dream; placed some coins on the counter; muttered, 'Pardon,' once more; and walked from the shop.

How he got there was a mystery, but he found himself once more at the café on Place du Cirque. Rather than his usual window table, he sat in a booth at the back, which, on this morning, suited him down to the ground. He hardly noticed as the waitress served his coffee, his whole attention on the article.

'Hello.'

Startled, Olsen jolted his coffee at the interruption; the young Israeli waitress stared at him. This morning she looked as though she'd been crying non-stop. Their eyes locked on the same headline.

'You've seen?'

He nodded, and she cried openly now—long drawn moans wracking her tiny frame, causing people to turn and look.

'Sit down,' Olsen advised her, glad of the momentary distraction from his own misery. He moved so she could sit next to him and be partly hidden by the sidewall of the booth.

The woman leant against the cold wood, as if all the rigidity of her body had left her.

'You okay?' Olsen felt very ineffectual as the weeping continued in the corner.

She nodded, still sobbing, so that Olsen's discomfort increased. Self-consciously, he pulled on his coffee, scalding the tip of his tongue on the still hot liquid.

'I'm sorry, just seeing the headlines, and you reading them, made me sad.' Her voice was small and lonely.

He lifted the paper. 'This is terrible. So many people killed. And the accord was agreed between Israel and Palestine. What now?'

The young girl shivered. 'I don't know.'

Olsen looked at the pictures, and his thoughts went to Judith; he shuddered, and then tears overwhelmed him. Tel Etz, the new settlement, a new chance, a new future for her and the children. 'I have to get to the Israeli consulate.'

Sharon Horowitz peaked at the Norwegian. 'Why?'

Olsen looked at her. 'Tel Etz was where my wife went with our children.'

Horowitz wondered how far to take this right now. Push too far, too fast, and Olsen could become suspicious and bolt. Hold back, for fear of saying the wrong thing, and he could walk off, never to be seen again. *Think girl, fast.*

'I could help.' Her voice was small, timid.

Olsen looked at her sharply. 'How?'

'I have a friend—at the consulate. If you tell me what you want to know, I could ask him to find out.'

The Norwegian paused and looked at the girl. 'Why ... why would you do that?'

She tipped her head, as if the question was the most ridiculous one she'd ever heard. 'You are a Jew, your wife Israeli as well. We have no one else in the world.'

Olsen shrugged. Why not? Rather than wait for the system. 'Who is your friend?'

'Binyamin Rabin. He deals with expats and visa applications for residency . He might be able to get me some information about the attack—casualties, survivors, if I ask. Do you want to know?'

Did he? Olsen realised that he probably didn't want to know the worst, because that's what it would be in all likelihood. And yet, he would need to know, would have to be told at some point anyway. Perhaps knowing now would make a difference, help him adjust. 'Y-yes.'

Sharon gauged his demeanour. 'Okay. Let me give him a call. I'll be back shortly.' She paused. 'You okay?' Her hand touched his forearm lightly, just enough concern, a tear rolled down her cheek.

Olsen nodded. 'It's just that ... Benjamin ... is my son's name.'

Sharon rose and smiled, a good caring smile, and patted his arm. 'Let me see what I can find out.'

Olsen watched her walk outside, her head tilted as she spoke on her mobile to someone. His emotions were in turmoil, and he suddenly found himself shivering uncontrollably. Shock. He was in shock, and he needed to do something about it. He felt his insides cave into the horror of what he'd seen in the papers; bile stained his mouth; sickness threatened to overwhelm him. God! What if they were all dead? What if he would never see them again? He fretted, biting his thumbnail, staring into the seemingly incongruous sunshine of Geneva's morning. The coffee cup shook as he lifted it to his mouth, concentrating on the act of drinking.

'I got through.'

Her voice jolted him back to the here and now, and he stared at the girl, uncomprehending for a moment.

'Benjamin … at the consulate,' she explained. 'He's going to call me as soon as—oh!' She reached in a pocket and pulled out her mobile, answering the call. 'Yes? Oh, hi, Benjamin … Yes … Yes … Okay … Okay … Thanks. I'll— Yes … Okay … I'll let him know. Bye now. Speak soon.'

Olsen looked at her, understanding, immediately, that something was up. He looked away. If he didn't look, it hadn't happened.

'Johannes.' Her hand was again on his arm. 'Johannes. That was Benjamin again. It … it isn't good I'm afraid.'

Gathering what little strength remained, Olsen held the gaze of the diminutive waitress. 'What?' His voice was bleak and empty, washed of all emotion. All he wanted was to know the worst.

'Y-your wife's house was caught in a bomb blast … when the terrorists blew up the synagogue. Th-the house was demolished. They … they were there, asleep at the time.'

He bunched his fists, felt his nails biting into the flesh of his palms, biting, biting, biting until the dampness came, and he didn't know whether it was blood or sweat, until the first spot appeared and spread like a little virus on the newspaper.

'How many?'

'How many what?'

'Died in the attack. How may did the bastards kill?'

'Benjamin couldn't tell me any more than was in the paper. He said he'd do some digging. If you want to meet with him to find out more, give him details of y-your wife … and children … he'd be happy to meet wherever you wish.'

The silence wound itself round the two inhabitants of the booth until Horowitz thought it might suffocate them. Then Olsen looked round and there was something in his eyes that made her smile inside. When he spoke, Olsen's voice was low, guttural, like a feral animal, waiting to be unleashed.

'I'll meet him. I want to do something to help. I'll meet him here tomorrow.' He gathered up his paper and brushed passed the waitress.

Sharon Horowitz waited until he had disappeared out of sight, down the pavement, and then reached for her mobile again.

Moments later she was speaking to Rabin. 'We have him.'

Moshe held the mobile as if it were a precious artefact. It was still warm from the call, signifying a life presented like a sacrificial lamb. Johannes Olsen had been recruited, even though the poor Jew from the Norwegian diaspora hadn't a clue what was going to happen.

He would go tell David the news personally.

'The polls are not good. And there is no time for you to campaign to try and rescue the situation, even if that were possible after the attack.' Netayev's tone was bleak as he sat fidgeting in the chair opposite a silent, stone-like Malbert.

The prime minister said nothing, just gazed into the middle distance as if only his body was in the room.

Netayev coughed.

'I'm sorry, my friend. I did hear you. I was just thinking.'

Netayev inclined his head. 'What are your thoughts?'

Malbert gave a long drawn-out sigh, rose, and walked to the sideboard. This day called for a drink, even though afternoon had barely taken over. He poured brandy into a glass; offered one to Netayev, who declined; and went back to his seat.

Netayev noted the size of the drink. Not a good sign. Malbert's predilection for brandy was well known, and this would increase his melancholy, which had become more and more noticeable as the election approached. In the short time since the agreement had been reached at Camp David, much had happened to dispel the myth of victory. The attack on Tel Etz; the attempted assassination of al-Umari; and the overt, some believed crass, celebrations in Jerusalem of what was perceived a Palestinian victory had many Israelis seething. Calls for retaliation were mounting by the hour, many led by the forthright broadcaster Natalie

Epstein, who seemed to relish the idea. Still nothing from the government of Malbert, which acted like a deer caught in the headlights.

'Well, Prime Minister?'

'Hmm?' Malbert sipped on the drink.

And Netayev, briefly thanking God, saw that it was an affectation this time, a totem to hold onto. 'Your thoughts,' Netayev encouraged.

'My thoughts?' Pause. 'I'm too old for this game. Camp David has washed me out, Schmuel, left nothing for me to work with. How do I respond to this? I was doing this for my people. And now we're as much at war as the first day I left for America.'

What could he say to alleviate the despair in the prime minister's voice? 'That isn't the case, Ehud. These things happen around here; you know that. It is the brutality of just a few who want to see the old ways maintained. Change is coming, and you are its architect.'

'I feel I am the architect of destruction. People say how much I have sold Israel to the Palestinian cause.' Malbert took a large swig, wincing briefly. 'You hear what that bitch Epstein says on the TV every day, every hour now,' he finished sourly. Malbert slumped. 'I have nothing more to give, Schmuel. Israel has taken it all from me.'

'The elections are not until tomorrow. You still have—'

'Nothing!' Malbert drained the brandy, rose, and went to pour another. Netayev's heart sank.

'You've already shown me the ratings, the opinion polls. I am fucked.'

Netayev flinched at the obscenity. His boss was not given to using such words; this was worse than he had originally thought. 'Prime Minister, I—'

'Leave me.' Malbert waved a hand dismissively. 'I need time to think.'

Netayev opened his mouth to speak, the pause between understanding he had no words and closing his mouth again seemingly a lifetime. He rose, trying to maintain composure in his own defeat. 'Very well, Prime Minister. I shall be in my office if you need me.'

Malbert waved him away.

Shrugging, the aide closed the door silently behind him, aware that the single act appeared like the closing of a chapter. Where did he look to for his next?

David listened to the caller intently. Moshe was very deliberate and clear as he delivered the good news, spelling out what it meant for the plan. A smile played briefly across David's lips, and he allowed himself the luxury of a moment's contentment. Now they could plan for real. 'What happens next?'

'Our colleague in Geneva meets with our potential partner. If that is successful, then we shall arrange to bring him here and meet the design team.'

'How soon?'

'Could be as early as the beginning of next week.'

David savoured the thought. To think they could be embarking on their mission in just a few days filled him with a warm glow. 'Very well. Tell them all we need to meet. When you speak with Yitzhak, have him source the materials needed and give us a delivery date.'

'Of course.' Pause. 'Anything else?'

David considered the point. Things were delicate now, the forces of change in play. Tel Etz had been the catalyst, the martyrdom in Al-Bireh a stepping stone, but now wasn't the time to foment further clashes, for fear of causing all-out war with the Palestinians. After all, they were only the front door. His plan was to attack the occupants of the house, not the dogs guarding it.

'Tell Golda she's doing a good job engaging with our customers. It's just what we need now to ensure the competition is kept at bay. Other than that, no … And, Moshe?'

'Yes?'

'Thank you. You're doing a fantastic job. I couldn't ask for more.'

There was hesitation from the other end. 'I'm doing what you ask of me, what is asked of me.'

'I know, Moshe. I hope they understand.'

'I … I'm sure our customers will. Let's speak again tomorrow when, hopefully, I have more to tell you.'

The line went dead, and David considered Moshe's final words. Had he been too emotive at the end? It was unlike him, but there was so much at stake. He hoped that nobody had been listening.

B y the time Logan and Murtagh had passed gate security at the centre of USAF logistical operations for the UK, John Black had negotiated his way through the airport facility and was making his way towards the guardroom. As he flashed his credentials and opened the back door of Logan's Jaguar XF, the MPs viewed their unwelcome guests in a very different light.

'You might want to call ahead, next time,' Black observed laconically.

Logan laughed. 'It did occur to me, rather belatedly, it might've been better. I was hoping to rely on the credentials of my tame CIA officer. Oww!' He rubbed his arm and glanced across at a stern-looking Brooke Murtagh. 'What was that for?'

'I'm not your "tame" anything.'

The smile he was about to deploy remained hidden as he saw the look on her face—which quickly broke out into a grin as she witnessed the confusion writ large on his face. 'Just kidding.'

'See things haven't change a heap round here,' noted the big SEAL from the rear.

'Logan is just so hard to train properly,' offered Murtagh conspiratorially. 'He just gets all British on me when he can't have his own way.'

Black laughed. 'You expected?'

'Y'got me there,' agreed the CIA officer.

'When you've both finished,' Logan observed, grinning. It had been a long time since he'd been in the company of all those he'd helped thwart the threat to President Carlisle's life; it was good to renew the acquaintance with John Black.

The drive into London was uneventful as the three caught up, at first reminiscing over the events that had brought them together and then what had happened to them all since the honour ceremony, at the White House.

'So, you getting used to living in England?'

'Just about,' Murtagh said. 'There're a few things could be altered, but otherwise it's not bad.'

'Okay, what's he got to change?' Black laughed at the look on Logan's face.

'I don't have to change anything!' remonstrated the SIS officer.

Black leaned close to Murtagh and adopted a conspiratorial tone. 'It's okay. Whisper and I'll brief him later.'

'You'll be walking,' Logan suggested huffily, 'before it gets to that point.'

'Baby, it's okay you don't have to change anything. I love you as you are.' Murtagh turned her head away as if to address their passenger. 'John it's— Ow!' She started and laughed as Logan punched her.

'Okay, people, enough of the funnies. We have a situation brewing, and people high up want some sort of action plan.'

'What gives, Steve?'

Logan gave a quick résumé to the SEAL, who listened intently, interrupting only to seek clarification on a point. He grew serious when he heard of the missing ranger and again when they discussed the attack on Tel Etz and his theories regarding it.

'Seems like we have some serious business to attend to,' Black remarked, without any sense of irony.

'Yes, we have. And we're to be in Vauxhall Cross bright and early tomorrow. I'll get a driver to pick you up from the hotel.'

'You not putting me up at your pad then?' There was a glint in the American's eye as he queried his friend.

'Afraid not, my friend. Dispersal of assets policy.'

'You shitting me?'

'Not at all. Here we are.' Logan nodded out the window at the Sheraton. 'Room's booked. All you have to do is sign in.'

Black took in the facade and tried to maintain a bored air of indifference. 'It'll do.' He grabbed his duffel, which he figured was probably a tad understated for the hotel, and made to get out of the Jaguar. He reached over to Logan and held out his hand. 'Good to see you again, friend. Looking forward to kicking some ass with my favourite Brit.'

Logan felt the warmth in the shake. 'Same here. Get freshened up, and we'll do dinner later, catch up properly.'

Black shook hands with Murtagh before climbing out and heading for the entrance.

Murtagh regarded Logan. 'Nice to have him back again.'

Logan continued to watch the disappearing figure. 'Yes, yes, it is.'

'This was picked up by GCHQ at eleven fifty-nine yesterday morning.' Phil Okri flicked the transcript from his device to the large screen in the operations room. 'It was a scrambled message via satellite phone to an unknown number in Israel.'

Around the table sat those who had first convened a few short days previously, before the Tel Etz event. Now there was a more serious mood, into which John Black insinuated his tall uncompromising frame. 'This is from?'

'That's what we're trying now to ascertain. It's been given priority at GCHQ because of what it doesn't say, as much as for what it does.'

They all read the phrases that burned on the display:

I'm doing what you ask of me, what is asked of me.

I know, Moshe. I hope they understand.

'Do we have any idea who "Moshe" is?' Murtagh considered the words on the screen as if the answer might leap out of it for her.

Okri shook his head. 'Not at this time. There is nobody within the Israeli government or any known unit whose name can be linked to anything vaguely nefarious. From that, we conclude it's a code name.'

'How about the person addressing him?'

'That person wasn't decipherable, though we believe his code name may be "David".'

'There is one other thing.' The new voice attracted attention; it was Eddie Powell. 'We've been picking up unsolicited traffic, which mentions something—a group, unit, or media plug—called "The Seven". It's appeared, seemingly, from nowhere, but we can't trace anything. We're not able to ascertain if it's a group of people, a call sign, what really.'

'You're blind?'

Powell looked at the officer. 'Yes, completely.'

Logan leaned back in his chair, mulling over the words on the screen and those of Okri, who had shown a remarkable honesty bordering on naivety in this environment—not always a disadvantage. And he knew Nigerians for being uncomplicated in their dealings. Code names and no substance; in any other sphere, it might have been ignored. Here, in this room, at this time, that wasn't an option they had.

'Okay.' Pause, evaluate. 'So, what we have are three pieces of information. Can we bring just those up on the screen?'

Okri obliged.

'"David", "Moshe", and "The Seven". Two are connected, while this group, unit, or whatever seems to be drifting in the ether. Anybody got any ideas?'

There was a silence around the room as people studiously ignored Logan and concentrated on the screen.

When the answer wouldn't jump out at them, Eddie Powell ventured a question. 'Are we presuming the elements are connected?'

Logan nodded. 'Or not,' he continued hastily when he saw Eddie's expression, which slumped once more. 'We can't assume with any confidence at this stage. These two who were talking on the phone could be business people. They could be politicians from Ehud Malbert's government. They may not be code names, as we're assuming.'

'This group, "The Seven", we're presuming they are hostile to the accord?'

'Brooke, we don't know what to think at the moment.'

'Well, Steve, we have to start somewhere, do you think?'

Not a hint of sarcasm, though she made him stiffen. 'Okay, what are you thinking?'

Murtagh stared at the screen. 'I seem to remember, from my days in high school religious studies that seven was an important number for the Jews.'

'Religious studies?' Powell felt this was funny until he caught the look on Murtagh's face.

'Yes, Eddie, religious studies. Now, if we can get away from any jokes please?'

He nodded mutely.

'Thanks. As I was saying, this number is very significant.'

'In what way?'

'I was trying to remember, Steve,' Murtagh replied testily.

'Why don't we just google it?'

'Good call, Sally. Phil?' Logan enquired of the support officer, who, with a quick nod of his head, pulled up the search engine on the screen.

Seconds later, an entry flashed up. The group read through the listing.

'We're talking about some thing or group signifying spiritual perfection? Bloody hell! That's all we need—nuts on the other side of the divide.' Powell shook his head.

'Let's keep this unemotional please,' cautioned Logan as he caught the rising mood. 'We don't know that's the case, but it's a starting point. Eddie, can you and Phil work with GCHQ and NSA to see if you can find anything more about The Seven. And get them to run any voice or background analysis on the conversation between that David and Moshe.'

Both men made notes on their idevs.

Logan looked around the table. 'Anything else?'

As if on cue, Des Farrow appeared in the room with his customary breathlessness. 'Sorry … I'm … late,' he managed as he sat down. A film of perspiration had formed on his flushed face, and he dabbed at it with a handkerchief. 'I was just looking at some info that had come in from Europe.'

'Anywhere in particular?'

Farrow's eyes gleamed as he spoke. 'Yes, as a matter of fact. Geneva. One of our officers picked up some traffic while having breakfast at a café on Place du Cirque in the centre of the city. He only caught some snippets.'

'Can we?'

'Just a minute,' breathed the little man. He quickly flicked information from his idev to the main screen. 'Here. This is a short report, the gist of a conversation he heard between a young woman and an older man, discussing an event that had transpired the night before. There was a lot of crying, which attracted his attention, but he couldn't make out too much because of his distance and the fact they spoke in hushed tones.'

Logan's attention was on the script on the screen. It seemed the officer had used good judgement in reporting it. Two people; a slither of words—*consulate, wife and children*—a name, Jo; nothing more. Maybe Joanne. Perhaps the wife? Then the final words from the man—that he wanted to help out. The man had gone then, and the woman had talked to somebody on her phone. Suddenly though, she'd appeared not to be as distraught as before.

Like Okri's information, it could be something, nothing, or everything. It was damned infuriating.

'Do we have descriptions of the man and woman?'

Farrow nodded hesitantly. 'Yes and no. We don't have any faces or detailed descriptions—just general height, build, hair colour, that sort of thing.'

'It's something. Get working on it, and see if we can start by matching Israeli agents to the descriptions, particularly the woman. Sally, do you have our covers ready yet?'

'Yes, Steve. Call by my office after, and I'll run you through the background stuff.'

'Excellent. Okay, people, do I have to tell anybody what they've got to do?'

He was answered by a line of shaking heads.

'Good! Let's get to business and see if we can make any sense of this.'

Logan, Murtagh, and Black trooped into Sally Nugent's office to sit at the desk while she presented their cover information. The three slim boxes she placed on the table contained everything they'd need to impress upon people their credentials were spot on. Nugent pushed the boxes closer, encouragingly.

Opening his, Logan scrutinised the contents. According to his passport, he lived in Ealing and was thirty-eight. The AP press card identified him as a freelance news photographer, specialising in current affairs and politics. Nugent noted the expression on the officer's face.

'Don't worry. We have kit for you to take with you … It's quite a bit of stuff,' finished Nugent apologetically.

'Great.' Logan secretly wondered about his innate ability behind the lens. It probably wouldn't do any good to admit to being completely rubbish.

'It might be better for me to be the camera person.' Murtagh winked at her partner's surprised look. 'Come on, Steve. Your photography does leave something to be desired.'

Nugent looked uncomfortably from one to the other, while behind them Black merely smiled. 'Is that okay with you, Steve?'

Logan nodded to the operations manager and suddenly laughed. 'Yes, it would probably be better the other way round.'

'Okay. I'll make the changes. They'll be ready this afternoon.' She turned to Black. 'Your cover has been provided by your consulate.'

The SEAL took the box and looked at the contents, smiling as he took them in. Logan raised an eyebrow in inquiry. Black showed him.

The British officer laughed. 'Somebody stateside has a sense of humour.'

'Huh?'

Logan took the visa from Black and showed it to Murtagh, who burst out laughing. 'There is no way I would ever buy a holiday from you.'

'I'm hurt. I think I'd make a real good tour advisor.'

A hesitant cough brought them back in the room.

'Sorry, Sally.' Logan handed Black his papers back.

'That's okay, Steve. You said you wanted to change things. What are you thinking?'

'We need to get to Geneva. Follow up on Des's findings.'

'Okay …'

'Who's our contact over there?'

Nugent considered her idev. 'Jim Souster is our man at the consulate.'

'Signal him. Tell him we'll be there this evening. He's to meet us at Geneva International. Let him know when our flight will land. Do we have an aircraft?'

Nugent nodded. 'I think we can get you a flight early afternoon.'

'Good. One more thing. Hold on those changes to our cover till we get back.' There was little point in them being rushed, and things might happen in Switzerland that would pre-empt their use. Logan glanced at Black. 'How about you?'

'I think I'll make my way a bit further south. Suddenly I feel the need to see what the tourist options of Tel Aviv and Jerusalem are.'

The White House South Lawn shone in the morning sun as its rays caught the tops of the trees. Carlisle stood at the window, hands clasped before her, attention only half on the inhabitants talking earnestly behind her. Rather, she was wondering when there would be a moment in her presidency when things might quieten down. It had all been so promising when Kemble asked her two years ago to use Camp David. The idea of a Middle East peace program and an accord between Israel and Palestine was too good to give up after the horror of home-grown terrorism and the schemes of a rogue Chinese general. He was selling her a fail-safe presidential victory, and that had captured her attention.

That was, until the NSA came along to spoil the party. And now the Brits were in on it, confirming the initial fears of her National Intelligence director and suggesting that somebody might be deliberately sabotaging the peace process. Carlisle had resolutely refused to believe it—until the news of Tel Etz hit. That had been a blow, her conversation with Malbert suggesting he was nonplussed by the whole event but that even he couldn't believe it was anything to do with his Palestinian counterpart. For his part, al-Umari was bemused, even shell-shocked, recalling the attack on him as he triumphantly entered Ramallah. The talk of the bullet had fed her memory of Drew Faulkner, and she'd stiffened to prevent the shudder from being visible.

But what to do? Foreman wanted overflight with drones, to launch a strike at whosoever could be found to be the perpetrator. That had gained a lot of support from her team. For her part, Carlisle wanted to think before she acted. Too much was at stake to jeopardise the relationship with either Israel or Palestine. That was before considering the relationship with the countries around the two antagonists. The administration had done as much work to secure a healthy rapport with Iran. The wrong actions, injudicious words could spoil years of work.

Carlisle was aware the room had grown silent. As she turned, sunlight caught her face, and she felt the last warmth of autumn touch her. Was it a premonition? A sign time was running out for her and the accord? It was decision time. Much depended on her ability to lead and reach the right conclusion.

'Ladies and gentlemen, thank you for attending at such short notice. You all know the reason Senator Kemble has called this meeting on my behalf. We have a situation developing in the Middle East that could damage the work of this administration to end centuries of conflict. I'm going to ask Bill here to bring us up to speed.'

The director of National Intelligence acknowledged his president and took centre stage in the Oval Office. The audience wasn't anything he wasn't used to, and yet this time he felt nervous, as if there was something more to be lost by saying the wrong thing, making a poor assessment. He coughed self-consciously and breathed deeply. *Concentrate on the boss*, he told himself and turned to the president.

'Okay, so the problem we have'—*fuck, weak start*—'is that we weren't sited on the Tel Etz atrocity. There's no clear perpetrator, a concern on its own, and I'll come back to that. However, what we do have is posturing by the three main protagonists, underlined by activity from individuals or very small groups. The situation is quite fragmented, and therein lies the problem.'

He dropped his idev on the low table, which Carlisle had put in as a working feature. The dark glass surface was designed to project information to everyone gathered around and, as Foreman placed his device on its face, the other senior team members took in the information scrolling before them.

Foreman allowed everyone a moment to read and visualise before he spoke. 'Tel Etz isn't the problem, per se. It's what we think might be behind it.'

'What's that?'

Foreman regarded the interrupter. A small serious-looking person, Rose Cundy was the new Homeland Security director, someone determined to impress. Like Markham, Foreman kind of liked her but was aware of her reputation for vindictiveness. After all, it was she who had orchestrated the downfall of her predecessor, David Chandler. Foreman would need to exercise caution.

'There is increasing evidence of a group forming in the shadows.'

'What sort of group?'

Foreman denied himself the shrug. 'It's not clear at this time, Rose. Just snippets of information, metadata, etcetera, untraceable to any known number.' Even as he used the words, he knew what they meant to those listening. NSA was snooping once more. There was much discomfort in the room as he stopped.

'Are we saying we're collecting data from calls and emails, without presidential authority?' Carlisle looked fit to bust. and Foreman coloured.

When he remained silent, Carlisle continued. 'This information had better result in something, or I'll require somebody's head.'

'We were left with few options, Madam President.'

Carlisle regarded the quiet interruption. 'Sarah, when I require apologies and excuses, I'll ask for them. Until then, please restrict your comments to the facts.'

Sarah Markham coloured, and everyone realised this was going to be a most uncomfortable meeting.

'Does anybody have any facts, anything that translates into actions?' The president's gaze swept the room, with no one willing to talk first.

'Ma'am, Sarah is right. We're struggling in the dark, trying to find information about something we cannot grasp.'

'Which is no excuse for breaking the law, Bill. If this gets out, we'll be crucified. No, actually, I'll be crucified, by a public who justifiably needs to know we're above criminal activities for our own purposes.'

'I appreciate that, ma'am, but—'

'No "buts". I don't want to hear about us doing anything like trawling phones and email traffic again, without seeking my express permission. Nor do I want to hear that you're using an ally to do what I've told you not to. Now, can we stop this turning into schoolroom politics and get on with what we ought to be doing?'

'Anybody want coffee?' Kemble rose from the cream couch and went to the jugs on the sideboard, pouring himself a coffee.

One or two joined him. It was a welcome break from what had been destined to turn into a farce. As he sat again, Kemble realised that he was the only calm one in the room. Tensions were high on the misuse of intelligence collecting, and the focus had gone from the real reason for being here. Despite the feeling his accord could be crumbling around him, he remained at ease. It had been a long time coming, and he wasn't about to get carried away. A level head was required right now.

'I agree with you, ma'am. We can't be seen to be doing anything that isn't lawful.' Kemble sipped on his coffee. 'So we need to get people in there, and we need to get some drone overflight of Israel.'

Markham shuffled on her high-back chair, deeply aware of the meaning behind Kemble's words. Should she retort that her people were doing those very things, and she hadn't been given chance to say so? She still smarted from Carlisle's rebuke but had to say something.

Deep breath. 'We are doing those things. A stealth drone is constantly over the country, gathering electronic intelligence. But that is very limited in extent because of the way in which this group is working. We're moving to insert operatives into the country.'

'How come the ELINT is so limited?'

'This group appears very well organised. They keep changing phones, using burners destroyed after each use. Currently we've picked up on these things only because of the continued use of the names "David" and "Moshe" across a few different calls.

'We've also tracked a number of satellite calls from Geneva to Tel Aviv supporting our assessment and suggesting there is an Israeli group working on a project in the Swiss capital.'

'Who might that be? And what are they after in Geneva?'

Markham faced her interrogator, Rose Cundy, whom she saw as a threat to her position. 'We don't have sight on that yet, but part of a discussion overheard in a city centre café referenced Tel Etz. We aren't the only ones interested,' she continued as if an afterthought. 'The Brits are also wondering what is going on.'

'What's their take?'

'They have little more than us but think it's worth investigating on the ground, so they're prepping to send somebody to Geneva as we speak.'

Cundy huffed. 'And do you think it would be a good idea if we did the same?' The brittle tone spoke of disdain.

'We are sending somebody,' Markham kept the smile in check. 'One of our officers will be on the same flight as the MI6 operative. We're also putting a person into Israel to carry out recon on the place.'

'Who's going to Geneva?'

'Brooke Murtagh, ma'am.'

Carlisle nodded. 'Let me guess. The MI6 person isn't Logan by any chance?' Markham nodded, eliciting a smile from the president. 'That's some good news then. Do you know who is going to be going into Israel?'

'Lieutenant John Black.'

'Another good choice,' Carlisle commented, remembering the work the SEAL had put into her personal protection. 'Okay, people, there's some work to do on this. I don't want anything to interfere with the work of these people. They must be protected at all costs. If something is being done to threaten the accord, we must do all in our power to prevent that from happening.

'Is that understood?'

Nods rippled around the room.

'Okay, let's to it!'

As people began to file from the room, Carlisle caught Markham's attention. 'Can we speak please, Sarah?'

They waited until the room was clear of the others, and Carlisle indicated for Markham to sit with her. The CIA director sat stiffly, still uncomfortable with the dressing down she'd received earlier.

'You clearly didn't agree with my earlier words.'

Markham thought for a second. 'No, I didn't, ma'am. But you're the president, so I accept what you said.'

Carlisle regarded her director. 'Sarah, you and I don't really have any kind of relationship going, and that's my fault. You were instrumental in helping me when I had to take over from Jonah.' The mention of the last president, assassinated aboard Air Force One, made her pause. 'I repaid you by ignoring you, and for that I'm really sorry. But what I said today I stand by. We can't afford time apologising for past actions. What's done is done, and we move on.'

Sarah felt her stomach churning and wondered why she was so concerned. Maybe being director of the CIA had been a step too far, and she was now finding it difficult to maintain her usual persona as a hard case. Whatever it was, she knew she had to sharpen up and that Carlisle was right; apologies didn't win wars. 'What do you want the CIA to do?'

'We both know that Logan can get to the bottom of this better than anyone and that Murtagh and Black couldn't be a better team for him to work with. But he's a Brit, and I need an American leading on this. I want them to be coordinated by our consulate in Switzerland. Can you set that up with the station chief in Geneva as quickly as possible?'

Markham nodded. 'I'll get on it straight away. Anything else?'

'Can you put together profiles on Malbert, al-Umari, and the Jerusalem Palestinian mayor, Qureshi? I want to know everything I can about them, just to be on the safe side.'

'Sure. End of the week?'

'As soon as you can. Friday at the very latest.'

'Okay.' Markham rose, feeling her professionalism cloaking itself around her once more. Again, she felt more her old self.

She'd reached the door before President Carlisle stopped her. 'One last thing, Sarah. No mistakes. We cannot afford them this time. If something is threatening the peace in the Middle East, I want to know before it happens.'

A cold wind wrapped icy fingers of greeting around Logan and Murtagh as they descended the steps of the chartered business jet into the dark of a Geneva evening. Floodlights painted isolated pools of illumination on the wet tarmac and the sounds of a busy airport cloaked them as they moved towards the lone car waiting for them.

A young man wearing a pillowed North Face jacket and a serious expression moved to greet them. The outstretched hand, encased in a thick glove, was limp; the officer adjusted his grip accordingly.

'Logan? Jim Souster, British embassy. I'm here to take you to your hotel. I'll pick you up in the morning. London has advised me of your mission, and I'll brief you further tomorrow.'

'We'll do it tonight at the hotel.' Logan looked at the man, biting back his disdain at a man who was yet to greet his partner. 'Brooke and I want to hit tomorrow running, if you don't mind.' His tone made it clear he didn't care if he did or not.

'Oh, sure.' There was a tremble in the man's voice as he turned back to the car, hurrying as Logan trod close on his heels.

The journey into Geneva was short, and after leaving the car in the hotel's parking lot, the three were in the lobby checking in.

'I've got you two rooms.'

'One will be enough. Thanks.'

Souster muttered an apology and informed them he'd wait down in the bar while they settled in. They nodded and made their way to their room.

But in the lift, Murtagh exploded. 'The little shit! Where did you guys get him from?'

Logan understood what she meant. He'd had to restrain himself as the embassy official continued to blank her. The man's behaviour was unfathomable, abnormal in the extreme. Was he anti-American? Did he have a thing about women?

'Look, it is shitty, but we don't have to work with him beyond tonight. So let's get what we need and get shut of him?'

'Suits me.' Murtagh glowered.

She was still moody fifteen minutes later as they approached the young man in the bar. He was sat hunched over at a table, a beer, hardly touched, in hand.

'You go sit with him. Make him uncomfortable. I'll get drinks. What do you want?'

'Bacardi and coke, long please, plenty of Bacardi.'

Minutes later, Logan passed Murtagh her Bacardi, took a sip of his Malbec, and turned to the man. 'So, what gives?'

Souster coughed and reached in a pocket. 'We believe there's a Mossad unit at work in the city and they're about to recruit somebody.'

'We figured, from the reports you sent in to London.'

Souster spoke only to Logan. 'Well, we've done some trawling and identified this person as the head of the unit. His name is Danny Levine.' He pushed a photograph across the table to Logan, who pointedly passed it to Murtagh. She glanced at the face, instantly recognisable as Middle Eastern—jet-black hair, olive skin, and prominent nose, along with deep brown eyes that spoke of a shadow, hiding something.

'How many are there in the unit?' Murtagh handed the photo back.

Souster looked at Logan. 'We think ab—'

'Hey, fella. I'm over here.' Murtagh placed a hand on Souster's forearm.

She felt him stiffen under her touch, but his face flushed with embarrassment. For the first time, Souster looked at her.

'You got a problem with me?'

'N-no.'

'Fine. Well, talk to me when I'm asking a question.'

'S-sorry. W-we think the unit has about four or five in it, but Levine is the leader. He's been identified at several locations at or around Place du Cirque.'

'Anywhere in particular?' Logan regarded the young man closely. How on the ball was he?

'Yes, a café. We think he, his team has been watching somebody.'

'Do we know who?'

Souster shook his head at Murtagh's question. 'It's unclear, but you heard of the incident in the café on Monday?'

They both nodded.

'It may be connected. Afterwards, Levine was on a satellite phone to Israel. We're making a tenuous link.'

'But a link nonetheless.' Logan paused for thought. 'Okay, I want to visit this café tomorrow. Leave us directions and keep on trying to find the rest of the Israeli team. Be careful though, if they're Mossad.'

Souster looked uncomfortable. 'I'm instructed to accompany you to the café and be with you at all times. How long are you expecting to be in Geneva?'

Logan refrained from venting his disdain at the man and, instead, drained his drink and looked squarely at the young embassy contact. 'As long as it takes to get answers.'

Ten minutes from the centre of Tel Aviv, David was sat in the air-conditioned security of his limousine. Next to him, his lieutenant, Moshe, was deep in conversation on a cell phone. David allowed the words to wash over him without comment; Moshe would advise him soon enough. For now, the older man contented himself with watching the city pass him by. Tel Aviv was not a city he loved, except as any Israeli would. Rather, he kept all his respect and passion for Jerusalem, the place soon to be ruined by the accord.

'It is done.'

David turned and took in the serious expression on the face of his lieutenant. 'Expand.'

'The transfer of our expert is under way. He'll be on a flight by lunchtime today. Meanwhile, Yitzhak has begun the process of sourcing the raw materials required to build our product.'

Code, forever code, lamented the old man silently. A necessary evil that would perhaps pass. 'Good, Moshe. How do you feel about our expert?'

Moshe was disassembling the phone. He destroyed the SIM, methodically twisting the little piece of metal and plastic until it was unrecognisable. 'He's a safe bet after Tel Etz. He was informed his family were killed there. He will do anything for us.'

David listened to the words. Even though he knew the car was protected from surveillance, he winced as Moshe spoke.

'Let us hope so. For the sake of Israel and Jews everywhere, let us hope so. Very well. As soon as he is in the country, make him secure. I want him focused on the job in hand. That is imperative.'

'Our people know what to do. He will be given the best of everything when he arrives on site, and he will provide us with the capability to silence our critics and enemies once and for all.'

David looked at the traffic around the car, the packed streets, and the last of the lights winking out as Tel Aviv readied for another busy day in the world. Would all these people understand the sacrifice he was making for them? The difficult decisions to be made in the coming days and weeks would, inevitably, culminate in Israel's vilification by the world. Could they understand the necessity of the actions? Maybe not today or next week or even next year—but eventually it would become clear to everybody, not just Israel.

'And Dimona? What of the preparations there?'

Moshe smiled, a slim almost bleak expression. 'That's all according to plan. Olsen should have everything he needs when he gets there. Ariel and Uzi are on their way there as we speak, to finalise plans.'

'Good.' David considered the traffic still, anxious that Moshe did not see his sudden unease. 'Good. Make sure everything is in order.'

'I will.'

'Now, what is next on today's agenda?'

The vehicle in which General Topol and Major General Miranda Klein travelled had been provided, driver and all, by the one known as Moshe. The vehicle was driven neither too fast nor too slow, nor so perfectly as to draw attention to it. Everything was considered, Topol reflected, and that made him feel confident enough to embrace what was required of him.

He was pleased in a way that he had been given the codename "Ariel" and that it was for Sharon that he was named. The one-time general and leader of Israel was a hero of his, and Topol admired the choice; it showed perception on the part of the individual doing it.

What about his air force comrade? Did she have the characteristics of Uziel, man or gun? He glanced across at her, face half-hidden behind aviator glasses. She was an unknown quantity to him, but he felt they would get on really well.

The SUV was fast approaching their destination, and Topol tensed slightly. Excitement coursed through him; at least he thought it was that. This project promised to change life for many people, and it looked as though his would be one of the first.

At the brand-new security checkpoint, the driver brought the vehicle to a halt as two guards approached. In the gatehouse, two more soldiers stood, alert, assault rifles at the ready position. Farther back stood two Hummers with roof-mounted fifty cals, the barrels trained menacingly at the SUV's windscreen. The two figures approaching were not military like the other guards. Rather, they were obviously trained operators of some sort, man and woman. After a moment, he decided on for Mossad. They had that sort of bearing that didn't exist with Shin Bet operatives. They would be far more useful.

'Papers.' Statement, not request.

The driver handed their passes through the open window, letting the heat of the Negev beat the air conditioning into submission. The man studied the photographs until it was almost rude. Topol coughed impatiently, loudly enough for the guards to hear. If they did, they chose to ignore it.

Finally, the guard passed back the papers, looked directly at Topol, and spoke. 'Welcome to Dimona, General Topol. We've been expecting you. The site manager's office is on the right, about a kilometre down this road.' The man stepped back and saluted smartly. 'Enjoy your stay, sir.'

The general nodded quietly and motioned their driver on. As they moved forwards, he noted that the other guards, obviously IDF, kept their weapons trained on the fast-moving vehicle. It pleased him to see such disregard for authority and person.

At the site manager's office, Topol and Klein stepped into the full heat of the midday desert. A short portly man appeared at the door to the office complex, smiled, and scuttled across the sand-dusted tarmac towards them.

'Welcome to the Dimona nuclear facility, General Topol. I trust your journey was uneventful?'

Topol regarded the little man. He was a picture of rude health, despite his portly stature and ruddy complexion, bounding up to them and pumping the general's hand with vigour, as though he were a long-lost friend. His grip, the general noted, was firm and gave the impression of someone totally at ease with himself.

'For sure. You're Walter Kiegel?'

The little man smiled. 'Correct! And you must be Major General Klein?' he asked of Topol's companion, who dipped her head briefly in acknowledgement.

'How are preparations proceeding?'

There was that smile again, as if they were talking about the weather. 'Very well indeed. The reactor is up and functioning at 98 per cent efficiency. We will be able to produce our first graded uranium in the next two weeks.'

'That quickly?' Klein couldn't conceal her surprise.

Kiegel's face grew smug. 'Oh yes. But then the facility was never truly offline, despite what was publicised. It was always known there would be a need for it at some point.'

Topol considered the statement, almost throwaway, yet not so. It spoke to Israel's need to always be prepared to strike their enemies first—a good strategy. But the scientist was too ready to talk. He allowed Kiegel to usher them, away from the heat, into the cool of the building.

If it was a structure from the early days of the facility, its decor didn't speak of neglect. The walls were freshly painted, pristine tiles and carpeting and new furniture all through. Topol remarked on this as they entered Kiegel's office.

'We didn't want to give the impression of a facility on the brink of decay. Dimona has been dormant, not abandoned. I'm pleased to say that everything has been accomplished on time and made easier by the fact that the teams assigned here were so well organised and effective.'

'You had a moment though, a few weeks ago.'

Kiegel's face clouded momentarily. 'A mo—? Ah, yes! Nothing the IDF detachment wasn't able to resolve efficiently though.'

'I heard. What happened to the body?'

A half-smile clung to the corners of Kiegel's mouth. 'What usually happens in the desert, of course. He won't be traced till long after it's important.'

Klein kept her expression blank, finding the man distasteful. 'We expect our expert to be in country very soon. We're also sourcing important materials, to be shipped in. Is everything ready to receive them?'

Anger flitted, bat-like, over Kiegel's visage. 'As I said, everything is ready,' he rebuked pointedly.

'Can you detail for us everything that has been done?' Topol enquired.

'Even better,' responded the manager proudly, drawing a dossier from his desk. He handed it to Topol, who began reading quickly. It was a dry, detailed document, full of checklists, risk assessments, evaluations, and readiness reports. Kiegel was right, Topol noted as he took it all in.

The general drew in his breath, slowly, deliberately. 'You're aware the military is taking over the facility?'

Kiegel's head bobbed vigorously. 'Actually, the teams are in place now. The construction teams left a few weeks ago, the management team last week. There's just me to complete the final handover to you.'

'Then this will come as a surprise.'

Evidently it did, Klein surmised, as she saw Kiegel's eyes bulge.

The general's revolver barked twice, Kiegel fell backwards against the wall, surprise writ large in his dead eyes.

18

Breakfast was a silent affair. Brooke Murtagh ate eggs and toast without comment, Logan knowing better than to engage her in conversation. The previous night's encounter with the British consulate official weighed on her. Truth be told, she was fuming at the official's rudeness. If Steve hadn't been there, and if the case wasn't so important, she'd have either walked out or punched him.

Probably the latter, she decided, and the thought brought a smile to her face.

'Something's brightened your morning!'

The smile broke into a grin. Just hearing his voice made her feel light-hearted. Murtagh hadn't believed anyone could have made her feel like that again, let alone the sometimes-acerbic Brit who could border on stuffy. He was very different from Brad, her ex, a sanctimonious, self-absorbed asshole from Quantico.

'Want to tell?'

She glanced at him. 'You.'

He raised an eyebrow, clearly doubtful at her easy reply. 'Okay, it's definitely me. It doesn't have anything to do with wanting to give a certain British consulate official a good slap does it?'

'Maybe.' Murtagh laughed as the arch on Logan's eyebrow threatened his hairline. The Brit shook his head. 'But seriously; you make it all worthwhile, my love.' Murtagh leaned back and ran fingers through her hair.

Logan laughed but remained focused on the previous night. 'He was a bit of a twat, I have to admit.'

'A bit? Understatement of the century, honey,' Murtagh reflected sourly. 'Look.' She stood abruptly. 'He'll be here shortly. I'm going back to the room while you chat up your friend. Let me know what the score is.'

Logan tipped his coffee cup at her in acknowledgement and watched as she weaved through the tables and out of the restaurant. Almost on cue, the young consulate official appeared in the opposite doorway, his neck craning, presumably making sure Brooke didn't double back, figured the officer. Satisfied, Souster made his way over to where the MI6 officer was pouring his second coffee of the day.

'May I?' Souster indicated the chair Murtagh had been sitting on.

Logan nodded curtly. He admonished himself; *keep a clear head*.

'Coffee?'

The younger man nodded.

Logan attracted a waiter and then drew his first question. 'So, what was yesterday about?'

'Uh, what do you mean?'

'You know very well what I mean. All the shit with my partner. You were pretty damn rude, and she's about this far'—Logan measured a very small gap between thumb and forefinger—'from slapping you good and proper.'

Souster blushed, concentrating on the freshly poured coffee.

Logan allowed him a brief moment before coughing impatiently.

The young man looked up sharply. 'I, uh, was following orders.'

'Which were?'

Gathering himself, the official launched into his explanation. It transpired his boss, the SIS station chief, had received a message from London informing her that the case was being passed over to American control. When no real explanation had been offered, she'd done as instructed, giving Souster orders to do the briefing, rather than come and meet Logan and Murtagh herself.

'So, you see, I'm just here to ensure you have all our intel before I take you to meet with the CIA station chief.'

'I suggest you apologise to Brooke if you get the opportunity, not that I think she'll take it kindly now.'

'I know,' replied the younger man with feeling. 'I'm really sorry.'

Logan waved away the apology. 'Save it for Murtagh. Where are we meeting the CIA station chief?'

'He's setting up an observation post on the café.'

'Presumably in a vehicle close by,' Logan ventured.

'Sorry, yes. We're supposed to meet him there at nine. It's thought the Israeli's are going to move their asset today.'

Logan consulted his watch. 'We'd best get a move then. Is your car out front?'

Souster nodded.

'What is it?'

'BMW 3 Series, dark blue.'

'Okay, we'll meet you there, ten minutes.'

'There,' observed Murtagh ten minutes later, and they headed over. A BMW pulled out of its parking space and waited as they climbed in, before driving smoothly away. The journey through the heavy morning traffic was quiet and fuss-free, and some twenty minutes later, they pulled up in Rue des Rois, leading off Place du Cirque. A short walk back along the road, and Souster rapped his knuckles on the rear doors of a white Sprinter van parked near the junction.

It opened, and a voice spat testily from the interior. 'Get in.'

The three found themselves crammed in at the rear of the van. It was a tight fit. One side was occupied by a bank of surveillance equipment, screens, listening devices, and communications equipment, before which sat two individuals. The female was slim and nondescript, in a classic spy way, and focussed on the scrolling information. Her companion, a large bull of a man, was red of face with an angry demeanour. He barely gave them a second glance as they jostled for position.

The air in the van had that stale quality that came with long-term surveillance, and the cold bitterness of old coffee drifted through the tiny eddies of discomfort emanating from the occupants.

Finally, Logan could take it no longer. 'I'm Steve Lo—'

'I know who you are, Brit,' growled the man, eyes fixed resolutely on the monitor before him. 'The great Steve Logan, who came over and saved

America and its president from the enemy.' A low sneering laugh, bark almost, underlined the cynical comment.

'Steve Logan, Secret Intelligence Service,' the Brit continued after a moment's pause. 'This is Brooke Murtagh, CIA, and Jim Souster from the British consulate. You are?'

'Paul Rickman, station chief from the US embassy.'

Control your temper; losing it won't help right now. 'Jim here was telling us you've been watching a suspected Mossad team.'

Rickman merely grunted in acknowledgement, keeping his attention fixed to the screens.

The Brit continued. 'I presume they're somewhere close by.'

With a speed belying his bulk, Rickman rose and thrust his large frame down the van at Logan, who stood his ground impassively. Sour breath assaulted his face, but he didn't move, didn't waver.

'Presume what you want, *Mr* Logan. You just need to know this is our play now, and you're providing support.' Speckles of spit dusted Logan's chin.

Enough was enough. 'In case you hadn't noticed, Rickman, this is a dual-nationality operation. We have as much invested in this situation as do you Americans.'

'Course you do. Like Britain is the big arbiter of world peace. You were so clued in that you were right on top of this Mossad shit and didn't see it.'

'Washington has expressly advised you tha—'

'Washington can go screw itself.' Rickman ground the words out in a deadly monotone. 'I'm the station chief here. This is my operation, and I intend to suck you dry and spit you out the back while I get on with the real work.'

Logan struggled the urge to punch the man and wondered what the two behind him were doing. He couldn't expect much from Souster, but he'd been hoping for more support from Brooke. 'I'm not sure quite what you mean by real work, Rickman, but the best thing we can do is come together on this. We're both after the same outcome.'

Rickman had been moving back down the van. Nonetheless, he whirled and squared up once more. The interior of the vehicle was overheating fast, but Logan concentrated only on the threat before him. 'I'm not working with anybody, and you and I are not after the same thing. All I want from you is all your information and then to fuck off.'

Logan wondered again where Brooke was in all this; she was, after all, CIA, and perhaps she could calm this idiot down. Even as he thought this, he believed he could hear her on the phone. At a moment like this? But his adversary required all his attention, so he pushed a little against the man's presence. 'You have to listen to me. All the time we spend bickering plays into the hands of the Israeli team, whoever they are. So why don't we calm down and get to business?'

Rickman's face grew a deeper shade of red. 'You are not going to take this one, Logan.'

'What the fuck is your problem, Rickman? Why are you so bloody wound up over this?' He felt his temperature rising in the highly charged atmosphere.

But before Rickman could retort, Brooke gently moved Logan aside and offered her cell-phone to her compatriot.

'Somebody for you,' was all she said as Rickman took the device from her outstretched hand.

Rickman raised the phone to his ear. 'Yes? Who is this?' He was clearly unhappy that his tirade at the Brit had been cut short, and then his face fell.

Logan turned to Murtagh and mouthed, *Who?*

Murtagh smiled knowingly and replied soundlessly, *Director Markham.* He repaid the expression.

They waited while Rickman took the one-sided call, occasionally making acquiescent noises to his boss in Langley. Eventually the conversation came to an end, and Rickman handed the phone back to Murtagh with a barely polite, 'Thanks.' Without another word, he left the van.

Putting the cell to her ear, Murtagh listened as she received instructions from her boss. Like Rickman before her, she made only brief acknowledgements of the conversation, before ending the call. She placed the device back in her pocket before sitting where Rickman had been just a short while before.

Logan walked down the van to her. 'Well?'

'Well what?'

'What about Rickman?'

Murtagh scrutinised the screen before her displaying the front of the café. 'We don't need to worry about Rickman anymore. Director Markham heard everything. She doesn't take kindly to that sort of behaviour.'

'Thank God. It was a bit over the top. What the hell had I done to piss the guy off anyway? I've never met him before in my life.'

'No, but he knew Faulkner, understood some of the history between you two guys, and blames you for the radicalisation of his friend.'

'Shit.'

Murtagh looked at her lover and shrugged. 'Hey, it happens. We have no time to worry about that right now. We have an operation to sort out.'

He nodded. 'You're right.' He turned to the woman who was operating the surveillance equipment. 'Hi. Steve Logan.' He smiled.

She returned the look with not a little relief.

'You are?'

'Stacey Lincoln.'

'Well, Stacey, what gives?'

The young woman turned half towards the Brit, keeping an eye on the displays. 'We got mikes in the building, and we're building transcripts. It seems there's a waitress, by the name of Natalie, talking with one Johannes Olsen. He is the man your field operative picked up on the other day. It seems they are talking about moving immediately and flying out to Tel Aviv.'

'When?'

'As far as we could make out, today.'

Logan turned to Murtagh. 'So we must move, and quickly.' To Lincoln. 'What else has been said? Who is this Olsen?'

'We've done some digging in records. Johannes Olsen was registered as a scientist at CERN, nuclear physicist to be exact.'

'Was registered?'

'Yes. We spoke with his director. He resigned as of yesterday; his desk was cleared by five. He's also given a month's notice on his flat in the Jonction area of the city, though that was later withdrawn.'

'Somebody wanted to make it look like he was still around for a while,' Murtagh opined.

Lincoln nodded agreement.

'Fortunately, it was too late to hide it from you guys.' Logan looked at the front of the café, bright in the morning Geneva sunshine. People were going in and out, each scanned by facial and physiological recognition software and checked against Olsen's profile, displayed on another screen. Nothing yet.

'When CERN said he'd resigned, did they give a reason for his departure?'

'Family issues, apparently. They said he was unsure when he'd be back so preferred to resign, rather than leave his options open.'

'Unusual behaviour, unless you have no intention of returning.'

'Possibly.' Logan mulled over Murtagh's words. 'Seems odd they picked up on the flat but not the job,' he said to nobody in particular.

'At least we're not playing too much catch-up.'

'Sure.' Logan looked at the café. 'Why don't we get some coffee?'

Murtagh glanced at him curiously and then nodded.

Logan turned to Stacey. 'Do you have any earpieces?'

The young American nodded and handed a couple to the Brit. He passed one onto Murtagh and put the other in place. Then he turned and rapped on the window that separated the back of the van from the driver. The latter turned and opened the slat.

When Logan felt he had everybody's attention, he addressed them. 'People, listen up. This is a delicate situation. We don't know what Olsen and the woman working him are going to do, but we can assume it probably involves them leaving the country, presumably for Israel. The most obvious route is the airport, either a scheduled flight or a charter. Other than that, they'll plan to get him over a border. France is easiest but obvious, so they could try Italy.

'Jim, I want you to check all flights out of Geneva International. Check for last-minute seats on scheduled flights bound for Israel, aircraft that have recently been chartered, or where flight plans have been changed last minute. Stacey, if he finds anything, get it to us straight away.' Logan looked at the driver. 'How good is your driving?'

'Good.'

'Okay. When the targets leave the café, you follow and keep them in sight. Don't worry about us.' He turned. 'Jim, I need the keys to the Beemer.'

A moment's reluctance from the consulate man before he delved in a pocket and handed them over.

He nodded his thanks and headed for the back doors, Murtagh following. As he stepped to the road, he passed a last comment to everybody. 'Remember, you're following them, not taking them down. Keep your distance and report to us how you're doing. Jim, is there equipment in the car?'

Souster nodded.

'Thanks. Okay, let's to it.'

He swung the door closed and both he and Murtagh walked to the end of the road. They stood on the corner, next to Rickman, who was on his third cigarette. He addressed the two without looking.

'Guess you think you're gonna save the world again, huh?'

'Just having a coffee,' Logan rejoined laconically and crossed the road.

19

Danny Levine packed the satellite phone in a side pocket of his rucksack, pulling the Velcro flap down hard to ensure it wouldn't fall out—an affectation of his. Everything had to be safe and secure. Pretty soon now, their prize would be wrapped up too, and he would be starting his journey to Israel. Levine allowed himself a quick smile. A job well done; not long now.

He walked slowly around the apartment they had inhabited for a couple of months now, ensuring everything was wiped down. Covers had been removed and disposed of; cutlery, pots, anything that might hold a trace of their presence had been methodically removed and trashed over the last week. All that would be left after this morning would be an empty apartment, ready for its next inhabitants.

That had also been arranged.

He gathered up the sleeping bags and took them down to the car, a Passat, a nondescript blend-in type of car, but with the biggest engine available. Rabin was in the 3 Series, with a three and a half-litre engine and would pick up Sharon and Olsen. Levine was the backup—in case they were followed. The other team members had gone ahead of them to prepare for the exfiltration. Checking his watch, Levine bounded back up the stairs one final time.

He hoisted his rucksack, locked the door, and headed back to the car. Time to take up station.

Logan and Murtagh sat in the window of the café, drinking, laughing, and acting like a couple of tourists pouring over a map of the city he'd picked up from a tabac. Periodically, he'd look up and sweep the room. He'd already clocked Olsen as they walked in and took a table. He wanted to make sure he recognised the guy wherever they might see him.

'What's our friend doing?'

He kept his attention on the map. 'He's talking to a small blonde woman with a good Mediterranean tan. I suspect she's his handler.'

'Reasonable. Do they look like they're ready to move?'

'Not yet, though she is checking her watch quite a bit. Wait, Olsen is moving.' Logan watched as the lanky Norwegian rose and walked away from the cubicle, but he headed for the toilets, not the door, and the woman remained seated.

Five minutes, and Olsen returned. As the Norwegian came back into the shop, his eyes rested on the couple by the window pouring over a city map, so that the Brit thought he'd made them. Absurd. His hand reached across the table to Murtagh's and squeezed it before pointing out the window. They both laughed at an unseen spectacle. Olsen, Logan could see, was already sat and talking with his companion. Their conversation was more animated now.

'Officer Logan. We're picking up transmission from the two. They're heading out. No idea of destination yet, just the woman saying it's time to go.'

Even as he got the message from Stacey in the van, he noted the pair preparing to leave. He and Murtagh had to be out first, moving back to the consulate car. He nodded to Murtagh, dropped some money on the table, and scooped up the map. They walked hand in hand to the door and out into the sunlight.

Just like any other tourists, they headed back over the road to Rue des Rois. All the time he could hear Stacey's commentary running in his ear, telling him their targets were on the street, a car approaching, drawing up next to them.

He clicked the remote. And while Murtagh got in the passenger side, he retrieved a couple of sidearms from the secure box in the boot. Climbing into the driver's seat he stashed one in the centre console and passed the other to Murtagh. She checked the mag and safety, then holstered the weapon and hung it on her belt.

The Sprinter was already turning left onto Place du Cirque, and despite the heavy morning traffic, Logan followed. Fortunately, Stacey was meticulous at relaying their position to him, allowing him to maintain a discreet distance. Soon he could make out the van, several hundred metres ahead. Satisfied, he held his position and checked the satnav. They were heading out of town on Boulevard James Fazy. Ahead, the sweep of the railway line advanced across their skyline, and then they were parallel to it, heading for the next junction. The sign for the airport appeared, advising he turn left; Stacey's voice in his ear told him they were still with the target, a few cars ahead.

Murtagh touched his arm. 'What do we do when we get to the airport?'

'Let them go. We can communicate to London and John in Tel Aviv.' He followed a blue Audi ahead and pulled onto Rue de la Servette. Ten minutes from here. 'So long as we know what flight they're on, it will be enough.'

'Agreed. Let's hope we can find that out.'

As if on cue, Stacey's voice reverberated in their ears. 'We have a flight, chartered yesterday evening. Its flight plan takes it to Athens. Due off the ground at fourteen ten today.'

Logan glanced across at Murtagh and grinned. 'There we go. Let's go see them off.' Brooke Murtagh returned the smile as he pushed his foot down on the accelerator.

As he looked ahead, he saw brake lights coming on, faster and faster until he had to slam his own on to avoid the Audi in front. What the ...?

He got out and stood on the sill and tried to see what was going on.

'Can you see anything?' Murtagh had joined him. He shook his head.

'No, nothing ... Wait!' As traffic parted briefly, he could make out a vehicle lying on its side—a van, white. And with a sudden realisation, he remembered he hadn't heard from Stacey in the last few minutes.

'What is it?' Murtagh sounded impatient.

He looked at her across the roof of the car and shook his head. 'Somebody took out the van.'

Danny Levine watched from his buckled Passat as Rabin, Horowitz, and Olsen disappeared towards the airport. Time to get out of here, he figured as traffic started to build up around him and the CIA van barricading the carriageway, back end warped where his vehicle had tapped it round. The driver was holding his head, a bloom of blood on the door glass where he had slammed against it. One back door was open; a woman crawled out, dazed. Everybody would be okay, decided the Mossad agent as he put his vehicle in gear and drove away, down Rue Hoffman, as if nothing had happened.

After driving a couple of kilometres, he parked the car near the railway line, transferring himself and his rucksack to another vehicle parked close by. Checking the car was locked (collateral needed to be limited), he reached one final time in the boot, clicked the wiring connectors together, and flicked the arming switch on the bomb that nestled in the sleeping bags.

Five minutes.

Levine jumped in the other nondescript car and drove away without a backward glance. He also had an airport rendezvous to make.

'That was Stacey. They got taken out by a car, single occupant, which took off down Rue Hoffman.'

'We've lost them?'

'For all intents and purposes,' Logan agreed with his colleague's assessment and shared her frustration. 'Stacey is going to try and discover what happens when this charter flight arrives in Athens. Do they swap Olsen to another flight? Is it a stopover and where does it go in Israel? Tel Aviv? Or somewhere else … ' He left the sentence hanging.

'It's not much use though. They won't—' Murtagh's words were abruptly cut across by a flat, low crack and rumble. Both turned to the east where the noise seemed to emanate from. 'What the?'

'Bomb?' It was easy to speculate, but in such circumstances two plus two often made five. Still, his immediate thought was that whoever had forced the Sprinter off the road had also caused the explosion. It wouldn't be impossible to find out if the events were linked. But would it be useful to know now? He knew the look on Murtagh's face and agreed. 'We ought to get back to your embassy. There's nothing we can do here.'

Levine settled in for a long drive. He would be making his own way back to Israel, via Rome's Fiumicino Airport and an open-ended return. He was quickly out of Geneva, taking the E25 heading south. Ahead lay about eight hours of driving—a good job he enjoyed it!

Levine allowed himself a smile. The mission had been successful—no body count, foreign interest only when it was too late, and not a trace of their presence would be found to click the bricks of suspicion together.

His boss would be pleased with the professional way in which they had executed the plan.

'That's a real clusterfuck.' Rickman's blunt analysis hurt all the more for the fact they both felt the same about it.

Logan shook his head slowly. 'It was an outside chance that we'd even catch up with them at the airport, but we had to try.'

Rickman grunted. 'That the best you got? Man, we had these guys in the bag, and if it'd been left to me, we could have found out the easy way, but no.' The American let the word draw out, long and meaningful. 'No, you had to do some James Bond shit, make like the big secret agent.' He laughed, low and hard.

Logan ignored him, but inwardly he was seething.

Murtagh, however, faced up to the station chief. 'So, what have you got for us?'

Rickman cast a sideways glance. 'What makes you think I got anything for you guys?'

'Two things. You're certainly sitting on something for one.'

A look of smug self-satisfaction settled on the big man. 'And the other thing?'

Murtagh took her mobile from her bag. 'A call to Langley.' She consulted her watch. 'It's mid-morning stateside and I'm guessing Markham will be eager for news. She's already had your ass once in the last twenty-four hours. You want for her to take another piece?'

'You wouldn't.'

Murtagh dialled and held the phone to her ear. Rickman visibly paled and raised his hands in surrender. 'Okay, okay. For fuck's sake!'

'So, give it up.' Murtagh's hard expression showed there was not about to be an amnesty for her colleague.

Rickman paused, gauged the steel in Murtagh's eyes, sighed, and drew a book from his jacket pocket. He thumbed through the pages. 'Okay, we did a bit of scouting when your boy here'—Rickman jerked his thumb in Souster's direction—'called in the intel. Like he said, a flight was chartered hurriedly, about thirty-six hours ago. It lifted off'—he consulted his watch—'fifty minutes ago, bound for Athens.'

Murtagh and Logan exchanged exasperated glances. 'We already know about Athens. And?'

'And what?' rejoined Rickman innocently.

Murtagh bit her lip. 'Who chartered it?'

'Oh, yes!' Rickman smiled like a cat about to pounce. 'It appears to have been chartered by Westmann Industries, a German light engineering company that specialises in precision equipment for the scientific community.'

'Really?' Logan hunched forward.

Rickman grinned. 'It gets better.'

'How?'

'Westmann is a fully owned subsidiary of Perez Global, a major industrial conglomerate based in Haifa, with its registered office in Tel Aviv.'

Logan considered this information. Perez Global, as far as he was aware, was predominantly a transport and logistics company, which had branched out into chemicals and raw materials first and then engineering and design. But why was the company looking to bring a Norwegian scientist from Switzerland to Israel? What was in it for them? Perhaps … 'Do we have a photo of Olsen on file?'

Rickman tapped on his idev and swiped it to Logan's device, who angled it so Murtagh could see. The face staring back at them was wan, the skin pallid beneath unremarkable light brown hair. Light grey eyes, hiding beneath drooping lids, seemed to hold a misery that gripped the man's soul.

Logan glanced at Rickman. 'There's an operative in Tel Aviv. He's our forward scout. Can you send him that photo?' He turned to Murtagh.

'I think he'd be in the right place to catch up with our Nordic friend, don't you?'

Murtagh smiled. 'He'd be very interested to have a picture of our friend here.'

Their grins broadened as they saw the look of bewilderment on the station chief's face.

'Don't worry Rickman,' Murtagh assured him laconically. 'John Black will keep this US. He's Navy SEALs.'

T he Gulfstream arced its way south-east away from Athens, flying into the night that spread its dark hand over the eastern Mediterranean. On board all was quiet. Olsen had succumbed to the excitement and adrenaline rush of the journey to the airport, his bundling on the flight, a quick change in Athens and introduction to his new handler. Now he was dozing in a small bed, in the rear. Sleep was for the best they'd agreed, and Rabin had turned the heat up to a slumber-inducing level in the small sleeper cabin.

The Mossad agent nursed a whisky and regarded Sharon sitting across from him. As the mission entered its final phase, she'd cooled off considerably, leaving him confused by her demeanour. He knew it was his pride that was hurting, and he also knew Danny would admonish him over his emotional involvement. "Never mix business and pleasure," he would have said, were he here.

But, he had to say something, anything. 'Can you check on our guest?'

Horowitz raised her head from the magazine she was engrossed in, regarding her colleague with a mixture of pity and amusement. 'Why? Are you afraid he might get off?'

Rabin coloured up and shook his head. 'No, just want to make sure we deliver the goods in top condition.'

Horowitz shook her head. 'I'm sure he'll be fine.'

'What are you reading?'

'A magazine.'

Rabin sighed angrily, and Horowitz placed her magazine carefully on the seat next to her. 'You have a problem Binyamin?'

The young agent remained silent but knew his colour was rising in his cheeks.

'You're wondering why I'm paying you no attention now we have our man,' she indicated to the back of the plane. 'Oh, Ben, I was playing you, baby.' She laughed, a light uncaring sound, or so it seemed to him.

'You cow.'

The laughter came again. 'Come on. We're on an op. Did you think there would be anything else? I needed some relief, needed you to support me with Danny. You've done that for me. I gave you the opportunity to fuck me. We all win, don't we?' Her attention fell back to her magazine, precluding reply.

Rabin huffed, drained his whisky, and headed to the back of the craft.

The end of this mission couldn't come soon enough.

It was a scene familiar to him for many years, yet tonight Avi Perez had little time for the lights of downtown Tel Aviv. His thoughts dwelt on the developing plans of The Seven, rather than the traffic and sodium glow of the city's streets, which battled with the steel blue of the night. His eyes roamed over the skyscrapers puncturing the dark sky, symbols of the rising regional power of the city, but his attention remained riveted on the caller whose voice infiltrated his ear from the mobile. Perez scorned the influence others spoke of. If The Seven were successful, the control Israel would exert would dwarf the petty machinations of local businessman attempting to make it big.

'Our ship has docked?' His question filled a lull in the other's monologue.

'Yes, two hours ago. We are unloading to the trucks now, and the convoy will leave in the morning.'

'What about security?'

'We have a private company providing armed escort. That has been cleared with the IDF and Shin Bet officials. We should not meet with any delays.'

Perez nodded slowly for his own benefit. 'You're comfortable with the company?'

The caller paused long enough for Perez to be concerned.

'Tell me if there are any concerns,' he advised sharply.

'Their costs for anonymity are high, that gives me some concern. But this was short notice, Mr Perez.'

Perez snorted. 'What do they know of the goods?'

'Nothing. We do not release anything from the manifest until tomorrow morning. And even then, they will only know of its nature. We will give them general directions, which will be firmed up within fifty kilometres of the destination.'

'Hmm. Do nothing else till you hear from me. When are you scheduled to move out?'

'We can move any time after eight.'

'Okay, I'll get back to you on that. Now, another matter.' Perez hesitated. It was an issue, moving so much of The Seven's mission into the realm of his public work, yet it had to be done—and managed carefully. 'There is a flight coming in to Ben Gurion chartered by Westmann. It should be landing'—he consulted his watch, a Breitling chronometer—'just after midnight. Cars and escorts will be arriving for my guest. Ensure that nothing delays them please?'

'Certainly, Mr Perez. Will that be all?'

'For now, yes. But, I'll call you back about the other matter shortly.'

The line went dead, and Perez toyed with his mobile as he pondered matters. Putting it to one side, he pulled another, a cheap mobile from his pocket. His manager's actions, while in no way wrong, could compromise the operation. Bringing in privateers, whose only desire was the size of the wallet, was a weak link. Better to have individuals who were more controllable.

After a couple of rings, he cancelled the call, waited, and then rang again. At the second ring, his call was answered.

'Ariel?'

'Yitzhak.'

With pleasantries quickly dispensed, Perez explained the reason for his call.

General Topol, code name Ariel, paused. 'What is it you expect from me?'

Perez thought a moment. Had he heard right? 'I expect an escort for our product, Ariel. It is to the benefit of both ourselves and the group.'

The industrialist continued, explaining to Topol what would happen the following day.

Topol was silent. Yitzhak was right. It would be beneficial, but he would need to be careful who he chose; he'd been given precious little time to sort anything. There was perhaps one thing he could do. 'You expect to move after eight tomorrow?'

'That is correct.'

'I will have a team on site before then.' Now he knew exactly who to use, but it would need Moshe to negotiate it. 'You can let the others go.'

'That's good. One other thing, our specialist is arriving tonight. Do you have the people?'

'Of course, Yitzhak. That is excellent timing. I'll let Moshe know everything is running accordingly.'

'Very well, Ariel. I'll look forward to your people arriving in the morning.'

The call ended, and Perez performed the ritual destruction of the mobile. Pouring a whisky from the cabinet in a corner of his fortieth-floor office, Perez wandered to the windows and drew slowly on his drink. Now he could appreciate the city. Far below the red and white streams of light confirmed his desire for motion in the moment. Perez felt connected to the movement, felt the dynamics of the project running through him, unhindered, unfettered. It was time to change the world, and there was no better place to affect that than here in Tel Aviv.

Midnight had just passed as the chartered Gulfstream touched down on the tarmac at Ben Gurion Airport. The new handler had been satisfied Olsen was still committed, so much so she had been confident his acclimatisation to Israeli life could begin.

Olsen had been only partly attentive, or so it appeared to Rabin as he watched the handler assess him. There was a slight drowsiness to the man, intermixed with a little nervousness. But she persevered, informing him where he would be staying and who he would work with initially and laying on the benefits of working with them on the project.

What is the project?

Scientific, was the answer he had received from his handler.

At the mention of a project, Olsen had seemed to wake up, become focused. He'd quizzed her back: What was the science involved? The aim? Who were they directing it against?

She couldn't answer such questions now. *Johannes, later, when we are safely in Tel Aviv.*

He had then subsided back into his former lethargy, and the work had been curtailed. Now, as the aircraft touched down at Ben Gurion, Rabin felt at least a bit more confident that Olsen would be committed. His worry, though, was that the man was only doing this for his dead family. Would he also transfer allegiance to his adoptive country?

It was a big risk and one that had taken on greater prominence now they were on Israeli soil. Still, he and the team had done their part. They would hand Olsen over to local assets, and that would be that. Whatever Olsen was going to do was beyond Rabin to figure, and he liked that just fine.

Horowitz and he escorted Olsen and his new handler, from the aircraft, to a fleet of waiting vehicles parked in a quiet corner of the airport. The three SUVs stood, engines idling, everything dark as if they had been discreetly abandoned—doors closed; lights off; not at all like in the movies, reflected Rabin as they got closer and he could make out the shadows of people in them. The handler made to the middle vehicle with Olsen and, without another word to any of the Swiss team, opened a door, guided Olsen in, and followed. The closing of the door was a signal, akin to flicking off a light switch. And as one, all three vehicles moved off, leaving Rabin and Horowitz to watch them head off the airfield.

'I guess that's our part over,' Rabin observed as the vehicles passed through a gate and onto the road from the airport.

Horowitz chuckled. 'Thank you for your contribution to the security of Israel. We'll call you when we need you again.' Not a note of irony made its way into her voice, yet she echoed Rabin's disillusionment. 'Anyway,' she continued, forcing her tone to be light, 'it was a good job. I need sleep though. We need to be ready for Danny getting back tomorrow for the debrief.'

Rabin watched her go, not for the first time longing for just one more night.

It had taken John Black a while to track down where the hangars of Perez Global at Ben Gurion were before finding somewhere he could hole up and watch for suspicious activity. He'd been there from late afternoon, scoping the movement of people around the isolated hangars, noting registrations of vehicles likely to be of interest and the numbers of people who arrived with them. Late in the evening, three SUVs had arrived and parked almost regimentally, before the occupants had dismounted and disappeared into an office block attached to one of the hangars.

Something was about to happen.

Black's patience had been tested and then rewarded when the Gulfstream had arrived. Two individuals had climbed into one of the SUVs, and the three vehicles had departed the airfield.

Black started his car and headed for the road.

Shlomo Yakin and Peter Goldstein watched as the hire car turned on the airport access road and followed the SUVs. They had no doubt concerning the identify of those three vehicles; the hire car was a different matter. The occupant, a single Afro-American, military or ex-military, had been their target since arriving in Tel Aviv, two days prior. They and another team had built a dossier of his activities, troubled by his not-so-random circuits of the city, which had paid only lip service to the usual sights and sounds of the Mediterranean's top spot for the high life.

Then he'd abruptly taken to the airport and, seemingly without any pretence, had (how did Americans say?) cased the joint. When he had become ensconced around the back of Ben Gurion, the two agents had placed themselves on the airport itself, parked two hangars down from Perez Global, where they could both scope the American and the area he was interested in.

But what had piqued his curiosity in Perez Global? What could a US operative find interesting with an Israeli logistics company? Their own inquisitiveness had been aroused when the three SUVs had arrived. Yakin had scoped the vehicles and turned to Goldstein. 'Mossad?'

Goldstein had glassed the vehicles in turn, nodded, and regarded his colleague. 'What do you think they want with Perez … this time of night?'

Yakin considered the vehicles. It didn't help. 'Your guess is as good as mine,' he had told Goldstein.

Now it appeared they might get some answers. It was easier to take down the American than to stop and question Mossad. What was unquestionable was that Mossad was running some sort of operation on home turf and that was a 'no-no'. What was also without question was that two Shin Bet operatives would have no success confronting a Mossad section.

So, the American it was.

Yakin and Goldstein slotted in behind the hire car and radioed for their partners to join them. They would then follow the guy for a while before isolating and taking him. No doubt the American would come quietly.

The convoy of vehicles headed through the lightly populated streets of early morning Lod and Ramla. Yakin was sure he'd heard there was a Mossad safe house in Rehovot, only a short drive south of their current position. He wanted to stop the American before they left Ramla behind. There was a Shin Bet facility not far away, which would make a good place to interrogate their 'friend'. He told Goldstein, who nodded approvingly.

'I'll tell the others. When do you want to stop him?'

'Now. If we leave it any longer, it'll be a long detour back to the safe house.'

'Okay.' Goldstein got on the radio to the other car.

Black knew he was being followed. He just hoped he could make out where the SUVs might be headed before the inevitable happened. He checked the details he'd collected on his idev—vehicle types, registration markings, distinguishing colours, numbers of occupants, direction of travel, and roads taken. Everything was there.

If he could get the file to Logan before he was taken down, they might stand a chance.

The second car pulled out and overtook Yakin and Goldstein, without acknowledging them. The two watched as the car pulled alongside the American's automobile, seeming to match its speed for a minute, making no real effort to pull away. Yakin closed on the back of the American.

Black noted the car, the two occupants talking away, preoccupied by their own journey. He wasn't fooled; he'd noted how those behind had narrowed the gap to him. He was also aware a slip road was approaching.

Any moment now.

What should he do? Try to outrun and risk a shooting match? What was he going to be able to do about the Mossad convoy ahead? Nothing. It was perhaps better to plead ignorance and risk being deported. There were always other ways to do things.

The car overtaking him still leisurely made its way past him.

'Okay, now.'

There was the 100-metre marker for the slip road. Black was doing about seventy. Time was running out for them. How would they work this? Fifty metres.

The car overtaking suddenly closed on him, and Black felt the bump, grimacing at the screech of metal on metal. His vehicle was punted towards the off ramp, and he braked to try and escape the manoeuvre. After all, he had to try and put up a fight.

There was a crunch from behind as he was contacted by the vehicle that had tailed him. Another shove from the side, and he was descending the off-ramp. He regarded the face, now very close. The Israeli returned the stare, raised a hand, and made braking motions. Black complied; after all, what else did he have in his repertoire?

With his car stationary on the verge and cars to the front and rear, Black awaited the inevitable.

Goldstein exited the motor and advanced towards the hire car, hand on the butt of his Glock 19. He approached the driver's door slowly and rapped on the window.

Black slid it down. 'Is anything wrong?' Black looked up at the Israeli. Small but powerfully built, the man looked as if he was more than capable of dealing with him. And given that there were three others available to assist, Black figured ignorance formed the best policy.

'Nothing at all. Would you mind getting out of the car … slowly, sir.' Goldstein backed away in case the other tried to take his gun from him, though that was unlikely, with so many other agents around them. Still, best not to take chances. Black slowly exited the car.

'Turn around. Place your hands on the roof.'

Black did as ordered, waiting patiently as the Israeli patted him down. 'Right hand.'

Black raised his hand and then held it out behind him. The inevitable snap of handcuffs sounded.

'Left hand.'

Black did as bid. The hand on his shoulder turned him and directed him to the car behind his. This was like something out of an episode of *CSI: Wherever.*

Then they were all a convoy heading … 'Where are you taking me?'

Nothing from the front, and Black guessed that was how it would remain until they got to wherever they were going—a safe house of some sort. And then the questions would begin.

Not exactly a holiday in the Med for him then. He just hoped that Logan had gotten the transmission by now.

21

'Is that all the transmission?'

Just a nod from the operative. Logan stared again at the screen. There was a log of information, some photos of vehicles, but they were so nondescript that, had Black not sent registration details and other markers, it would have made little difference. Even so, he didn't expect them to be able to use the data in any meaningful way. It was highly likely they would be swapped for others as a matter of precaution. It was safe to bet that, if some Israeli operatives had picked up Black, then the Mossad unit would change its tactics, including transport. Still …

'Is there any way we can find out where these vehicles are?'

'What you thinking?'

Logan turned to Murtagh. 'If we find these vehicles, we might have an idea what's happing with Olsen right now. If we can re-task some surveillance we might be able to continue to track Olsen, even if they change vehicles.'

'It's an option,' Murtagh concurred. She turned to the operative. 'All Mossad vehicles have a tracker, don't they?' When he confirmed that, she continued. 'NSA will have details of all trackers for Mossad vehicles.' She leaned over the operative. 'Upload those tags to NSA and let's see what we get.'

It took only a few minutes for the operative to get through the NSA portal and upload the data. Three matches came up fast, and the operator dropped them into a new window. Beneath each registration was an eighteen-digit unique identifier code. Once that tag was uploaded to a satellite, they could follow the tracker wherever it might go.

'How soon can we get a satellite re-tasked?'

'Anyone's guess, Steve.'

'Not exactly the answer I was expecting, if I'm honest,' Logan retorted, instantly regretting his tone. It wasn't Brooke's fault. 'Sorry. Do the best you can. We mustn't lose Olsen.'

The Norwegian felt disoriented and wondered for a moment if he had been drugged. He could remember only shards of the journey from Geneva. But, he reasoned, that could be because of tiredness and emotion. A good meal would be nice right now, he advised his guard, who remained stoically uninterested.

'Look. I haven't eaten properly since yesterday breakfast. If I'm a guest, as your colleague said, then the least you can do is get me something to eat.'

The guard glanced at Olsen, made to say something, thought better of it, and rose to rap on the door. It opened, and the guard spoke in low tones, with someone just out of sight. Olsen guessed they were talking in Hebrew as he only made a few words out; *food* was one of them, thank God.

Satisfied with his personal little victory, Olsen settled back to wait.

Black leaned back in the chair and smiled. It did nothing to improve the mood of his interrogators. He wondered how long they'd hold off getting rough. They'd done magnificently well so far.

'Let's try one more time,' said the taller of his two captors. 'You were found surveilling a private area of Ben Gurion Airport yesterday and this morning. Then you followed three vehicles. You've no papers on you, but there was a bag in the car with binoculars, night vision equipment, and maps. You're obviously some sort of operator, and you are particularly interested in something our colleagues in Mossad are doing.'

'I was just on the same road from the airport.'

Yakin shook his head slowly, sadly. 'We have been following you since you came to Tel Aviv, my friend. We're just being polite here, John.'

Black hoped he showed no emotion as the Israeli mentioned his name. He hadn't expected to keep his identity from them—that would be too much to ask—but little victories mattered.

'Let's get real, shall we? You were watching Perez Global, and you were very interested in the gentleman brought in on the Gulfstream—so interested, in fact, that you decided to follow them.'

Black noted the man's language. 'You keep saying "them". So you're Shin Bet. Right?' Right, he concluded, clocking the little sideways glances between the two. 'Therefore, the question actually is, "How much do you know about what your friends in Mossad are up to?"'

'What makes you think that?'

Black smiled at the shorter, one who was visibly perturbed; the taller one was much more controlled. 'The fact you said that only confirms what I'm thinking. Mossad is up to something, and they haven't invited you to the party. You must ask yourselves, why would they want to bring a Norwegian Jewish scientist all the way from Geneva to Tel Aviv in the middle of the night and spirit him away so quickly? Surely you have enough scientists here?'

The two Israelis retired to a corner of the room and spoke softly in Hebrew. When they'd finished, they both headed for the door. As they went through, the taller one faced Black. 'We'll be back shortly.'

Black raised his manacled hands and rattled the chain r=that bound him to the table. 'I'm not going anywhere.'

Olsen bit into the sandwich as if he'd never eaten before, washing down each mouthful with still water. It felt good to be filling his belly. As he took in his surroundings properly for the first time, he wondered what the hell was happening to him. Things had seemed to be so black and white back at the café in Geneva. Now, he couldn't help but feel he was a prisoner in a foreign land, guarded by people who didn't have his best interests at heart.

That was so at odds with the words of Natalie, the small waitress—agent. He would have to concede that he'd been played to get him here.

No, wait, the deaths of his wife and his children were real. He'd seen the newspaper telling how Tel Etz had been razed by Hezbollah, the information Natalie had passed him about the attack corroborating the news. That and the entries in the settlement's records—they all pointed to the death of his family at the hands of cold-hearted terrorists who didn't want any peace in the Middle East that might include Israel having its rightful place at the political table.

Olsen ate, considering the injustice that had left him so bereft and then the determination in his heart, fuelled by hatred, that had brought him here. Yet, here he was, being held like a criminal. Or an enemy?

Enough!

He rose from his chair and headed to the door. Immediately the guard (what else was the black-garbed individual with a semi-automatic at his hip?) cut him off, staring impassively at the taller man.

Olsen mustered as much indignation as he could and stared directly at the man totally unfazed by the Norwegian's height advantage.

'Step aside.' When the guard steadfastly stood his ground, Olsen fulminated. 'You can't hold me in here forever. I haven't done anything wrong. In fact, you need me apparently. You need to let me go if you have changed your mind, so I can get on with my life.'

The guard returned Olsen's stare but didn't budge. Olsen backed away and searched the room for something, anything, to use as leverage or to attract someone else's attention. He caught the tiny black half sphere in a corner of the room and advanced towards it, summoning as much anger as possible.

He stood right in front of where he hoped the camera lens was. 'Let me out! I said I would help you, and I will. But you have no right to hold me here against my will. Either give me a job so I can repay those Hezbollah bastards, or let me go to mourn my family.

'Come on!'

He whirled as the door clicked; the woman who'd joined the team in Athens was standing in the doorway.

'Johannes Olsen, come with me. There is somebody you need to meet.'

22

A return flight to London was the only option left Logan and Murtagh since Black had gone dark. The last transmission suggested he was being held by someone, but at least the information he'd sent had turned out to be useful.

No. It had been more than useful, giving them the opportunity to remotely track Olsen, taking over in part from the now absent Black. The three vehicles had been traced, by satellite, to an address in the small town of Rehovot. Getting the re-task done had been far easier than either had expected. A stealth drone had been tasked to hold station in the area, monitoring activity at the safe house. Nothing had happened, hence the pair was heading back for a hastily arranged meeting at Vauxhall Cross.

Just five people occupied the situation room. Galbraith and Logan sat on one side of the table, and the officer noted his uneasiness at sitting across from his girlfriend and partner in a very overt show of nationalism. One of her compatriots he knew; Sarah Markham had been an ally of sorts in their hunt for Drew Faulkner. The other was an unknown quantity, but he'd heard that Charlie Eissenegger was a highly intelligent and formidable director of NSA. *Be careful what you disclose in this environment*, a little voice told him.

It was Galbraith who opened proceedings, thanking everyone for taking the time to come here today. 'Where do we want to start?'

'Perhaps with how we managed to lose an operative in Israel.' Markham was clearly trying to head off any shit from Eissenegger.

'We haven't lost him.'

'Oh, could you clarify, Steve, because I always considered not knowing where somebody is was tantamount to losing them.' Markham was clearly unamused.

The reply died on his lips as Murtagh stepped in, just in time. 'Steve's right. We haven't lost John. We're almost 100 per cent sure he's at a Shin Bet safe house in Ramla.'

'That's supposed to ease our concern, miss?' Eissenegger regarded her without humour.

Galbraith raised a hand to forestall any retort. 'I think we should possibly look at the information we have to date before we carry on the debate concerning Mr Black. Steve, will you please?'

Logan nodded, recapping recent events in Geneva, the information about the flight chartered through Westmann to Athens and then to Tel Aviv, and contacting John with the information concerning Olsen's predicted arrival.

'John confirmed that with his data stream prior to capture.' Before anyone could respond, he carried on, explaining the use of the NSA satellites and drones to identify where Olsen was believed to be held.

'Believed?' queried Markham.

'That's right, ma'am,' replied Murtagh. 'We used the UICs on the three vehicles to track them to Rehovot. They've not moved from there, and we have a drone overhead. That will inform us if they try to move Olsen.'

'Let's hope he's there, shall we?' Eissenegger was clearly reserving judgement.

Galbraith bit her tongue. 'We have to work on that presumption for now, Charles. The right action now is to get more people into Israel. Time is of the essence if we want to save the accord.'

There were nods around the table at the remark. This was the real reason for their actions, and they couldn't forget that. After the destruction at Tel Etz and the attempt on al-Umari, tensions were understandably high in Israel and the West Bank. If there was a group trying to overturn the agreement, they had no option; they had to act.

'We have to act.'

'You're right, Moshe. This provides us with a welcome opportunity to destabilise the accord's progress. Are you confident in your team's report?'

'Yes.'

David smiled. God was certainly smiling down upon him today. 'They have a plan?'

Moshe nodded.

'And you can trust them.'

The arch of the eyebrow was all David needed to see to confirm that Moshe was on the case. 'Okay. I don't need to know anymore then.'

'I'll get on it. Now, our other matter.' Moshe flicked an image from his device to David's. 'Our Geneva team extracted our target without issue. He appears quite willing to work with us, but my team is keeping him on a short leash.'

David stared at the face on the paper before him. An earnest individual, white skinned and intellectual, thin, who looked as if a good meal wouldn't do him any harm stared back at him. Alarm bubbled to the surface. What if … 'Is he going to cause trouble?'

Moshe shook his head. 'Not at all, but we want to be careful, don't we? After all, the guy has just lost his family, been brought to a foreign country. I'd rather have tight control of the man.'

'You're right, Moshe.' He flicked through the résumé that had come from the Geneva team. 'So, he's on side.'

'The Rehovot team thinks so. Said he was getting quite animated, vehement even. They have him on the way to our rendezvous even now. You should meet him, and then we can get everything in motion.'

David checked the face one more time. Diaspora or no, it was putting things in the hands of someone who had not lived on the West Bank or through the intifadas. He wondered how much faith he should place in this unknown individual. Now the moment was upon them, was it the only way? Perhaps a natural death could be arranged for the accord.

Moshe listened as his leader gave vent to his disquiet. 'Yes, it is. It is what we put the operation into motion for. Do you think our enemies will be content with the death of the accord? They will press now for more power over us, because this is what our so-called friends have offered them with this process. No. We must continue, David. And this person gives us the means. He also gives us distance should anything go wrong. He was brought here to head up research. If things go sour, we say he went rogue.

'Johannes Olsen is expendable.'

David pulled a big hand over his chin. And for once, the warnings and pleadings of his doctor and wife came back to trouble him. He ate too much and loved his drink as much. David knew there wasn't too much time left, but this one thing ... 'Okay. Let's get to the meeting. I want to see what size this scientist's balls are.'

Moshe chuckled as he picked up a walkie-talkie and spoke into it. 'We're moving out now. Get the cars ready.'

The two Israeli agents hadn't been long at all. When they returned, the tall one had immediately un-cuffed Black, who demonstratively rubbed at his wrists. His faux displeasure was soon pacified by a strong coffee, bread, and meat. He ate slowly, gauging the change in demeanour of his captors. Had roles changed? He would find out soon enough.

Finishing his food and licking his fingers for good measure, he turned to the tall Israeli, who'd been reading a magazine while Black ate. 'What gives? Why the sudden change of pace?'

Yakin regarded the American and smiled. 'You are right, Mr American. We are wondering why our brothers in Mossad are doing what they are doing. However, not all of our illustrious colleagues in that organisation are aware either.'

Black frowned. 'You mean?'

'Yes. We're talking about a very black op. Question is, who, what, and why?'

Black smiled wryly. 'That's three questions.'

'And they all require answers,' Yakin retorted evenly. 'But first, why don't we introduce ourselves?'

'Reasonable enough request,' concurred Black. 'You go first and tell me why you're interested in what your colleagues are doing.'

Yakin considered the American. This was a tricky situation for both parties. He knew their guest didn't want to throw his hand away; after all, it could be a ploy to get incriminating information from him. For Yakin, it was a calculated gamble—admitting, potentially, that his government was blind to something happening under its nose while trying to prise information from the American.

'Shlomo Yakin and this'—he indicated his stocky compatriot—'is Peter Goldstein. And yes, we are Shin Bet.'

Black reflected on the words, the admission. Was it enough yet? 'Good to meet you, gentlemen. I'm John Black, and I'm a freelance travel operative.'

Yakin's face darkened as he registered the words. He leaned back in his chair and considered the now silent Black. 'Well, John Black, thank you for that. Perhaps we can help jog your memory about your real job. Or would you reconsider?'

Black didn't move, but this was the pivot point. He hoped his poker face was in place as he waited for Yakin to speak.

The Israeli dropped his idev on the table between them and swiped the screen to life. There in front of him was John Black's military résumé, his SEAL photo and action profile. 'So, Lieutenant John C Black, apparently leader of US Navy SEAL Team Five, would you like to maintain your charade? Or are you going to tell us what you're actually doing here?'

Black considered his options—slim, if he was honest. But what could he gain from them? 'Why do you think?'

Yakin sat back, his eyes never leaving Black's face. He noted the American hadn't actually confirmed his identity. 'John, you're a special operator in a foreign country, without permission. You were observed undertaking acts that could be construed as against the State of Israel. That would be enough to incarcerate most individuals with only a cursory trial.'

'For sure, but you are not going to do that.'

Yakin said nothing, just sat staring at the American.

'So, if you're not going to jail me, what are you going to do?'

The Israeli leaned forward, elbows on the table, glowering. Yakin was getting pissed now. 'I think we need a lot more honesty, John, before we decide that. Are you going to talk to us?'

Black ran his hands over his head and let out a long sigh. He needed to come clean. It was dangerous certainly, but he was out of place right now. If he came clean, they either would handcuff him and march him to prison or … 'If I tell you my reason for being here, what happens next?'

Yakin shrugged. 'Let's see, shall we?'

Black drew himself up, more from trepidation than bravado, glanced at Goldstein and then began. As concisely as possible, he went over the facts of the situation, starting with the loss of a ranger so many weeks ago in the Negev, right up to Murtagh and Logan trying to track down what had transpired in Geneva. All the while he spoke, Yakin made no movement, no noise, merely listened while his colleague ensured everything was recorded. He was deliberately sketchy over the CIA and NSA information; it was enough that he was singing like the proverbial canary.

Finished, Black braced himself for whatever riposte the Israelis would unleash. Instead of a thank you for coming clean, the silence remained unfilled.

At last he could contain himself no longer. 'So?'

Yakin fixed his eyes on the American, reached into his shirt pocket, and pulled out a packet of cigarettes. He leaned over and offered one to Black, who shook his head. The Israeli smiled sardonically. 'Clean-living American, eh?'

When Black remained quiet, the Shin Bet agent shrugged, lit a cigarette, and pulled on it slowly. 'You say the Mossad team in Geneva was recruiting a scientist?'

Black nodded.

'For what purpose?'

Black shrugged. 'I have no idea.' He paused. Should he give them anything? What the hell? He'd given them everything else. 'We believe he's a nuclear physicist from CERN who has an Israeli connection.'

'He's Israeli?'

'No. Norwegian. But our intel shows he's Jewish by birth and that he was married to an Israeli woman.' Again, he paused, drew in a breath. And then, as Logan would say, in for a penny, in for a pound. 'Reports suggest she was killed in the attack on Tel Etz, along with their children.'

Yakin raised an eyebrow and shot a look at his partner. 'Peter, we could do with some coffee.'

The younger man raised his eyebrows in a way that asked, *Me again, eh?*, but left the room anyway.

Yakin leaned closer to the American. 'We were investigating the attack on Tel Etz. There are things about it that don't ring true, if it was terrorists.'

'You mean like the size of the ammunition casings found?'

Yakin nodded.

'Yes, we thought that was suspicious. What else have you found?'

Yakin's smile was tired. 'A blank wall. We've been told to let it rest by our superiors. Nobody is happy about the situation, but we cannot take matters any further.'

Black considered the Israeli's comments. They explained a load about this odd set of events, one hell of a load. 'I'm taking it was no coincidence that you were at the airport last night?'

Yakin pulled on his cigarette again. 'Peter and I have been following you all the time you've been in the country, Mr Black. You led us there.'

'But you had a team at the airport?'

Yakin neither confirmed nor denied this, which Black took as an affirmative.

'So, you're interested yourselves. I was a little diversion for you guys.'

Before Yakin could reply, Goldstein re-entered and placed two cups of coffee on the table before sloping off with his own, back to his recording device.

Yakin twisted in his chair and stared pointedly at the young man. Goldstein appeared to be confused—until Yakin jerked his head towards the door, making it clear he shouldn't be here.

When the door had closed once more behind the truculent agent, Yakin turned his attention back to Black, who saw something in his eyes. He wasn't clear if it was indecision or not. Eventually, having lit another cigarette and drained most of his coffee, Yakin coughed, a self-conscious act, or so Black figured.

'Goldstein'—Yakin jerked a thumb, which Black noted was calloused and grubby, probably from handling pistols—'is an earnest young man but a promising operative. However, it is sometimes best not to know too many things.'

Black's mouth cracked in a wry grin. 'For real. And what is it the big boys know that would be bad for Mr Goldstein?'

The cigarette glowed red as Yakin took a moment to enjoy his passion. He liked to smoke, partly because he liked the taste and smell of a real cigarette, but mostly because it pissed off a lot of people who were too uptight to enjoy life. His thoughts wandered to his head of operations, Avi

Brun, a short, ascetic individual who was waiting for retirement to catch up with him. Brun didn't want anything to spoil his record at Shin Bet, so when Yakin had ventured that Mossad was running a black operation that they had no eyes on, Brun had ordered him to leave it be.

That wasn't his way—never had been. And he saw no reason to start now, just to protect some blinkered old guarder wanting a quiet life before fading into obscurity.

Yakin finished the cigarette, crushing it resignedly on a saucer, along with the remains of the other. 'There have been a number of events recently—'

'The Camp David talks were always going to bring out the worst in those who don't respect compromise. Malbert was a very strong prime minister. He knew agreeing to the accord would be the final nail in his political coffin.'

'That doesn't ring true. Yes, we expected some sort of response, but the Palestinians pretty much had what they wanted. It was we Israelis who'd lost the most. Then there's Tel Erz—' He caught Black looking at him and realised there was another cigarette in his hand. He stubbed it out, hardly smoked. 'I guess what I'm saying is that I'm as intrigued as you about the events of the last few days, and I'm saying I'm not going to get any help from my boss.'

'What about Goldstein?'

Yakin allowed his coffee to fill the pause created by the American's question. He placed the cup on the table. 'Goldstein is with me, but I don't want him compromised by anything we agree in here. He and I will continue our surveillance. You, I think, will give us a different perspective on the situation.'

'Except you've had me sitting here for the best part of a day while our scientist friend is moved to—wherever.'

'Don't worry, John. We are watching that particular problem. We know exactly where they have Mr Olsen.'

23

*T*his was your country? Our birthright? A place all Jews aspire to be part of, are drawn to throughout their life? As he watched the kaleidoscope of colours, green and sand, white and blue, stream past the car, Olsen realised he knew little about his wife's country of birth. Nor had he ever dwelt on his own heritage, even when Judith asked. It was passed-down memories, stories heard at the knee of a grandparent back in Oslo, old folk who'd heard of the 'homeland' from their parents and grandparents. He'd never understood the attraction, the need, to be part of this continuing journey back to a heritage he had disregarded since the school science department.

He'd discounted it entirely, until he had met Judith. She'd told him of Tel Aviv's vibrancy, its breathlessness of business, culture, change, and sexuality, which challenged the old concepts of Hebraism. The ideological melting pot that was Jerusalem came alive in her words, how uneasily cultures lived in juxtaposition in the hot, humid walls of an ancient city, dominated by the golden symbol of another religion. And every time she spoke, there was love in her eyes. He couldn't have helped himself if he'd tried, as he watched the brown eyes glow, the olive skin crease with happiness at the name of her beloved country. Through her, he had begun to realise what it was like to be a man out of place, out of time; he had come to know he had a connection that had been lost since before his birth.

Now, it was the place of her premature burial and that of his two children. He didn't know what it was these Israelis wanted of him, but he knew that, if it was within his control to provide it, that's exactly what he would do.

Since leaving Geneva thirty-six hours previously, he hadn't cast eyes upon his children's photographs. He had vowed to look again only when he'd completed the task yet to be set. Speaking briefly to Judith's parents, Olsen had left to them the particulars of arranging her estate, saying he would contact them when the time was right. He'd sensed her father's opprobrium (they had never been comfortable in each other's company), but he couldn't deal with that yet.

The interior of the vehicle was silent as the convoy made its way out of the town where they'd overnighted and into the hot, dusty countryside. After a while, the vehicles made a turn off the highway, generating even more dust as they headed towards several buildings set against hills, protected by trees. The main house, their destination, seemed uninhabited. Olsen wasn't given to spy games, but guessed he was probably involved in such as all three SUVs came to a halt. He noted black-garbed security personal with rifles and weapons held easily but with purpose. Uneasiness fell over him as he was encouraged out of the vehicle.

The house was a plain affair, nothing remarkable, Olsen figured, as he followed his two guards (keepers?) through the front door. The interior was just as basic; a lack of furniture and decorations confirmed, to his limited experience, the house was used infrequently and perhaps only for meetings such as these.

The room he was taken to held one chair and a table, on which sat a laptop. Olsen stared at the door closing behind him, leaving him to his own devices, and then paced the room, taking in his surroundings.

It didn't take long. When he'd checked the uninspiring view from the locked windows and tried the handles on the other two doors in the room, he sat, resigned to whatever happened next.

As if on cue, the laptop flickered into life. A silhouette was discernible but nothing more, no matter how hard he tried to make out any features.

'Good afternoon, Mr Olsen.' The voice was muffled, presumably to protect the identity of the speaker.

Olsen relaxed. There was no point in trying to figure it out. 'Hello. I'm guessing I won't get to know who you are.'

The laughter was low and not unfriendly. 'It isn't strictly necessary for our little venture, but you can call me David.' The figure paused. 'May I call you Johannes?'

'Jo.'

'Very good, Jo. Thank you.'

Olsen tried to relax into the chair, to appear nonchalant, but all he felt was confused. 'Your people said there was something you might need me to do. Would you like to expand?'

Silence emanated, a tangible thing, from the device, as if the other was breathing into the ether, trying to figure what his response might be. 'Jo, you've come a long way to offer your help. And I understand that … your family … lived in Tel Etz.' The voice softened, seemingly secreting sorrow to win him over.

Olsen didn't need that; it was the moment to let 'David' know that. 'David, whoever you are, I don't need your sympathy. You brought me here for a reason. What is it?'

A grunt. 'I can see we are both men of singularity. We both need a solution for a problem.'

'Yes, yes. What do you want?' Olsen retorted tetchily, pressing to know. All this obfuscation was beginning to drag on him.

The other stopped and then laughed, a hearty sound, even with the distortion. 'Very well, Jo. You are a direct man. I like that. You won't suffer fools or delays. Okay, Jo Olsen. We've brought you here because we want you to build something for us.'

Olsen leaned forward, intrigued. 'What?'

The silhouette was silent for a moment. 'Before we get to that, let us talk about you. You must understand, Jo, that, for us, we must be sure of you.'

'I'm here, aren't I? It was you who came looking for me.'

'We did, because you have a very special set of skills. But I'm aware you have had to come to terms with a special loss, and I cannot in all conscience ask you to do something if you are not in the right place.' David at once regretted the words.

Olsen looked at the screen and laughed, a harsh empty sound. 'Not in the right place? You mean that I might be affected by the death of my children and their mother.' He bit back the tears. 'Yes, I am. It's robbed me of any chance of reconciliation, something this area of the world seems to be so fucking useless at.' Olsen paused, to quell his inner turmoil. 'So, in answer to your question, I am in the right place—the right place for doing what you request, for delivering an answer to the people who killed my wife and family, and the right place for revenge.'

Silence seemed to fill the room until it hurt.

Olsen refused to speak first, waiting for animation from the screen. At last he could bear it no longer. 'Tell me. What you want me to build?'

'A very special bomb.'

'When did he arrive in Israel?'

'Yesterday.' Murtagh referred to her idev, scrolling through the data she'd received from John Black before Shin Bet had cut short his reconnaissance. 'Olsen was in a three-vehicle convoy that left Ben Gurion headed for a safe house in Rehovot. Following Black's transmission, we tasked a drone to an oversight position and tracked Olsen to this farmhouse south of Tel Aviv.' She flicked an aerial photo to the main screen in the situation room at Vauxhall Cross.

From her Langley office, Markham inspected a copy photo before addressing London. 'Where is this farm? Who owns it?'

Murtagh checked her notes. 'It's an isolated farmstead twenty kilometres or so south of Rehovot, owned by a leasing company.'

'Who?'

'A franchise.'

'What you're telling me is, you don't know.'

Murtagh averted her gaze. Markham's reputation was well known, and she had no plans to have her head chewed by her new director.

Markham harrumphed. 'Not knowing isn't an option. So I suggest you get on with finding out. For God's sake!' Markham let her anger get the better of her momentarily. 'This is escalating out of our control right now, and Kemble isn't happy. It's fucking with his accord, and he wants us to put a stop to that here and now.'

Galbraith regarded Markham. The American, often quoted as a hard woman, struck her as quite brittle. Yes, there were issues. But taking it out, in public, on her officer was unbecoming behaviour. Still … 'It's unfortunate indeed, Sarah. However, there are many occurrences over which we have less control than we would wish. Take the outbreaks of violence in Hebron and Ramallah since the massacre at Tel Etz. We can't control that.'

Sarah Markham's face darkened. 'That's exactly what we need to do. For Christ's sake! What is happening here? Let's get a grip.' Her hand waved indiscriminately in the air. 'We all have a responsibility to ensure this accord works out. Israel and Palestine can't just keep ducking the issue. They have to wake up and smell the coffee.'

'I'm sure that's the case, Sarah. But it doesn't help us much at this time.'

Markham knew this and cursed her outburst. She needed to calm down. Didn't do for the Brits to get smug; it was something they were exceptional at. 'Okay, so where is your man while we're here and Black is talking with his new Israeli friends?'

'Steve's currently at GCHQ, working with them on the drone surveillance. Your NSA is coordinating real time between Cheltenham and your drone squadrons to make sure we get as much information as possible. Unless and until Black is released, it's the best we've got.'

Markham dragged a hand through her hair, feeling all her forty-eight years and more besides. One thing was clear; she had to get on top of the situation somehow. Stateside would be expecting information and options.

'Is that it?' Markham searched for some comfort in the activities of the operatives and, finding none, felt another outburst coming on. She managed to control the urge to explode.

Galbraith wished she'd had more time to have discussed events and actions with Markham, without a junior officer in the room with them. But what was, was. 'We don't know what Olsen is being asked to do at this moment in time, but we might as well start with a link to this group called The Seven. Another objective must be to monitor levels of violence, which are increasing in the West Bank, particularly in Hebron. They will link up at some stage; it's inevitable. Let's not forget that any new government, Binyamin Olmet for instance, is likely to be more hard-line in the aftermath of the attacks.'

All three women recognised the truth of that. Olmet was a traditional Israeli, not a religious Jew by any means, but one who used his interpretation and portrayal of faith to rally the population to the defence of the country. In the run-up to the election he had been seen at synagogues, listening intently to the rabbis, taking prayer at the Wailing Wall, meeting enthusiastically with religious leaders and acknowledging their important role in the strengthening of Israel.

'So, what else have we picked up concerning this "Seven"?'

An uncomfortable silence descended around the table once more. Markham fixed her compatriot with a hard stare. Murtagh turned away, and it was Galbraith who came to her rescue.

'Sarah, there is a lot of work being carried out in the background, and what Steve and Brooke have been doing is linked with this group.'

'Which is hardly enough, Amanda. This is a group we know virtually nothing about, one Director Foreman wants to know more about. Meanwhile, we're sat here swinging dick.'

Galbraith coloured at the obscenity but had no comeback. Her counterpart was correct. It was perhaps time to ramp up activity. 'I understand your ire, Director Markham. I would remind you that there are three operatives, one in this room, who are actively trying to find out.'

Markham, still truculent, avoided Galbraith's gaze. 'They're not doing enough, and that needs to stop now. All this remote surveilling, while one of our people sits in an Israeli prison cell, isn't progress.'

Murtagh coughed gently, almost reverently; she knew when to play to the boss. 'Director, Logan and I are prepped to go to Israel. Our cover is good; just the situation with John is what put us back. Both of us would like to get the chance to find out what is happening on the ground.'

The director of the CIA mulled over the words. Flimsy and lacking in substance but pinpointing their potential need, the young officer had perhaps said enough. What else was there for them to do? The older woman huffed. 'I guess you'd best get on with Plan A then.'

'Thank you, Director.'

'What are you planning?'

Murtagh nodded and quickly flicked information from her idev to her audience. The display filled with faces of men and women, young and old. Beneath each was a name, followed by a line detailing his or her political persuasion and then a biopic—political and personal histories for each. A series of arrows formed the relationships. Murtagh quickly talked them through each of the photos. All were influential figures in Israeli and Arab politics in the Middle East.

'But these are the people we are particularly interested in.' Murtagh swiped the screen, and the number of faces reduced to sixteen. 'These have a confirmed anti-accord stance and are absolutely opposed to the creation of an autonomous Palestinian state, some more than others.'

Markham considered the smiling faces, bathed in an innocence only achievable if you were politically astute. Which of them wanted to bring down the accord? Who had resurrected Dimona? As she gazed at the names, she knew it was entirely feasible for any or all of them to have formed a shadowy group of Israelis determined to crush Palestinian ambitions. They came from a wide background—politicians, industrialists, military personnel, celebrities. How did you work out who it might be? What was the starting point?

'Why these individuals? I notice they're all key influential leaders. Could cause something of a problem back home.'

Her officer shrugged. 'That can't be helped. We believe these individuals are most likely to form The Seven. They have all, to varying degrees, avowed an anti-Palestinian, anti-accord dialogue. Currently, we've insufficient evidence to implicate any of them in such a group. That's why we need to get on the ground.'

'You're absolutely sure of this seven idea? You don't think we're chasing the wind on this?'

Murtagh shook her head vigorously.

Markham regarded the young operative for what seemed an age. 'Well, I guess you'd better go find out.' The screen blanked as Markham dropped the call cursorily.

Galbraith and Murtagh exchanged glances. The need for results, fast, was only too evident.

It proved an awkward start to what needed to be a growing relationship between two powerful Palestinian Arabs, if anything positive was to come from it. Al-Umari had been tetchy and restive all morning, nestling his strapped arm as if it were a baby, desperate for protection. In the convoy, his ill humour had morphed into pensiveness and a silence overpowering everyone else. Hamid worried their president was suffering too much with his decisions and thought processes. He needed to be pin-sharp to deal with Qureshi.

Things had improved little upon arrival in Jerusalem to meet with the city's prospective mayor. Qureshi had vehemently opposed the president's plea for restraint over celebrations of Jerusalem's new status, and steadfastly refused to condemn the rising violence across the West Bank as disaffected Palestinians challenged both their own police and the Israeli Army and settlers in the aftermath of the Tel Etz massacre.

'But it is in our own interests to ensure that we are not seen to be reacting to—or even provoking—Israeli actions and negativity.'

Qureshi leaned forward, intent on the president, for whom he felt only contempt. 'No, Mr President,' he retorted with some relish. 'It is in your own self-interest for us to be seen to be passive and allow them'—he resisted the urge to spit—'to do whatever they wish.'

Hamid saw his leader waver, doubt his own understanding of the situation, his credibility even. Al-Umari's reply was stilted, full of uncertainty as he fought to protect his record in promoting Palestinian interests in the US-led talks, and the rights he had won for a stateless people.

Qureshi had listened impassively, allowing al-Umari the courtesy of finishing. When he finally spoke, it was only to rebuke the president yet again, and Hamid had cringed inwardly. 'Mr President, you have spoken for your people on the world stage; you have signed your name on the same page as the Jewish Prime Minister, in a display of solidarity that is not echoed in the everyday lives of your people. Even the Jews reject their prime minister, with his high ideal and desire to bring us all out of the shadows.

'For what reason did he do these things?' Qureshi had fulminated.

'You forget their losses,' al-Umari had responded meekly.

'Pah! You believe their word over that of our brothers? There is no evidence that the attack on Tel Etz was anything to do with Hezbollah. The views of those who might be seen to be the most reliable witnesses avow that a team of people, well armed and well versed in covert tactics, attacked the settlement. Our brothers have not claimed victory—'

'Or denied involvement.'

'Who would believe them? Not even you want to be seen with Hezbollah, perpetuating the rift of your predecessors. No. This is not something of Palestinian making. But we shall finish whatever our enemies have started.'

The meeting had degenerated into a sparring match, won, Hamid felt, by Qureshi. And al-Umari had led his small delegation forlornly away. Now they were heading back to Ramallah. Hamid, for the first time that morning, felt he could relax.

He cast a quick glance over at his boss, deep in thought, and decided to leave him to it. Retrieving his idev from a jacket pocket, he began reading the latest headlines.

'Do you think I have betrayed our people?' Al-Umari's voice was low, weak, the voice of someone for whom power was an ill-fitting jacket that threatened to slip off.

Hamid considered the question. What did he think? When Jamal had said he was entering full negotiations with Israel, brokered by the United States, people had expressed reservations. A major departure, he had embraced Jamal's decision, and it had looked as if it might succeed. The final meeting had been a major success for the Palestinians. But coming home?

The attack on the president should have shown that irreconcilable differences remained between the government and the people. Hamid and his leader had chosen to ignore that possibility. After all, who would not want to end centuries of turmoil? Such a thought seemed folly now.

'You did what you thought was the right thing, Mr President.' Though al-Umari always insisted on being called Jamal when they were in private, Hamid felt the need to remind him of his position—the stature and the power it conveyed to and demanded of its occupant.

'For who, Faisal? Is Qureshi right in what he says? Who am I really doing this for?'

Silence engulfed the back of the SUV as their driver drove towards Ramallah. Hamid stared out the window at the construction site they were passing. More houses for more settlers. Who were they kidding? he wondered. The Israelis were never going to stop their burgeoning programme of settlement building.

The vehicle came to a stop at temporary traffic lights, positioned for site traffic to cross the highway. A hot wind drew up sand and dust in quivering eddies that made the distance shimmer. Hamid loved his birthplace, but this was not his future. Right now, he longed to be with his wife and two children, perhaps tending a smallholding—a few chickens, a goat, and vegetables growing.

Perhaps he'd resign.

The light was green, and the vehicle started moving again. Soon they would be home.

The cement truck hit the back flank of the vehicle just behind where Hamid was sitting, the force rending the metalwork and punching the bench seat forward. Hamid cried momentarily as he was forced into the bulkhead separating them from the driving compartment.

Across from him, al-Umari made the mistake of putting his hands out to protect him. His wrists snapped with the crack of dead twigs; his screams filling the air as if it would never be calm again.

The vehicle slowed in its spinning. But just as it seemed the mayhem was over, another truck smashed into the driver's side, spinning the SUV in a cacophony of tearing metal, squealing rubber, and groaning engine noise. The driver buckled under the impact. Twisting horribly in the maelstrom, blood spraying from the crushed skull.

Silence fell. Hamid attempted to move. He could shift his head just enough to see his president lolling forward, spittle falling from his half-open mouth. A light dust, perhaps atomised glass or merely sand from the desert outside, whirled in the still air.

'Jamal.' Just speaking sent pain stabbing through Hamid's chest, intensifying as he tried to draw in air. Broken rib? Punctured lung?

Al-Umari didn't move, didn't acknowledge, made no sound.

Hamid exhorted him again. 'Mr President!'

A faint stirring.

'We have to move. We must get out!'

Hamid pawed at the door and then realised it was hopelessly buckled. The back windscreen was shattered. Perhaps, if he released al-Umari's belt, they could scramble clear. What idiot had changed the lights on the junction?

The sound of a car stopping attracted his attention. Hamid mustered all his strength and called out. 'Hey! Hey! In here. Quick, the president is injured.' Pain burned in his chest.

Shadows flitted through the bright sunlight, closer and then far away. Quiet once more.

Hamid waited, trying to look and identify what was going on. 'Hey!' His voice was more strident now, though it hurt him to shout so. 'Hey, President al-Umari is hurt. We need help!'

The sound of boots on tarmac assaulted his ears, and Hamid experienced both elation and fear at the same time. Were they rescuers or executioners? The sound ceased.

'Hey!' Hamid tried again, pleading to their better judgement, whoever they were. All around him was an eerie quiet, which was gradually filled with the beating of his heart, cascading through his consciousness. 'Hey, help us. The president needs help. He's dying.'

The sound of shoes scraping on the tarmac came to him, and in his dimming vision, he caught the shadow of a figure appear in the mangled space that had once been a door window.

'Please.' Hamid could feel himself losing the battle with consciousness. With a great effort, he opened his eyes and tried to turn his head to where the person was. 'Please help.'

He caught a movement from the figure, and something reaching towards him. A hand. His vision cleared. No!

The bullet sliced efficiently through his forehead and blew out the back of his head, but Faisal Hamid was already dead. A look of sadness remained on his face.

Satisfied, the shadow moved away from the wrecked vehicle and joined the others, who climbed into a pickup and drove away without another glance.

'Jesus Christ! Are you sure?'

John Kemble studied his new secretary, Kathryn, who had appeared, almost apologetically, in his doorway, as if the news about to be imparted had been her doing. The secretary of state suddenly felt his age as she made a quick, affirmative flick of her head before averting her gaze.

'Thank you.'

'Will there be anything else?'

Kemble shook his head, slumping heavily in his chair as the aide began closing the door behind her. 'Wait! Yes. Get me the president.'

Fuck. This was a real shitstorm and no mistake. Kemble rose purposefully from his desk, headed for the sideboard, and poured a whisky. It was late morning in Washington, early evening in Jerusalem where the shit had spectacularly hit the fan. The first stories would be appearing on Twitter, Snapchat, no containment; everyone would know a version of the truth. Carlisle would have to be told and quickly. It wouldn't do for her to hear from anyone else.

This marked the end of the accord.

It was the venom of a man scorned that caused the tumbler to be hurled from his hand, to crash against the wall and burst into shards of glass.

President Carlisle sipped her coffee. It was hot, too hot really, but sipping it meant she didn't have to look at Kemble, as if the man had grown another head. She wanted to say something, anything, but she didn't know what would help the broken man in the blue-and-cream-striped chair before her now. The silence threatened to engulf them.

'This is a fuck-up.'

No response.

'Do we know who is to blame?'

A slight shake of the head.

'John! Anything, anything at all would be a help.'

Kemble seemed to heave, as if raised from a deep slumber, his demeanour slack and defeated. Carlisle couldn't believe how quickly he'd succumbed to the news. Sure, it wasn't good, but she expected more of her secretary. 'John, you have to get your shit together. We have to know what's happening now.'

Kemble's body heaved again. 'My apologies, Madam President. It's all something of a shock.'

Carlisle smiled in what she hoped was an endearing and engaging way. 'Of course it is, John. But we have to respond—quickly.'

Her secretary of state drew in a deep breath and another and then looked her straight in the eyes. 'Madam President, I have to tell you that the Jerusalem Accord is dead and buried.'

'John, we don't know that yet.'

'Ma'am, Jamal al-Umari has been assassinated, that's plain, possibly Hamas if the reports are correct. There are so many acts of violence happening across the whole of the West Bank right now. Add to that a change of government coming in Tel Aviv, a new mayor in Jerusalem, and we're looking at a whole new political situation in the region.'

In the lull, both politicians considered the altered landscape of their political lives.

Carlisle leaned across her desk to her bemused secretary of state. 'I hear what you're saying, John. And, yes, it looks like shit. But let's wait until all the facts are in. This cannot be the end of it. Too much is at stake for the Middle East, you, me, the whole goddamned world. You must bring this deal back home.

'As soon as possible.'

The pictures were all over the news—smoke rising from behind police barriers, Israeli soldiers and Palestinian police officers moving in a ballet of restless unease. Crowds had gathered, under the early afternoon sun, around the pyre, and it was clear there were few who mourned the violence brought on al-Umari.

Israeli Prime Minister-Elect Binyamin Olmet stroked his chin reflectively. He'd seen off a late surge from Malbert in last week's vote and would now be officially sworn in as Israel's premier in the next month. Despite his own feelings on the accord, much trumpeted by his predecessor, the death of the one person he could renegotiate with was a major blow to the safety of Israel. Qureshi, the most likely benefactor of the attack, would be much less willing to sit at the same table as a Jew.

And how did he react? A statement would be required, one balancing commiseration for his counterpart and concern for the Palestinian people, with the need to be seen to be protecting Israelis and defending the interests of the state. He could have wished for a less tumultuous start to his tenure as prime minister.

His team had left him alone, by his own request. Olmet wanted space to think and not be swayed by advisors who figured they might have the answer he wanted—always dangerous. Picking up a pen, Olmet began to write his response. Fifteen minutes and two corrections later, he was finished.

How would the world greet his words?

The young man, dressed in black and with a Kalashnikov slung over his shoulder, dropped a folded sheet of dishevelled paper on the desk. Qureshi regarded it as the man left and then retrieved the missive. He unfolded it and took in the few words scribbled on its off-white surface.

A smile broke his usually serious face. The paper dropped to the tabletop, but Qureshi was already gazing out the window, planning his next move.

Ambulances delivered the bodies of al-Umari and his entourage to the emergency department of the Herzog Hospital, it being closest to the accident. Hamid and the driver were pronounced dead on arrival, while the bodyguard died in theatre soon after, amid unsuccessful attempts to save him.

The surgeons crowded round the broken, mutilated body of al-Umari. The feeblest of pulses had been found and maintained in the ambulance, beyond all right thinking, and continued as he was rushed to surgery. Now they were in a race against time to mend the wrecked form, a contest in which they were playing an impossible game of catch-up with fate.

25

The late-afternoon sun flooded the office, heating a chilly environment, though Kemble knew the cold was his own. How had this happened? Al-Umari's naivety in travelling, without other vehicles and security, was literally unbelievable. But that was only the start. And Kemble was aware of how casual and uncaring that would come across to anyone. The secretary was a man who hated investing in things that were subsequently subjected to the stupidity of others.

This was one such situation. Al-Umari had, by his actions, ensured that the work of the last three years could, potentially, come to nothing. Except, as Carlisle had made clear, that wasn't an option.

So, what to do?

Kemble sipped on his coffee, considering what he knew and what options existed. There were few. Rumours were surfacing from Israel and the West Bank, about the end of the peace process, both sides blaming the other for the assassination of al-Umari and using it to either espouse greater violence or better defence—one and the same thing to many. They appeared to amount to the same thing in the end—more bloodshed.

There was a call from leading hard-line columnist and broadcaster Natalie Epstein for Israel to take back control of the West Bank and Gaza. Her reasoning seemed to revolve around unfounded threats involving ISIS, the Syrian Muslim Brotherhood, Hezbollah, Hamas, and the Iranians. Kemble had mulled this over and quickly dismissed any threat from ISIS as irrelevant. They were small beer when considered against some of the bigger players in the region.

Iran and Syria were different propositions. Iran espoused violence against Israel, and Syria was acknowledged as a puppet of Tehran. Even so, offering all-out support of al-Umari's assassins seemed a step too far, even for them.

Hezbollah had made no comment about the assassination, but many observers felt this was just a matter of time, rather than any fear of a backlash from the world community.

No. Iran was the enemy with the most to gain or lose from however this played out. Iran wanted, still, the demise of Israel—an accord between Israel and the Palestinians might put paid to their ambition. Then again, the Israelis weren't the pushover other Middle Eastern powers could be in the face of fanatical attacks.

The CIA/NSA report, muted in its conclusions, suggested many faceless antagonists, half-formed threats, and suppositions, which, he conceded, was typical of the region and the politics. However it might appear, it was clear that, unless something drastic was considered, there would be no accord. Any possible solutions seemed to revolve around three individuals—two American and one Brit—to save the day. It didn't make for good reading, and Kemble felt even more resigned to his original prognosis.

A sigh emanated from his lips. He'd never felt quite so helpless as he did now—not that he could afford to dwell on how hopeless everything was. He had already been contacted by CNN, Fox News, the BBC, and Al Jazeera, to name just four channels, all eager to know what his thoughts were. His eyes were drawn back to the words he had typed on the screen of his device. All were inadequate—all lacked political gravitas for the moment—even though he knew Carlisle wanted him to convince the world the accord still had legs. Did he have the talent remaining to accomplish that feat?

The knock on the door was light, hesitant. That would be his secretary, Kathryn—Kathryn Tatchell. Nice enough girl, but not Sarah, though she'd do for now. 'Come.'

The door opened slowly, and Kathryn peeped round the jamb, apology blooming large in her brown eyes. 'I'm sorry to disturb you, Mr Secretary, but there are some gentlemen to see you.'

'Who?' Kemble tried and failed to hide his irritation.

Before his secretary could answer, there was a slight commotion as another squeezed through the small gap she'd left. He was a short man in an ill-fitting suit, balding and definitely "reserve team". But the smile told another story.

'John Harrington Kemble?' The little man advanced purposefully towards the secretary's desk.

Behind him, two DC Metro officers checked their progress just inside the door.

Kemble tried to suppress the turmoil his thoughts had become but was sure his face shouted confusion, much to the other's glee. The secretary's eyes evaluated the two officers, standing as if to prevent flight. Kemble felt his heart thump in his chest. 'Y-yes … And who are you?'

'Detective Sergeant Aspen, DC Metro. And this' (he placed an envelope he'd retrieved from a jacket pocket almost reverentially on the secretary's desk) 'this' (he tapped the surface with his finger) 'is a warrant for your arrest.' Aspen loved doing such things to powerful people; it brought them down to his level.

Kemble felt the colour drain from his face, his body suddenly sweating with fear. 'Warrant?' His voice was small and powerless.

'You know a Sarah Anderson?'

Kemble nodded mutely.

'Miss Anderson alleges rape, which has led to her pregnancy with what she firmly believes to be your child. As of this moment, you are under arrest, Senator.'

'Breaking news this hour—the collapse of the Jerusalem Accord. Is it about to become another casualty of the road crash that is Middle East politics? In Tel Aviv today, Israeli Prime Minister-Elect Binyamin Olmet issued a stark and uncompromising warning to those who had attacked President al-Umari that any similar action against Israeli personnel of any stature in the country would be met with swift and decisive action. He also called on the United States to broker talks as soon as possible on the future of the long-heralded treaty, intimating the attack warranted a pause and a rethink in the negotiations on the region's future.

'Matters get worse for President Carlisle's administration, as Secretary John Kemble was sensationally arrested at his Washington office, following allegations of rape from former secretary Sarah Anderson. Anderson, twenty-eight, claims she was dropped by Kemble when she refused his advances. So, is it rape, or an affair that went wrong?

'Whichever way this falls, Kemble is looking over the abyss, and we'll be bringing more ana—'

'Turn it off.'

Carlisle's mood was as black as a stormy day in Maine. What had Kemble been thinking? There was little that could be done about a diplomatic process, stymied by outside forces. But to get entangled with your personal assistant at the same time was just sheer stupidity.

The Oval Office had only a few individuals in it. Foreman was ensconced on one of the two cream sofas, sipping black coffee. Bill she would have trusted with her life, so steady a rock was he. Next to him was her chief of staff, Carol Fleischmann, who'd been with her a year now; her insight into the political landscape of Washington, as well as her legal background, made her irreplaceable in such calamitous situations.

Opposite them were defence secretary Warren Mitchell and Kemble's understudy, Robert Weiss. It was no secret within the White House that Weiss had struggled with Kemble's diplomatic efforts, and Carlisle wondered whether the young man had secretly let out a whoop of delight at the lunchtime news. If he had, he kept it well hidden—a true politician. But while a solid performer, he was no career politician; Carlisle knew he'd progressed on the back of Daddy's money.

'Views?'

Coughs and harrumphs greeted her question. What could you say? Foreman wondered. For him, it was a clear-cut situation. Kemble was a liability while this rape case was hanging over his head. They would have to do something about that and quickly if there was any chance to rescue the accord. 'If that's what we want to do,' he finished calmly.

'Thanks, Bill. Succinct and to the point. You're saying, then, we sacrifice John as soon as possible.'

Foreman fixed Carlisle's gaze. 'Ma'am, I'm not saying anything, just my perspective on the situation. On the battlefield, if a commander screws up or circumstances arise that threaten the overall strategy, you move fast to minimise the risk. We have to consider that.'

'Bill's right, Madam President,' insisted Carol Fleischmann. Mitchell, Carlisle saw, nodded emphatically as her chief of staff spoke. 'As difficult as it may appear, John now threatens your administration's credibility. Issues around his accord are bad enough, and that's unravelling fast. However, his inability to keep his dick in his pants at a time like this is a major mistake. He has to make the right decision.'

Carlisle considered the blunt delivery. Fleischmann was right, albeit she could have taken a more measured approach perhaps. Kemble was a good man, and she had always appreciated his knowledge and easy humour. Was that enough to stand by him and … 'What about your view, Bob, you've been fairly quiet till now. What do you think?'

The deputy secretary shuffled his bony frame uncomfortably in his seat. Weiss knew he was seen as pro-Israeli, a view he'd done nothing to dispel. How could he? His family was from Hebron; family on his maternal side still resided there and across the West Bank. Kemble's diplomatic activity would have a direct effect on his relatives and, ultimately, himself. It had been a struggle to maintain impartiality, though he perhaps preferred ambiguity. He had to be careful.

'Madam President, John's work for this accord has been tireless. His ability to bring together disparate parties in such an encompassing way is without parallel.'

'You can cut the bullshit in here, Bob. What do you really think?'

'First assessment? It's going down faster than the *Titanic*. Olmet won't support it because his Likud Party was voted in on the back of strengthening the settlements and clamping down on the West Bank. Qureshi has been against it from the beginning. So, no surprise, he's already coming out to say he will not be negotiating on behalf of his people if he becomes Palestinian president. Syria and Iran are known to back Qureshi, so we have work to do there.'

'No middle ground then?' Carlisle retorted acerbically.

Weiss shook his head ruefully.

'And what about Kemble's other problem?'

'I can't comment on his personal interactions, ma'am. He's still my boss at this moment.'

'Okay, I've heard that loud and clear now. John's position over his personal stupidity is my responsibility. Anything else? How likely are Iran and Syria to get physically involved?'

The silence was deafening, with each official looking to the others to respond first.

Weiss shrugged. 'Iran is eager to see the downfall of Israel. But al-Umari is a stumbling block. And they're only just now recovering from the setback on the nuclear deal. They'll hang back from anything other than utterings of support for Qureshi.

'Syria. They're a different matter. The new Muslim Brotherhood government isn't pro-US and is unlikely to become so any time soon. Their backing is predominantly Russian, so what we say is not going to sway any affiliation they might feel towards a new Palestinian administration. I think they could sponsor any Hezbollah claim to assassination of al-Umari—politically and practically. That feeds into tacit Russian support. And bang goes the UN vote for any initiative in the Middle East. Your feelings, Director?' Weiss passed the poisoned chalice to Foreman, who scowled.

'Bob's right, Madam President. Iran covertly wants our dollar, and Syria couldn't give a rat's ass. But what about Israel? That's my issue. What are the Israelis going to do? If the reports coming in are to be believed, Olmet will be seeking a renegotiation of the accord at the very least.'

'This action does enable Prime Minister-Elect Olmet to promote Israeli interests in a way his predecessor couldn't.' Weiss's tone was measured.

'Self-interest,' interjected Foreman disparagingly, encouraging a rare display of frustration from the deputy secretary. 'Olmet will pander to the right and the religious lobby, and that will be the end of the only deal that has been anywhere close to resolving the fuck-up that is the Middle East. Jee-sus, he's already intimated that we should broker another round of talks!

'Am I right?' The director appealed to Mitchell and Fleischmann.

The latter remained silent.

Mitchell opened his mouth, paused, and shut it again.

'Don't be shy, Warren. Let us know what you think,' Carlisle encouraged.

Mitchell coughed. 'Madam President, we know Israel will come out strong from this. They've already raised concerns recently over Iran, citing, as yet unconfirmed, evidence they're recommissioning Fordow's nuclear programme. We've kept a lid on that. With the Umari incident now, who knows what they'll be emboldened to do.'

Foreman drew breath. 'I agree with the secretary. Now isn't the time to withdraw from the Middle East peace process.'

'Nor is it time to push ahead regardless,' retorted Weiss. 'We should take our lead from the area, on the matter of the accord.'

Carlisle digested the words, keeping her thoughts to herself; she decided to ask Fleischmann what she thought later. 'Very well. Thank you all for your contributions. I guess it's down to me to find a way forward.' She walked over to the Resolute desk, feeling more than a little let down by her advisors; sat; and pointedly concentrated on the information on her desk display. The meeting was over. She heard the door close and, feeling the strain go, allowed a sigh to fall from her lips.

The cough startled her, and she raised her head from her reverie. Foreman stood just in the doorway in the middle of the room, regarding her. Carlisle raised an eyebrow. 'What gives, Bill?'

'May I have a moment of your time, Madam President?'

Carlisle indicated an ornate wooden armchair opposite her. 'Please.' She waited as he took his place then. 'What is it you want?'

Foreman settled himself, considering his next words carefully. Carlisle was astute. She'd know if he was showboating or bullshitting. Now was not the time to get things wrong. 'Ma'am—'

'Angela,' she encouraged.

Foreman breathed deeply, smiled despite the seriousness of the moment, and started over. 'Angela, doesn't all this worry you? I mean, Kemble being cited for rape at the exact moment the political situation on the ground in the Middle East is going belly up?'

Carlisle considered Foreman's question. Was it conspiracy or just circumstance? 'Go on, Bill. You have something you're dying to say.'

'I'm concerned that Bob Weiss is playing for our team now that Kemble is on the bench. He's completely pro-Israel.'

'Bill, America is pro-Israel. Bob is the automatic choice if John is out, and he is. Let's not forget; it's his fault that we're in this position.'

'Granted, that's how it seems. That doesn't mean we have to jump so readily into abandoning him. You need to speak with Bob before you make any rash decisions.'

Carlisle allowed herself a moment as she digested his words. 'What do I tell the press?'

Foreman smiled briefly, almost bleakly. 'Anything you damn well please, ma'am. After all, you are the president.'

Carlisle laughed. 'Your sentiment is understandable; however, I shall try to be circumspect.'

'Just be sure to make decisions for the right reasons,' Foreman admonished.

'Thanks. As ever, your advice and support is much appreciated.'

The press conference, Carlisle could see as she waited for her introduction from her chief of staff, was well attended. This was going to be difficult, no mistake. She shuffled in the shadows, worry gnawing at her as Fleischmann prepared the audience.

'Good afternoon, ladies and gentlemen. Thank you for attending at such short notice. The president will shortly deliver a message and then take questions from the press.

'Ladies and gentlemen, the president of the United States.'

Carlisle stepped from the wings, and with a quick nod to Fleischmann, she took her position before the cameras and the world. After all, this was not just about the United States of America.

'My fellow Americans, I come before you today with grave news concerning one of my most notable and able diplomats and a cornerstone of this administration. John Kemble has been accused of a crime none of us would condone or dismiss. You will forgive me if I do not go into the details now. That is for another time and place, and enough speculation abounds right now. Much more important are the concerns John has spoken with me about, for the Jerusalem Accord.

'As you will all appreciate, this presents issues for my administration's Middle East initiative. Given recent events in the West Bank, the sustainability of the accord, which John worked so tirelessly on, is something that I believe is my responsibility to carry on. The world has been waiting for this historic initiative to bear fruit, and I will not allow the work of my close friend and confidante to suffer.

'While John resolves the issues that confront his personal life, it is my intention to carry on the work he so ably began. I ask that you support

John at this time and the efforts of this administration to usher in a new peace in the Middle East.

'Thank you.'

The pause was what she'd hoped for, even so she waited the questions expectantly even as Sharone Caulfield, her press officer requested them.

A hand went up in the front row—Carey Swann, *Washington Post*, beat the rest of the pack to it. 'President Carlisle, how seriously do you take the arrest of Secretary Kemble and the allegations of rape?'

Carlisle adopted her best poker face as she smiled presidentially and responded. 'Carey, as you know, I'm not in the business of speculating on any ongoing investigation. This allegation will be dealt with by the proper authorities, and I'm sure DC police will do their utmost to get to the bottom of the case. My focus remains on the Middle East process and ensuring that doesn't suffer as a consequence.'

Another hand and hastily rehearsed words. 'But, President, doesn't this whole case put into question Secretary Kemble's judgement? Will you be asking him to formally resign?'

'Peter, it is Peter, isn't it?'

The reporter nodded—Peter Haines from *Sky News*, she remembered.

'John has already resigned this morning, so he can concentrate on this situation. Any more, I'm not prepared to say at this time. With regards to the peace process, I think the fact we got to the table and there is an accord, to be signed by all parties, is testament to his negotiation skills. I only hope that I can do John, and that process, justice.'

More hands shot up. But Caulfield stepped to the lectern and placed her hands in the air. 'Thank you, ladies and gentlemen, for your patience. As you will understand, the president has much to arrange. Thank you.'

She turned off the television and turned to the others in the room with her. Tears had smudged the mascara on Sarah Anderson's face, but she made no effort to clean the stains away.

Those with her looked on with disinterest—all save one, who leaned over and patted her knee. She recoiled at the touch and the person smiled. 'You see, Sarah, your actions have been of much use to us.'

'Why?! Why are you doing this?' Despite her internal admonishment, she felt herself beginning to lose it again. 'Why did I have to tell lies about John?'

The person seemed to recoil. 'Lies? You were not asked to tell any lies. Did you not have sex with your boss and are you not pregnant?'

Sarah nodded mutely.

'Well it is an almost truth. He was not your boyfriend, and he is married; therefore, it could be seen as rape'—there was a turn of the head to the others and a thin laugh—'if you don't think too hard. I'm afraid thinking hard isn't a forte of mine.'

'I don't want to do this, and I don't want you here anymore.'

'But, Sarah, you're implicated. You've taken our money and you have given a sworn statement to the local police. You can't back out now.'

'I didn't think it would go this far. I was just mad he sent me away.'

'And so you should be.'

'I'm going to tell the police this was a big mistake.'

'No. No you're not, Sarah.'

Sarah rounded on the other, with what she hoped was righteous anger. 'You can't stop me. This is America.'

The thin laugh came again. 'I'm sorry, Sarah. We can.'

Nobody passing the house on foot would have heard the double cough of the suppressed semi-automatic as it ended the unhappy existence of Sarah Anderson.

The person who had spoken rose and considered the silent form on the sofa and then turned to the others. 'You know what to do?'

They both nodded.

'Good. Get to it.' With that, he stepped from the house.

The call to the DC Metro dispatcher was logged at seven fifteen the following morning when Anderson's cleaner arrived and let herself in. Officers were quickly on the scene, but it was clear that Sarah Anderson had been dead several hours. Cartridge casings were found—two in number, which would later be traced to a .45 Browning 1911 owned by Senator John Kemble.

26

It was later in the morning in London when the news came through from Washington. Sir David was at Vauxhall Cross, along with Foreign Secretary Vincent Huntley. Huntley was a heavyset man, with thinning blonde hair and a drooping left eyelid that made his blue eyes look lopsided. The man had a habit of looking down at those around him, as if he owned them. Galbraith studiously ignored him. Logan could see Brooke was less than impressed. He also noted a coffee stain on the secretary's crumpled white shirt. He wasn't, figured the officer, the sort who inspired confidence in his peers.

When he spoke, that view was only further reinforced. 'You realise, everybody, that we're once again having to rescue the bloody Yanks. There is some serious ...' Huntley tailed off as Sir David leaned in to whisper in his ear. The secretary squinted, glanced sharply at Murtagh, and reddened, disguising his faux pas with a sudden cough. He continued as if nothing had happened. 'Analysis to be had in Washington. And, of course, we wish Senator Kemble all the best in the coming investigation.

'Notwithstanding that, we have a more pressing situation within the Middle East, which I'm hoping that you people are going to be able to provide some good intelligence and leads on.'

Oh dear, went through Logan's mind at the foreign secretary's words. He rather hoped that Huntley didn't want chapter and verse, because that might include a healthy portion of bullshit. How to play?

Galbraith rescued him. 'Foreign Secretary, you're correct in stating that we have a situation in the Middle East. However, there's much that remains operational in nature and, therefore, not what we can pass on, even to yourself. I'm sure you understand.'

Huntley made to speak, but Sir David cut him off, quickly and so urbanely Huntley was the only one who didn't notice the slur. 'Secretary, my director is, unfortunately, correct. We cannot possible let you know what is currently transpiring—safety of individuals, you know. In a situation such as this it's the old adage: "Careless talk costs lives." Hmm?' The look said it all, but Huntley was completely bamboozled by C's charm.

'Of course, I understand that, David. Don't want to do anything that might jeopardise anyone's life.'

'Quite so, Foreign Secretary.'

Huntley puffed his chest out. *The silly bastard thinks he's been part of something secret*, figured Logan. *He's happy.*

'Secretary, let me take you for a spot of late lunch at the club. I'll fill you in on a few more details while we're there.'

Huntley's eyes gleamed at the mention of lunch. By the time they were eating, a bottle of good wine consumed, he would be in no fit state to comprehend the misdirection so deftly completed by Sir David.

They all stood as Huntley made to leave, everyone seeming to heave a collective sigh of relief.

It was Murtagh who spoke first. 'Please tell me that guy isn't for real?'

Galbraith blushed apologetically.

Logan had no such reserve and laughed. 'I'm afraid he is. What can we say? New money, inherited through the business of his father, who was an arse to his workforce by all accounts. Huntley went to university in Birmingham, studied law, and managed to get a half-decent result. Politics was his real thing, though, and he used Daddy's money to fund his election to Parliament nine years ago. Typical small-town England but managed to cultivate friends in the right places, which got him in the prime minister's sights.'

'The rest is history,' Murtagh observed laconically.

''Fraid so. Anyhow, C will keep him "in the know", so he should be less trouble for us now he's done his obligatory visit.'

Murtagh didn't look convinced.

Galbraith changed the subject. 'Never mind our illustrious master; we have work to do.' She pulled up a number from 'contacts' on her device and swiped it over her dialler icon. The tone sounded twice before the call was answered.

'Philip? Can you get up here please? Thank you.'

The young officer was quickly in the room and, after placing an aluminium case on the floor and syncing his device with the room, smiled at the small gathering. 'What?' he asked.

'Brooke and Steve have the go-ahead from C to head for Israel. We need to finalise their cover and contact the local office for support.'

Okri smiled again. 'For sure, ma'am. I have everything already for them, as per Miss Nugent's orders.' He reached for his case and lifted it onto the table, flicking the clasps open. Reaching in, he brought out two dossiers, checked the names, and passed them over to the officers.

'These are your updated covers. Brooke, you are a freelance photojournalist who has worked with AP, Reuters, Sky, among others. Steve, you are a freelance political writer, and the pair of you have been given an assignment to report on the changing scene within the West Bank.' Okri's delivery was clear and precise, exactly what was needed, Logan figured, when you were having your non-official cover constructed.

The younger man continued his narrative, informing them their employer was Fox News, whose CEO had been approached personally by President Carlisle to support their cover. Danielle Hardy had readily agreed to Carlisle's request, presumably imagining the scoop the two officers might bring her way.

An itinerary was included of places to visit and people to meet, those who could possibly furnish them with leads or background information. Finally, their passports; Logan leafed through the document. It was a masterful disguise with stamps from all over the world. One or two he could equate to real events; there was an entry for Ukraine, February 2014, another for Syria in May of the same year. On another page was a stamp roundabout the time of the Nigerian massacre. At least then, he had some reference, and that was positive. He feared having to make up too much.

Murtagh caught his attention. It seemed she was equally happy with the cover story she had been given. The extra time from their Geneva sojourn had obviously been worthwhile.

'Everybody happy?'

'I am.'

'Me too,' confirmed Murtagh.

'Good. Let's look at the latest information we have. What did you get from GCHQ?'

Logan gestured at Okri. 'Philip and I went down there yesterday. The drone information was only partly useful. We couldn't directly identify Olsen from the images. There was voice data, and GCHQ are running through voice analysis now. First indications make them fairly confident it's him.'

'Anything on the people he was meeting?'

'We think that whoever he was talking to, it was by some sort of communication link. They certainly weren't on site.'

'You're sure of that, Philip?'

'Very definitely.'

Galbraith arched an eyebrow at Logan. 'What do you think?'

'It is highly likely that whoever Olsen was talking with wouldn't be there. Too high a security risk.'

'Okay. Do you think he might have been talking to somebody from The Seven?'

'Anybody's guess. Likely though,' he replied truthfully. 'The bigger question we need to ask is why Israel need's a nuclear physicist.'

'Whoever Olsen spoke with means we're moving into a new phase of operations,' Murtagh ventured. 'Let's not be circumspect. We've already identified there's a group of individuals against the peace process. So should this come as any surprise?'

Logan chuckled. Brooke keeping it real again, he figured. 'No. And, we need to get out there to find out who is making contact.' He gathered his papers together. 'Do we have a flight?'

Okri nodded. 'Yes. Tickets are in your packs, including hotel and car hire.'

Logan caught Galbraith's gaze. 'If you'll excuse us, Brooke and I need to finalise our arrangements.'

Galbraith indicated the door, almost dismissively. Inwardly, she admitted to herself the concern tugging at her when she had to send officers to a potential conflict zone. Logan recognised her internal turmoil but was also aware Murtagh wouldn't understand. He'd talk with her later.

As he and Murtagh made to leave the room, Galbraith reached out to him. 'Be careful,' she told him.

27

As a nuclear facility, Dimona was as good as it got, Olsen decided as he continued his virtual tour of the plant on the television they'd provided him. Had he expected anything else? Perhaps not, now he thought about it, but then he hadn't known what the Israelis had lined up for him. What little he'd gleaned about Israeli technology should have told him the Israelis would have put everything into their nuclear endeavours. As the disembodied voice guided him, he was impressed by the attention to detail in the plasma and design physics labs, the calculating power of the supercomputer and hydrodynamics. These were all his playground.

He was less interested in the manufacturing facility, though systems engineering was something he had grown to endure, purely because it enabled him to move from the theoretical to the hard practicality of delivery. When the show finished, the screen went blank, leaving the Norwegian to his own devices once more.

Since his sojourn to the farmstead, life had been quite dull—two days of nothing much. He'd had very little contact with his keepers (guards? Olsen was still unsure which, if he was honest), just the ritual of daily ablutions and meals. Fortunately, Olsen was good with his own company. That and a pile of research papers, periodicals, and his one pleasure—Jo Nesbo novel. The moments that really disagreed with him were his indoctrination sessions with Ruth. Perhaps it wasn't her intent, but he appeared merely a task to her, one she was disinterested in and wished to complete as quickly as possible. Learning language, customs, and the politics of the country, Olsen felt he was a refugee from a Cold War spy story.

When the television had been placed in his room by the uncommunicative duo of removal men, Olsen had tried to ask them why. What was it for? They'd departed with the same silent deliberation with which they'd arrived. He had switched it on in the hope of seeing something of the outside world, rather than the four walls of his room.

Now, having communicated his destination and purpose, the device was blank, dead. No other channels were available, and Olsen found he was vaguely unsettled by its presence—the eye of the world, blinded and unresponsive. A metaphor?

No. He was here for a reason; the pictures and the tour had confirmed his little conference at the farm. But all this cloak-and-dagger stuff was starting to piss him off. He wanted to get out to the facility and start designing. Sitting here, waiting for the bus so to speak, was not his idea of revenge.

The door clicked open, and Ruth entered. Unlike Natalie, this woman was almost ascetic, not prone to small talk. Olsen knew the dynamic was much different to the one in Geneva and was embarrassed now by the ease with which the waitress had sucked him in. But to be courted by Natalie had boosted his ego a little, at a time he'd needed it. Now, it appeared, something different was required.

'Hello, Ruth. How are you?'

'Fine.' No effort at small talk or niceties, and this irked Olsen.

He jerked a thumb at the TV. 'So, nice programme, but the channel choice is a bit limited,' he quipped.

Nothing.

'What happens next?'

Ruth, if that was her name, which he doubted (after all, he'd watched *24* and knew the drill), pulled a chair round from the small table and sat down facing Olsen. 'We prepare to move you.'

'Excellent!' It truly was—action at last. 'When do we go?'

'Another day, while preparations are finalised, and then we head south.'

Olsen wanted to know what the delay was about. It looked as if they had everything in place, and he could start work on the project now.

His questions must have been written across his face because Ruth pre-empted him. 'There is security and materials to put in place before we can move you down there.'

'What security? What materials?'

Ruth ignored the question as she delved into her shoulder bag.

Olsen rolled his eyes. 'You might get more out of me if you were a bit more forthcoming with some information, you know. What do you think I'm going to do? I'm here to help you people, to avenge in any way I can the death of my family. Instead you treat me like a prisoner. Why?'

'The materials you'll find out about when you arrive at your destination. The security? You don't need to know.' Her last comment just pricked his curiosity, but she steadfastly refused to expand. Instead she retrieved an idev from her bag, placed it on the table, and pushed it towards the scientist. 'Make a list of clothes, toiletries you need, and any other equipment you may require on here. I'll make sure it's brought to you before we leave.'

Olsen nodded, and with that exchange, she was gone.

All that filled his mind as the door closed was the question: What was it he didn't need to know?

John Black lay back on the bed in the small room and considered the ceiling. It wasn't the most exciting thing he'd ever had to study over his thirty-four years on the planet, but it gave him space to think. There was much to consider while he was being interrogated by Yakin and Goldstein, not least what had happened to Olsen. It would be difficult to pick up the trail again; of that he was sure.

A knock came on the door.

Black smiled ironically, these guys had come 180 degrees in their treatment of him. Not that he was complaining. 'Come.'

The door opened. Yakin entered, carrying a mug of coffee and a bowl, both of which he set on the small table. In the bowl were some rice and vegetables and meat, the smell of what he thought was lamb.

He picked up the spoon and looked at his one-time captor. 'Thanks.'

Yakin dipped his head. 'We need to move soon.'

Black regarded the small Israeli. 'Today?'

The other nodded.

'How come?'

'Our friends are moving Olsen. We picked up movements at the safe house. Two vehicles left thirty minutes ago, heading back to the main road.'

'Did you see Olsen in the vehicle?'

Yakin paused. 'No. He's still at the safe house for now.'

'Really? Why do you think they've done that? There were three vehicles that I followed the other day. What are they doing with Olsen?'

'Perhaps they're scouting … ' Yakin tailed off, indecision writ large on his face.

'Perhaps, perhaps not,' rejoined Black, his face dark with misgiving. 'Can we get eyes on them?'

'Why?'

'I have one bad feeling about this.'

The two SUVs took the off-ramp for Ramla and headed into the town before turning towards a suburb that nestled in between two large industrial areas. The houses here were anonymous blocks, sandy coloured, with dun windows and looms of electric and telephone wires looping from one to another. There were few people around and even fewer cars. Ideal situation, decided the front passenger in the lead vehicle.

They turned into a side road, and as the leader carried on, the other vehicle blocked the entry. Just passed a house on the right about halfway down the street, the lead vehicle stopped, blocking the street. Quickly the black-garbed occupants disembarked, holding automatic weapons at the ready.

'We have to get out of here, now.'

Yakin glanced at Black, and the latter saw common sense dawning on the Israeli. 'Okay. Our car is out the back. Get your things and follow me. Peter!' Yakin called his colleague, who shouted back. 'We're going. Get the car ready.'

Black laid a hand on the Israeli's shoulder, who turned sharply, eyebrow raised. 'I need a weapon,' the American told him.

There was a pause, and then Yakin took him by the arm and propelled him to another room. 'Here,' he said, handing Black a Heckler and Koch MP5 9mm Parabellum.

The SEAL hefted the weapon. It was good for close-quarter work but showing its age now. Still, needs must—

'You might need this too.'

He turned and grasped the hilt of the Glock 19 Yakin offered him. A little better, though he would have preferred a Beretta.

'Okay. Let's move.' Yakin led the way to the back door, heading through the kitchen, with Black in train. The sound of a car horn came from the alley behind the house. Yakin's hand fell on the handle and turned.

At the front door, two Mossad agents stood either side, guns at the ready as a third brought a ram to bear on the latch. With a nod from his section leader, the agent slammed the weight into the door.

Yakin whirled as Black bundled him to the floor just as the first bullets whistled over their heads. He turned and raised the Glock, loosing off three or four rounds, he wasn't sure initially, in the direction of the door. There was a moment's silence as the intruders fell back. Black grabbed Yakin propelling him through the back door, even as shells screamed over their hunched forms.

He landed in the dirt outside the house, scrambled to his feet, and brought his automatic to bear on the doorway. His finger pulled back on the trigger, and bullets fanned across the corridor towards the black figures. Accuracy was furthest from his mind; all he wanted was for them to keep their heads down.

A sound made both swivel, weapons ready. Goldstein was stepping towards them from the car, pulling his automatic from his holster. 'What—'

'Get down!'

Even as the words left Black's mouth, the first bullet hit the young man's torso, forcing him backwards, surprise etched large on his face. The second scythed into him, a flower of blood bursting from the back of his head. Goldstein was dead as he hit the ground.

'Fuck!' Black brought up his MP5 and sprayed the interior with bullets, feeling satisfaction as the sound of pain emanated from deep in the house. 'Yakin!' The Israeli was staring, shocked, at the prone form of his colleague. Black kicked his foot hard. Yakin jolted, and anger spread across his face. Black didn't care. 'Let's go, man! Get the car!'

It seemed Yakin would shoot him and then nodded.

Black smiled encouragingly at him. 'Go! Go!'

As Yakin moved, a flurry of shots chased him to the car. How they missed him, Black didn't know. The American loosed off more wild shots into the safe house before he jumped into the car, and Yakin skidded off down the alley, away from the house.

The Israeli gunned the car at the rectangle of road that showed at the end of the street, careless of damage to the car in his desire to get away. The hard ping of metal against metal as their pursuers fired on them assaulted their ears, the splintering of the back windshield alarming them. How were they still alive? Black wondered as Yakin shot the car through the gap.

They were clear!

The impact on the rear quarter jolted them, but its effect was lessened by the speed Yakin was carrying. He fought hard as the vehicle fishtailed down the street. 'What the fuck?'

Black looked around. 'Another crew!'

'Hang on.'

Yakin whipped the wheel and pulled hard on the handbrake, slewing the car around before accelerating down another tight alley. The driver behind wasn't so lucky, slamming the SUV into a corner building. Their pursuers got smaller in the rear view, but Yakin kept his foot planted on the accelerator, skidding out the alley and onto the next main drag.

After another five minutes of manic driving, Black placed his hand on the other's forearm. 'We need to slow down, or we'll draw attention to ourselves.'

For a second, the words seemed not to register. Then, gradually, Yakin slowed to match the speed of the other vehicles around them.

Black smiled reassuringly. 'Let's get coffee somewhere.' If only he felt as calm as he sounded.

They were high over the Mediterranean, making good time with a following wind. Even so, it would be another two hours before they'd touch down at Ben Gurion, and Logan was restless. Taking a public flight meant he couldn't check information as he'd have liked. Looking across, he could see Brooke had no such issues—earphones in, eyes closed, and a relaxed expression.

He uncrossed and crossed his legs for what seemed to be the umpteenth time.

'Are you gonna keep that up all the way?'

The Brit glanced across at his partner and blushed. 'Sorry. I can't relax, sat here, doing nothing.'

Murtagh frowned, and Logan realised he liked the way the little creases deepened between her eyebrows; it gave her the look of a quizzical monkey. He guessed he shouldn't tell her that. 'Well, that's what happens with flying, honey,' she advised sagely.

'I know. Doesn't make it any easier.'

'Do what I do and employ distraction; it helps.'

'What you listen to, then?'

She turned her idev screen towards him, pulling an earphone delicately away from her ear. At that moment, he wanted her.

'Softengine?'

Murtagh smiled shyly. 'Yes, they're Finnish; they were in your Eurovision a few years back.'

Logan arched an eyebrow. 'Not my Eurovision,' he advised her forcefully, and she laughed. 'You never shared that love with me before.'

'You never asked,' she observed. 'Anyway, is that it?' Murtagh made to put the earpiece back in place; his hand stopped her.

She looked at him quizzically as he leaned in towards her. Their lips caught, and he drew in the vanilla scent that stained her skin.

Drawing away, her eyes stared deep into his and she smiled. 'What was that for?'

'Because I love you.'

The words were simple and unadorned, and caught unawares, she reached out to touch his face. 'You goddamned romantic, Mr Logan. I love you too.' Murtagh kissed him again, placed her earphone back in, pressed play, and settled back in her seat with a smile.

Logan considered her as she reclined and grinned. He was one lucky guy.

A coffee and a sandwich at an airport restaurant was their reward for a journey endured. Both had slipped into their persona at customs as their papers were checked. Murtagh had resisted the urge to sling a camera across her shoulder to reinforce the evidence of her credentials, though it had been a close-run internal debate.

'So, what do you think we should do first?'

Flicking his idev out, Logan dropped it on their table and swiped it on. He tapped a Reuters icon and loaded a series of files to the fascia. 'This has to be our best bet.' He pinched a photo that showed a trim man in his forties, tanned and immaculately dressed. A certain arrogance exuded from him, and it was apparent that he considered himself important.

'Ah yes, Mr Perez.' Murtagh considered the image. 'I think you're right. Do we get to meet him?'

'Perez has given us all the reason in the world to want to interview him. Israel's businessman of the year, a company that has lately dominated the logistics and technology industries; he's recently been quoted as Forbes' business person of the decade. He has form in right-wing anti-Palestinians views but employs many in his company. Our man has a lot going for him, not least that one of his subsidiary's provided transport to a nuclear physicist, smuggled from Europe.'

Murtagh finished her coffee. 'What's our line then?'

'Let's meet our contact first. They'll be able to give us more information.' He looked around the airport restaurant; nobody appeared to be watching them, though he was conscious of the CCTV and the IDF personnel who patrolled leisurely.

A television screen showed the national news programme. There was some continuing news on the attack on the Palestinian president and the power vacuum that had been created, but it was very much about opinion, not worry. It wasn't a country that looked as if it were concerned about the current situation, which demonstrated they were ahead of the curve in searching out potential conspiracies. That pleased him.

'This isn't a country that sees problems the way we do in the West. What's been happening is normal for them, even in the face of the negotiations we're judging events by. An attack on a settlement; two attacks on a Palestinian president, whose people want the death of your country; a potential spying operation, the outcome of which might have brought you up against your biggest supporter—it's all nothing out of the ordinary for Israel, which always looks for issues and ensures it stay one step ahead.'

'Does it make you think we're following a ghost?'

A shake of the head. 'Not at all. Look what's happened recently, not least that we lost contact with John. Something is happening, and it's important we get ahead of the curve.'

Murtagh watched the news for a moment. He was right; there was no sense of urgency in the atmosphere, and that went to the demeanour of the two news readers.

'When do we meet with our contact?'

Logan checked the clock on his device. 'Half past.' He pulled it from the table, folding it into a strip, which he bent around his wrist. 'When we get to the hire car, we need to connect.' Murtagh nodded, he was right. Activating the tracker device, recently inserted in their shoulders, which allowed operatives to be located quickly should contact be lost for more than a day, was imperative in this situation. If only Black had been able to activate his prior to his capture.

Murtagh rose and collected her things together. 'Okay. Let's do it.'

He watched her head for the door as he gathered their litter together and placed it in the bin. Then he followed her. He felt the tension in his belly as he walked out into the Mediterranean autumn heat. Things were about to change again.

Black studied his reluctant colleague. Shock was playing out through Yakin's deep brown eyes and across his furrowed brow as he came to terms with the death of his partner. The big American allowed the Israeli his inner turmoil, for now. He knew how hard it was to lose a partner, the person you relied on to cover your back. But Yakin would have to snap out of it—quickly. He needed help tracking Olsen to his destination.

He drained the last of his drink, waving his cup to attract the attention of the bored waitress. 'Can we have more coffee please?'

She slouched off, returning with two refreshed cups, before clearing the empties and withdrawing to the safety of the counter. Black looked again at the man across the table from him. 'You're going to have to suck it up. Goldstein is dead, but it don't change what's happening here. We need to find the guy who landed at Ben Gurion the other night and figure out where he's headed.'

Yakin glowered at the American. 'My partner just got killed.' His teeth ground out the words, almost making them visible. He picked up the coffee, a slight shake causing liquid to drip to the table.

'I'm sorry, Shlomo. You're right. And I shouldn't have said suck it up. But you have to leave your grieving till after we've accomplished what we need to.'

The silence stretched time, and Black felt his breath catch, waiting for the Israeli's response. Yakin pointedly ignored the American, holding his cup and looking at the late-morning traffic on the motorway outside— thousands of Israelis going about their daily business, expecting to be protected against all enemies. What was he doing here, sat in a roadside café with an American operative?

'We've accomplished?' The words were low, desperate, and Black was immediately wary. 'We've accomplished? Do you know that I'm breaking the laws of my country being here with you?' Yakin stabbed the tabletop with a finger, immediately regretting the gesture. He leaned forward, pinning Black with his gaze. 'All this shit you're talking about a conspiracy—how do I know it's for real? Olsen might be in our country for legit reasons.'

Black arched an eyebrow. 'You think?' He shook his head, hoping the incredulity registered on the other. 'And that's why he was smuggled into the country.'

'That's strong. We haven't ascertained that.'

'No. We haven't asked them if they were doing that. But … you were watching the arrival. And whoever it is didn't wait to identify themselves or hesitate to try silence you and me. Doesn't that strike you as, at least, odd?'

Quiet washed over the pair again as Black waited patiently for a reply. After a long moment, Yakin leaned back in his seat and let out a long sigh, drawing a hand wearily over his face. He felt a lot older than he had yesterday. Black was right; he had to get over this, or he would put them both at risk. 'Okay. What's do we do first?'

It was Black's turn to consider in silence. 'Is there anybody you can trust in your organisation?'

Yakin shrugged. 'There are a couple I could think of, but I'll have to be careful.'

Black nodded. 'Think on it, how you'll contact them, but don't take too long. Sorry,' he concluded as he saw the look on the other's face. 'I need to meet up with a couple of people who are arriving today.'

'Fuck! More of you? Great!' Yakin was clearly upset by this news.

'Buddy, if you can't get your people onside, you're going to need these two.'

Yakin frowned. 'Really? How come?'

'Because they're the best we got.'

28

Murtagh brought the rental car to a halt outside an innocuous building on King George Street. It was close to lunchtime, and the temperature was a balmy twenty-seven degrees Celsius. The humidity made her feel damp, a feeling she decided she disliked, unlike her partner, who appeared unaffected—which pissed her off a little.

'Ready?'

She nodded, following Logan as he made for a small door overshadowed by trees and shoehorned in a gap between two shops. He pressed the button on the intercom. A voice answered.

'Steve for Adam.'

There was a click, and he pushed open the door, revealing stairs supporting the two grubby white walls. Foreign press offices, he noted laconically. At the top of the stairs, they entered a reception area occupied by a woman behind a large desk, complete with computer screen, printer, and two phones. Her right hand sat beneath the desk while her left held a pen. Her smile didn't extend to her eyes.

'Hello. The editor is ready for you. If you'd just check in for me, please.' She indicated the visitor log, old-fashioned paper, giving the camera he'd noted in the corner over her right shoulder opportunity to photograph them both and for the operators to check they were who were expected.

'If you'll go through now.' Her left hand pointed to their right.

Logan nodded his thanks, leading Murtagh through the door. A corridor opened before them, and he strode down it, looking in the windows of the offices either side.

'Who you looking for?'

'Steve!'

The interruption belonged to a big man, broad shouldered, close-cropped, fair hair, and a ruddy complexion, broken by a huge white smile.

The British officer grinned in return. 'Adam! Long time, no see. How are you?' He grasped the proffered hand and pumped it enthusiastically.

'Adam' guided them both through a doorway into a hot primitive conference room, which held only one other person, whom neither recognised. 'I'm doing fine, thanks, if you can say living in this heat is fine,' he replied as he pointed to chairs. He turned to Murtagh. 'You must be Brooke Murtagh. Pleased to have you on board. I'm Adam Promerole, station chief for Six.' He shook her hand firmly, a move that endeared him to her.

'This,' Promerole continued, indicating the other person in the room, 'is Kerry James, CIA station chief.'

The woman he introduced was small, with wide-spaced brown eyes dominating an otherwise narrow face and long dark brown hair. She seemed to be in a perpetual mode of ironic amusement. James nodded to both.

Introductions over, Promerole brought coffee and fresh cups to the table. Everyone filled up.

Suitably refreshed, Logan opened business. 'I gather you both know what our brief is here?'

They nodded, but it was James who replied. 'We do, Steve, and we've been running background checks on the people you passed to us.'

'Excellent. What about investigations into Tel Etz?'

'We'll come to that in a mo, friend. First off, let's have a look at those people you asked us to check on.'

Logan shrugged. 'Okay.'

Promerole pointed to the projector screen at the end of the room as James flicked a photo on to it. Avi Perez was instantly recognisable. The MI6 man spoke first. 'David Perez was the first target you gave us to check. We went through all the usual stuff about his background, family, business issues, proclivities, and political persuasion. David is, as you know, a hardliner, a paid-up member of Yisrael Beitenu. The party is pro-settlements, pro-Jewish immigration, or aliyah, and anti-talks with the Palestinians. We'll give you a dossier on him before you go. What we can tell you right now is that you were right to single him out for attention. Not only did one of his subsidiary companies smuggle Johannes Olsen out of Geneva, but the parent company recently imported materials into the country, ostensibly construction materials, but which our sources suggest may be something else.'

'Do you know what?'

Promerole turned to Murtagh. 'Not as yet, though we have some ideas.'

When it was clear the man wasn't going to open up, Logan questioned him. 'Can you give us any clues? Anything?'

Promerole and James exchanged glances, and it was the American who spoke, Logan finally placing her accent to the West Coast. 'We … believe Perez is bringing in material conducive to the production of enhanced fissionable weapons.'

The words choked the atmosphere, stifling all thought. It was a development neither officer had countenanced. It was their worst nightmare.

'You say you "believe"? How confident are you?'

Again, there was a quick look. 'Over 80 per cent confident.' James's face remained poker straight.

'Is there something you're not telling us?' He glanced from one to the other, trying to read them. But they weren't senior officers for no reason. The silence deepened, a palpable living thing haunting the spaces around the table.

Promerole heaved a sigh. 'Whatever's happening, Steve, we can't get close enough to confirm it. A consignment left his dock earlier this week, and we tried tailing it. Our guys were quickly blocked off by individuals unknown. Armed.'

Logan took in his old colleague's crestfallen visage. 'Unit?'

Promerole shook his head, measured, so he'd had time to think this over. 'No, at least not legally.'

'Shit.' The admission was terrifying. The Unit, or Sayeret Matkal, was Israel's elite special operations force: justifiably feared and respected by those in the know. If Sayeret agents were operating rogue? The question tailed off in his head.

'Oh, it gets better,' Promerole continued, now seemingly over his reticence to share information. 'This morning, what appeared to be a

Mossad unit raided a known Shin Bet safe house in Ramla. There were reports of gunfire and one body dead at the scene, later identified as a Shin Bet agent.

Logan and Murtagh exchanged glances. What the hell were they walking into? 'Mossad and Shin Bet fighting?'

James shook her head. 'We think this is a Mossad team off reservation. When we rang our contact, she was really defensive—obstructing. Kept saying that it was a training exercise gone wrong.'

They all smiled grimly at the euphemism.

'Some training,' Murtagh opined.

'For sure,' concurred the big Brit. 'However, the electronic trail suggests otherwise. The team involved seem to have disappeared. And, after furious exchanges between the head of Shin Bet and the director of operations at Mossad, Peter Halfin waded in to diffuse the situation.'

'Who's Halfin?'

'Halfin is the minister for security and director of Mossad.'

Logan frowned as Promerole offered up this information. 'Does that strike you as suspicious?'

Both Promerole and James smiled quietly. 'You could say that I couldn't possibly comment,' the Brit confirmed.

'Okay. So Perez is shipping in dodgy stuff that we can't track, and Mossad and Shin Bet are offering to brain each other. Got any more good news?'

James grinned. 'It does all sound a bit fucked up, sure. Our next target is this guy.' She flicked up a picture of a large man, balding, with doleful eyes and heavy jowls. 'Benjamin Kompert is a senior director of Israeli Aircraft Industries. American by birth, he came over as part of the aliyah movement we spoke of earlier and lives in one of the newer settlements.'

'What's the connection with Perez?'

'Not clear, though there is a potential link in their support of Yisrael Beitenu. However, we're more interested in what he's been saying to this person.' Promerole swiped another photo to the screen, and the face of a youngish woman appeared. 'Here we have our very own anti-accord, Anti-Palestine, and pro-everything Jewish commentator who, in the last few weeks, has ramped up her rhetoric as events change. Her view is that Israeli political support of the accord and Malbert actually shaking hands with al-Umari has led to this level of terrorism and political upheaval currently being expe—'

As if on cue, the sound of an explosion rattled the windows of the first-floor office. Logan and Murtagh immediately flinched, while the local team waited patiently for their attention to return.

'Just another day in Tel Aviv,' Promerole noted sardonically. 'You're lucky. This is a quiet morning.'

'How many do you normally get?'

'Perhaps four or five, on average, directed against people, buildings, or transport. It's pretty small stuff at the moment, and you get used to it.'

Logan raised an eyebrow but offered no views. The sound of sirens drifted through the partly open windows, reinforcing the fragility Brooke and he had suddenly found themselves in. 'Anyway, you were saying,' he encouraged the others.

'Oh yeah, Natalie Epstein'—Promerole waved a pen in the direction of the screen—'interviewed our Mr Kompert on a couple of occasions in the last fortnight. Superficially, it concerned the State of Israeli technology. But a proportion of both interviews was given over to discussion of the attack on settlements (how bad it is and disruptive, boohoo) and the political situation (how difficult the accord will make business in the State of Israel).'

'Okay, could be something, maybe nothing. How does it tie in?'

'Well, Brooke,' James said, picking up the story, 'it was a specific comment by Kompert talking about the strategic value of a strong Israel in the face of all this Palestinian and Islamic upheaval to the rest of the world. He went on to say the state should be developing a response that makes clear Israel's intent and determination to defend its status at all costs.'

'At all costs? Those were his exact words?' It was important.

She matched him stare for stare, swiping a document from her idev to his. 'Certainly. Here's a transcript.'

Logan skimmed over the document and nodded. 'How did Epstein react?'

'She absolutely loved it and played the segment several times afterwards.'

He read through the words again. They were tight, perhaps scripted, giving nothing away, and yet perfectly encapsulating the need of every Israeli to feel safe and protected by their state. Enemies on three sides, to be

187

defeated; would the situation justify a first strike? He ran a hand through his hair. 'What about the others?'

Promerole shrugged. 'We're still working on the rest of your list. But if you want our honest opinion, these three are your best "in".'

Logan shot a glance at Murtagh. 'What do you think?'

'I still think Perez. He's vain and likely to let his guard down in the right circumstances. Kompert, he's our second string. But Epstein may see straight through us.'

She was right, and he told her so. He turned to Promerole. 'What's our best tactic to get an interview with Perez?'

By way of an answer, the station chief turned to his American colleague, who handed him two passes. He passed them to Logan. 'There's a dinner held at the Hilton tomorrow night. We've got you exclusivity with Perez—an exposé on the face of Israeli industry.'

'You mean—'

Promerole grinned widely. 'Hope your credentials are good, my friend. You're interviewing your prime suspect for television tomorrow.'

29

lack sat passively as Yakin manoeuvred their car through the streets of Tel Aviv, made busier than usually by the activity of a bomber. Reports on the radio suggested the perpetrator was backed by ISIS, a new enemy of Israel, one needing to be countered aggressively before the Jewish nation was pushed into the Mediterranean.

He reached out and switched off the news. Yakin glanced over, made to speak, stopped, and returned to his driving. Moments passed.

Then, 'So, who are these two we're going to meet?'

Black smiled, thinking back to his first meeting with Logan and their ensuing partnership, which had spawned a deep friendship. 'Steve Logan. He's ex-SAS, now MI6. He's been in some serious situations, and he has his head screwed on properly. Brooke Murtagh, CIA and you don't wanna mess with her.'

'That may not be enough here,' Yakin advised him morosely. 'We're talking about determined military-trained people, ready to kill their own to get what they want.'

Black sighed. 'We've been through this. If you're not up for it, say so, because I need to get the hell on with business.' He realised he was being curt with the guy. But shit, Yakin was beginning to become a burden. 'Look, just get me to this address,' he showed the Israeli what he'd written on his palm. 'Get yourself sorted out. If you can, get in touch. If you can't, just give us the space to do what we need to.'

Yakin nodded slowly as he manoeuvred through the streets. Another day, another bomb, more slaughter. He'd often dreamed of an Israel where these things didn't take place. That seemed further away than ever.

'I will drop you there. After that … ' An uneasy silence draped itself over the remainder of the journey.

As he watched the Israeli disappear in the traffic, Black wished for the very best for his new friend. And now …

He turned to the innocuous door that had been used only once before that day and pressed the buzzer.

The relief surrounding the three as they embraced was conspicuous. Logan seemed particularly overjoyed, hugging the big man for what seemed like several minutes, before letting him go self-consciously. Promerole and James allowed them their moment.

Black regaled them with his trials and tribulations as they all sat back round the table, pausing when he got to the part where the young Goldstein was killed by his own people and the escape from the Mossad team.

'And I ended up here, right on time,' concluded the SEAL with a wry grin.

'For which we're grateful.' Logan chuckled. 'So, you think you can trust this Yakin character?'

Black nodded. 'Yes, I do. He just needs to get his head straight right now. My feeling is we crossed an irregular Mossad operation.'

James nodded. 'We can confirm that, John. The Mossad is in some turmoil following what happened in Ramla; its relationship with Shin Bet is at an all-time low. The minister for intelligence and security, Halfin, eventually had to wade in and separate them.'

Black mused on the point. 'So just like that, everything is smoothed over?'

'We don't believe so,' Promerole responded. 'Our surveillance is still picking up internal Mossad communication trying to identify where the units involved have received their orders from. There is a suppression of the investigation going on, which says to us there's definitely some sort of outside influence on the activities.'

'Which surely points to someone high up in Mossad being in The Seven.'

Everyone nodded at Murtagh's observation.

'Who do we think that is then? Halfin?' Her question hung over the table. 'If we know the who, we can remove that part of the problem?'

'Even if we knew, especially if it's Halfin, we'd never get close enough to act. Also, such an action would (a) make finding Olsen almost impossible and (b) bring a real shitstorm down on us.'

Murtagh frowned. 'That may be the case, Kerry. It doesn't mean we shouldn't at least try to identify who the person is. This is a key individual, currently out of reach.'

James flushed briefly but quickly recovered, glancing at Promerole before replying. 'You're right, Brooke. We'll task part of the team to investigate.'

Murtagh hesitated. 'Fine. Thanks,' was all she said.

Logan stepped up. 'Okay. Now let's coordinate our fieldwork'—he swept a hand to encompass his colleagues—'with your intel gathering. John.' He turned to the SEAL. 'Brooke and I are meeting with Perez before a function. Andy and Kerry have some information relating to goods Perez has had shipped into the country and transported … down south?'

Promerole nodded.

'The question is, big fella, what do you need now?'

Black grinned his big white grin. 'I got me a shopping list, friends, and it's long.'

Olsen flicked the idev to Ruth, who looked down the list and nodded.

'This is doable,' she informed her ward. 'Anything else?'

Olsen shook his head.

Ruth turned to leave, folding the idev and slipping it in her pocket.

'Wait. Yes, there is one thing.' It was something he'd found himself thinking more of over the last few days, in the times he had to himself. What had happened to … 'Natalie?' he finished lamely.

Ruth looked him over. Was that amusement in her eyes? 'What about Natalie?'

'I wondered where she was, what she was doing.'

'You don't have to worry about that. You have far more important things to concern yourself with.'

Olsen leaped from his chair and grabbed hold of the woman. Really, he didn't know why he was doing this. But in his gut, he had to know. 'Why can't you just tell me? Why can't you just say?' He didn't know whether that sounded like anger or pleading, but this Ruth was pissing him off more and more.

'It's not her name, you know.'

Olsen shrugged. 'I don't care, at least sh—' He bit off the dig at his handler quickly, but his unspoken words weren't lost on the Israeli.

'You don't need to concern yourself with her,' Ruth reiterated coldly.

Olsen was sure he was angry now. 'I want Natalie back now.' He'd had enough with this ignorant woman.

'Not going to happen.'

'Now.'

'Go sit down, Jo. Read something. Do some research.'

'I want you gone and Natalie back.'

Ruth seemed to waver, an uncertainty on her face. 'You can't demand—'

'If you want me to do the job, get Natalie back.' He turned to the CCTV camera in the corner of the room, addressing it directly. 'You hear me. I want the woman you sent to me in Geneva. Get Natalie.'

How long he stood staring into the camera he couldn't tell. But when he turned, Ruth was gone.

'We've sent for Sharon.'

Ruth had learned many years ago not to show emotion; it didn't go well when you did. She allowed herself a small affirming movement of the head as her commander delivered the news. It had been inevitable, if she was honest, and a welcome relief. She didn't have anything personal against Olsen. The guy was innocuous, bland really. It was clear that they weren't going to gel; that was her problem, not his.

'When do you want me to leave?'

Her boss sat back. 'Sharon will be here midday. When you've briefed her, I have another assignment for you, something you may prefer more.' With that, she was dismissed.

The two vehicles in the compound exhibited the signs of long-term wear and tear. They'd blend in on any Middle Eastern street. Logan knew they would have been worked on, tinkered with, in order to do the job when necessary, but their anonymity was what he desired the most. Mercedes-Benz C-class versus BMW 3 Series. It was a hard decision; either was a good car, with strong three-litre engines. In the end, Black's decision to take the automatic Mercedes forced his hand in the best possible way.

Under the protective awning, keeping out prying eyes and surveillance, they each checked out the credentials of the vehicle's boot lock-up, which were impressive. Satisfied with the selection, Logan slammed the boot shut and looked over at Black, who smiled the smile of a man content with his lot.

'Happy?'

Black nodded. 'Your guys have excelled themselves here.'

'Let's hope we don't have to use anything,' That sounded as unlikely as possible, given their situation. But you could always hope. 'Have you activated your chip?'

Black nodded. 'You'll be able to keep tabs on me wherever I go.' The American grinned as Logan coloured up. 'Sorry, buddy, you checking up on me?'

'Not at all,' retorted the Brit fervently. 'Just making sure we're able to find you if there is another issue.'

'There won't be.'

Logan nodded. 'You heard from your Israeli friend?'

Black shook his head. 'Not yet.'

'That's a shame.'

'You know it! Hey, it is what it is. If Yakin wants in, he'll find me. If not, I'll have to work on my own. No biggie.'

Black was a good operator, more than capable of looking after himself. Having somebody from the inside, so to speak, would have been a godsend though. He said so.

'I think he'll be back. He lost a colleague to rogue agents. That's gonna hurt. And there are questions he wants answered.'

'Hi, boys. You finished pumping testosterone at each other?'

They turned as Murtagh called to them from the doorway of the building. She laughed at their expressions and walked over to join them.

'Checking your guns and things I see,' she remarked as Black finally snapped shut the boot locker.

'You need to take these things seriously, Brooke,' Black admonished her.

'Oh, she does,' Logan confirmed with a slap on the man's back. 'She really does.'

Black eyed her suspiciously. 'You think?'

'He knows.' Murtagh laughed. 'But while you play "boy scout" in the hills of Israel, your sparring partner and I will be interviewing our chief suspect at a swanky dinner here in town.' She waved a pair of VIP tickets under the nose of the SEAL.

'I'm envious,'

'You're just saying that.'

'Yeah, I am.' Black laughed as Murtagh took a swipe at him, and he climbed into the Mercedes. He looked up at Logan. 'Man. I thought you were gonna be in the fight?'

A grin. 'I reckon there'll be plenty of fighting before this is over.'

The engine started first time, and Black shut the door, powering down the window. 'You know it. Well, I'm off to find our elusive scientist. Watch out for any dodgy canapés or buffet tonight. And when you two girls get bored, give me a shout. I may let you join my party.'

He slewed the vehicle round and, with a wave, was gone from the car park.

Activity at the Rehovot house was heating up, and Johannes Olsen waited anxiously for the signal to move. Ruth hadn't returned, and another had brought the items from his list, depositing them on the bed and departing after saying, 'Be ready'. Now, packed and prepared, he was merely waiting for his escort to take him to the vehicles.

The knock on his door came about three hours later while the afternoon marched relentlessly towards evening. Olsen could feel the heat of the day crowd into the room as the door opened and a black-garbed individual, wearing wrap-around glasses and toting some sort of weapon, beckoned him out. Following the guard, he shielded his eyes against the glare of the sun in the azure sky. Quickly he felt his head being forcefully lowered.

'Surveillance,' was the perfunctory answer when he protested.

Quickly, he was bundled into the back of a Land Rover 110. The door closed on him, leaving him alone with his thoughts. He settled back on the bench seat and closed his eyes, wondering if Ruth had really left after his complaint and who might be her replacement. He hoped for Natalie. But that hope, perhaps, was a vain one.

He heard the door on the other side open and a body climb into sit next to him. Resolutely, he refused to look to see who had joined him—another surly Israeli guard probably.

'You're not going to say hello then?'

Olsen started and whirled. There, sat smiling in that familiar way, was the small waitress from the café in Geneva. He felt his heart skip slightly as he took in her face, her form, the easy way in which she sat next to him. 'H-hello.'

'I hear you weren't enamoured with Ruth.' The way her eyebrow rose made him smile despite himself. He didn't want to feel anything for the diminutive Mossad agent, but …

'We didn't see eye to eye, no.'

'Well, you don't have to worry about that any longer. I'm here for as long as you need me.'

Or you me, thought Olsen. It was a sobering thought but one he'd entertained for a while now. What would happen to him when he had fulfilled what was required of him? He pushed the thought back down again; such thinking would only cause him to freeze. 'Thank you, Natalie—'

'Sharon.'

So matter-of-fact. Sharon, not Natalie. 'Okay. Yes, it's reassuring to have someone I know, at least a little.' The irony of the comment was not lost on him.

'Quite, and we will need to get to know each a lot more on the journey to Dimona. So, Johannes Olsen, tell me more about who you are?'

Olsen paused. He disliked being asked to say much about himself; it didn't figure in his psyche. 'W-what do you want to know?'

She opened the perfect lips, displaying perfect teeth, but her attention slipped momentarily as the driver and escort got in up front and settled in. 'You can start by telling me what the T stands for?'

Olsen's brow furrowed. 'The T?'

'In your name. You are Johannes "T" Olsen, aren't you?'

That T. It was a while since he'd uttered it or been asked about it. In fact, he rarely admitted to a middle name. 'You really want to know?'

Sharon's smile widened. 'Of course. Why would I ask otherwise?'

Olsen glanced at the two up front, hoping they weren't listening. 'Thor.'

The laugh was at once delightful and knowing. He thought he caught a quick ironic chuckle from the people up front.

'Really? That's very Viking.'

Olsen shook his head vigorously. 'No, not at all is it Viking. And, yes, really, which is why I don't use it.'

The Land Rover coughed into life, and the driver scraped it into gear, before releasing the brake and accelerating behind another sand-coloured four-by-four ahead. Olsen looked over his shoulder, partly to see what followed them but mainly to try and deflect attention from his ridiculous middle name.

'How come?'

'What?'

'Why were you named Thor?'

Olsen feigned interest in the view from the window. White buildings, red pantile roofs reflected the sun back at him; in between the shadow of trees flowed a steady stream of alien culture he was trying hard to assimilate. Yet his past was almost as outlandish. How did he tell her about his father's obsession that had burdened him with bullying at school and introversion during his teens?

'Marvel.'

'Sorry?' There was a hint of humour in her voice as Sharon responded.

'My dad was really into the Marvel Comics and thought it would be fun to name me after a character with ties also to Norwegian folklore.'

'Parents can be odd.'

Olsen laughed cynically. 'Odd or self-serving; I'm not sure which. Perhaps both. Anyway, I dropped it after I went to university. I'm impressed you found out about it.'

'Thank you, though it wasn't that difficult if I'm honest.'

Olsen frowned. 'I guess you know most things about me, don't you?' When Sharon nodded, he regarded her, seeming to pin her with his eyes. 'So, why does what I say make a difference?'

Sharon shrugged. 'It's your story, Jo. It's who you are and only you can tell it.'

He laughed, a short harsh sound. Drawn from some past experience? She couldn't be sure. 'I'm sure that you know all there is to know about me.'

'Try me, Jo. Tell me about yourself.'

Olsen sighed and began to talk. After all, what else was there to do until they got to Dimona?

Yakin stood and walked to his bathroom. He poured water in the sink and then dipped his face below the surface. It felt good to hold his breath, to experience the draining of power from his body, as Goldstein must have. The bullets would have punched the power from him, expelled his breath into the air, and left him to fall to the ground, an empty sack.

Why had they been targeted by Sayeret Matkal? What was a Mossad unit doing taking a foreign national from Ben Gurion to a safe house in Rehovot? Was the American correct with his evaluation? If so, who was running this operation? There was nobody in Shin Bet who could answer those questions. Worse, the minister, Halfin, had peremptorily shut down any discussion.

Which placed him where?

Yakin regarded the tired face staring back at him. He had options, and he chuckled when he considered their baldness. One, he could go back to work, as if nothing had happened. But who might be waiting for him? Two, he could complain to his boss and really draw a large target on his back with no understanding when he might die or be captured and tortured. Or …

Or, fuck the target on his back, find the American, and uncover what the hell was going on.

So, where to find the American?

John Black sat in the coffee shop opposite the MI6 station on King Charles Street, downing a steady stream of bitter coffees as he waited. Despite Logan's doubts, Black had no concerns that Yakin would contact him. Here was the only place the Israeli knew that he was contactable, so it made sense to wait a while.

He drew on the coffee, savouring the tartness, different to the stuff back home but what he favoured when he could get it. The traffic was thinning after the late afternoon hiatus, and he allowed himself a small smile as a car came to a halt outside the office and the tall Shin Bet agent eventually exited the vehicle. The man casually locked his car, after the briefest of considerations of the door through which Black had entered hours before, and walked along the pavement. A couple of minutes later, he had returned to his car, before continuing in the other direction.

Black rose, dropped some money on the table, and walked out. He paused, checking the traffic but also looking for tails. Nothing showed itself. He stepped closer to the curb and tried to pinpoint Yakin.

There he was, carrying a newspaper. Black watched him as he got back into his car and started reading. Checking the traffic, the American stepped across the road, passing directly in front of the Israeli before heading to his car. Without checking on Yakin, Black got in his Mercedes and slowly, smoothly pulled out into the evening traffic. Checking his mirror, he saw the Shin Bet agent replicate his manoeuvre, a couple of cars back.

After a half hour, they were out of Tel Aviv and in the hills to the south-west, heading to a spot Black had clocked on a previous occasion as a rendezvous spot. He sat as Yakin pulled alongside, got out of his car, and climbed into Black's car.

'Hi.'

Yakin turned. 'Hello, John.'

'How's things?'

'Shit.'

Black stared out the window at the deep blue of the night, the lights of Tel Aviv a distant contamination behind them. 'How d'you want to play this?'

Yakin considered the question momentarily. 'I want to get the bastards who killed my partner.' It was that simple.

Black took a moment to consider his new comrade. Was he worried? 'Is that it?'

Yakin nodded. 'I know what you're thinking. You're wondering why it isn't about state security?'

Black nodded.

'It is, but finding those bastards will enable me to understand why Israelis needed to kill an Israeli. From there, we can find out who's behind all this shit.'

'They may be well hidden,' Black cautioned.

'They may, but we Israelis are a tenacious people. It's what has enabled us to survive so much throughout history. Whoever threatens our country, foreign or domestic—isn't that what you Yanks say?'

Black dipped his head.

'We're sworn to protect the nation against them all.' Yakin's face was set in the in the cold night light.

Black felt grateful to be on the same side, mindful of the nature of those they would be up against. 'It'll be tough. You have some real hard people we're going to be up again.'

Yakin nodded. 'I know. But sometimes you have to do the hard things to make sure.'

'Okay. You're the man on the ground, Shlomo. Where do we start?'

'We need to find your scientist, where they're taking him.'

Black thought for a moment. 'I guess the answer to that is Dimona.'

Yakin nodded. 'It would seem appropriate for Olsen's skills.'

'Getting in there is probably a no-no, so we're going to have to gather intel where we can about his involvement, his work. How will we do that?'

Yakin sighed, a deep and heartfelt motion. 'Your guess is as good as mine,' he replied eventually.

30

'He's on his way to our facility as we speak.'

'Is he content?'

Moshe considered the question, reminded of Olsen's demands over Ruth and Sharon. The escort had declared Olsen happy when Sharon had joined the team. The two had chatted in the back all the way south, the scientist opening like a split melon. All things considered, Olsen was their man, and he told David so.

The older man grunted his appreciation. 'You've done a good job, Moshe. Now it's down to our friend. Can he do it?'

The younger man nodded. 'Very definitely.' He smiled. And when David raised an eyebrow, Moshe told him the story of how Sharon had teased out of the Norwegian the name behind the middle letter.

David roared with laughter. 'Thor? How marvellously ridiculous!'

Moshe concurred. 'But he'll provide us a mighty hammer to smash our enemies.'

'Without doubt, Moshe. This will be the operation of Thor's Hammer.'

'What do you need to begin your work?'

Olsen considered the old, high-ranking Israeli officer sitting behind the desk that dominated the office. The face was impassive, bored almost; Olsen tried not to feel intimidated. 'I need a while to settle in—'

'You have this evening, and I'll expect you ready in the morning. Breakfast at nine, as a concession,' General Topol cut Olsen off.

200

Olsen shrugged. After all, what was the point of remonstrating? 'I'll need to acclimatise.'

'You were given that opportunity. Time is of the essence. We must have a response as quickly as possible.'

Olsen sat back. 'You realise how long this will take?'

The officer shook his head.

'I'll need at least a month to test your designs and modify before we're even ready to run tests.'

'You have a month, tops, for the whole thing. We have a working design anyway. What we need is for you to design the enhancement that will send a clear message to those enemies who still doubt our resolve.'

'But your enemies are close. How will you use such a device on your own doorstep?'

'It isn't for those on our doorstep. It is for those who would help them. We can deal with the ones close too. We are going to teach Syria and Iran that they should stay at home.'

Binyamin Olmet settled into the chair, smiling at the poised figure of Natalie Epstein. She returned the look as she waited for the count in. There was a restlessness in the studio audience, as if expectation was weighing on the response of the new prime minister to her questions. She had no concerns for her guest. But as always, political expediency counted; her job was to push that pragmatism over the balcony and watch it die. The two-minute signal came from the floor manager.

'You okay, Mr Olmet?'

A bead of sweat slid down the side of his face, dampening the white collar. To his credit, he ignored it completely. A grunt. 'Yes, Natalie, fine. Thank you for the opportunity to talk about my party's response to the recent events and the future of the accord.'

'You're welcome.' Epstein caught the thirty-second signal from Tomas. 'We're on air shortly. There's nothing to worry about. We're on the same side.'

They were words no politician enjoyed hearing, and Olmet felt his stomach jolt. This was likely to be a visceral affair, and he felt the cold sweat run down the back of his shirt.

Natalie Epstein experienced the tingle through her frame. She lived for this; it was her reason for her being—challenging, eviscerating politicians. The floor manager completed his countdown, and she faced the camera with the 'live' light on.

'Good evening, Israel. And welcome to "Nine with Natalie". Tonight I speak with Avi Drum, a fresh artist from Haifa currently sweeping the club scene in Tel Aviv with his own brand of techno, who also runs an organic farm near Bethlehem. Finishing the show is our own "Dolly Parton", Misha Chekov who sings about the hardships of living on the West Bank and, unusually, being in love with a Palestinian.

'However, we launch tonight's show with Prime Minister Olmet, fresh from election victory, who has agreed to discuss the escalating tensions on the West Bank and the Jerusalem Accord. Good evening Prime, Minister Olmet.'

'Good evening, Natalie.'

'Prime Minister, congratulations on winning the recent elections.'

Olmet nodded his thanks.

'You've been an opponent of the Jerusalem Accord from the beginning, haven't you?'

'I'm concerned that the concessions my predecessor signed up to at Camp David open up our country to potential threat from its enemies.'

'Can you quantify them Prime Minister?'

Olmet settled in his chair. This was familiar territory, and he silently thanked Epstein for leading him here. 'The very ones we have all experienced these last few days and weeks. Death in the settlements, the proclamations from the mayor of Jerusalem, even the attempt on al-Umari—all these things destabilise our lives, our livelihoods, and peace.'

'We've heard tonight that President al-Umari may make a recovery. Are you pleased he isn't dead?'

'Of course, Natalie. We must celebrate all life. I welcome the fact that President al-Umari, who counted us Jews as his friends, looks to have survived.'

'So, do you believe your predecessor went too far in conceding to the Palestinians?'

Olmet nodded vigorously. 'I do. Look, Natalie, Malbert entered into these negotiations with the best of intentions. And, I'm sure, so did al-Umari. But ultimately, the Arabs cannot hide the fact they want Israel wiped from the map. Despite al-Umari, the Palestinians haven't renounced that objective, but now they're being used. Syria and Iran see this as the opportunity to defeat Israeli, and the Palestinians are too jealous of their martyrdom to see they're being used by the Brotherhood and Tehran to do their work for them. Malbert thought he could overcome that jealousy and hatred.'

Epstein nodded her head vigorously, almost in supplication to Olmet's creed. 'And you're suggesting he couldn't?'

'It was a dream, nothing more.'

'Turn it off.'

Perez stood by the window, conscious Natalie Epstein's dialogue with Olmet had fled the room. The old fool had no idea but, like all politicians, was good at appearances. He glanced at his watch—the charity ball would be starting soon. Before that …

'So how can I help you?' He looked at his two guests on the sofa, a man and a woman, the latter holding a camera, like a lame bird, in her lap.

Perez was assured and controlled, bored almost at everything around him. Logan regarded the cool, well-dressed businessman. Would they learn anything? 'I'm Mike Clarke for Reuters. This is my colleague Stacey Allen. Stacey will take—'

'No photos. I do not allow people to take photos of me. We will release our own to you, if you provide an email.'

'Okay.' It wasn't the end of the world. The drone, some thirty miles out over the Mediterranean, with the latest imaging technology, would be able to get any images they needed. He placed a voice recorder on the glass coffee table before him.

Perez shook his head. 'No recordings either. You'll have to do this the old-fashioned way.'

The MI6 man resisted the urge to tut as he reached into his bag and pulled out a pad and pen. Fortunately, Okri's information about Perez's hatred of recordings had been spot on. Still, no harm in testing the intelligence or playing the part.

He glanced momentarily at the glass of red wine, brought to them by Perez's assistant. He resisted. Murtagh had no such restraint, her services no longer required.

'You've recently been voted Israel's number one businessman and you're currently listed by Forbes as having a personal wealth of around $11.2 billion. How does that feel?'

'Which part?' Perez smiled self-deprecatingly. 'The status or the wealth?'

Logan returned the smile. 'Both. Either.'

Pondering the point, Perez tapped a finger to his bottom lip. 'Being Israel's top entrepreneur is an achievement for which I am justly proud. But I realise I owe that to generations of my family before me. The wealth, is … incidental.'

'Both must give you a certain amount of influence within the country?'

Perez frowned. 'Perhaps. Not as much as you might think.'

'But it's true, isn't it, that the new prime minister, Binyamin Olmet, has spoken to you on four separate occasions since his election?'

'It is. He asked for my help in securing the support of Yisrael Beitenu to build his government. I was happy to oblige.'

'Was that because you believe the accord is dead?'

Murtagh caught the look that flashed across Perez's face. Had they peaked too early?

'The accord was never alive in many people's eyes, Mr … Clarke?'

The Brit nodded.

'Malbert was being foolish if he thought the agreement would bear fruit.'

'You sound like this is a done deal—that the accord is no more.'

The industrialist paused, taking in Logan's expression. What was the reporter angling for? 'No deal is ever done, Mr Clarke, but the accord was not what anyone in this country really wanted. And apparently, neither did our Palestinian brothers.'

An arched eyebrow. 'Two things surprise me there, Mr Perez.'

'Really?'

'Yes. You say the accord was not what anyone wanted. Do you really believe that nobody in Israel wanted this agreement?'

'Nobody that matters,' Perez retorted haughtily. 'I have been following this matter for the last three years, and those who wanted it will want it still. The rest of us, the majority of Israel, know the accord was bad for us.'

'So you believe Israel, and you as a business, will benefit if the accord dies?'

'For sure. You must understand, we don't believe when our enemies make displays of conciliation and friendship. Too many times have people been friends of Israel, only to show their true colours when our guard is down.'

'And the Palestinians?'

'You know, my company employs many Palestinians, in a variety of positions, including two board positions. The ordinary Palestinian doesn't want the accord any more than the ordinary Jew. It restricts the normal man and woman, while the politicians gain.'

Logan acknowledged the earnestness of the Israeli. 'So, what's the solution?'

Perez shook his head. 'Whatever it is, sitting down at the same table with the Palestinian Authority isn't it. Israel must show its strength. In that way, it will be capable of living in peace.'

'You really believe that?'

Perez stared at Murtagh, at first unsure of her meaning. The look on her face persuaded him she wasn't about to launch an attack. The man he was less sure of. 'Miss Allen, I do, and perhaps your friend should be readier to accept that Israel will, ultimately, do what is right for its own security.'

'I'm sure Mike does, Mr Perez. In what way do you think that Israel should show its strength?'

Perez's eyes narrowed, and for a second, Murtagh thought she'd brought the interview to a premature end. 'I mean, in what way could that strength be shown that doesn't impact on your trade. Local business leaders have expressed concern that the accord's failure will significantly damage Israel's standing within both the Middle East and the wider global community.'

The businessman smiled, the expression striking Logan with its smugness. 'My dear, it isn't for me to say how Israel responds to potential threats. What is clear is that they are real, and remain so, regardless of the accord. That misguided piece of work has merely masked continuing issues.'

'And do you think those are soon to be resolved?'

It was the merest of moments, but the pause was noted by both officers. 'Who can say?' Perez consulted his watch. 'If you don't mind, I have an event to go to.'

Murtagh smiled sweetly. 'We know. We have press passes for it ourselves.'

'G-good. I would be happy to escort you both,' Perez offered, masterfully recovering his surprise.

Logan shook his head. 'I'm sorry I'll have to decline. Something's come up. I need to leave.' He caught Murtagh's look as he packed his pad and pen away, briefly shaking his head.

Perez looked to Murtagh. 'I would be happy to accompany you to the event, Miss Allen, if you still wish to go?'

Murtagh nodded enthusiastically. 'That would be great. Thank you. Perhaps we can continue our discussions?'

'Surely. I would enjoy that, Miss Allen.'

'Please, call me Stacey.'

'Well, I can see you two will get along fine,' Logan remarked coolly as he picked up his case and headed for the door. 'I'll catch you later, Stacey, at the hotel.'

She smiled sweetly as Logan headed for the door. As it closed behind him Murtagh let out an exclamation. 'Thank God for that!'

'You're glad he's gone?'

'Oh, like you wouldn't believe! I mean, don't get me wrong, he's a good reporter—most of the time—but when he gets a bee in his bonnet, well.'

Perez nodded slowly. 'Yes, yes. I was surprised at how fixated he was.'

Murtagh smiled. 'When he gets his teeth into something, he won't let go. Tell me, is there any more wine?'

Perez gave his watch the merest of consultations before topping Murtagh's and his glasses. He sat next to the American. 'Stacey, tell me your thoughts on the accord?'

'I tend to agree with you,' replied Murtagh, wondering if that was the case. 'It is a good principle, but like you say, ordinary Israelis and

Palestinians won't be moved by it. Do you think there could be a movement against the accord politically?'

'It's already begun. Olmet will attend talks with America, for the sake of the friendship, but will struggle to maintain a positive outlook, even if he really wanted to.'

'What about Qureshi?'

'Pah, "the Jerusalem Mayor"'—Perez clawed the air with stiff hooked fingers, punctuating his own vehemence, 'will gladly nail the lid of the accord's coffin, as he would of those who died at Tel Etz.'

'Was Tel Etz a turning point in the relationship?'

Was that a pause from the businessman, as if revising a script? Murtagh remembered the reports that questioned Hamas or Hezbollah's role in it.

'What do you think, Miss Allen?' came his disparaging reply. No Stacey this time; obviously he was irked by the reference.

Murtagh shrugged. 'I just ask. Obviously, it was a heart-rending event for this country. But it was a settlement, built close to Ramallah and fairly new, something that Kemble had warned against during his talks.'

Clouds gathered across Perez's brow. 'Perhaps we leave this subject now, please.' He drew heavily on his wine and walked to the window.

Recovery mode, now! Murtagh rose and walked over to stand by him. 'Apologies. It must be difficult to talk about.'

'It is.' And he offered no more. 'Now, I presume you wish to find out more about me and my company?'

Murtagh nodded.

'Good! Then please, accompany me to the charity ball. There will be fireworks and drama in great supply.'

31

The operator had picked up the unidentified drone some hours before and relayed the message to his commander. In turn, the commander had sought clarity from her superior. There could be only one source of a drone of the type being shadowed right now, and that caused concern for all three. They pondered the images coming from their own UAV—high-resolution long-range shots from above and behind, silhouetting the device against the glow from Tel Aviv.

'What do you think?' Major Regev continued, looking at the screen, but his words were directed to his Captain, Miriam Stolz, and the operator, who studiously ignored them both.

Stolz cursed Regev for his indecision, and for trying to make the choice hers. 'Definitely not ours,' she replied noncommittally, inwardly smiling at the fleeting frown that dimpled his brow.

'No.' His voice trailed off.

God, he was completely fucking useless, Stolz decided. 'So, what do you want us to do about it?'

'Can we tell what it is surveilling?'

'Hard to tell. We know it's been on station for several hours to our knowledge. Nor do we know where else it's been.'

Silence shrouded the three, and Stolz was only marginally aware of the activity in the rest of the room. To her, it was a clear case of 'seek and destroy'. They'd done the seeking. What was Regev waiting for? Line up the target, lock weapons, flick the trigger. Job done.

'Well, sir?'

Regev pondered. He knew what Stolz was thinking—take it out. But what did they know about this aircraft? Nothing. It could be a joint operation with the Americans, though that was doubtful. If it had been, he'd have been informed of it—which meant it was an operation against Israel.

Still.

He considered calling his boss. What about the intelligence being gathered by the vehicle though? Who was collecting it? And for what? Had their craft been seen? The longer he prevaricated, the more chance that the craft would leave. Decisions had been so much easier on the ground in Lebanon or Gaza, where the enemy was known, even if you couldn't see them.

'Okay, take it out.' The words tumbled reluctantly over his lips.

Stolz seized them with enthusiasm, before they could be recalled. 'Gabriel, it's all yours,' she informed the pilot.

With a nod, he turned to his screens. The strange UAV remained in view of his aircraft. He tracked it as it moved gently back and forth, lazily ascribing an ellipse in the dark sky. With a flick of his thumb, he armed a short-range air-to-air missile and targeted the vehicle. The tone sounded in his ear, and easily his thumb caressed the firing tit. The missile shot into view, streaking towards its target.

The three watched as the weapon homed in on the target. The pilot of the other UAV seemed not to have noticed, and suddenly the vehicle erupted into incandescence as the warhead detonated in its side.

Stolz grinned and the young operator, Gabriel, allowed himself a quick smile.

Regev was not as ebullient. He wondered what the fallout might be.

'They took it out with an air-to-air.'

Galbraith considered Okri's words, delivered without emotion. It was a blow, but perhaps … 'What did we get from the drone?'

'Some stuff, but we won't know how useful till NSA and GCHQ have analysed the data. We managed to confirm the interview. Logan left; Murtagh stayed with Perez. We lost the feed but got photos of Perez, before it went.'

As satisfactory as an empty glass in a whisky bar, Galbraith judged. 'Okay, Philip. Keep me apprised of developments.'

The young man nodded and excused himself, leaving Galbraith with her thoughts. What had they discovered? How had Murtagh got on with Perez? Time would tell.

'Are we certain it was American?'

Moshe nodded. 'The crew who took it out had followed it for some hours, as it moved from Rehovot to Tel Aviv. It seems they had a good idea what they were looking for, David.'

The admission made David stop. Were they becoming too careless for their own good? 'Is our friend in place?'

Moshe nodded.

'Do you think it was noticed?'

Moshe considered the question. 'We know the Americans were concerned about our resurrection of Dimona, yet they did nothing about it.'

'No, they didn't, did they. What do you think that means?'

Moshe shrugged. 'I have no idea. They're playing a cat and mouse game with us I'm afraid, but perhaps we can outwit them.'

'How come?'

'The UAV was off the coast and could have been watching anything. Let's face it. Perez has his headquarters there, and he was active with a curious pair of freelance journalists last night.'

'Curious?'

Moshe paused. 'I had some of my people do some background checks. There are scant records for Michael Clarke and Stacey Allen prior to today.'

David frowned. 'That's odd. What do you mean by "scant"?'

'I'm being polite.'

'Well don't. Just say,' retorted the older man testily.

Moshe flushed. 'What we found are background stories, nothing more. Quickly pulled together, and plausible if you only scanned it. Otherwise, they are not reporters.'

'Shit!'

Moshe didn't respond, smarting still from David's rebuke.

'Are they under surveillance?'

'I have a team mobilised and a unit standing by, just in case. Our problem is more than that.'

David made to speak, paused, and nodded. He knew what was on Moshe's mind. 'Yes, yes. What do you propose?'

'I have another lined up. It will be most unfortunate, but Perez has done all we needed of him. Do you agree to a termination of his contract?'

It sounded so ordinary, just for the sake of any eavesdropper, yet the intent was not to be misunderstood. Pity. He had grown to like the industrialist. Unfortunately as Moshe intimated, it was a problem they didn't need.

'Yes, do it.'

'Thank you.' Moshe made to leave.

'And, Moshe.'

'Yes?'

'Ensure our other colleagues get the message.'

It was early, or late, depending on your point of view as Perez's driver brought the S-Class to a stop before the gates of his mansion. The gates were opening slowly, and Perez attended his idev rather than fret at the tardiness of the electrical system. His mind was preoccupied by thoughts of a certain American photojournalist.

The two men in the parked Toyota Land Cruiser had been waiting since they had received the early-morning call. It had been a quick, simple message. 'Contract termination: Perez.' The details had been decided many months ago; nothing else was necessary.

Each checked his Kalashnikov. No errors this time. The passenger nodded, and his partner gunned the vehicle at the S-Class.

Perez's chauffeur began to ease the car forward through the widening gap. Soon, he'd be in, and it would be time for a relaxing bath.

The impact threw Perez forward against the front passenger seat; he felt the pain shoot back over his head, and a stickiness trickled down his cheek.

'What the—?!'

The driver looked around wildly, revving the car, which was patently unable to move anymore. Perez reached to open his door, but it was jammed against the gate pillar. Shaking his head, he shuffled over and made to open the door into the street. A shout from the front stopped him; a hand motioned him back. Drawing his Glock 17, the chauffeur opened his door to confront the driver of the other vehicle.

Leaping from the Toyota, the two assailants closed on the vehicle. The Land Cruiser's driver clocked the chauffeur, the gun, and opened fire without hesitation. The shells scythed through the man's torso, kicking him back into the vehicle and against the wheel. His head hit the horn before slumping into the passenger foot well.

His partner, thwarted by the pillar, ran around the Mercedes and reached for the rear door handle.

Perez's ears rang with the hammering of the Kalashnikov and the horn as his sight filled with the corona of blood around the image of his fallen chauffeur. He couldn't make sense of anything. Who would want him dead? Why?

He heard the handle being pulled and was glad of the self-locking— until he remembered the driver's door was open. Panicking he dropped into the space behind the front seats. Vainly, he wondered if they would leave it at that.

The staccato response registered only momentarily on his scrambled mind.

The driver of the Toyota pulled the dead chauffeur unceremoniously out of the way. They had only moments. Reaching in, he looked to see that the back appeared empty.

But no. Scanning quickly, he caught the bulk lying on the floor. Bringing his rifle up, he let loose with the rest of the magazine, emptying it into the prone form of David Perez. A quick cough of surprise from Perez, and then just the *hack, hack, hack* of the bullets drilling the prostate body. Blood fountained across the back of the car, and then all was quiet.

Without a word, the two climbed back in their vehicle and reversed away, before driving off in the direction of the West Bank.

Looking across at the slumbering form of her lover, Murtagh mused that, if somebody had told her a couple of years ago she'd have a fling with a Brit, never mind fall wholesale for him, she'd have suggested said crazy person go for therapy before she slapped him or her. Now, staring at the relaxed figure, she couldn't imagine being without him. She smiled, leaned over, and kissed his brow. Logan smiled sleepily and gathered her into his arms.

'Morning, handsome.'

He grunted a sleepy reply.

'Fancy a cup of tea?'

He grunted, lifting his arm as she made to go.

'Toast?' she called out as she left to busy herself in the rented apartment's kitchenette.

'Please.' He rolled over and retrieved his idev from the bedside cabinet as she disappeared, shaking it out and swiping the app. His fingers scrolled through the news items and stopped.

Murtagh carried the two plates and two mugs expertly back to the bedroom, mindful of the heat and the movement of the liquid. No matter how careful you were, the liquid always slopped over the side of the cup. Really annoying.

She bumped the bedroom door open. 'You'll never guess what I managed to get out of Perez last night.' Carefully Murtagh placed the cups on her bedside cabinet and passed over a plate of toast. 'I said—'

'I heard,' he replied.

She almost rebuked his curt reply, but she recognised the tone in his voice. 'What gives?' She looked at him earnestly.

He threw his idev across the duvet. 'Here,' he said by way of answer.

Searching his face for a clue and finding few, Murtagh picked up the device and scanned the article it held. She'd often wondered what it meant to feel the colour drain from your face; now she knew. 'Perez is dead?'

Logan shrugged and bit into his toast as if it was a cornered animal. 'Seems that way,' he observed between bites. 'Thing is, who?'

'And how much do they know about us?' Murtagh felt the bile rise in her throat at the thought.

He considered her a moment. This was her first overseas assignment, he reminded himself. 'They know something but not enough; else there would be more in the release.'

'Or they're fucking with us.' Her tone was urgent.

'Calm down,' he rebuked her gently. 'You're right. They figure that Perez was talking to somebody. They don't know who or where they are. We might have to extract, but we have to contact John before we make any decisions.'

'You really believe we might have to leave?'

Sensing her shock, Logan wondered how he might break the news. There was no easy way. After all they were now in enemy territory to all intents. He nodded.

'Fuck!'

'Easy. We don't know. And we don't panic—first rule of operating.'

Murtagh nodded.

He reached over and grabbed his tea. 'So, baby, let's drink up and organise our day.'

32

Galbraith cursed and slapped her desk. Okri merely waited for some sort of cogent comment he could respond to.

'Have you heard from Logan?'

He shook his head. 'Steve hasn't made any contact with us yet, but it's early days and he probably wants to take stock locally before he calls.'

Galbraith nodded. Of course he wouldn't want to attract attention. Whoever was responsible—and it wasn't Hamas; she knew that much— would be waiting for Perez's contact to make a move. She found herself caressing her earlobe again. She quickly dropped her hand to the desk and resisted the urge to drum.

'Thoughts on who?'

Okri sat still, mulling over the words. 'Israeli.'

Galbraith caught the sarcasm in her voice. 'Really?'

Her analyst nodded. 'Oh yes, but not government. From what GCHQ has picked up, they're as mystified as we are.'

'Oh good.'

He flushed. 'I think that puts us ahead of the game, ma'am. We knew all along it wasn't the Israeli government; we're just trying to figure out who.'

'Well, when you have, let us know?'

Okri sat in his chair for a moment longer than was comfortable, before he realised he was dismissed. Self-consciously, he rose and exited, annoyed by Galbraith's manner.

Galbraith didn't move, but she knew her analyst had left. In the space he'd left her, she allowed herself to slump. If they'd killed Perez so soon after Murtagh's contact with him, it could only mean they were onto a foreign team working in their country. She needed to talk to Logan. But until he made contact, there wasn't a damned thing she could do.

Topol considered what he was hearing from David and realised there was fuck all they could do. The vice was so tight he could feel it constricting his balls. Klein kept her feelings to herself, but the others, Epstein and Kompert, were visibly shocked.

It was the latter who filled the sudden gap. 'You mean you had Yitzhak killed?' The incredulity in his voice made it crack, an unnatural sound in the enclosed space.

David made no reply, merely looked over at his lieutenant.

Moshe hunched forward. 'You have to realise, Shimon,' Moshe said, using the man's cover name, 'that Yitzhak had potentially compromised our group and our operation. You had all been warned of the need for secrecy, hence the use of code names and the other precautions we have put in place. Talking with reporters, whether real or otherwise, unless with Golda here, must never take place. It is too dangerous. In this case, Yitzhak let his pride get the better of him. He didn't speak to David or me about this. These people were not reporters; therefore, we can only conclude they were agents from a foreign power.'

'But was it necessary to—dispose of—Yitzhak?'

'Don't whine, Shimon. It ill becomes you.' David ground the words out. 'His actions were a threat to our security and a threat to our integrity—exposing us to surveillance, whoever that was. That threat has now been neutralised.'

'Will you do that to the rest of us?'

David registered the truculent tone in Kompert's voice, and it angered him. But he knew he could not show it. 'Is there a need?' He waited. 'I shall take your silence as meaning no.' Hunching forward, he surveyed the assembly. 'This work is vital for the defence of Israel, for our future. Nothing must prevent us from showing our enemies that we will not be crushed. You all understand that, don't you?' When they had concurred David continued. 'Accord or not, our enemies press ever closer to the gates of Jerusalem. We now have the means to crush them.'

'Who will take Yitzhak's place?'

'Moshe has someone in line, Ariel,' David told the general. 'If the approach is accepted, when contact is made, you will know of it.'

Topol nodded.

'Is there anything else on this matter?'

Heads shook around the table.

'Good. Then let us attend the remainder of our business. Golda, your interview with Olmet was exemplary, as ever. It gave grist to our mill. But now I want you to do some exposé on Hamas, something that links them to Perez's death. Can you do that?'

Natalie Epstein nodded, her thoughts still filled with the awfulness of Yitzhak's demise. For the first time, she wondered what it was she had gotten into. For sure she knew she wouldn't be able to get out of it.

'Ariel,' David continued, oblivious to the depressed air of the room, 'how go our preparations?'

Topol grunted. 'Uzi and I both interviewed our friend when he arrived and since. He continues to insist he needs more than a month to test design, modify our weapons, and run lab tests.'

'I presume you advised him of our timetable?'

Topol nodded. 'As much as I thought expedient. When I told him the weapon wasn't directly for those who killed his family, he was less than impressed. I think he wanted something that struck directly at them.'

'How you handle it is up to you, but you have to convince him that this is his revenge.'

Moshe chimed in. 'I have some evidence I can get to you that may convince him more.'

Topol inclined his head. 'Much appreciated, Moshe.'

Klein raised her finger.

'What is it, Uzi?'

'We've talked about the situation Yitzhak placed us in but not about the reporters in any detail. What is happening there?'

David made to speak, but a cough and light touch on the sleeve made him turn. David leaned back and allowed Moshe to take the stage.

'We have units mobilised to track them down and eliminate them be—'

A noise interrupted Moshe, and all heads turned to Kompert, who coughed again and reached for a glass of water. 'Apologies.'

Moshe frowned and then continued. 'Before they discover our plans. We must assume they are tracking down what we are doing at our facility, and this cannot be allowed to happen. Golda'—he waved in her direction—'has agreed to get her station to run a bulletin on these two in the hopes it will flush them out.

'Could they be linked with Yitzhak?'

That was a good idea. 'We're looking into that option,' Moshe replied. 'I think it is possible.'

'I can do a link for the piece,' confirmed Epstein.

'Excellent!' David allowed the pleasure they couldn't see on his shadowed face to leak into his voice. 'Moshe will contact you further with your work. That is all for now.'

The meeting at a close, the other four drifted out, leaving David and Moshe with their thoughts.

David turned to his lieutenant. 'Shimon concerns me.'

Moshe nodded. He knew what David was saying. He was concerned more about what the industrialist hadn't said than with what he had. Yet another high-profile death, so soon after Perez, would make people talk. He voiced his concerns to David.

David ruminated on the idea. Moshe was right of course. Even so, undirected speculation was better than focused narrative. And Kompert could provide their opposition with the latter were he allowed to vent his concerns to anyone. Was that worse than another body?

'Keep an eye on Shimon,' David advised Moshe. 'If you have any suspicions, then please, give him his papers.'

Moshe nodded, rose, wished David a good day, and departed.

The old man continued to sit in the darkened room, thoughts rumbling through his head. Nothing could stop them realising the downfall of their enemies. The accord had been a reasonable excuse. But now they were so far down the line that it was immaterial what had sanctioned their action.

All he knew was an implacable hatred of the Palestinians and their supporters.

Soon, they would understand the wrath of God.

33

The sun was hot and threatening more of the same for the rest of the day. Black was partially thankful for the shemagh covering his bald head and adding another layer of cover to his shoulders. They were handy bits of kit, cooling you in summer and warm in winter. His eyes were sweating into the rubber cups of the dun-coloured binoculars, and he was aware of the gritty, rubble-strewn ground beneath his torso.

It was a good thing, he figured sardonically, he was a highly trained operative; otherwise, it could be easy to get pissed at the inactivity, the temperature, and the discomfort. The industrial complex shimmering in the heat haze was dominated by a large silver dome and high stack, a bit like a balloon that had fallen from its stick. Amazing to think something so innocuous could hold such an apocalyptic secret.

Slowly, easily, from beneath the camouflage cover, he traversed the plant and the ground around and in front of it, searching for movements, anything unusual. There were regular patrols, every five minutes, from one direction or the other, four guards to each. Helicopters were dipping in and out of the site as if it were a small airport, which signified major activity of some sort. Black smiled to himself. *We all know what*, he thought.

A nudge in his ribs made him move his head slightly. Next to him, Yakin also watched the nuclear facility. A quick nod of his head directed Black's gaze to something closer to them. Black focused his bins on the point. Two people were leaving the track about a mile away and heading over the rough terrain in their general direction. Hikers, he decided quickly, as he took in the wide-brimmed hats and backpacks, shorts, and stout boots. He continued to watch them, making sure they were what he thought. After all, the Israelis had a track record of disguise and deception in this regard.

'What do you think?' Yakin's voice whispered in his ear.

'Walkers.'

'Me too,' whispered the Israeli.

They watched the two walking serenely up the slope, taking their time, picking a course between the rocks and boulders that gradually took them away from the hidden position. Black started to feel relieved. There was no way he wanted to be forced into an anti-civilian situation.

Again, a nudge in the ribs. Black glanced round, and again Yakin dipped his head in the direction he wanted the American to look. A patrol vehicle was making its way across the desert plain below, towards where the walkers were slowly picking their way up the slope. The vehicle stopped, as did the two hikers, who watched as soldiers got out and walked towards them. Black figured there had to be some drone keeping overwatch on the area, which concerned him. Had they been pinpointed already? It was a worry.

He watched the soldiers call the two hikers down. They came on smiling and gesticulating, presumably telling the soldiers where they were going. As they got within a few steps, one of the two soldiers, at a time hidden slightly behind the other, pulled his pistol, ran forward, and hit the man against the temple, knocking him out. The woman's hands flew to her mouth. But before she could do anything, run, the soldier dealt her a similar blow to the head. Her body crumbled next to her partner's.

Black and Yakin watched as the two camouflage-clad figures dispassionately went through the pockets and personal effects of the two hikers. They pocketed wallets, papers, and so on and took the rucksacks and deposited them in their vehicle, before coming back to the bodies. Securing them, the soldiers placed sacks over their heads and dragged them into the shadow of the truck. They resumed their indifferent vigil of the desert, but Black wasn't fooled.

Focused, methodical, there was only one outfit that would carry out such an action—the Unit. He felt the stiffening of his new partner behind, perhaps arriving at the same thought he had.

Neither man dared move. Black even wished he could stop breathing. Every small itch, every trickle of sweat seemed magnified as they waited for the two soldiers to leave.

But they didn't. Instead the two men lit cigarettes and stood talking, as if they were waiting for something.

The thought returned that they were being watched.

'They know we're here.' Yakin's voice sounded in his ear.

'For sure. Just not where. But that'll change soon.'

'Yes. A drone will be hunting us, and there'll be another operator somewhere to come behind us.'

Black considered the words. What to do? Were they being suckered in? Made to concentrate on the two guys before them, while they were outflanked. If they moved, their position would definitely be given away, an opportunity for a sniper to pick them off. He itched to move from this place, but his training resisted desire. Instead, he reached slowly into a trouser pocket, pulled a small device from it, and placed it on the sandy ground. With infinitesimal movement Black pulled his idev from his wrist, configuring it to a ten-centimetre square controller. His fingers tapped an icon, and immediately the motor of the little device sprang into life, buzzing like the mosquito the drone took its name from. Another icon, a window opened, displaying video from the little drone. He piloted it away from their position, higher into the sky.

Circling the machine higher, he tried to pick out motions around them, other than those they already knew of. Wider and wider went the mosquito and then—

There.

High up in the hills to the north of their position, two shapes, well camouflaged but not well enough, lay prone, obviously scanning the area for them.

How to get out of this?

The 3 Series made its way discreetly through the traffic, Logan careful about drawing unwanted attention. After all, they were freelance reporter and photographer. They sat dutiful in the mid-morning Tel Aviv traffic listening to the news, which kept repeating the same details of the David

Perez killing. A lot of speculation abounded, though it remained just that. And as with the Tel Etz attack, both began thinking about the possibility of the death being an inside job.

'Why would the Palestinians want to kill somebody like Perez?'

Logan concentrated on the cars in front as he considered the question. 'They wouldn't. There's no capital in it for them, if Perez is to be believed about his employment of Palestinians across his organisation. We are looking at another group carrying out this action, perhaps The Seven. It's an act of political terrorism.'

'Is it linked to Tel Etz?'

'Very probably. Proving it will be the issue. So, what is it Perez told you?'

'Umm?'

'Before I showed you the article, you said that you'd managed to get something out of Perez. We never got to finish the conversation. Is something wrong?'

His partner turned, a frown creasing the usually smiling countenance. 'I think we're being followed.'

Logan nodded. 'Black 5 Series, inside lane, about three cars back? Yes, I noticed it too. Just bear with me.' He dropped down a gear and changed lanes, accelerating as he did. A junction was approaching. Indicating, he positioned the car to exit and took the off-ramp. The BMW joined them, now two cars back.

At the bottom, he took a left and, maintaining a steady thirty, waited for the 5 Series to follow. It nosed around the corner, settling into position. *Scan the traffic. What looks suspicious?* He saw the blue Toyota that drew alongside the BMW. Two people in each—time to appraise.

'So, are we being followed?'

'Not sure yet.' *Turn off the main drag.* The shops and people on the side street here offered better good protection. Behind was the blue Toyota, not the BMW. A switch? He carried on down the road, trying to glimpse the car behind in the windows of the shops. But there were too many people in the road, bikes, scooters, all vying for position and hooting, as people carried on with their lives.

'Can you check what the blue Toyota behind is doing? No! Don't turn around.' He checked Murtagh's first instinct to look behind. 'Check in the shop windows if you can. Use the vanity mirror. Just don't let them know we know.'

A T-junction was fast approaching, and Logan debated which way. The thrum of his device, wound round his wrist, made his mind up. Glancing at it, he saw Black's call sign flashing red at him. An arrow directed him to the point where his colleague was requiring assistance; it showed an hour away.

Decisions, decisions.

'What are our friends doing?'

'One seems to be on a radio or telephone, chatting. Neither has taken their eyes off us.'

Logan bit his lip, deep in thought. Turning right could potentially put them in contact with the 5 Series again. Turning left would take them away from Black. John had to be in trouble to have sent him a signal. But anything could happen in an hour, and they were under immediate threat.

Potentially.

He flicked off the device and handed it to Murtagh.

'John's in trouble. Access code is four nine eight one. Signal him. "Compromised. Unable to support at this time. Secure and wait." Got that?'

Murtagh nodded and set about sending the message. Logan closed on the junction, positioning for a right turn.

Slow, slow, quick, quick, slow, one of his instructors had once advised him. Lull potential pursuers into thinking you were unaware. At the last moment pull a quick manoeuvre and then blend back in when safe to do so.

The Toyota was three cars behind. Ahead the lights were red.

Slow. 'Hang on,' he managed to warn Murtagh through his concentration. He was aware her hand gripped the door handle, prepared.

He flexed his fingers. The car was in drive, and his fingers encircled the handbrake. The lights turned to amber on the cross traffic. First gear, pressure applied on the accelerator, depressing the handbrake, left foot balancing the brake.

Green.

He pushed the accelerator straight into the carpet, the car bounded forward. With a wrench, he pulled the wheel left and slid across the traffic with much honking of horns. He ignored it, concentrating on the gaps in the traffic ahead. The car's three-litre engine kept pulling as his foot stayed firmly down on the accelerator, the car slipping and wriggling, fishlike, between cars, buses, and lorries. Second, third.

A turning to his right across traffic—Logan wrenched the wheel, second, pulled on the handbrake briefly, and the car slewed, in a cacophony of tyre squealing, to point across the road. Release the handbrake. Depress the throttle. Slot through the gears—just like Gran Turismo. The car leaped forward, narrowly missing traffic, fishtailing as it slid into the minor road. Traffic was lighter here, but he couldn't afford to slow just yet.

'Anything?'

He allowed Murtagh the luxury of turning this time.

'Yes. They're just turning down this street. Some way back now.'

'Okay.' Logan kept pressure on the accelerator, conscious of the proximity of pavements, people, and other vehicles. His senses prickled with adrenaline as he sought out all threats to their progress.

Another turn ahead. Right this time, the tyres protesting once more as they juddered over the tarmac under his determined driving.

Accelerating again, he slotted the car in and out of gaps, hoping to God no cops were in the vicinity. His eyes searched the road signs, looking for one that would take him out of the city and away from his pursuers—towards his friend.

'Are our friends still there?'

A pause. 'I think so. Just a— Yes. I can see them about ten to twelve cars behind.'

Before him, a sign proclaimed a junction ahead for the main motorway. Five hundred metres to go.

Decide. Decide. Wait for it.

Smoothly he pulled the car in front of a lorry indicating to exit, not dangerous enough for the driver to blare a horn at him but enough to be hidden from pursuers. He kept inside the profile of the truck and dropped down the ramp.

He joined the traffic heading south out of Tel Aviv. Time to slow down and look like an ordinary couple out driving.

'You think we lost them?'

'Maybe.' Logan frowned. 'I'm more worried about John.'

'He can take care of himself, can't he?'

224

'I guess. But he sent that signal, and a ranger has already been lost in that area. It makes me uneasy.'

'Can we send support?'

Logan gripped the wheel. 'I'd love to be able to send in a drone, but who are we hitting? We don't know what the situation is out there, how many he's facing. He may well be on his own.'

Time had not improved the situation, and the signal from Steve had increased Black's concerns for their predicament. He realised he and Yakin had to make their own destiny. He smiled at the thought, despite the gravity of their position. Soldiers to the front, soldiers to the rear.

Stalemate.

Unless he and Yakin moved, the Israelis could do nothing. If the Israelis moved, it was their game.

Who would blink first?

'They are hiding in the hills to the east, expertly.'

Topol regarded the report on his idev and glanced at the captain, who stood at ease in front of him. 'Another special forces team?'

The man shrugged. 'Could be. There is a complication however.'

Topol looked up sharply. 'What?'

'One of the men, we think, is Shin Bet.'

'Fuck. Are you sure?'

'Not 100 per cent, no.' The captain moistened his lips, careful of Topol's reputation as a ball-breaker. 'Our Rehovot team lost sight of the second operative after the shoot-out.'

Topol ignored the words, concentrating on the image on his device. The man who stared back at him was a fighter—even features, determined look. He expected no quarter and gave none; that much was clear. The résumé put together by the Mossad team painted a picture of John Black that made both grim and intriguing reading.

What was a SEAL doing here? How much did the outside world know of Dimona? Perhaps they needed to find out.

'Okay, I want the SEAL brought in. We need to know what he knows, who is behind him.'

'What about the other one?'

General Topol looked the captain squarely in the eyes. 'He's expendable. Make sure he isn't found.'

The two soldiers down the slope hadn't moved from their vehicle, the bodies of the two hikers remained where they had fallen. Dead? Or just knocked out? Difficult to say.

On his idev, the mosquito continued to beam back pictures of the snipers and the backup. Nobody moved. The heat intensified, and Black felt the sweat trickle down his flanks and the sides of his face.

No movement.

Time seemed to stand still, the sun beating down on their camouflage netting, pieces on a board, waiting for the first move.

A plume of dust rose in the west, heading towards them from the plant—a vehicle, travelling at speed. As it grew bigger, they both made out a troop truck. Black sent the mosquito over. It had six heavily armed soldiers on board.

'End game?' The words from Yakin whispered into his ear trickled down and brought a tingle of adrenaline to him. Black embraced the feeling—he'd always loved the surge of chemicals the body produced when the moment approached for action.

'Looks like it,' he whispered back.

What to do? Either they broke cover and chanced the bullets, or they waited and tried to fight it out from cover. How easy would that be?

Wait.

The truck came to a halt by the patrol, and an officer jumped down from the cab. The troops clambered from the back and began final weapons checks.

'You ready?'

Black felt his new colleague nod.

'Do we know where?'

The patrol sergeant nodded at Captain Geller. 'Yes, sir. Up in the rocks, about half a klick away. The sniper has had eyes on for the last three hours. They haven't moved, but he figures he can take them. We have a back team about a klick further, with line of sight. Just waiting your orders, sir.'

Geller regarded the fresh-faced woman. She looked as if she was straight out of university, but that was the way of things. She was a clinical killer, that much was clear, and good at taking orders. He pointed at the bodies of the hikers. 'What about our friends here?'

'They're knocked out but should come around shortly.'

Maybe they would be useful later, Geller mused. 'Do you have a bullhorn?'

The woman nodded and retrieved it from the cab before handing it to her superior.

Looking around in the sun, Geller wondered how things had worked out the way they had. Killing random people, opening up nuclear facilities, taking out the soldiers of friends, protecting a scientist, and now this—capturing civilians and preparing to kill fellow Israelis. He shook his head at the insanity but knew he would carry out his orders. The sanctity of the State of Israel required his obedience even though his government was in the dark. His heart hadn't the qualms of his head.

Okay. Time to act.

David woke with a start, the ringing of the bell sound like a note of doom in the vestiges of a disturbing dream. The insistent note of his mobile's ringer drowned out the last of his visions. He looked at the name on the display.

'Moshe, what gives?'

'David, we are closing in on a US operative in the Negev.'

The old man paused, the ramifications roiling around his mind. 'What does Ariel intend to do?'

David knew that Topol had to make the right call here. Would he be up to it?'

'He's ordered a snatch.' A pause. 'There is another issue.'

Moshe could really drag things out sometimes, David decided grimly. 'What?'

'The other Shin Bet agent has surfaced with the American.' Moshe waited for his chief to respond.

'You have a plan for him?'

Moshe considered the plan—kill the man, bury him in the desert, and concoct a story of the man's sacrifice in the face of enemy action. Palestinian action would be the best, stoking the discord among Jews and their Arab neighbours. 'We have a plan,' was all he said over the phone.

David considered the reply and nodded slowly. 'Very well. See it is completed quickly and quietly. There should be no loose ends.'

'I'll control it myself. It will be tight.'

Black regarded the tall Israeli, who walked slowly towards where he and Yakin were hidden. The bullhorn in his hand indicated that the man knew they were there somewhere. Should they fight or surrender? The officer stopped and waited. Behind him, four soldiers fanned out across the rocky slope, weapons at the ready.

'What do we do?'

'I guess we're about to find out.' He nodded to where the Israeli officer was bringing the bullhorn to his lips.

'American!'

Geller's voice seemed to fill the still, empty air of the Negev. There was no answer; nor did he expect one—this was all one-way traffic for now.

'American, we know where you are. Why don't you come out of your hiding place? There is really no point in carrying on with this charade. Come out, and we will talk this over.'

A few hundred metres up the hill, Black stifled the grunt of derision that rose in his throat. It was less than he'd expected.

'He's a nice guy, isn't he?'

Black allowed himself a smile at Yakin's dry humour.

The bullhorn sounded again, carrying the voice over the dry rocks to them. 'Come on. You cannot escape from there. If you try to fight, then you will die. And for what?'

The inactivity that followed stirred Geller's anger. Who the fuck did this American think he was? Hiding out in the desert, snooping on what was being done here? Time to get real.

'Okay, John Black. John Black, we want you to come down now, and you can bring your friend with you—your Shin Bet friend.'

For the first time, the two men moved and looked at each other. That sounded like the game was up.

Yakin sighed. 'How do you think this will end?'

Badly, was the first word that ran through Black's head, but he pushed it away. Every minute they remained alive was a minute more to respond. There was always a way.

'Let's find out?'

Logan took the exit for Autoroute 6. The route would convey them to Beersheba, from where they could access routes towards Dimona. It was where he had to hope Black still was. The indicator on his idev, which he'd synced to the BMW's satnav, concurred—for now.

He worried that he'd heard nothing from the SEAL. They'd been driving for forty-five minutes with no contact whatsoever. Brooke had tried to make contact, to no avail. He hoped to God it didn't mean what he thought it did.

Slowly, Black and Yakin walked down the hill towards the Israeli officer. When they were still fifty yards away, they were ordered to stop.

'Kneel on the ground; interlock your hands behind your heads.'

They did as ordered and waited as soldiers surrounded them and began to pat them down. Dragged to their feet, they were divested of their webbing, belts, knives, water bottles, and other accoutrements and pushed towards the officer.

'I'm Captain Geller of the Israeli Defence Force. You're in a restricted area. Why are you here?'

Neither man spoke, and Geller smiled at their obduracy. He turned to the SEAL. 'We know who you are, John Black. Save us all some time and come clean.'

'Sightseeing.'

The blow from the butt of a Galil shuddered through his knee and dropped him to the ground.

Geller knelt and looked into his face. 'Lieutenant Black. You are a foreign operator working a clandestine mission on Israeli soil, with no sanction from the government as far as I know. However'—he looked across at the still silent Yakin—'you do seem to have recruited a member of our internal security. Interesting.'

Turning, Geller took in the Israeli, as if for the first time. 'So, Yakin. It is Yakin, isn't it? No matter; you don't have to reply. It's unimportant. You are known, and you have committed a treasonable act by working with a foreign agent. Do you have anything to say?'

Yakin refused to acknowledge his interrogator. His mouth was dry, and he wondered idly if it was just the desert air that made it that way.

'This is ridiculous!' One of you will speak to me. One of you will tell me what the fuck you are doing here!' Geller drew his pistol from its holster and pointed it at Black. 'You, American! What are you doing here? Answer me!' He ground the muzzle into Black's forehead. 'No?! No?!'

The movement was instantaneous, fluid, unavoidable. In a split-second, Geller whirled and fired the pistol.

Yakin's face registered no surprise as his legs crumpled and a fountain off blood sprayed from the side of his head. Pieces of flesh and brain spattered in the sand. Bloodstained, it a dark red.

'You still wish to say nothing?' Geller regarded the silent American. And for a second, he faltered—the look on Black's face told him all he needed to know. He backed away, and his resolve came seeping back, his vision taking in the soldiers at his command. 'Okay, Lieutenant Black, how many more do you wish to see die?' Geller nodded towards the patrol vehicle and the two bound hikers.

The sergeant walked over, dragged the man to his feet, and walked him over.

Black watched as the man fell forward before Geller, could hear him calling for his life, and saw the stain on his trousers.

'What are you doing, man?' The words forced themselves through his clenched teeth. 'He's a civilian. What's he done?'

'Like you, he was in the wrong place at the wrong time. This is a restricted area, and we like to keep it that way. Now, are you going to tell me why you're here and who sent you?'

'Black, John. Lieutenant, first grade, serial number 0—'

The shot rang out, cutting his words dead. He watched blankly as the hiker dropped to the ground. Somewhere, some way off, a keening sound, starting low and rising to a querulous crying seeped into his conscious. He was blank.

'Still prepared to say nothing? Would you like to see the woman go too?'

Something in the captain's voice told Black that he was becoming unstable. Perhaps it was time to offer something up. 'You don't have to do that. Let the woman go. Take me back to the compound, and I'll tell you what you need to know.'

'That's more like it,' enthused the Israeli. He motioned two soldiers. 'Get him in the truck, hooded and secure.'

Hands grasped hold of the SEAL and started to haul him towards the transport. Geller smiled at him as he was dragged past. Black wanted nothing more than to throttle the bastard, but that wouldn't happen any time soon.

He hung his head, determined they should think he was compliant. After all, he was—for now. A time would come.

The *crack*, *crack* of a pistol rent the still air yet again. And despite himself, Black turned in time to see the woman sink slowly to the desert sand.

34

'Call it in.'

Murtagh looked from her device to Logan and back, glanced out the window of the car, and bit her lip.

The words came again, and she forced herself back into the space her body was sharing with the Brit. Even as the words sank into her consciousness, she wanted to shout out, deny the possibility Black was gone.

Logan knew what was crashing through her mind; the same thoughts marched relentlessly through his own. The beacon had been dead a while. What if Black was dead? Captured? Which could be worse for Brooke and him? Then he challenged himself. Had they put him in harm's way? Had there been a better way to gather the information they required?

Stop it.

Nothing was to be gained from all this soul-searching. That would have to wait till later. For now, they had to figure the best course of action, and that meant contacting London. They'd stopped at services as it became apparent they weren't going to raise Black. A dark mood draped itself over them.

'Brooke, you need to call now.' It probably seemed heartless to her, but he had to get her to do this, the most harmful part of operations—calling in the loss of a friend.

'I can't.' Her voice was small and lost.

'You must. London, Washington, both need to know.' He rested a hand on her shoulder, aware of how contrite and contrived that one gesture would appear. What else was there at a time like this?

'What if he's still alive?'

'He may be, but it's a call we can't make right now. We have to call him as "missing in action".'

'I know … I just hope he's not … ' Her voice trailed off.

'Me too.' Fear and concern filled the space between them.

'Okay.' Murtagh drew a deep breath and flicked her idev into life. Tapping the secure transmission icon, she constructed a brief flash communication, paused, and then swiped the transmit icon. 'Done,' she informed Logan quietly.

'Thanks. Now we need to get coffee and think what to do next.'

Galbraith looked up as Okri burst into her office, raising an eyebrow as the out-of-breath analyst slid to a halt. He dropped his idev on her desk, syncing it to her device.

'Flash communication from Israel. Black has gone missing. Logan and Murtagh are going dark.'

Galbraith read the words and looked up at the young Nigerian. 'Speak to me.'

He returned the gaze, a little unsure, and then the light of understanding clicked on. 'Oh, right. Yes. Black sent out a secure transmit saying he was in contact with hostile Israeli forces. That was just over two hours ago.'

'And?'

'Nothing else was received from him. We do have drone surveillance on overwatch of the Negev area, and we can confirm there was military action to the east of the Dimona facility but nothing more than that.'

'And the others?'

Okri shook his head. 'Nothing after we received that flash comm'—he pointed at the device—'from Murtagh, twenty minutes ago.'

The director nodded, and her thoughts turned to her officer in Israel. Did he believe Black was gone? Was the message premature? And what did she say to Washington?

President Carlisle sat in silence at the desk in the Oval Office, her hands clenched before her, lest she hold her head in her hands. The news from London had rocked and angered her in equal measure. How could the man have been so careless and how could the planners have been so naive as to think this wouldn't come around and bite them all on the arse?

Her eyes constantly flickered to the telephone, waiting for the call from Israel to ask what the hell she thought she was doing sending a Navy SEAL into the country to spy on them. What would she tell them? "It's okay, there's a CIA operative hanging out with somebody from MI6 too?" What hope for the accord now?

There was a knock on the door; she looked up at the sound. Best face on. 'Come.'

The door was eased open, and her chief, Carol Fleischmann, appeared, followed quickly by Foreman, clutching his slim calf leather briefcase in one hand, as if it held the plates for hundred-dollar bills.

'National Intelligence director for you, Madam President.'

'Thank you, Carol.' Carlisle indicated the sofas that inhabited the centre of the office. 'Take a seat, Bill.'

'Will that be everything, ma'am?'

Carlisle asked Foreman if he needed a drink, which he declined. 'Yes, thanks, Carol.'

Fleischmann dipped her head in acknowledgement and departed. Carlisle joined her director of National Intelligence on the sofa.

The silence that followed the aide's departure threatened embarrassment, until both decided to break it at the same instant. It brought a sliver of brevity to the situation.

'So, what's on your mind?'

'I figure you've heard about Black?'

Carlisle nodded.

Foreman continued, without any sense of irony. 'It gets better. NSA believe he's been captured by armed Israeli's near Dimona. However there's no traffic from IDF, Shin Bet, or Mossad concerning this.'

'So, conspiracy theorists would say?' Carlisle arched her perfectly manicured eyebrow.

'We have something rotten in the State of Israel.'

Carlisle smiled weakly at Foreman's poor reference to Hamlet. He probably thought it would appeal, given her fondness for Shakespeare.

Now was not the time to re-educate the man. 'Thanks for the update. How does NSA make that assessment?'

By way of reply, Foreman reached into his briefcase and pulled out a folder, which he handed to his commander in chief. Carlisle opened it and regarded the A4 photos that lay within. High-definition black-and-white photos, the first showed a couple of vehicles and a cluster of people.

She flicked through them—each one showing a development of the act, until three bodies lay on the sand and rocks of the desert and one body was bundled into the back of one of the vehicles. Foreman was watching her closely, and she realised that the hand holding the pictures was shaking. Was it anger or fear?

Carlisle placed the photos on the low table between the sofas and clasped the quivering hand in the other. Anger, she decided. The incident with Faulkner had taught her to suspend her fear. Nobody was going to threaten her or her people.

'You're certain that's John Black?'

'Yes.'

'How much?'

'One hundred per cent.'

Carlisle considered the assurance, picked up the last photo, and regarded the tiny figures frozen in the grey wilderness. How sure could you be? she wondered.

'I absolutely need to be 100 per cent. Too much will rest on this.'

Foreman looked his commander squarely in the eyes. 'One hundred per cent,' he repeated, 'ma'am.'

Carlisle fixed his gaze for a moment longer than might have been polite. Finally, she said 'Fine. So, what's your call on this?'

'Call Tel Aviv.'

'Go on.'

'Speak with Olmet. This is the chance you need to resuscitate the accord before it's pronounced dead formally. Say we have information relating to a possible treasonable event.'

That was a deal more than she felt confident saying to the Israeli prime minister, but she saw Bill's point. Olmet would want to know how she had come by the information, and telling him there was a covert operation being conducted on the sovereign territory of a friendly nation would not be the best opening gambit. 'What does London say about this?'

'Our contact in MI6 was called to a meeting of COBRA today. We should hear soon.'

Carlisle hoped London's analysis matched their own. Otherwise, it was going to be a long day.

The prime minister looked distinctly unhappy as he listened to Sir David's monologue. The rest of the Cabinet Office Briefing Room A group wasn't in any better humour, Galbraith decided, as she surveyed them from behind her boss. Sir David's urbane and unflappable manner was just what was needed at times like these. Being able to hide behind his considerable mental and diplomatic presence was also very helpful.

Sir David came to a smooth halt as he finished describing the activities of the last few days. How somebody could provide so fulsome an account without having in-depth knowledge and without imparting any, Galbraith didn't know, but C had somehow managed it.

Tony Adams, the prime minister, turned to his foreign secretary. 'You knew about all this?'

Vincent Huntley nodded reluctantly, desperate not to be aligned with anything that might come back to bite him on his, not inconsiderable, arse. 'I was aware that there could be an escalation of the issue. We were in direct contact with Washington.' He offered that as an appeasement; it was clear Adams wasn't about to be pacified so easily.

'Well,' the prime minister said after a deliberate pause, 'I'm glad we coordinated with our American colleagues over this.' His words dripped with heavy sarcasm. 'So, let me be clear about this. We have an MI6 officer on the ground, in Israel, working with the CIA and a military operator who, it appears, has been captured by Israeli Defence Forces—correct?'

Huntley flushed and briefly nodded.

'I have only one question to ask you therefore. When the fuck did you surrender British intelligence operations and policy to Washington?'

The silence was deafening as the secretary prevaricated, his discomfort clearly apparent for all to see.

It was Sir David who came to his rescue. He didn't like Huntley particularly, rather felt that the PM was an overbearing bully in such meetings, at odds with his public persona—wasn't that often the case? 'PM, the secretary was only superficially aware of the operation. I'm afraid it came within my purview, and I informed him as I saw fit. The omission is mine.'

Adams stared at Sir David as if he'd just crawled from under a stone. 'Do you answer to me?'

The head of MI6 dipped his head in acknowledgement.

'Regardless of your excuses, I expect my secretary to have all the answers at his disposal when he needs them.' Adams rose and went to a sideboard along the rear wall of the room; he poured himself a coffee from the flask there, thumping it back on the tray. It clattered, making everyone jump.

'What galls me,' Adams continued, taking his seat at the table again, 'is how unfocussed you all seem about this situation.'

'Prime Minister, we know so little about it.'

'Thank you, C. If we know so little, why do we have boots on the ground?'

You'll have to try better than that to catch him out, Galbraith observed from her position of safety.

'We alw—'

'Thank you, C. However, I was directing the question at your director of operations.'

Galbraith flushed. *But you can catch me with relative ease, apparently.* Fortunately, she was prepared. Sir David had advised her that Adams would try to ambush the pair of them, so they'd rehearsed their responses prior to attending.

'Prime Minister, we had considered relying only on drones, but the information we were getting back was both sporadic and unreliable. Our big break came with activity in Geneva, where a Mossad team recruited a scientist from CERN.'

'What sort of scientist?' Adams's interruption was brusque.

'Johannes Olsen is a nuclear physicist.'

'Why?'

'I'm sorry—'

'Why are Mossad interested in a CERN nuclear physicist, who presumably hails from Scandinavia somewhere?'

Galbraith handed over Olsen's file for Adams to consider. The PM flicked through it, pausing and reflecting every so often. Finally, he dropped the document to the desk and turned to Galbraith. 'It would seem our man has every reason to want to work with this Israeli group, whoever they are. What is his speciality?'

'He wrote a thesis evaluating the viability of salted nuclear weapons.' When Adams continued to look blankly at her, Galbraith expanded. 'Salting a nuclear device with the isotope of certain substances is believed to extend the period in which the radioactive fallout is deadly to humans. Some typically extend this period by a matter of days.'

'Others presumably don't?'

'No, sir. Cobalt emits as gamma radiation and is radioactive for over five years.'

'What does that mean?'

'All life where the device is exploded could be wiped out. Such a weapon is also known as a doomsday device, because detonating enough could wipe out life on earth.'

Several faces around the room went ashen. Adams remained unmoved. Galbraith was impressed by his reserve. All eyes turned to him expectantly. Adams sat motionless, almost not breathing, like an automaton, Galbraith decided. Time dragged.

The silence gave way. 'Sir David, your prognosis please.'

All eyes turned to the head of MI6, who steepled his fingers in a display of deliberation and reflection.

'You talk to President Carlisle, PM. Nothing has come from the Israeli government, which means this is not on their radar. Both we and the Americans need to buy time so that our assets can find out what is happening on the ground. Our drones will support them from the air.'

'You take this threat of a bomb, or bombs, seriously?'

'Very seriously, Prime Minister. What we do next is pivotal to the sanctity of life in that region, if not the world.'

35

The days were all the same in this sweat shop, only the artistic licence of his role allowing him any respite from tedium. Olsen sat ruminating in the canteen, his eyes looking at but not seeing the calculations on his device. He sipped absent-mindedly on a Coke.

'Can I?'

Olsen started, glancing up at the interruption. It was Sharon, smiling expectantly. He felt a little buzz of excitement, though his head told him she was no more interested in him physically than a cat really wanted to play with a mouse. He was a job, a number, and nothing more. Even so, he gestured towards an empty chair, at the same time trying to appear disinterested.

The young Mossad agent settled into the chair and regarded her charge. Duplicity normally came easy to Sharon Horowitz. On this occasion, she felt troubled by the whole scenario around him. This had puzzled her, for in Geneva there had been no doubts, no struggle of conscience. Why now? Was it the enormity of the mission she was part of? A nuclear strike on the enemies of Israel was often in the collective psyche of the country—a last resort against the enemies at the gate.

This time, things were different. The enemies were at the gate for sure, but with hands outstretched and not with guns in them. Oh, certain events had taken place but nothing that wasn't normal in the life of the average Israeli or Palestinian for that matter.

So what?

So nothing. *You have a job to do, Sharon, which is the defence of your country. Remember that.*

'So what?'

'Huh?' She focused on Olsen for the first time since taking her seat.

Olsen regarded her quizzically and permitted himself a short smile. 'You asked to sit down. I figured you had something to say to me.'

Sharon smiled back, and when she did Olsen found it hard not to feel his resolve melt. 'Sorry. I was just thinking.'

'About?'

She bit her lip. 'Just wondering how you were getting on with the work. I haven't seen you for a couple of days. I've had other things to do. Saw you sitting here, and you looked miles away, so thought I'd just come and see.'

Frowning, Olsen pursed his lips. 'The general has been cracking the whip. It seems there is a timetable to which I'm not privy, but which is paramount.'

The agent nodded knowingly. 'I'm afraid he can be like that, and he's not accepting when events aren't going his way.'

'I understand that. But my God, does he have to be so bloody-minded about it?'

Sharon laughed. 'It's his job.'

'Hmm, and mine is building a bomb that will work. You can't rush these things. This plant has been mothballed for some time and needs time to be brought back into weapon manufacturing.'

'What are you saying?'

'That I need time, more time than the general appears willing or able to give.'

'But you're just building a nuclear bomb, aren't you?'

Olsen stared at the agent, in the way of people who had just found their space invaded by idiots. He was on sure ground now. 'Not just any nuclear weapon, a salted weapon,' he continued as he saw the mystified look on his audience's face. 'We use isotopes to increase the lethality and longevity of the fallout. You have plenty of scientists who can build a common, or garden, bomb. For what the general requires, a different approach is needed.'

'And you've made this sort of thing before?'

The scientist shook his head. 'Nothing like this has ever been built, though the theory is sound. It was first promulgated by a Hungarian scientist in the fifties but the then feasibility and, more importantly, the consequences of such a weapon put a break on even the most hardened Cold War advocate, and the plans were quietly shelved.'

'Why now?'

Olsen shrugged. 'A weapon that reduces fallout decay after the initial explosion has the advantage of making an area dangerous to enter for a longer period after the initial explosion.'

Sharon shook her head. 'I don't understand. Won't the area be contaminated anyway?'

'Yes, it would. But in a typical bomb, the fallout decays rapidly, and the contamination is in the ground, water, plants, etcetera that were in the area at the time. With a salted bomb, it keeps the fallout, if you like, radioactive for much longer.'

'How long?'

He made a face. 'Depends what you use. It can be anything from a couple of days to years.'

Years? The thought of somewhere being so contaminated for years made Sharon shudder involuntarily. 'What do they want you to use?'

A pause. How much did he tell this woman? If she didn't already know, was it his place to do so? 'I-I'm not sure I should say.'

Sharon felt her face heat up at the gentle rebuke. 'Okay. I'm sorry. That was wrong of me to put you in that position. Do you think it's a right response?'

The scientist's brow darkened. 'There was an accord, supposed to bring centuries of hatred and conflict to an end. Some Palestinians put paid to that, and to my children also. Yes, it is the right response. These people need to know that they can't fuck with us.'

It was the first time she'd registered the Norwegian being obscene, and it took the young woman by surprise. Radicalisation could come in all shapes and sizes, and from all backgrounds apparently. She stared back at him hard. 'You're right of course. It is the correct thing to do. We must show all the enemies of Israel that we cannot be dictated to, threatened, or abused in any way.' She reached over to him and grasped his hand in hers. 'You are a great man, Johannes, and your name will be remembered in Israel.'

'Thanks.' Olsen's voice was flat, emotionless.

When he got like this, she worried. 'Hey, you know what we could call this weapon, to make it yours?'

His eyes looked through her uncomprehendingly.

'Thor's Hammer. You could make use of that name your father gave you all those years ago, something that strikes fear into our enemies. What do you think?'

Olsen pushed the tray with his half-finished rice and cola on it away from him, and the legs of the chair scraped loudly on the tiled floor as he abruptly rose to go. 'I have things to do,' was all he said as he left, his idev balled up in his clenched fist.

Sharon Horowitz had spent a while in the canteen after Olsen's abrupt departure, waiting for the attention of everyone else to leave her. She admitted to being shocked by his vehemence to her innocent questions and wondered what he would do if pushed. The man carried a lot of power in his hands. Leaving the canteen, she wandered the corridors deep in her own thoughts. She knew it was important to keep Olsen onside. She was, after all, his keeper for all intents and purposes. Pissing him off would make that task even more difficult. *Best think of something, Horowitz*, she admonished herself as she rounded a corner.

Ahead of her, General Topol and his aide, Major General Klein, were headed towards her. She saluted as she passed the two, who were in deep conversation. Horowitz drew a sigh of relief, short-lived, as Topol's gruff voice brought her to a halt.

She turned back. 'Yessir?'

'Have you seen Olsen recently?'

'Yessir.'

'How is our friend?'

How is he? 'He seems committed, General.'

Topol frowned. 'How do you mean?'

Horowitz tipped her head on one side. 'I mean he's determined to build a bomb to pay back the people who murdered his family, General.'

Topol scrutinised her, seemingly satisfied with what he'd seen and nodded. 'See to it that our guest gets some R & R.'

Her eyebrow arched at the implication. But Topol had already moved on, deep in conversation with Klein.

Horowitz carried on her way, rounded a corner, and found herself in the security wing. Two guards stood at the doors to the cell area, Galils held at ease. She nodded at them; they returned stony stares.

'Is this where the American is?'

The two men looked at each other, as if determining whether she was friend or threat. One turned his head in her direction, indicating the other to respond.

'Who wants to know?'

'Horowitz. I'm local Mossad.'

'Don't worry. Your guys are already in there.'

'Good. Can you let me through then? I'm supposed to be helping them out.'

Again, the look passed between them both. Talker turned back to her. 'ID?'

Horowitz showed her papers. The guard took them from her, perusing for what seemed longer than friendly. Finally, he passed them back, opened the door behind him, and jerked his head at the gap.

Smiling sweetly, Horowitz slipped through and found herself in another antiseptic corridor of grey and steel doors. She hesitated in the unfamiliar territory, trying to get her bearings. Why had she done this? she wondered. What did the American operator matter to her? *Come on. Girl. It's just curiosity. After all, so many have been talking about him.*

'Can I help you?'

She turned and examined the face of a black-clad agent. 'I'm looking for the team who are interrogating the American prisoner. General Topol wants a sitrep.' *God, how much trouble could I be in here?* The thought dragged itself through her brain like sandpaper.

Her counterpart smiled back at her. 'Sure. No worries. Come with me,' he said and headed off down the corridor. 'What's your name?' Hand out.

'Horowitz, Sharon Horowitz.'

'Avram Klotz. Well, Sharon, our friend is proving to be a particularly tough nut to crack. But we're getting there, we think.'

'What was he doing?'

'Good question. An even better one is, what was he doing with a Shin Bet operative, out in the desert scoping this place?'

'Shin Bet? What did the operative say?'

Her colleague grinned. 'He was quite uncommunicative at the time. We made that permanent.'

The cold in the pit of her stomach seemed to reach out and inhabit every part of her existence. This wasn't what she'd been expecting on this assignment. Killing their own people? What the fuck?

'Here we are.' They stopped outside a door, which Klotz opened, waving her in. It was a standard observation room with a large one-way glass window. Two people sat at a shallow countertop below the window. One lounged, dispassionately watching the activity in the interrogation room. The other wore headphones and was working recording equipment.

'Guys, this is Sharon Horowitz. Sharon, Simon and Peter.' Avram indicated the two, who nodded in her direction. 'Take a seat and watch the action,' the agent offered and took his own position staring through the glass.

Horowitz turned her attention to the room beyond theirs. It was a standard white brightly lit interrogation space, occupied by three pieces of furniture—a metal oblong table, bolted to the floor, and two metal chairs. Both chairs were occupied. One occupant was dressed in standard black, but it was the other, wearing an orange jumpsuit, who drew Horowitz's attention.

The man was big and powerful, hair shaven so that his dome shone. Large clear brown eyes pierced the atmosphere from beneath brooding brows. But it wasn't his features that made her stiffen.

The bruises and blood glistened on his dark skin. Water drenched the front of his jumpsuit and dripped from nose, lips, eyebrows, and ears, suggesting he'd been tortured. As she surveyed the remainder of the room, items and the appearance of the four others confirmed her fears. A trough of water, pools on the floor, soaking towels, and the rolled-up sleeves of wet shirts all pointed to waterboarding.

'You seem to be having fun.' She hoped the quiver wasn't too evident in her voice.

Klotz grinned. 'Yes, though he's a tough motherfucker for sure.'

'Not spoken then, yet?'

Klotz shook his head, anger filling his eyes momentarily. Horowitz knew then he would be a dangerous man to cross. 'What else have you tried?'

There was the smile again, a malicious living thing that spoke of dark intent. 'Well, they say water and electricity should never be mixed.' Laughter rippled in the close environment, bouncing off her mind.

She smiled, but inside she felt cold, and all she wanted was to get outside in the warmth, out from this vision of hell.

John Black wasn't sure what was going to happen next. He just knew everything hurt—his face, his arms, his ribs, his kidneys, and his legs. They had given him a good beating with rubber truncheons, careful to leave superficial marks on the surface. But he was sure that two of his ribs were cracked, and he'd spat out a tooth after one particularly visceral exchange of gloved fist with face.

The waterboarding had been uncomfortable but, for a SEAL, was a way of life, and he cared little for the experience one way or the other. His biggest worry was not what torture they might use next, but fatigue. He could feel himself succumbing to the big mental pillow, beckoning him in to its downy folds. If he allowed them to tire him out, then they might learn more than he wanted them to know. It all depended on what they thought they needed to do to drag information from him.

A sound made him glance out of the corner of his eyes. The door opened, and a man entered carrying a car battery.

That should do it.

36

'We can't do anything for John right now. Wherever they're keeping him, he's effectively out of sight. We have to regroup and find some means of establishing more secure contact with London or Washington.'

Logan admitted to himself that Brooke was correct in her evaluation, though every sinew and muscle screamed for him to find John and rescue him. Reason told him the American was either dead or being held under interrogation. Either way, they couldn't help. All they could do was ensure they kept abreast of events, in case Black resurfaced somehow. He refused to believe the American was dead.

'You're right. What we need now is a safe place and to make contact with Langley or London. We need them to keep watch on Dimona. We know there's a drone out over the Med with long-range surveillance capability.'

'What are we going to do?'

'Let's reprise our reporting role and visit Tel Etz. Something tells me that wasn't all it appeared to be.'

'Okay.' Murtagh sipped at her coffee and surveyed the car park outside the café. They were both sat back from the window, so they would see others before they were spotted themselves. Logan had line of sight on the water closet, and he faced the door from the car park. No one had driven in or stopped on the road who seemed remotely interested in them. That was good, but she couldn't help wondering how long it would last. 'We don't seem to have any company.'

Logan drank coffee and watched the Land Cruiser that had pulled up about five minutes after them in the car park. Both occupants had decamped and were wandering up and down the road, looking in shops and acting like any other couple on a midday shopping trip. But as he'd watched, a shape had risen slowly, surreptitiously, in the rear and had appeared to point a camera towards the café. Should he tell her? He had to; he wanted to put the problem to bed before they moved off again. Something was different about this team.

'Look at me.' His voice was at once commanding and gentle, and Murtagh gazed into his eyes, becoming unsure of what she saw there.

'Keep looking at me.' He placed his hands on hers, as lovers do, but there was no love in the eyes, just steely determination. 'Sorry to burst your bubble. Brown Land Cruiser across the road, arrived just after us. Now the couple up front got out and are walking around. There's somebody else in the vehicle.'

'What do we do?'

'This. Listen very carefully.'

Murtagh stepped out of the café, looking back inside and smiling to somebody in the building. From where he was sitting, the occupant of the Land Cruiser tried to make out where she was looking. They were good, he decided, making the most of the cover they could find. Mary and Ruben would need to get back quickly if their quarry was on the move. He raised the walkie-talkie to his lips and made to press the transmit button.

A tap on glass made him glance around—into the barrel of a Glock 19. The eyes that stared at him from behind the matte black barrel meant as much business as the dark muzzle trained on his face. He wound the window down as bid.

'Put the radio down,' advised the figure quietly.

Uri complied, slowly and carefully. He cursed the fact that he was lying on his own automatic. Naive in the extreme.

'Sit up.' The face commanded again.

When he had, the figure relaxed back, checking the exterior of the car before addressing Uri again. 'Who are you?'

'Uri Gideon.'

'Who do you work for?'

'Shin Bet.'

The other nodded, as if the news placated him a little.

'Why are you following us?'

'You're on the radar. Disturbances, activities involving other units. One of your colleagues has disappeared with one of our operatives, somewhere out in the Negev. We're—' Gideon faltered as he crushed his desire to tell this man about the noose tightening around him.

'You're what?'

'You don't have much time left. Put your gun down and come in peacefully.'

Looking out the window, Logan saw where the Israeli's compatriots were starting to return, walking brusquely through the afternoon crowds. He saw the sudden urgency in their faces; they knew. He looked at the young agent's earnest expression. 'You need to look a little closer to home,' he advised him.

Gideon made to speak, but the butt of the pistol clattered into his temple. He resisted the urge to vomit and coughed, before the second blow came across the back of his head.

The lights went out.

Logan jumped from the vehicle. The two agents were pushing people out of the way, moving fast. He drew his knife from a pocket, knelt as if searching for something, opened the blade, and quickly slashed the tyres. There was a roar of engine and screech of tyres, and suddenly Murtagh was alongside him in the BMW. He leaped in, and she sped off down the busy street.

They had parked the car half a mile from the safe house and approached under the cover of darkness. At the door, they'd given the response to the challenge and had been quickly ushered inside.

It could have been an ordinary home, owned by any Israeli family. However, the specially constructed basement belied its innocent appearance. After greeting the keeper, they were shown to rooms where they could shower, change, and prepare for the next instalment. That wouldn't take place until they had been debriefed and a report sent to Langley.

The shower was welcome, and Murtagh took the opportunity to dye her shortened hair a darker colour and drop different-coloured lenses into her eyes. When she dried and brushed her hair, she looked in the mirror and smiled. It would throw Logan straight off.

The Brit had done what he could, shaving his head and picking clothes he would never normally have been seen dead in. He gave a cursory glance in his mirror before heading to the kitchen area. Food was the number one priority.

They both burst out laughing when they saw each other.

'Bloody hell, Brooke, that is different!'

Murtagh grinned. 'You can talk! Never thought I'd see you in a blue Liberty shirt and chinos. And the hair. What have you done to your hair?

Logan ran a hand self-consciously over his baldness. 'You like?'

'Meh,' she retorted, 'though I may get used to it.'

'Well, I like yours, and the eyes.'

'Right answer,' Murtagh advised laconically.

'When you two have finished patting yourselves on the back about your disguising skills, we'll do a debriefing downstairs in ten. Grab yourself coffee, and there are some microwaveable meals in the fridge.' The housekeeper, Rick Salmon, wasn't an advocate of backslapping, and the two irked him somewhat. He disappeared, oblivious to the face pulling of the two officers.

The debrief was completed inside an hour, Salmon looking increasingly grim as they told him of the events that had befallen them and they discussed the reports of fighting in Ramla. He filled them in on the capture of Black and the death of both the tourists and the Shin Bet agent. Silence sat heavy in the lined room.

Logan eventually opened the discussion. 'Is there an update on John?'

Salmon shook his head. 'We only know that he was taken inside Dimona. There's been no comms traffic out of it to inform the authorities of his capture. There's a drone on overwatch.'

'Shit.' Rubbing a hand over his face, he suddenly felt very tired. Hope had dictated that Washington or London had done, or seen, something by now. Yet, they were just as blind as he.

'What about Olsen?'

Salmon checked his device. 'He's confirmed on site. Drones picked him up being dropped there, a few days back. Apart from a few forays into a high-walled compound for exercise, nothing's been reported.' He paused and looked at Logan. 'What will you two do now?'

'We're heading out to Tel Etz; see what we can find out.'

Salmon shook his head. 'That's a high-risk strategy. The Israeli authorities are working closely with Palestinian Police to keep the area locked down. Truthfully, it's IDF in there, and I doubt you can get past them. They're even keeping relatives of the deceased out of there at the moment. All the bodies have been transported to a military hospital.'

Logan screwed his eyes tightly shut. 'That only leaves us with the option of extracting and heading back to London.'

'Yes, it does.' Something in the man's voice told them both it was a done deal. 'Following high-level discussions between Washington and London, it's felt that you guys roaming around an allied state spying isn't good for relations.'

'Good for you. Aren't you at all bothered by any of this?'

Salmon frowned. 'Any of what?' His tone was tetchy.

Logan regarded him for a moment and thought better of contesting the situation. 'Nothing. What are the plans to get us out of here then?'

Salmon outlined the extraction plan to them both. 'Your transport will be here at zero five hundred, tomorrow morning. Until then, you'll not move from here. Understood?'

Both he and Murtagh nodded mutely.

'Good. You make use of the facilities here until then, but stay inside.'

'They can't do this, it's absolutely ridiculous!'

Watching Brooke pace the room like a caged animal, he realised he'd not often seen her in this mood, but he loved watching her being so passionate—about the situation they found themselves in, the plight of their comrade. He sympathised with her but, for the moment, was content to sit and conserve his energy. When she challenged his inactivity, he advised her so.

'But there must be something we can do,' she railed at him.

'Put the telly on and watch the news.'

'What—'

'Please?'

Murtagh glared at her partner but did as he bid, sitting with a flounce in the one chair in the bedroom. For several minutes, they watched one of the local networks, not taking in the content, and then Logan got up and walked to the bathroom. She watched him bemusedly as he went in, switched on the light, and knocked about for a few minutes before he called out to her.

'Can you turn the sound up? I can't hear.'

'How's that?'

'A bit more … Fine, thanks.'

She heard taps going on. He was using a lot of water. What the—

The door to the bathroom opened, and from inside the dark interior, she could just make him out beckoning to her. Knowing better than to call out to him to find out what the hell was he doing, she merely rose and joined him, sitting on the side of the bath.

'What gives?' she asked in a low voice.

'Do you want to get out of country?'

She shook her head mutely at his question.

'Okay. This is what we do.'

The sky was dark, save for the odd star glinting through the fog of sodium lighting as Logan opened the window in the bathroom and looked out on night-time Tel Aviv. The street was about a hundred metres away, and between them and freedom was a flat area of concrete with no cover—deliberately so. When the security lights came on, it would give the defenders clear sight of any intruders and enable them to take the necessary precautions.

Twisting his head, he searched for the lights and cameras. There and there. Another there on the corner of the large garage complex to his right. But that one they could probably refrain from triggering by judicious use of the wall on which it was attached. Possibly, given his next actions, that light would be the least of their troubles.

He judged they'd need at least forty seconds to climb down from the bathroom and across the concrete. That was easily within his capability, and Brooke appeared to harbour no qualms about completing the task. All they had to do was wait in the dark of the bedroom until three in the morning, when everything would be quietest.

Now was the moment to find out whether he was right about that last point. Leaning carefully out of the window, so he didn't set off the lights, he aimed his suppressed pistol at the closest device. There was a soft tinkling as the glass smashed and fell like ice to the ground below. He turned and despatched another just as quickly. One more thing left to do, and then they had to move, and fast.

'You ready?'

In the soft glow from the street, he saw the resolute Brooke Murtagh nod her bobbed hair in affirmation. They were on.

'Okay. Drainpipe is to your right. I go first, and then you follow as soon as I'm down. Nothing fancy, just get to the ground as quickly and safely as you can.'

'I'll be fine,' she hissed. Logan was abashed, and then her lips brushed his cheeks. 'Let's get on with it.'

He leaned out and found and drew his aim on the camera housing. The short *phut, phut* of the suppressor sounded in his ear as he made sure of the camera. Quickly, he passed the gun to Murtagh—no time for him to stow it away safely—and then swung out; grabbed the drainpipe; and, hand over hand, dropped quickly to the ground. He kept watch as his ears picked up the faint scrabble of his partner making her way down the pipework.

Her hand rested briefly on his shoulder, and he felt her close by as he moved along the side of the garage wall. Stopping her, Logan edged forward to the corner and checked around for potential guards. Nothing to see. This was suspiciously easy. Somebody should have been alerted to the camera going out. Still.

The gates and wall were just a few yards away, but the gate was right in the beam of the garage light. Should they chance it? They'd gotten this far. If somebody saw them now, what did it matter? They wouldn't be shot, and they could be away.

Do it.

Logan shot a glance at Murtagh and mouthed, *Gate, now.*

Without another word, he sprinted for the barred opening. The light sprang into life, bathing the hardstanding with its glow; it was like noon as he threw himself at the gate, grabbed the top, and hauled himself up and over. He could hear Murtagh's rasping breath as she followed him.

Lights were coming on in the house, and raised voices could be heard. Gunshots. Murtagh was at the top of the gate and dropping over as a light went on in the bedroom they'd used. A body appeared in the window and stretched an arm towards the gate.

Another light came on in the hallway, and figures could be seen moving to the door. It opened, and armed men appeared, raising weapons.

Murtagh was on the ground in a crouch. As she started to straighten, Logan barrelled into her. Shots flew overhead. Quickly, they scrabbled in the dirt, placing the wall between them and the shooters and then straightened and sprinted, hell for leather, away from the building.

They ran through the streets for what seemed like an age. But then they were back at the car. So much for changing it.

'What the fuck was that about?' Murtagh was sucking breath in after the arduous flat-out run to the vehicle, her chest heaving and falling like an old bellows.

He sat in the dark, hands on the steering wheel, wondering just the same.

Who the hell were they fighting now?

37

Moshe placed the mobile on the concrete outside the back door of his garage, bringing his heel down on the device again and again, venting his anger on the inanimate object. It was better that way than excoriating the caller. But why had they let it happen? Within their grasp, and they let them escape. A breach in the safe house of an ally, a body to dispose of—a diplomatic incident in the making.

He knew he had to make the call, and his chief would not show such leniency to him. Nor should he. A man should always take responsibility for his own mistakes. But ... fuck! He gave the remains of the mobile another stomp for good measure.

Removing another device from his jacket pocket, he took a fresh SIM from his wallet, slipped it into place, and powered up. Dialling a number from memory, he waited patiently but with a little trepidation as it rang.

'Yes.'

'It ... failed.' Moshe couldn't help the hesitation, cursing the sign of weakness. David hated such recognition of failure, considered it a trait that his people should never show.

Deep silence emanated from the other end of the line before David coughed. 'Is this under control?'

'It's being sorted as we speak.'

'It was a foolhardy option. We should have waited for more favourable circumstances to prevail. They would have come, may still come. What about our competitors?'

'They will believe it was a hostile takeover bid.'

'Hah,' came the characteristic grunt. 'We need to accelerate the project.'

'That may be difficult. Ariel believes our developers are going as fast as they can.'

'I'm not interested in what Ariel believes, only what he can deliver. Our competitors from the US are getting increasingly agitated and ready to move, to deliver that contract. We must be able to deliver before that happens. Understand?'

'Yes, David.'

'On no account must that damned piece of paper be signed. I don't care what we have to do to stop it, stop it we must.'

The line went dead, and Moshe was left staring at the sun rising in the east and wondering where the two had got to.

Galbraith looked up at the rap on the glass door of her office. Her operations officer, Sally Nugent, stood on the other side, and it didn't look like good news she was bringing. Galbraith beckoned her in.

'Sit down, Sally. What can I do for you?'

'It's Tel Aviv, ma'am.'

Why did they call it a sinking feeling? Galbraith wondered as the words pierced her mind. It was more of a free fall. 'What of Tel Aviv?'

Nugent dropped her idev to the desk and swiped her information to Galbraith's own device. 'We got a communication yesterday afternoon from the CIA safe house. Logan and Murtagh came in, got debriefed. They were give the extraction plan for five o'clock this morning. When the extraction crew arrived at the house, there were signs of weapons discharge. The housekeeper was … killed.' Nugent faltered ever so slightly.

Galbraith chose to ignore it; it was her first major operation. 'What of our officers?'

'No sign of them.'

Galbraith read the report in silence, digesting the information contained therein. 'Was there anything to suppose that Logan and Murtagh had broken out of the facility?'

Nugent looked taken aback. 'Fire came from the building only, suggesting that whoever was shooting was trying to stop somebody from getting away.'

Infiltration. It was the only possible explanation. What would Langley do? A housekeeper killed, ostensibly by an ally. Markham must be sick to her core. They had no time to mourn him though; their concern had to quickly move to their now isolated active team.

Where are you guys? What are you up to now?

Logan pulled the car off the road and into a short track that threaded between olive trees near the top of the hill. A sign there indicated that Tel Etz was another kilometre. He turned and looked at Murtagh.

'You okay?

Murtagh drew a hand over her brow and yawned. 'Yes, just tired is all.'

'No time for that, missy,' Logan informed her, grinning. 'Here, take these; we have some work to do.'

Murtagh looked at the tablets suspiciously. 'What are they?'

He took a slug of water from a plastic bottle and handed it to his partner. 'No questions. They'll keep you awake.' He headed for the boot.

Reluctantly, Murtagh downed the tablets with a hefty swig of water and stepped into the morning air. Already it was warming up, the dusty air cloying her mouth. Who the hell would want to live in a place like this, where the only greenery was a bunch of decrepit old olive trees? The sky was light and blue, the night almost chased away in the west towards the coast, but she felt an oppressiveness, palpable and not just a figment of her imagination.

'Hey!'

Murtagh looked up. Logan was holding up her camera bag. So, he meant to go through with the charade. She walked up to him and took the bag, placed it on the ground, and fixed him with an earnest questioning look. 'You're determined to carry this through then?

'Whoever is after us, it isn't the Israeli government. What they're doing here is a cover-up, yes, but for reasons different to the ones we think. They don't want people to see they're not in control of their own country.'

'Okay. So, what do you hope to find?'

There was a long pause as Logan continued searching the car's boot for something. Eventually he reappeared. 'I have no idea. But I guess we'll know it when we see it. Do you have your press pass sorted etcetera?'

Murtagh contained her surprise. 'Are you just going to march up to the front door and ask the guards to go in?'

'One of the checkpoints should be manned by Palestinians. They're more likely to let us in the place—I hope. That's why I came this way. Do you want to walk or go by car?'

'Car,' Murtagh replied fervently.

'Right. Let's go. Let's see what we can find!' Logan pulled the car back onto the main road and, with a big grin on his face, accelerated the vehicle over the brow of the hill, towards Tel Etz.

The small town straddled the road they drove along, its white buildings showing, even from a kilometre out, the scars of the attack. The synagogue, which had occupied a piece of land to the left of the road, atop a rise, was devastated. Its blackened ruin stood like a shard thrust into the side of the hill, the land around a disturbed rupture suffering from the attack.

Inspecting the view, they could make out pockmarks in the walls of the sleek structures, signs of attack. But had there been a response? A checkpoint spanned the tarmac, blocking progress towards the town. As they drove closer, a guard, wearing-dun coloured fatigues and a beret, rifle held loosely in one hand, raised his other arm to indicate they should stop. Logan noted the police either side of the road and the heavy machine gun mounted on a truck, which the operator used to sweep the area in front of the checkpoint with studied regularity.

Bringing the car to a halt by the guard, Logan wound the window down and smiled at the man, a gesture that remained unreturned.

'Hello.'

'What you do here?'

'I'm free press,' the Brit replied in Arabic, handing over their press passes and passports for inspection.

'We're not supposed to let anybody in here you know,' the guard noted as he inspected the paperwork.

Logan nodded. 'So I'd heard. Not the only thing that's being said.'

The guard squinted at the officer, frowning at the use of words. 'What do you mean?'

'I've heard from colleagues, just after the event, that the ammo casings found here were five, five-six, not'—he indicated the man's Kalashnikov—'seven, six-two.' He raised an eyebrow to emphasise his point.

Resting his arm on the door sill, the guard looked closely at Logan. 'You have heard correctly. What of it?'

Logan shrugged. 'It's not usual for Hezbollah to use weapons of that calibre. I'm just curious as to what actually happened here.'

'You'd have to ask the Jews that.' The man hawked and spat on the tarmac.

Hoping he gave what was a winning smile, Logan stared the guard in the eye. 'I'm not sure they'd give me a straight answer.'

The guard looked at him and then laughed out loud, before turning and indicating for his colleagues to raise the barriers.

Driving the car carefully past the Palestinians and off into the town, he looked across at Murtagh, who looked relieved the moment had passed. 'They don't seem to think it was their side, anyway.'

'Nobody ever does,' opined the American flatly.

They parked the car on a side street in the deserted community and, hefting rucksacks, set off towards the synagogue. Logan reasoned they would be best doing that, to work outwards from there. Everything seemed to be full of bullet holes; structures were blackened where explosives had been deployed or fires set. The stench of burned bodies still hung in the air, like an invisible cloak, and Murtagh dragged her shemagh over her mouth and nose to fight off the smell. An eerie silence haunted the buildings and streets, as if the whole place had been contaminated, and no one wished to venture in.

At the synagogue, they spent some time inspecting the ruins. He picked up small slivers of wire and the remains of detonators. If he'd been an expert investigator, he might have been able to identify where the charges had been laid. But he could only guess, and he wasn't clear how much value there was to that. It was while walking the outside of the remains of the building that he saw more evidence he could interpret. Structures he assumed to be homes were quite close to the place of worship.

But on one side, there was much more damage to the home than on the other. As if—

'Look at this.'

Murtagh joined him and stood staring.

'What do you see?' he asked her.

She turned and looked at the other buildings the other side of the synagogue and then back. 'There's much more damage this side of the synagogue than to the other. Somebody was targeting something, or someone?'

'My thoughts exactly. Shall we go have a look what's in there?'

With a nod, Murtagh walked with him into the ruins of the house. It had been a beautiful place, the bones of furniture seemingly jutting from the floors. Picking her way through the charred remains, something caught her eye in the debris. Murtagh bent and pulled a ring of gold, a man's wedding ring from the depths of the rubbish. She pocketed it.

Logan was making his way through the remains of the kitchen. At the point farthest from the blast, protected by a wing wall, some cupboards and drawers had survived, burned but relatively intact. He picked his way through them, discarding most of the contorted and damaged contents.

The bottom drawer came up trumps. A photo album sat beneath warped place mats and blackened serviettes. He pulled it out and carefully prised the heat-moulded leaves apart. Many of the pictures were damaged and misshapen beyond recognition. As he got to the back, the photos were in better condition. They were old, taken elsewhere than this settlement, showing a smiling family—man, woman, girl and boy. Squinting, he made out what appeared to be snow and some chalets in the background. A tourist photo perhaps, taken in the … Alps?

He looked at others, and gradually the man's face came to him with a jolt.

'What you got there?'

Logan turned.

Murtagh was looking over his shoulder. 'Is that –'

'Olsen. We've found where his family lived.'

What else could they find, he wondered as he surveyed the wreckage that had suddenly become a home violated. 'Okay, let's see what else is here.'

Murtagh nodded. 'I'll see if I can get upstairs, check the bedrooms.'

'And I'll comb through these drawers and check for other clues as to their background.

Murtagh left to pick her way up to the second floor. He turned his attention to his search. In all they spent a full two hours methodically going through the structure, Murtagh back in her element with her FBI training to the fore.

They met up again in the back garden. Logan sipped at a water bottle from his rucksack.

'You found anything?'

Murtagh cast her head to one side and frowned. 'I did, and I didn't,' was all she said.

'Go on, expand,' her partner encouraged.

'Well the bedrooms are pretty devastated, particularly the largest, which is at the front of the building. It's difficult to tell from that whether there were any occupants at all.'

'However?'

Murtagh smiled at his encouragement. 'Well the bedroom farthest from the blast is least damaged. Looks like a small boy's bedroom from what I can see but—and here's the odd thing—I can't immediately find any evidence of human remains.'

Logan arched an eyebrow. 'You sure?'

Murtagh hesitated. 'Not very, but there's no fabrics like pyjama fabrics visible and no marks of skin or hair that I can see.'

The Brit nodded at her words. 'Strangely, I found no casings from gunfire in here like in the other dwellings. Unless somebody was very methodical, then there was no shooting here.'

Murtagh frowned. 'Doesn't make sense. If this was Hamas, or Hezbollah, they wouldn't have cared.'

'Agreed. So they were either never here or were abducted. Question is—who took them?'

'We'd have to presume Israeli?'

A nod. 'Question then is, Why?'

The American screwed up her nose. 'Ransom?'

'Maybe,' Logan concurred. 'Make it look like they've been murdered but then have a bargaining chip if Olsen looks to waver at all.'

'It's a risky play, especially if they escape, or somebody finds them.'

'It is, maybe. But given what our conspirators are fighting for, perhaps they believe it's one worth taking.'

Murtagh rose easily to her feet. 'Okay. What did you find?'

'His wife's parents' address. It might be worth having a look at. See when they last saw the woman and the children.'

'What are we waiting for?'

38

The phone call to Binyamin Olmet had been a stilted affair, niceties quickly over, and President Carlisle wondered if she had conducted herself in the right way. It was perhaps a little late for her relationship with Olmet, which, she surmised laconically, would require a lot of work to re-establish. It was easy to determine where it had all gone wrong—mention of rogue units within the Israeli defence forces and then an admission of US operators on Jewish soil, which had been met with undisguised anger from the recently appointed Israeli prime minister.

Carlisle could see the Jewish lobbyists marching to her door even now, demanding to know what US forces were doing on the soil of a sovereign country that was also an ally. AIPAC, the American Israel Public Affairs Committee, would be first to the door, with its chief, Daniel Rosen, demanding that the administration do something about Palestinian aggression against the Jewish state.

Which brought Carlisle to her next difficult phone call. The leader of Jerusalem's Palestinian government, Mohammed Qureshi, was becoming increasingly vociferous and anti-Semitic in his rhetoric, while dismissing the words of President al-Umari broadcast from his bed in hospital. Al-Umari was the one person who might be able to salvage all this shit, she figured.

But that wasn't the issue right now. At this moment, she had to try to wind in Qureshi. She picked up the phone.

'Yes, ma'am,' came the calming tones of her chief of staff.

'Do you have Mr Qureshi for me yet, Carol?'

'Ma'am, you're being connected.'

There was a pause on the line, and then the gruff, deep voice of Qureshi sounded in her ears. Carlisle had a sneaking respect for the embattled Palestinian leader, while understanding he wouldn't just do what the United States demanded. Also, he was vehement in his opposition of women in positions of power. There was a real need for diplomacy.

'Mr Qureshi, good evening.'

'President.'

It had started already, his first words, demonstrating his disrespect for her. She couldn't rise to the bait. She had to show she was his equal. 'Are you well, Mr Qureshi?'

'The weather is good, and our people are oppressed. The blessings of this day have been mixed.'

Carlisle drew a breath. 'I've just spoken with Prime Minister Olmet.' Had he heard? The silence lingered between them, as deep as the physical distance between their two continents. 'Hello?'

'I am still here. What did *Mr*' (emphasis) 'Olmet have to say?'

'We were discussing the validity of the Jerusalem Accord.'

'Does it have any, Madam President?'

He used her title for the first time, but there was little politeness or deference in the usage. Perhaps she expected too much, she considered. After all, what had she given this politician to deserve such recognition? 'That's why I'm calling—to find out, Mr Qureshi. We understand there is much ground to be covered, and there have been divisive activities taking place. But the accord itself does not rely on the actions of a few but the concordance of the many.'

A grunt emanated from the speaker. Was it dismissive?

'Big words, Madam President. Do you understand what has happened over here? The Jews accuse us of destroying one of their illegal settlements, of slaughtering the settlers themselves—'

'Did you?'

'No, we did not. Do you think, if we had, we would have remained silent? Do you think we would have not spoken in glorious terms of the death of those who would take our country from us?'

'Taking life is never glorious, Mr Mayor.'

'Ha! The great America, preaching morals to those who have only the strength of their convictions. And yet, it is always the Palestinian who is the aggressor, always the finger points to us when the truth is more complex.'

Carlisle realised she was losing him by being drawn into a fight over right and wrong. And he was correct about one thing. 'You're right, Mr Qureshi. We're in no position to take the moral high ground on this subject. We've made enough errors of judgement on that one. As for the case of Tel Etz, we are doing what we can to investigate that incident, as we are with the attempt on the life of President al-Umari. These things take time, but we will get there. Can we talk about the accord?'

Again, the silence threatened to overwhelm their discussion.

'Very well. What?'

Carlisle drew a breath. This had to be carefully managed. 'Mr Qureshi, we would like to get everybody around the table again, to discuss what happens between your people and the State of Israel. President al-Umari remains clear he wishes to seek a signing and a rapprochement between your two people. The fighting has gone on longer than anybody should have to endure.'

'You know nothing of enduring.' The words conveyed generations of suffering, but there was something in his tone. 'As for our president, does he need me to do his work for him? All the time, this man begs from those around him. He is our leader.'

'Who somebody tried to kill only too recently because of what he stood for.' Carlisle paused to let the words sink in. 'Mr Qureshi,' she continued, 'you are as important as President al-Umari in ensuring parity for the Palestinian people, with the Jews and other nations of the Middle East. Signing the accord is a step towards full membership of the United Nations, when your people can stand with all the other nations of the world on equal footing.

'And your first friend on that stage will be the United States. For too long have we let you languish uncared for. My commitment to you is that hand of friendship that will see a strong Palestine.'

'What of your Israel lobbies and the feelings of the Jew?'

'They will have to come to terms with a new world, Mr Qureshi. If you do this, you will be speaking for common sense and what is right. Politically, you will be strengthened immeasurably.'

'I can give you no response today, Madam President. I must consult before I answer yes or no. You understand?'

'Yes, sir. I do. When do you think you will have an answer you can communicate?'

'Perhaps tomorrow, perhaps the day after, certainly before the weekend.'

'Very good. I look forward to speaking with you again in due course. Good day, Mr Mayor.'

'Ma'a salama.'

When she returned the phone to its cradle, Carlisle was aware of an overwhelming tiredness, and she felt the dampness of stress cooling on her skin. That had been as difficult as she'd expected. If Qureshi came back with a yes, she had to deliver on her promise. Only one thing remained to haunt her.

What of President Jamal al-Umari?

Loneliness had been a word people had presented to him on many occasions to describe the position of Palestinian president. And how it did express completely the position he held. Today, as he sat, feeling better for the first time in weeks, Jamal al-Umari truly understood what the word meant.

Since the attack, only fleeting memories of that time had come to him. Slowly but surely, they had increased, creeping into his mind as if to unsettle his recovery, to cast doubt on his power and conviction. The television in the corner of the guarded hospital room showed his dreams being slowly but methodically torn apart, and he despaired of ever being able to do anything about it.

The door opened, and a young nurse appeared, clutching a clipboard and pen. She appeared at once surprised and pleased to see him awake and watching the TV.

'Mr President, salaam. And how are you today?'

Al-Umari smiled at her. 'I am well, thank you.'

'It is good to see you awake so early.'

'Have I been sleeping a lot then? I can't really tell. All the days appear the same.'

The nurse blushed slightly and nodded. 'You have been very sleepy. But that is good,' she added hastily as he raised a concerned eyebrow. 'Sleep is good for the body when it has been through … what you have been through.'

Al-Umari nodded. 'It has been through a lot. Tell me, what of the others in the … crash?'

The way she ripped her gaze from his told him all he needed to know, and the isolation fell upon him so hard a tear slipped from his eye and rolled down his cheek.

The nurse moved closer and placed a hand on his shoulder. 'It is okay to cry.'

Al-Umari nodded, understanding that she thought he cried for his friends in the attack and not for his own sense of abandonment. He had to shake off this feeling. The only way to do that was to immerse himself in the work he had committed himself and his administration, even his people, to.

'Nurse, can you do something for me?'

The young woman looked unsure. 'What do you want, sir?'

'I need to contact my office and ask them to bring some things over here for me.'

'I'm not sure I should do that without Dr Barak's permission.'

'Then bring the doctor here, and I shall explain to him what is required and why I must work.'

The doctor was as reluctant as the nurse had suggested to acquiesce to al-Umari's requests, concern etching itself into his features. 'Mr President, you are still convalescing. There is much still to be done with physiotherapy and observation before we can even think of you doing any work.'

Al-Umari smiled the smile that had gained him so much popularity and trust from his people. 'I understand what you are saying, Doctor. And believe me, I know I can do only so much. But do something I must. You know of the accord?'

Dr Barak nodded his head.

'Good,' continued al-Umari. 'So you know how important it is that I continue to work for the benefit of Palestine and for the peace of this region?'

Barak nodded again, mutely.

'Excellent. I promise to work with your people, Doctor, to ensure that I recover as well as you can expect. Now, please, I need a phone so that I can contact my people.'

'I have a call for you, Madam President.'

Carol Fleischmann's deep, calm voice sounded in her ear, and Carlisle wondered who was phoning her so early in the morning. The news caught her by surprise.

'Put him through please, Carol … President al-Umari, it is very good to hear from you.'

'Thank you, Madam President. First, I'm sorry to hear of the circumstances surrounding John. He is a good man, and I do not believe the stories that people are telling of him.'

'Thank you—may I call you Jamal? These formalities can get in the way.'

The laughter, though sounding tired, was genuine. 'Yes, if I may call you Angela?'

'Deal,' responded Carlisle with humour. 'How are you doing, Jamal?'

'A good deal better physically than I was, thank you. The psychological scars will be harder to heal, I fear.'

'That so often is the case I'm afraid. I wish you godspeed with your recovery, Jamal. If there is anything we can do to help—'

'I will let you know,' al-Umari concluded the statement for her.

'So, to what do I owe the pleasure of talking with you now?'

'Angela, I wanted you to know that this attack on me changes nothing. I have my suspicions as to who was behind it, but they will not succeed. The accord is the best hope my people have for peace and status. I shall not let that go.'

'Agreed. I said as much to Mr Qureshi yesterday.'

'You did?'

'You sound a little surprised by that, Jamal.'

'It is nothing. What did he say?'

Was that a harshness in his tone that belied the words? Carlisle wondered. 'I advised him this was more than the actions of a few Palestinians determined to fight, but the struggle of the whole Palestinian state. He said he needed to consult.' Silence from the phone. 'Jamal. Are you all right?'

His answer was slow. He found thinking took a little time now. 'Yes … yes, I am fine. Do not worry.'

Carlisle allowed herself a moment of reflection. Perhaps it would have been better to wait for al-Umari to contact her first, rather than go to Qureshi. Hindsight—it was a damned fine and exact science, she told herself. 'Jamal, if I've placed you in a difficult position, I apologise. With everything that has happened recently, I needed to try to get things going again.'

'It is okay. I understand.' His tone was much warmer, and Carlisle understood the depth of feeling and regard with which Kemble had always spoken of the Palestinian. 'My call was really to tell you that my administration is being pulled together once more. I have some good people able to fill the places of Faisal and the others who lost their lives.'

'That is good news in terrible circumstances. I admire your courage, Jamal, to do so much with such good grace.'

Al-Umari allowed himself a chuckle. 'Angela, the accord is all I have for my people. We cannot continue to fight a losing battle. So many people die in Gaza whenever there is a dispute. It cannot continue. For Israel, it has to decide whether it can live peacefully with us or whether extermination of our people is the only route for it. Who knows? I, for one, cannot surrender to that thought.'

Carlisle's mind went back to her conversation with Olmet, twenty-four short hours previously. The Israeli Prime Minister had been quite bullish about not backing down and placing the murders of Tel Etz firmly at the door of the Palestinians. He would take a lot of convincing to set that particular rub to one side. Like her caller, though, Carlisle felt there was ground on which to work a common story for the benefit of all.

'Your dedication and power are notable, Jamal. And my administration will do everything in its power to ensure that there is peace between Palestine and Israel and that your people are finally recognised as a state in their own right.'

'Madam President, I can ask no more. You have answered all the concerns I had before this call. Thank you for your time.'

'And thank you, Mr President, for yours and for your commitment to this cause.'

'I must bid you farewell. I have much to do. But hopefully I shall be well enough soon to visit.'

Carlisle smiled. 'It would be wonderful to see you, Jamal. I wish you a speedy recovery. And, please, keep in contact.'

'I will, Angela. Ma'a salama.'

The line went dead, leaving Carlisle with her thoughts. Three very different leaders, three very different approaches. Jamal al-Umari was the younger and exhibited the unfettered wisdom of youth. That he had survived two assassination attempts would give him unparalleled status with his people; of that she was sure.

If anyone could use that status, it was he.

39

The unexpected stand-off vexed him greatly. General Avram Topol disliked being bested by anybody, least of all a weak-chinned, whining Scandinavian. Still, his career had taught him when to be patient and when not. While he admitted he was getting close to the latter, he was determined to hold on to the former, for now.

He merely hoped that David would offer him such clemency when the time came.

'Johannes, you must understand we have certain constraints that dictate against our prevaricating over the production of this weapon. This was made clear to you, I thought.' Topol smiled in what he hoped was a friendly way.

Olsen scowled briefly in reply, before returning to his state of supercilious indignation. 'What you have to understand, General, is that salting a weapon is unproven technology.'

Topol prevented the sigh from rising. 'It is appreciated, Johannes. But you are an expert, are you not?'

Olsen hesitated momentarily. 'In the theory. Nobody has ever done this since it was first postulated by Leo Szilard in 1950.'

The general crossed his arms expectantly. Let the overbearing shit expend his energy telling him what he'd spouted a thousand times before. 'Thank you. That is all very interesting,' he said when the scientist had finally run out of steam, 'but time is short for us. The weapon must be completed as soon as practical.'

'And it will be,' Olsen retorted stubbornly. 'Just not in the timetable you have in mind.'

The sigh came. He just couldn't help it. Placing his hands on the desk, Topol levered himself upright and stared squarely at the scientist, who was becoming more trouble than he was worth. Why they had to go through all this, he didn't understand. But David had a plan, which was enough. Getting this Norwegian arsehole to play along could derail it, though.

Time for a different tack.

'Very well, for now. Keep us updated with your progress daily please.'

Olsen's nod was perfunctory at best, dismissive if you wished to look on the dark side. 'Can I go now?'

Topol dismissed the man with a wave of his hand. When the door had closed behind the Norwegian, Klein looked at the general.

'What do we do now?'

'Get Horowitz in here. She's been half useless up to now. Time for her to earn her money.'

'And if that doesn't work?'

'We always have Plan B,' the general replied grimly.

Horowitz walked into the canteen area, searching the tables. There he was, alone as usual, staring at his idev, thinking about his dead kids. Something had to give eventually, but bending wasn't his way.

She pulled out the chair opposite Olsen and sat herself on it, purposefully making a noise. He looked up; she smiled.

'Hi.'

'Hello.' His voice disappeared as he dropped his head to regard his device again.

'You okay?'

'No.'

'How come? What's made you all grumpy today?'

Olsen's head rose sharply, and she instantly regretted her words as she saw the venom in his gaze. Mentally she took a step back, and her guard came up.

'Oh, I don't know. Maybe the fact that my kids are dead somewhere in this godforsaken country, or possibly because that fat fool of a general wants me to hurry up, so they can bomb the fuck out of somebody with some half-finished, half-baked concept of a weapon.'

'So, it can't be done.' It was a statement, meant to draw him out.

'I can do it. I have, if I'm honest.'

Horowitz felt a little breathless. Just the other day, he had been adamant about how untried the technology was, just a theory, and now. 'How far?'

He smiled, a shy thing that hadn't seen the light of day much. 'I've managed to salt an existing bomb with a gold isotope. It should be ready to test day after tomorrow.'

'Why didn't you tell Topol?'

'Because the man is an overbearing twat, and I wanted him to sweat a while longer.'

Horowitz laughed aloud. People looked up at the commotion, and she put a hand over her mouth, her body shaking with the humour of the moment. Then, on an impulse, she grasped his hand and rose, pulling him from around the table.

He looked at her quizzically. 'Where are we going?' he asked her.

She turned, reached up, and kissed his lips, smiling as she dragged him from the canteen. 'I think you deserve a little present.'

General Topol listened as the Mossad agent divulged her secret, fingers drumming on the desk surface in perfect syncopation with his temper. Part of him wanted to ring the scrawny bastard's neck; the other wanted to kiss him.

'We can test the device as early as Friday?'

'It would seem so, yes.'

Topol could see the energy sparking off the young woman. 'I presume Olsen is a happy man at the moment?'

'Oh definitely. He'll do anything for me right now.'

About time, thought the General. 'Good. Make sure you keep it that way,' was all he said, before dismissing the Mossad agent.

When she was gone, he pulled a cheap mobile from his desk drawer, dialling a number from memory. After a short pause, a voice answered.

'Listen. We have a test model ready for Friday. Let us know when and where you want the demonstration to happen.'

A short silence answered him before the voice buzzed in his ear. 'We'll get back to you.'

When he had destroyed the device, Topol went to the cabinet that occupied the wall opposite his desk. From there, he took a bottle of Courvoisier and poured himself a large drink. He sat at the desk, swirling the deep bronze liquid for a moment before swallowing.

At last, retribution was close at hand.

Come on! You don't normally take this long to answer the phone. What gives?

Moshe paced the lounge of his house, taking a moment to stare across the Tel Aviv skyline, flaming in the late-evening sun. He glanced at the clock on the wall; he'd hardly been on the phone any time at all, he realised. It must be the excitement.

'Hello.'

'We need to meet—now.'

The other hesitated, as if sensing the anticipation in his voice, and then, 'Do we have something?'

'We do.'

'Fifteen minutes, usual place.'

'Okay.'

The line died, and Moshe tapped the phone on his lips. A smile broke out, and he felt that golden moment of pleasure as he thought about the coming storm.

It was dark on the pier, and a light breeze came in from the Mediterranean. The two men stood away from the lights that extended in a chain down one side of the structure, speaking in low voices. Their escorts had blocked off the landside of the pier with large black SUVs. Automatic machine pistols were cradled in arms, and they prowled restlessly in the half-light.

'Are you sure of this information?'

David could be so cautious sometimes. But then, Moshe figured, it was understandable. 'I verified it several times with Ariel and Uziel. They are clear that we have a viable product. It is, if you like, a tester. Question is, where do you want to test it?'

Good question, David decided. There were so many who would benefit from the hand of God visited upon them. The predominant targets lay to the north or to the east.

In the end, there was but one benefactor of the ultimate cleansing device, designed by this brilliant young scientist. But this first product was only a precursor, so it would have to be the others laid bare by its power. He allowed himself the opportunity to bask in the glory of this moment. The people would see he had been right all along, and they would damn this accord to the dustbin of history from where it should never have been dragged. No. Now they had this weapon, Israel would never fear the enemy again.

'Is an aircraft ready?'

'We have three on the tarmac standing by for your order. Just tell us where.' Moshe waited patiently for the word.

'This will be only the start, Moshe, only the start. And we will start in Damascus.'

40

The sun was peeking over the umber hills, rousing life at the farmhouse as Logan and Murtagh regarded it from the confines of their dusty BMW. Lights shone downstairs, and up in the main house, while labourers prepared for a long day in the fields.

The Brit glassed the front of the building again and then the part of the back garden he could see. What he couldn't see was what he was looking for. He hoped it was just early. The fingers on his TAG Heuer read five forty-nine.

'Nothing yet,' he informed Murtagh, lowering the binoculars. 'Just the grandparents getting breakfast.'

'What do you want to do?'

He ran a hand over his face. 'Nice shower, big breakfast, and some orange juice while we're over here,' he quipped. 'How about you?'

By way of reply, she punched him in the arm. 'Stop fooling around. This is serious.'

Logan rubbed his arm. 'Ow.'

'Serves you right.' She regarded the farmhouse again. 'If the kids aren't there, then whoever is behind all this has them.'

He grinned at her. 'You're right, on both counts. So we go up there as journalists, looking for a story. But first off, I'm headed to that town we just passed through. I need a shower. Really!'

Two hours later, they approached the farmhouse again, this time driving up to the door. Logan killed the engine and surveyed the driveway, the front of the house, and the farmyard beyond. Nothing seemed out of place.

Cautiously he climbed out, grabbed his messenger bag, and waited for Murtagh to join him with her camera. He approached the door and knocked.

There was a short pause before a tall slim woman answered. Her greying hair was tied back in a short ponytail. The face, open and lined, was wearied by something more than farm life. A question squirmed across her face, and then she noted the camera.

'No reporters.' Her tone was flat; the expression exuded anger.

'We're sorry to disturb you like this, but we were won—'

'I said no reporters!'

'What's the matter, *ahuvi*?'

The woman moved to one side, her brow still creased with anger, to allow a large ruddy-faced man get to the door. In his hand was a cocked shotgun. He looked down on them both before turning to silently question the woman.

'There're reporters again,' she explained.

The man thrust forward, menacingly, with the gun.

Logan stepped back, wary.

'Can't you vermin leave us alone!? Can't you just let us grieve? What's wrong with you?'

The questions crashed over Logan, and he was aware of attention from the rest of the yard, farmhands dropping their tools and turning to look. It was a bit like a zombie movie, he reflected, trying not to smile at the incongruous image.

He held his hands up in front of him, an act of supplication. 'Would you let me explain why we're here … please?'

The man took a step forward, gun raised menacingly. 'No!' Spittle flew from his lips, his complexion turning a deeper red. 'Go! Before I call the police!'

Logan backed away and reached slowly into his shirt pocket. 'Okay. We're going. But I have news about your daughter and grandchildren.' He placed the card on the veranda's step. 'If you change your mind, call this number.' He beckoned Murtagh and headed to the car, aware of the weapon pointed at his unprotected back.

'That could've gone better,' Murtagh remarked as they drove back to the road.

'Hmm. Maybe.'

The American looked at her partner, a furrow developing on her brow. 'Maybe?'

'I'm surprised at you,' he admonished with a smile. When Murtagh remained mystified, he continued. 'Mr and Mrs Leibnitz obviously believe their daughter and family died at Tel Etz. If they are still alive, they're being held by people with the resources to make them disappear completely.'

'Of course! Sorry. I'm being a bit dim today.'

Logan smiled. 'No worries.' He pulled the BMW back on the road and headed back towards the town they'd visited earlier. 'Trouble is, finding out that information puts our pursuers closer to us than it does us closer to the conspirators.' He paused again. 'Perez was our best lead, and he's dead,' he observed ruefully.

'We have to find somebody else then.'

'Yes, but who?'

Murtagh studied the view from the window, the passing orange groves, rank upon rank of trees, perfectly set out, with the first fruits hanging from the branches. It was idyllic. She wondered how so much evil could exist alongside such beauty. She turned. 'How about Natalie Epstein?'

'The anchorwoman?'

Murtagh nodded. 'Yes. She had a lot to say about the situation, made no secret of her opposition to the talks or Palestinians in general.'

Logan stared ahead, rolling the suggestion around his head. They knew little enough about the woman. But after what they'd seen and heard, maybe it wasn't a bad idea to start with her.'

'Okay. Let's have a coffee and figure out how we do this.'

'They're going to do what?'

Olsen leaned forward, horror burning in his eyes as he searched Horowitz's face for … something. 'How did they find out?' His voice was dark and angry.

Horowitz wasn't fazed, but her tone was truculent. 'I told them. I do work for the government, if you hadn't noticed.'

'And they're going to bomb Damascus!?'

'I would've thought the West would be pleased. After all, we're dealing with the Muslim Brotherhood question for them … and you.'

'And killing millions of innocent people in the process.'

Horowitz leant back in her seat and burst out laughing. 'You hypocrite, you've just spent the last weeks developing an enhanced weapon of mass destruction, and now you weep for a few Arabs. Grow some, Johannes. Live up to your middle name.'

The Norwegian pouted. 'I don't care. This is not what I came here to do, bomb innocent people in another country.'

'Then you know nothing of how this situation works. Syria and Iran are our real enemies. They feed the Palestinians lies, bullshit, and the weapons to do their dirty work for them. We hit Syria and Iran, the Palestinian question disappears.'

'You believe you have nothing to do with the oppression of the Palestinian peoples in Gaza and the West Bank? You don't see the blood on your own hands?'

'That blood has kept Israelis alive, as will this mission. Don't forget you suffered because of the same struggle. Your precious children'—Olsen flinched—'are dead because of the Palestinian question. You weren't so squeamish when you thought it was Palestinians who would die. Though why you thought we would detonate a nuclear device close enough for us to be affected by the fallout too is beyond me.'

'It d-didn't occur to me.'

'Then you're a fool.'

Olsen stared through the window. The plant looked as it always did—busy but with the attentiveness necessary for such a place. Nobody would guess a decision had just been taken to destroy a city of several million people. The bile rose in his throat, burning, demanding an exit. He choked it back and wiped the tears from his eyes.

'There must be something I can do to stop this madness.' A statement—a plea—to the young woman, who had suddenly become much colder than she'd been previously. Now he knew why he'd been given 'a couple of days off'.

Horowitz smiled. 'The bomb is being fitted to an air force jet as we speak. They should be within range of Damascus inside a couple of hours at the most. The weather conditions are right, so the fallout will be blown over the sparsely populated Syrian Desert. Just a few goatherds and their animals to trouble you there.'

'Bitch.'

'Name-calling now? Really, Johannes, it's not what I expected from an educated man.' She glanced at her watch. 'Well, your handiwork should be getting airborne anytime soon. I'll leave you to enjoy the moment.'

Olsen watched her leave and then dashed to the toilets. Bursting into a cubicle, he vomited his lunch into the bowl. He clung to the porcelain, for fear that he would fall off the crazy world he had constructed for himself.

Topol and Klein watched the F-15 Eagle and its F-22 escorts lift off from the newly constructed runway at Dimona, swing over the plant, and head out towards the Mediterranean. The three would climb high first, as if to start a training mission, before setting course north, following the coast of Syria and then turning to run in from the north-west of the capital. At a range of a hundred miles or so, the cruise missile would be launched. The F-15 would turn back and dive to low level, making its escape over Lebanese territory. The whole operation would take a little more than an hour to conclude.

That was the theory anyway, Topol told himself as the aircraft became tiny dots in the blue vault. He turned away from the window. Despite his experience, the tension built a huge wave of anxiety in his belly. Was this the right decision for Israel? Was it showing their hand? What would the government say when the attack had been launched, the bomb detonated, and the casualties came pouring in? 'Not long now.'

Klein was still watching her birds disappear into the vast sky. 'Not long at all.' She sounded as unsure as he did.

The door to the control tower banged open. Both turned towards the intrusion. Olsen stood there, ashen-faced, wild-eyed, and dishevelled. He pointed at Topol. 'What are you doing?' His words seemed to despise their release into the air between the two men, grinding their way between clenched teeth.

'What any Israeli will do, defending my country.'

'By using a weapon of mass destruction on people completely unconnected,' Olsen scowled ineffectually as he spat the words out.

Topol laughed. 'Shut up, Olsen. You are part of this now. You cannot back out or deny your responsibility to the cause.'

'I said it was ready for testing is all.'

'And we are testing it.'

'I meant for underground testing. It's untried.'

'Not true, Mr Olsen,' Klein said. 'The weapon itself is proven; the warhead is proven. All you did was modify it for us. Either way, it will work. Don't forget that the people you are worried about are the very people who fund Hamas and Hezbollah—you know, the people who killed your family.'

'Yes, I know. Horowitz told me. Two wrongs don't make a right.'

Topol scowled. 'You should have thought about that when you signed up for this endeavour.'

'I was vulnerable. I was distraught. My family had been killed.' Olsen was close to tears, desperately seeking justification for his naivety. He slid back against the wall, knees buckling.

Topol looked disdainfully at the man, motioning two air force guards. 'Take Mr Olsen back to his quarters. Make sure he gets some sleep.'

The door closed behind the three figures, and Klein looked to Topol. 'What are we going to do with him?'

The general pulled a face. 'Same as with the American. When we have everything we need from him, the desert will make a very good place for disposing of our reluctant scientist.'

Black didn't think he could hurt anymore. His body was wracked with pain, while his head was a fug of tiredness and disorientation. The Israelis certainly knew their torture techniques. The light and the noise in the cell had been erratically but constantly tormenting him for so long now he couldn't remember when it had started. He knew he wanted it to stop, which was extremely unlikely. His death was more foreseeable; he was becoming hardened to the idea he wasn't much longer for this life.

It was a sobering thought, one he had worked to keep from his psyche—a losing battle. In his more hopeful moments, he wondered what he could do to prevent or stall the inevitable. In others, like now, he was glad he had no long-term partner or children, who would have to be told the news, be comforted in their grief. He could just about recall his father and mother if he tried hard. His death would kill his mom, and his dad would drink himself to an earlier grave.

You can't give up!

There's always a way, a route out.

Think, man, think.

The door to his cell rattled as a guard turned the key in the lock. It opened, and an armed guard appeared, motioning with his weapon for Black to rise. The SEAL did as bid and waited calmly for what would come next.

That was unpredictable. Sometimes it was a rifle butt to his stomach or side. Other times, a foot caused him to trip walking through the door. Or they'd just let him walk out, give him chocolate.

All part of the disorienting, nothing personal; he knew that. For these people, it was as much a job to do as it would be if he were in their boots.

This time, he was allowed to walk unmolested, before being directed to the left and through another door. As he passed through, one of his guards touched his arm, and he couldn't help flinching, much to both their amusement. The guard held out a towel, soap, and shampoo.

'Get yourself cleaned up,' he ordered Black.

The water was fantastic, enlivening. The big American just stood still and allowed it to rush over his tired muscles and skin. He grinned. Big mistake for them. A luxury and opportunity for him.

Five minutes later, washed, revived, and feeling immeasurably better, he joined his escorts once more. They marched him along corridor after corridor, until the smell of food wound its way up his nostrils and into his stomach. It rumbled.

The canteen was empty, save for a couple of technicians, who were quickly scooted out of the place. Directed to a table and chair, Black sat and waited while another guard went to collect a tray. He came back with food and juice. Black wolfed down the meal, hardly registering what it was; washed it down with the juice; and waited expectantly. His thoughts were as dark as his name. The only thing currently working for him was the fact they were in a public area. He had time for the food to settle before he was beaten or waterboarded. That would be back in the interrogation block.

Time went on, and he was kept in his seat. Then the canteen door opened, and two figures in army green walked in and sat at the table. Black recognised the captain who had captured him and shot Yakin so cold-bloodedly. The other, wearing the uniform of a general, he knew only vaguely from a couple of visits—once when he was first brought in and the second time during an interrogation.

The large man nodded to Black before turning to the captain. 'Captain, what have we learned from our friend here?'

Captain Geller stared malevolently at Black, who smiled back. 'Nothing, General.'

Topol shook his head as his attention returned to the American. 'You SEALs are as good as the rumours say then. I understand that you've had a bit of a rough time while you were here?'

Black said nothing, just continued to stare at the big man.

Topol smiled. 'Well, I hope the shower and the meal were some recompense?' He regarded Black closely.

He just stared back, lips shut tight.

'Your lack of response is a bit upsetting, if I'm honest, but not unexpected.'

Black continued his stony silence.

'Well, John Black, you present me with something of a dilemma.'

Here it comes.

'You see, you were here, illegally armed, with a member of our internal security services who was engaged in a treasonable act. Now, he has paid for that action. But what do we do with you?' Topol rose and paced round the table, before standing before the SEAL once more.

'Now, we could let you go and say goodbye, no hard feelings. Please visit Israel again soon.' Polite laughter accompanied the general's words. 'However, we both know that you would talk a lot about Israeli hospitality, and we can't have that, can we?'

Heads shook in agreement.

Topol leaned in. 'So, you are going to take a little ride into the desert with Captain Geller here. Enjoy the scenery for what little time is left you. Goodbye, Lieutenant Black. You won't be returning.'

41

The F-15 pilot checked his navigation system. It would soon be time to make the turn to the coast and drop below radar coverage. He looked out at the dark expanse of the Mediterranean, the last of the day's sunlight catching the tops of the Mount Lebanon range. He fancied he could make out Qurnat as Sawda' still glowing orangey pink in the rays of the setting sun.

The computer squawked his waypoint, and the pilot made the corrections, bringing the heavy fighter round and dropping it into a dive for the sea 30,000 feet below. As it bunted over, the twin Pratt and Whitney engines screamed furiously, and the altimeter reeled off the altitude like a berserk fruit machine. His eyes scanned the threat warning displays, alert to any potential warning of radar probing. Nothing.

That proved little. Any number of nations could be monitoring their movement passively.

On board the Turkish Air Force AWACS, the operator checked his screen again and made a note of the coordinates and plots his surveillance provided him. He looked round and attracted the attention of the commander, who approached quickly. 'What do you have?'

'A single plot heading north-east, made a turn starboard and a rapid descent. I'm getting some other plots too, but too intermittent and vague to confirm.'

The commander stroked his chin. 'Keep a watch on it. Let me know what it does.'

With a nod, the operator scrutinised his screen closely.

At 250 feet, the pilot set his autopilot to the course for the release point and allowed the terrain-following radar to maintain a safe height over the ground. He had clocked the large plot of an orbiting plane as he dropped altitude and surmised it was an AWACS, likely Turkish. There was nothing to be done now. The two Raptors would provide cover should anything untoward happen; he had to believe that, so he could concentrate on his mission.

The ride at this level was bumpy, and the ground flashed passed in streaks of light and dark. He kept his eyes firmly on the airspeed indicator, calculating the distance to release, even though the computer would give him adequate warning.

Five minutes.

He checked the fuel situation—sufficient for the return journey. Engines running sweet. Everything was fine.

Two minutes.

He reached for the weapons panel and armed the device. Green lights glowed, and the computer confirmed the flight path and coordinates for release.

Any time now.

High above, the lead Raptor pilot watched as the track of the Eagle got closer to the release point. Not long now, and the pilot would launch the cruise missile and turn for home.

He would receive a welcome he wasn't expecting.

The pilot punched details of the Eagle into his arming computer. Their brief had been very simple—the strike hadn't happened.

In the cockpit of the Eagle, the pilot's finger hovered over the release button. Any second now.

The warning sounded in his earphones, and he pressed the teat. With a whoosh, followed by the tremor of the release, the missile shot from beneath the aircraft, belching a stream of flame and vapour as it climbed away from him. At the same moment, the autopilot began the direction change as the Eagle reached its waypoint.

Back home and a late tea. The pilot smiled behind his mask. *Job well done*, he told himself. Now everything was up to the tiny missile. In its payload lay the future of Israel.

Jumping from his seat, the young operator rushed down the AWACS's cramped corridor to the commander, who turned at his approach.

'Sir.'

'Yes, what is it?'

'The target I was tracking has launched some sort of missile.'

The commander's eyebrows shot up. 'Are you sure?'

The operator nodded vigorously.

'Where is it headed?'

'Damascus.'

With an almost leisurely motion, the Eagle recrossed the Syrian coast, taking a southerly track back to Israel. From high above, the Raptor pilot checked the plot and went to active mode, selecting a medium-range missile. The head on the missile hunted as he closed on the aircraft, and then the tone came in his ears.

What the fuck? The Eagle pilot jinked in his seat, scanning the sky urgently. Why was the escort locking on him? It made no sense. The growl in his ears disregarded his mystification. He was being 'locked on' by his own escort.

The pilot reached for his communications panel. He had been told not to, but this was ridiculous. He had to reach them and figure out what was happening.

'Eagle to Rah-ahm, respond.' Nothing. 'Eagle to Rah-ahm, please respond.'

Silence greeted him.

What to do? He checked the scope. The Raptor was closing on him. Perhaps it was just fooling around. He dismissed that quickly. Who fooled around like this?

Countermeasures.

Quickly he threw every flare and strip of chaff that he could, to throw the pursuing aircraft off the scent. In a panic, he pushed the throttles through the gate, engaging afterburner, though he knew that would be futile. Outrunning a Raptor wasn't an option. He looked at the empty missile rails and a sinking feeling gripped him.

He wasn't meant to return.

Options.

To his port, he could see the coast of Israel, perhaps ten, twelve miles. If he could eject, then he could swim back, provided he got closer.

He pulled the aircraft round and dived, to get every bit of available speed from the ship. Behind the Raptor came on, inexorably.

Suddenly, the sky to the north and east was lit like the sun, framing the mountains of Lebanon in the deathly glow. He paused and watched in awe at the spectacle.

In his ear, the sound of the threat warning receiver blurted its message, but he wasn't listening.

The missile lurched from the Raptor. Satisfied, the pilot turned to starboard, even as the missile careered into the Eagle and detonated.

Still orbiting over Turkey's southern coast, the AWACS had turned east when the cruise missile had reached its target and detonated. The light was incandescent and unmistakeable, as was the cloud that spread outwards from the epicentre of the explosion.

Such was the effect nobody noticed the death of the Eagle farther to the south.

42

Black kept his eyes firmly on the receding lights of Dimona, framed by the two guards at the rear of the covered truck. In the cab, Geller and the driver were cut off from the back. This would give him precious moments for what was about to happen. He looked down perfunctorily at the cable ties round his wrists, thankful for those rather than cuffs.

'Hey,' he called to the guards.

They turned, bored and disinterested. Excellent. They thought him beat.

'Either of you got a smoke?'

He knew the one on the left had cigarettes; he'd smoked one before they'd loaded Black onto the wagon.

The guard stood and crabbed his way awkwardly towards the front of the truck, placed a cigarette in Black's mouth, and reached for his lighter.

Black puffed on the lit cigarette and smiled contentedly. 'Man, that is so good! You don't know.'

'Make the most of it.' The guard grinned and turned.

As he did, Black raised his arms high and, with his right foot, kicked the guard's leg forward so that his weight fell back towards the SEAL. Black dropped his hands over the startled man, who screamed for help and started thrashing.

Black brought his hands back up and then forcefully down on the man's nose. The crack as it broke was satisfying, but there were more important things to do. The other guard, shouting now for the vehicle to stop, was trying to get a bead on Black, who kept his captive between him and the gun.

Got to get rid of the ties somehow.

Rising, he pushed the guard along the bed of the truck, running at the other, until they both slammed into him. The Israeli wobbled and cried out as he fell from the tailgate into the road.

One down, one to go. Black slammed the man's head against the upright of the frame, once, twice, and was satisfied to feel the knees go on the third attempt. The man fell through his arms to the floor.

Using the cigarette, Black burned through the ties and rubbed his wrist. He flicked the stub out the back with a casual, 'Filthy habit.'

Quickly he relieved the unconscious guard of his weapons, found ties in a pocket, and repaid the gesture. He strapped himself into the man's webbing and holstered the semi-automatic, a Baby Eagle. So half-decent, he figured. The rifle, a Galil, Black had little faith in. But beggars couldn't be choosers.

The truck came to a stop, and Black heard the cab doors open and close again, the sound of boots scrunching on the gravel road.

'What the fuck is g—'

The bullet scythed through Captain Geller's forehead, erupting out of the other side as Black loosed off a second shot. Geller crumpled to the desert floor, blood forming a black halo around his head.

'And fuck you.' Black ground out at the dead body. He turned to the startled driver, a young woman whose hands slowly extended skywards as Black pointed the semi-automatic at her.

'Back away,' he instructed her. When she was far enough from him, he vaulted over the tailgate and advanced towards her. 'On your knees.'

'Are you going to shoot me, like you did the captain?' Though she tried damned hard, her voice wavered slightly with anxiety.

'He got what he fucking well deserved,' an angry Black informed her. 'You might think you're lucky you've survived this long. But, no, I'm not going to shoot you. Over to the truck.'

He ordered her to drop the tailgate and climb aboard. Swiftly, he pulled her hands behind her back and secured her wrists with zip ties and then her ankles. Unceremoniously, he bundled her next to her compatriot.

'Don't worry. He isn't dead,' he advised her as she looked in alarm at her comrade. 'Now I'm going to gag both of you … and put you to sleep with him.' The pistol cracked her forehead.

Satisfied with his handiwork, Black dropped from the back of the truck, made his way to the front, and climbed into the driver's seat. He grasped the wheel, thoughts swirling round. It was time to put some distance between himself and Geller's body, before setting out to find Logan and Murtagh.

Brooke Murtagh sat nervously in the Channel 1 studio waiting room. The idea had seemed a really good one when they'd discussed it in the café. Now, faced with only minutes of waiting before sitting down with Natalie Epstein, on her radio show, it seemed like the maddest scheme ever. It wasn't that Epstein could do anything to her, even if she suspected Murtagh's ulterior motive; it was more the fact that she felt completely naked, exposed. Not even her persona, Stacey Allen, seemed enough protection now.

Chill out, she told herself. *It'll be fine.*

A woman poked her head around a door and beckoned to Murtagh with a smile. Murtagh rose and walked over. Did she look unsteady?

'Okay, Stacey, Natalie has gone to a song, followed by an ad break. Then she'll interview you. You'll have about fifteen minutes, including music and another interval, but she'll run you through the routine.'

Murtagh nodded and followed the aide into the small anteroom. A large window let into the studio, and she could make out Epstein reading at the desk. She was a beauty, and Murtagh knew that would be difficult, bound to make problems for her. Nothing like two women who are competing.

Epstein looked up and beamed a greeting, beckoning for them to come in. The aide opened the studio door and ushered Murtagh through, closing the door behind her. *Into the arena*, flashed through her mind as she took the seat opposite her host.

'Okay, Stacey. Have you done this sort of thing before?'

'Oh yes,' Murtagh confirmed, sounding more confident than she felt.

'Okay. So, I have the gist of what you have to speak about. I'm going to talk with you for a couple minutes, go to a couple of tunes, and we'll talk about the next segment. It'll be about ten, fifteen minutes. Does that sound all right?'

Murtagh nodded.

Epstein gave a grin. 'Okay, here we go.' She turned to the desk and her mike. 'Good evening again, Israel. I'm joined in the studio by freelance journalist photographer Stacey Allen, who's just returned from Tel Etz. Stacey,' she looked at the agent, 'tell me, what were you doing in a restricted area?'

God, the woman is going for me straight away, thought Murtagh as she quickly put a response together. 'My colleague and I wanted to do an aftermath piece, looking at the place and talking to some of those connected to the settlement.'

'But you didn't find much there, did you.'

It was more a statement than a question—interesting.

'Well, we found no people, and the Palestinian Police at the checkpoint told us the survivors had been moved out sometime before, as had the bodies. So, no, there wasn't a great deal.'

Epstein gave a little laugh.

Mocking? wondered Murtagh.

'Well, if there were no people, no bodies, what did you find?'

'Well, Natalie, what we found was proof that the attack was not carried out by Hamas or Hezbollah.' *God this is a risky strategy*, Murtagh figured as she watched Epstein freeze.

'Not carried out by Hamas or Hezbollah?' Did Murtagh pick up caution, suspicion in the journalist's voice? 'That is not what our police and investigators say. What makes you believe they're wrong and you're right?' There was a coldness in the voice.

'We found evidence of NATO standard ammunition being used. By that I mean, five point five-six casings around the village, which is typical of the kind of cartridges used, for instance, by the Israeli Defence Forces.'

'If that's the case,' Epstein began, 'does that necessarily mean that Hamas, or Hezbollah, for that matter, haven't got hold of weaponry that fits the evidence?'

Murtagh gave what she hoped was a sincere but placating smile. 'That might be so, Natalie. However it plays out, it seems like an escalation, which is concerning. Is it not?'

'But you don't think that, do you, Stacey?' Epstein retorted, ignoring the question.

Again, more statement than question. *Tread very carefully, Brooke.* 'No, we don't, Natalie, because that wasn't all we found there.'

'Interesting. Well, listeners, on the evening of renewed efforts by the American government to keep the Jerusalem Accord alive, an American reporter finds evidence that she says points to a cover-up. We'll be back for more after this next song.'

Epstein flicked a switch and the 'On Air' light winked out.

'Okay, explain.'

Murtagh looked into the woman's eyes and didn't like what she saw. This could get nasty. 'I'm not sure what you mean.'

'Oh pu-lease. You're not a reporter, are you? If you were, you wouldn't have gotten into Tel Etz as easily as you did, and you wouldn't be saying what you are.'

'And what are you saying, Natalie? Is there a cover-up?'

Epstein ignored the question, but Murtagh caught the slight blush—result. 'What are you, Stacey? If indeed that's your real name. CIA? NSA?'

'Think what you, like Natalie. I'm telling you what we found.'

Epstein made to reply, but a light over her phone came on. She lifted the receiver. 'Hello.' For a moment, she listened to a voice on the other end. Murtagh couldn't make out what was being said, but it looked alarming. As Epstein worked up the next tune, it was obvious she was concentrating on the call. What was she being told?

Placing the receiver back in its cradle, Epstein turned to Murtagh. Her expression was hard to read; there was a—Murtagh struggled to identify the face—calmness to it, she decided.

'I'm afraid I'm going to have to pull the rest of the interview, Stacey.'

'Oh. How come?'

'There's been an incident in Syria.'

When Murtagh raised an eyebrow in query, she wasn't expecting the reply she received.

'A nuclear device has been detonated in Damascus.'

Murtagh realised she was shaking uncontrollably as she slid into the passenger seat of the BMW. Logan looked at her oddly. By way of reply,

Murtagh turned on the radio and tuned to a local news station. They listened in silence.

'Fucking hell.' He stared ahead blankly.

Her hands were shaking, and she pressed them hard against her thighs to try and stop them. It didn't work. The tears took her by surprise, seeping into her mouth and falling to her shirt, the salt bitter and wasted.

'She knew.' Was that her voice? she asked herself. It sounded so small and alone in the space between them.

Logan glanced at her. 'She knew?' He repeated the words back as a question, and Murtagh nodded mutely. 'How could you tell?'

'When the call came through, she was calm, empty almost, as if she'd been expecting something. In a way, it saved me.' God, what a callous thing to say!

'How come?'

'She kinda rumbled me and, when we went to a break, wanted to know if I was CIA.'

He let out a low whistle. 'That was close.'

'What do we do now? Doesn't this mean the end?' Murtagh felt Logan lean over and pull her towards him. Slowly the shivers subsided, and she allowed herself to relax. Some things needed a hug.

Looking out on the street, he asked himself the same thing. He wondered how John was. Was he still alive? Who could tell? One thing he knew; this couldn't be the end that Brooke was so worried about.

'No, it doesn't,' he said forcefully. 'It's just the beginning.'

Black killed the lights and drove the truck slowly over the brow of the hill, thankful for the light of the full moon. He came to stop in the lee of the hill where he couldn't be spotted. Picking up a pair of binoculars and flicking to thermal imaging, he scanned the road crossing his track some distance ahead. Nothing moved along its dark surface. Fantastic.

Easing forward, he drove down the slope. After a few minutes rumbling over the harsh desert, he came to the road and turned onto the ribbon of tarmac. Sometime soon, he would have to activate his beacon. First, he needed to put some distance between himself and Dimona. Only trouble would follow him from there.

The two Raptors aimed to cross the coast south of Ashkelon, fly east, and then turn south somewhere near Arad, to come into the strip at Dimona. As they closed on the coastline, the lead pilot flashed his IFF codes to military command and awaited confirmation.

No reply came.

He flashed them again and waited, bemused.

In the corner of his eye, he saw the light from the threat warning receiver just as the siren went off in his ears.

What the—

Contacts were moving towards their two aircraft, fast.

'Ravi, do you have the contacts?'

'Yes,' his wingman replied.

'What's going on?'

'Don't know. What do we do boss?'

'Break right.'

He flung the Raptor to his left and punched the countermeasures.

Nothing.

Fuck.

Wreckage from the two Raptors fell to earth, at Ashkelon, most falling in the sea, some on the beach, causing panic among the few people taking in the late-evening air. It would be reported as an unfortunate training accident. The pilots would be recovered and buried with full military honours.

Topol took the call shortly after the downing of the Raptors. He listened intently as the caller informed him of the success of the mission— all elements. Hopefully, Geller would be back soon with more good news, and they could move on.

But it was too good an opportunity to pass up on. He thanked the caller, placed the receiver on the phone, and pulled a cheap mobile from his pocket. He dialled a number from memory.

'Moshe? This is Ariel.'

Moshe listened as Ariel told him the culmination of the mission. It could not have been better news. David would be over the moon.

'Thank you, Ariel. I shall be in contact with you as soon as I have spoken with David.'

Moshe sat back in his chair, playing absent-mindedly with the mobile, contemplating the meaning of everything that had happened over the last few hours. How mad was it all? He felt the urge to laugh out loud. This was really sticking it to the accord.

On impulse, he dialled David's number. As he waited for it to connect, he knew he should have used a new device, but he felt a little reckless. Fuck it. What could anybody do now?

'David, how goes things?'

The older man grunted, but Moshe could tell he was pleased. News of the Damascus bombing was filtering through the news channels, and a storm of protest was rising. So be it. Who cared?

'Well, Moshe, well. It seems the product works.'

'Indeed.'

'What of the deliverers.'

'They've been paid off.'

'That's good news. We move to the next product.'

'Yes. Ariel confirms that it won't be a problem to go to that stage.'

'Very good. Proceed please.'

A silence grew between them, which threatened to become uncomfortable. 'Moshe, Golda had a visitor today.'

Moshe checked himself. Why had she gone directly to David? Everything should be routed through him. That was troubling, and he would have to speak with her. For now, he contained himself. 'Yes? What was the issue?'

'She wasn't sure but thinks the visitor was a competitor. There was some talk about the site we worked on a while back. Golda didn't get time to ask more though—events conspired against that.' There was that pause again. 'Weren't we supposed to have gotten rid of the competition?'

Moshe flushed. 'Yes. I was unaware our team hadn't completed the task.'

David grunted again. But this time, there was no doubting the meaning behind it. 'Well, it seems they're still out there. We need to tie off everything so that we aren't exposed. Does Ariel know that too?'

'I'll be sure to tell him.'

'Do.'

The line went dead, leaving Moshe feel considerably less excited than he had a few moments earlier.

The operative checked the entry and the codes, addresses, and other tags; they matched. She made the entry on to the record and passed it to her controller, who verified it. He passed it along the chain of command until it arrived at Vauxhall House.

Amanda Galbraith had just returned from an emergency meeting of COBRA, the main subject of which had been the Damascus bombing. Adams had been his usual cutting self and had enjoyed slicing the whole foreign department into slices, like salami. Phrases ranging from 'intelligence failure' to 'lack of oversight' to 'complete fuck-up' had peppered his observations. All in attendance had left Cabinet Office Briefing Room A with their tails between their legs and wishing they didn't have to return in only a few hours with the necessary answers.

When she saw the coded message from Cheltenham, Galbraith prayed fervently for a breakthrough. She entered her password, and the message opened. She smiled.

Swiping the comms icon on her device, Galbraith dialled up Nugent. 'Sally, we need to get hold of Logan as soon as possible.' She listened to her ops manager. 'Okay, get back to me ASAP. It's important.'

Ending the call, she flipped up another number and dialled.

President Carlisle looked at her first team and suppressed the urge to hold her head in her hands. The world was going to hell in a handcart, with a V8 strapped to it. She didn't know whether to laugh or cry at the news that a nuclear device had been detonated over the capital of Syria. Her first act though, had been to place all US forces on DEFCON 4. As her team congregated, the US Atlantic and Indian Ocean Fleets were steaming at flank speed towards the Mediterranean and the Gulf of Aden, while forces in Europe and Diego Garcia were mobilising for action.

Fuck the Israelis.

She knew that was prejudging the situation. But who else in the region would have access to such a device and target Syria? Oh, Iran for sure had the bomb but no reason to drop it on Syria.

Really, there was only one culprit.

'Okay, ladies and gentlemen, thank you for attending at such short notice. As you are aware, a nuclear weapon has been detonated over Damascus. Initial drone reconnaissance indicates that the city has been obliterated. We can only presume, at this time, that the population has been wiped out.'

A mobile rang, and all heads turned towards the sound.

'Sorry, ma'am.'

'No worries, Bill. When you're ready.'

Foreman looked at the caller ID. 'I need to take this call, ma'am,' he informed his commander in chief.

He slipped from the office. 'Amanda. To what do I owe the pleasure?'

'Apologies, Bill. I was trying to get hold of Sarah Markham.'

Foreman laughed. 'We're in the middle of something right now. Sarah is a little indisposed. What can I do for you?'

'So are we, so are we. But I have some news that may help out.'

The director's ears suddenly pricked up. 'Tell me.'

'We have a number and a location for one of the conspirators.'

'Fuck!'

'So how do we want to play this?'

Foreman fell silent, considering the information he'd been fed. 'Have you heard from Logan and Murtagh.'

'I've not heard from either. Then, I've heard nothing bad, so …'

The admiral nodded to no one in particular. 'We've no sight on Black either. Do you think our people are still active?'

Galbraith mulled over the point. 'We have to hope so.'

'Okay, well, I have to get back to the president. I'll call you as soon as I've had a think. Oh, can you send me details of the caller to this secure ID?'

A pause and then, 'Sending it now.'

Foreman checked his device and nodded to himself; it figured. 'Thanks. I'll be in touch.'

'Very well, Bill. Speak soon.'

'Bye Amanda.'

Foreman pocketed his mobile and stroked his chin, ruminating on the call. It was something they hadn't had moments before. But how useful would it be?

He walked back into the meeting and took his place at the table, aware of everyone's eyes on him.

'Anything you want to tell us, Bill?'

He regarded Carlisle and nodded. 'Oh yes, ma'am. I have something to tell you.'

43

They'd sat in the bar nursing their drinks for an hour now, staring at the telly and taking in the reaction of the crowds to the bombing. Overall, they both agreed, it appeared to have gone down a storm with the Tel Aviv audience—which was worrying, to say the least.

'This is really scary,' Murtagh observed as she drew on her lager. 'I mean, these guys are actually cheering the fact Damascus has been nuked.'

Logan considered the presenter of the late-night news channel, who was putting together a scenario. Interestingly, it was Iran being blamed for the attack. *Always ready to take the moral high ground against the Arabs.* Even more interestingly, though, the government had, as yet, made no comment.

'Why's that, do you think?' Murtagh asked.

He grimaced. 'I'm not sure. Oh, wait a minute.' He placed his drink back on the table and looked down at his device blinking on his wrist. Untwisting it, he placed it on the table and swiped the blinking icon. The information brought a smile to his face. Murtagh looked at him.

'Come on. Tell me,' she encouraged him impatiently.

'Mr Black is back on the grid.'

A night in a hotel in the middle of the biggest party he'd ever seen had kept Logan's nerves jangling constantly, so it was a tired, irascible officer who spooned breakfast away that morning. Brooke, he noted, appeared to have had a significantly better night's rest than he'd had.

She nodded. 'I slept like a baby, thank you. How about you?'

'Could've been better,' he remarked, draining his coffee quickly and standing up. 'More?' He indicated her cup.

She shook her head, and he walked over to the urn for an urgently needed refill. The television drew his attention. More analysis abounded on the bombing of Damascus and the political fallout resulting from it. Unrest had fomented in Gaza, West Bank, and the surrounding states. Iraq and Jordan rebuked the administration of Binyamin Olmet, who steadfastly denied culpability and appealed for calm. For once, Logan believed the man, but only because he knew something else lurked behind all this. That it wouldn't appear so to the outside world, maybe, was the point.

The newscast cut to an aerial view of Damascus. The devastation was immense, as if a meteor had hit, an extinction event in his lifetime. A shudder rattled through him. It didn't bear thinking about. How many years since Hiroshima and Nagasaki, and humankind had managed to keep from using such weapons?

Now what?

He took his coffee back to the table and drew on it in silence. Murtagh knew better than to disturb him at moments like this; she concentrated on her breakfast.

Finally, he stirred from his reverie. 'We need to move, and soon.'

She nodded.

'When we get back to the room,' he continued, 'I'm going to check where John's about and arrange to pick him up. Then we pay Miss Epstein a visit.'

His face displayed a grim determination Murtagh had seen before. Things were ramping up a gear. A buzz of excitement filled her belly. 'Let's go then.'

Black walked into the town just after eight. Things were busy, as was the way in hotter countries. They wanted to get business concluded early, have a break late morning and return when the intensity of the heat wore off in the afternoon. He found a small busy café and purchased coffee and fruit. He needed the caffeine and the sugar. Something told him it would be a busy day. As he pulled on the coffee, he considered the two he'd left in the hills above the town; at least they were still breathing. More than the chance Geller had been intending to afford him. Eating made him feel good; having activated his beacon made him feel better. There was still much to do before he could meet up with his compadres.

Sitting in the midst of the patrons, he noticed murmurs that showed he was becoming the subject of conversation. He grinned to himself. Perhaps it was inevitable, the size, colour, and all, he surmised. Finishing his hasty breakfast, he headed for the door and out. As Black moved passed the counter, he eyeballed the owner, who spoke rapidly to someone in Hebrew. He averted his gaze from the American.

At the door, Black glanced up and down the road, filled with people, cars, animals, and dust. Then he saw what he was looking for, and a slow grin spread across his face.

As ever, Natalie Epstein was eschewing journalistic convention and promoting a completely biased, even by Israeli standards, view of the situation. The two officers were impressed by her unapologetic stance towards the news of the Damascus atrocity and how she portrayed Israel as cornered and an innocent party in all the conjecture. She understood, she told the viewers, the depth of distress felt by the Syrian people. Who wouldn't? But there was no confirmation the atrocity was of Israeli origin. And thus, how could the state apologise?

Other channels, Logan noted, were less understanding, both Sky and BBC World News depicting the barbaric event and pointing the finger squarely at Israel as the offending nation.

So far, the Knesset had declined to respond fully to the situation and, save for Olmet's repeated personal denials, appeared unlikely to do so any time soon, as if the legislature had become ossified by the enormity of the event. The only action was the, almost inevitable, wholesale mobilisation of the Israeli Defence Forces, a shrewd and predictable move, given the circumstances.

He consulted his watch. Epstein would be finishing her show soon, and they were waiting, in a café over the road from her studio for the anchorwoman to make her appearance. She would be another five, ten minutes maybe.

'Time to go,' he informed his partner, who pulled some money from her purse and placed it on the table.

They headed for the car.

'You okay?' he asked Murtagh as he unlocked the BMW and climbed in.

Murtagh slipped in beside him, and it was a couple of seconds before she smiled weakly at him. 'Yeah, I'll be fine,' she advised him. 'I'm just worried about all this.' She waved her hand in the air, in desultory fashion, half embracing the outside world. 'It's completely mental. A nuke?' she finished lamely.

Logan digested her words. 'Yeah, it is pretty scary. The loss of those aircraft isn't unrelated either. Three military planes lost on one night would be coincidence enough; that they were lost after that missile struck is just too much unhappy coincidence.'

'Whoever is behind this doesn't give a rat's ass about consequences; that's for sure.'

The Brit made to reply, but at that moment, he nudged Murtagh and pointed. A white F-Type coupe had just pulled out of the studio's parking facility and was travelling away from them. Logan pulled into the traffic and followed a respectable distance behind. 'You got everything we need?' he asked as he concentrated to keep the coupe in sight ahead.

'Yes, everything,' Murtagh responded, 'to put a stop to this little show.'

'What do you need, General?'

President Carlisle was addressing her commander at Diego Garcia by secure satellite phone. Her team waited on her words as she sought the general's situational assessment. In command of squadrons of B52 and a detachment of B2s on exercise, as well as fighters and tankers, General Stuart Fletcher had just about everything he needed for a strategic response, should one be necessary. It was clear the man was cautious, placing emphasis on navy colleagues to project incisive force into the area.

'Ma'am, we just don't know how anybody would react now to overflight. This is a game changer.'

'Stu, this is Bill Foreman here. I understand your hesitance, but we're hearing that Russia is mobilising its Black Sea Fleet and has put strategic facilities on standby.'

'Hi, Bill. Good to hear from you. Been a while. I know. And we're getting some movement in the Indian Ocean from the Chinese. My concern is escalation. Currently we have a one-sided argument in the Middle East. It could get out of control if we flex our muscles is all I'm saying.'

Carlisle leaned forward, a gesture to the office alone. 'General, don't you think this is escalation enough? My God, somebody just nuked a sovereign state.'

'One we're in a state of phoney war with, ma'am.'

'Well, justification enough then.' Carlisle reacted sourly.

'Madam President, if I may?'

She turned to the latest voice. Admiral John Burke, her chief of the defence staff stared expectantly at her. He motioned for her to mute the call. She complied. 'What, John?'

'Fletcher is a good man, but you're asking the impossible of him. He's given you his report, but he's not going to make the decision for you.'

Carlisle leaned back in her chair, knowing what was coming and uneasy all the same. 'Go on.'

'Whether Binyamin Olmet admits it or not, Israel has effectively nuked another state and brought the world to the brink of nuclear catastrophe.' Even as he spoke the words, Burke was considering the fact that they'd always thought it would be Russia, China, or some breakaway group with a dirty bomb—not Israel. 'People are scared, and this is the time for us to be strong and to be the policeman that we always told the world we would be. You have to raise our readiness to DEFCON 2.'

'Shit, John, you want to place our finger on the trigger? For Israel?'

Foreman's face was a picture, Carlisle decided as she processed what Burke was saying. And maybe it was the right thing to do. What if Russia or China decided to teach Israel a lesson? She said nothing, waiting for Burke to continue.

'DEFCON 2 is proportionate, we've been there before. Madam President, when that's done, call a special sitting of the Security Council and demand that Israel is present to explain itself. At that time, you can place the Jerusalem Accord fairly and squarely back on the table. Given the situation, they are not going to be able to back out of it this time.'

Carlisle let the words roll round her mind, slowly nodding as she saw the sense of Burke's words.

'Okay, John, I like what you're saying. All except DEFCON 2. At this stage, it could look like provocation to Moscow and Beijing. I'm putting our forces on DEFCON 3. Does anybody else have anything to say? Any other options? Warren, Bill, what about you?'

The director of National Intelligence shook his head. 'I think you've struck the right balance.'

Mitchell coughed. 'Madam President, while I concur with what you've said, I think we need to raise our readiness with the Fifth Fleet. They're ideally placed to react to any threat posed in the Middle East, without escalating conflict wider. If we know what is happening in the damned country, we can be more precise in our response. What of our assets out there?' He addressed his question to Foreman, who shrugged.

'It's difficult to say at the moment, but they're all we have right now. The Israelis have taken out or suppressed our drones. We're currently in a stand-off.'

Mitchell snorted. 'Then we ramp it up,' he implored his commander in chief. 'We need to regain control in the Middle East before Russia or, worse, China does it for us.'

Of course, he was right, Carlisle decided. They needed to be 'eyes on' with the Israelis—and the Syrians, the Iranians, the Palestinians. It was difficult to know where to draw a line.

'Very well, Warren. That's a sound a proposition. Expedite it.' Carlisle lifted her phone. 'Carol, get Secretary General Oshikuro on the line for me.' She replaced the receiver. 'We convene the Security Council without delay, and we make goddamned sure Olmet is in the country by tomorrow morning at the latest to start answering some questions. Goddamn the man!' Carlisle rose and stopped, addressing the table. 'Ladies and gentlemen, we have work to do.' She swept her papers together and then looked back at her advisors. 'Let's trust the Russians and the Chinese are equally restrained.'

303

Admiral Viktor Timoshenko surveyed the fleet from his vantage point on the bridge of the *Moskva*, the Russian Navy's latest and biggest aircraft carrier. He was a proud man, a strong man, steeped in Russian tradition and patriotism, but even he was shaken by this latest turn in world politics. To think a state would launch an attack against another with such a terrifying weapon didn't bear thinking about, but it had occurred.

It would be a time again of hiding Jewish backgrounds, culture, all because one person needed to make a point. Timoshenko considered his heritage, the hard-fought battles to preserve their Jewishness through all the purges and pogroms. All for some crazy fucking Israeli to do this.

And what next?

He looked at his idev, as if the thing were a poisoned chalice, something to be discarded, thrown in the sea, lest it infect its owner. Yet it already had. The president had sent his demand and the Black Sea Fleet, restored to its former glory since the Ukrainian debacle, was to steam to the Mediterranean and protect Russian interests, discover who the perpetrator was, and dispense justice. War was only the tap of an icon away as Russia ranged its forces in preparation and the old enemy did the same.

The age of mutually assured destruction had been washed away once with the end of the Cold War, but the tide had very definitely borne it back to shore. And this war was likely to be very much hotter.

44

Ramallah was different. He couldn't put his finger on it, but Jamal knew something different was happening. He could see the people staring at his entourage, wondering at the health of their leader. He wondered that himself.

'Mr President, we're here.' His bodyguard glanced over the back of the seat and smiled.

Al-Umari smiled back, though he didn't feel confident. Confidence was a valuable asset he'd have to reacquire over the coming weeks.

The armoured Mercedes came to a halt, and security bustled around the vehicle. Within minutes, he was safely ensconced in his office. Al-Umari sat in his chair, now unfamiliar to him, and gazed through the window.

Everything seemed pointless and dirtied. He'd lost his closest friend and confidante in the attack. Most of his advisers had deserted him in the aftermath. What was left?

'Mr President. Mr Qureshi wishes to speak with you.'

Al-Umari grimaced. This might tell him just what was left to him—if he was lucky. 'Push his call to my device,' he advised his aide.

An icon blinked on his idev, and al-Umari swiped it into the centre of the device. Qureshi's face swam into view. 'Mohammed! To what do I owe this pleasure?' Despite his bonhomie, both men knew it was just show.

Qureshi's swarthy complexion glistened in the sunlight streaming in his office window. He looked like he'd just had a workout or sex. Al-Umari was unsure which and didn't want to know. The mayor's gruff, abrasive tone grated his nerves.

'I call to welcome you home, Jamal.' Was there a hint of hatred in that statement? 'It is good to see you up and about.'

Al-Umari doubted that but was determined to keep up the semblance of politeness. 'Thank you, Mr Mayor. It is unfortunate that I have not had time until now to congratulate you on your success in the elections for Jerusalem's new mayor.'

Qureshi's grunt announced the volumes his words served only to underline. 'It is time Arabs were given equal status in the city.'

'We can thank the Americans for that,' Al-Umari replied quietly, as if he didn't wish for his words to be heard.

'We can thank the Palestinian people—for their tenacity and their belief, Jamal. That is all. But enough of that. There are more important matters to discuss.' Clearly Qureshi had an opinion on his ability and naivety, concluded al-Umari, that wouldn't be discussed further here.

'You speak of Damascus?'

'You saw?

'Yes.'

'Damn them!' Qureshi looked as if he was about to cry. But al-Umari knew it was a game.

There was no real love lost between the Palestinian and his Arabic neighbours. While many deplored Israel's degrading behaviour of the Palestinian, few rushed to their aid. Conversely, al-Umari believed it very unlikely that the attack had been sanctioned by the Israeli government. What would they gain? he asked the Jerusalem mayor.

Qureshi sighed, as if he was addressing a backward child. 'They are not interested in the Syrians any more than they are interested in us. This was done, not to unite Arabs or to stall the peace talks. There is a greater motive behind this. The only thing we agree on is that this was nothing to do with the Jewish government. Something else, something much darker is behind this.'

'I will not believe it, Mohammed!'

'Then you are an even bigger fool than I originally took you for. It would have been better for the world if you had died in that attack!'

Al-Umari bit back the tears that threatened him in his weakened state. 'If I agree with you, then all our work has been for nothing.' His voice was small, shaking. There was nothing left.

'All your work,' Qureshi rebuked him. 'It is time for you to stand down, Jamal. Stand down and let others do the negotiating. There is only one thing these people understand—the sword.'

'W-what do you intend to do?'

'I have a conference call with the ayatollah this afternoon. It is time for us to respond.'

'Do we have any idea what he's doing?'

Galbraith's frustration was evident as Okri shrugged, and Nugent shook her head quickly, a birdlike motion that was over as soon as it began. Despite the ops manager's best hopes, it was not missed by Galbraith.

'So, nobody has anything to tell me? We have an international incident in the Middle East. America and Russia are squaring off. And when I ask about Logan, all you can do is shrug and shake your head.'

The embarrassment was a palpable thing in the room, brooding and foreboding. Nobody spoke. As Galbraith's ire rose, people felt even less like speaking. Eventually, one hand rose tentatively in the air.

'Yes, Derek.' Galbraith always used the Yorkshireman's full first name. 'Come on, speak up.' Her impatience growled across the table.

'Okay. We know Steve is in Tel Aviv. His locator shows us that. Also, he was outside the studio of Channel One when a certain Natalie Epstein was broadcasting. I suspect both he and Brooke believe she has information they can use.'

Galbraith arched an eyebrow. 'That is a big leap, Derek.'

Farrow grinned. 'I know it appears so. However, just thirty minutes ago I received a "flash" from him to say they were following Epstein and intended to have a chat with her when she got home.'

'Well, at least somebody has some idea of what is going on. Do we know if he and Brooke have succeeded?'

'Not yet.'

'Keep me informed then.' Galbraith leaned back in her chair. The whole situation tired her, and she didn't know what she was going to say to the prime minister that would, in any way, convince him that MI6 was on top of things.

Prior to that, she had to talk with her counterpart in the States. This was all completely shit, and she felt at a loss without contact with her best officer. Galbraith only hoped he was in control out there.

Logan kept a couple of cars between himself and Epstein's F-Type, hoping she wasn't going far. If they got on an open road, there was more opportunity of them being spotted, and he didn't fancy his chances against her sports car.

He needn't have worried. Epstein steered in to the Bauhaus area of Tel Aviv. Making a left and right, he followed her to a luxury apartment block, where he pulled into the kerb opposite and looked back.

'Bollocks.'

'What?'

'Gated security and she's parking in an underground car park. We won't know where her flat is.'

Murtagh smiled. 'Don't worry. I have her listing. She's a TV presenter, Steve, not a secret agent.' She showed him the building schematic on her idev—and an apartment number.

Logan's face set grimly. 'Let's pay a visit.'

Black considered the front of the small town's police station. It sat in a line of offices, similar yet different, with barred windows and a law enforcement sign over the heavy double door. He'd toured the block, scanning the approaches and the position of cameras. A municipal station, it was not subject to the rigours of control of a city centre post. The small walled parking area at the back held perhaps three or four police vehicles and maybe as many again of the officers' own vehicles. Watching the place for an hour, he had seen six officers in teams of two come and go. He reckoned there was another two or three inside and some admin.

Even so, there were enough people for him to give what he was going to do some serious consideration.

Logan rang the flat number Murtagh had given him, careful to keep his face partly obscured from the camera. The baseball cap and jacket from the "compliant" pizza delivery man helped him.

'Yes?' It was a young voice, bored and languid.

'Pizza.' Keep it short and simple.

'Okay, come up. Third floor and right out of the lift.'

There was a buzz, and the door opened. Passing through, he dropped the thermal bag in the gap and headed for the lift.

Murtagh followed him in, taking the stairs to the top floor. There, she checked the door numbers and smiled—bingo. The sound of the lift arriving started her, and she ran to the stairwell. She needn't have worried. Logan's shape appeared and passed her through the porthole.

She slipped into the corridor, coming up short as she stared down the barrel of a Glock. Her partner's grin was just visible behind the barrel. 'Where?' His voice was low and sibilant.

Murtagh pointed to the last door on the corridor.

'Let's do it.'

Natalie Epstein stepped from the shower and walked to the lounge. As she towelled herself down, she heard the tap on the door. Her brow furrowed. Who could be at the door? Adam, the concierge? She hadn't been expecting anything, so it was a mystery. Tying the towel round herself, she headed down the corridor calling out, 'Coming,' as she did so.

A cursory glance through the peephole told her there was a man there, very close so she couldn't tell who it was. She turned the latch and dropped the handle.

The door flew inwards with tremendous force, pushing her backwards and into the wall. She gave a small cry, and then the lights went out.

Slowly, oh so slowly, light started to filter back in. The pain didn't take as long to make itself felt. Natalie Epstein lifted her head, wincing at the soreness that accompanied the movement. She lifted a hand to investigate—well she would've had she been able to. Something constricted her, both arms, and she couldn't understand. She tugged at her right arm; it remained stubbornly fixed behind her.

'Easy.'

The voice came from one of two figures stood before her. He was slightly more than average height; that was all she could tell, given the light was behind him and the blinds were drawn. She tugged again, and the other person, a woman, laid a hand on her shoulder.

'Natalie?'

The reporter turned back to the man.

'Natalie, we don't have much time for this. We have somewhere else to be, so we'll be quick.'

'I don't have any cash on me.'

'That's okay, this isn't a robbery, though any you have in your purse will be welcome. I need something else from you.' He moved his hand, and Epstein glimpsed the gun, with silencer, for the first time. She swallowed.

'W-what are you after?'

'Information.'

Her eyes were uncomprehending, and Logan allowed her bewilderment to continue in silence—it helped.

'So, Natalie,' the man began eventually, but Epstein could concentrate only on the silenced gun, 'Quite a little piece this morning about Damascus.'

'What ... do you mean?' Her voice was small and lost.

'Railing against the Arab countries, suggesting that whoever had detonated the device was a hero for the Jewish people.' He paused. 'Doesn't it strike you that the ends don't justify the means here?'

Her brow darkened, even in the half-light. 'The fucking Arabs needed a lesson. They got one.'

Logan flicked a look to Murtagh, who raised an eyebrow fleetingly. 'Erudite. Anything further to say about that?'

Epstein glared at her.

'Well, okay. We're not here for that particular problem anyway. We've more pressing issues.'

'I don't know anything.'

'We think you do. You're going to tell us what we need to know, and fast. The first question is this. Who runs the cabal you're part of?'

'W-what cabal.' The hesitation was momentary but there nonetheless. 'What are you talking about?'

Logan nodded, and Murtagh went to the kitchenette, returning with a soaked tea towel. He continued. 'We know you're working with a number of other people to deliver a program of armed action to derail the Jerusalem Accord. So, once more, tell us about this cabal you're part of?'

'I'm not in any—'

Her voice was cut off abruptly as Murtagh packed the sodden towel into the presenter's mouth.

Logan ground the barrel of the silencer into Epstein's right thigh. 'Wrong answer, and I don't have time. Now, do you know who runs the show? Nod for yes; shake for no.'

Epstein's head shook from side to side vigorously, her eyes wide with the terror of what was to come. Logan pulled the gun away. She was telling the truth; after all, the leader would want to stay hidden from the others. However, their goals and objectives wouldn't be different.

'How long has the group been planning the attack?'

Murtagh took the towel from Epstein's mouth.

'Fuck you,' she spat at the Englishman.

'Okay, have it your way.'

The towel went back in, but this time Epstein glared angrily back. *Fucking do it, you shit*, the eyes said.

The soft bark of the automatic was greeted with a spray of blood from the fleshy part of her thigh, and Epstein screamed into the towel, over and over.

'It's just a flesh wound.' Logan ground the words out, his face close to the ashen visage of the Israeli. 'Next time you may not be so lucky,' he warned as he worked the hot muzzle into her left thigh. Epstein moaned again. 'Now, tell me. How long have the seven of you been planning this attack?'

The look in her eyes told him he'd hit the jackpot. 'How long?'

'Eighteen months.' The voice was small, bereft of fight.

'Whose idea was it to use a nuclear weapon? Don't worry about the blood; it'll stop.'

'It hurts, you bastard!'

'It was meant to. Now, you're wasting my time. If you don't want to be crippled for the rest of your life, tell me what I need to know. Whose idea was the nuclear weapon?

'I don't know his name. We don't know each other, and we meet in circumstances that mean we can't recognise each other.'

A sophisticated operation then, which meant government involvement at some level. How else did you organise such a group and launch a military nuclear strike?

'What about Olsen?' Logan pushed the muzzle into the flesh as Epstein hesitated; tears began to flow. 'Stop it. Concentrate. What about Olsen?'

Epstein sniffed. 'Th-that was a later meeting, but it felt like the decision had already been made.'

Logan glanced at Murtagh; interesting comment. 'Okay, what about his family?'

'What do you mean?'

'The attack on Tel Etz—how come Olsen's family don't appear to have been there at the time of the attack?'

Epstein shot a look at Murtagh. 'I don't kn— No! Don't, don't do it!' she shrilled as Logan placed his gun against her kneecap and pulled on the trigger. 'There was one, called Moshe, who said that they'd been kept safe as a device to use on Olsen, either for or against him, depending how he acted.'

'And you don't know where they're being held.'

'We didn't need to know.' She seemed defeated, slow now—probably onset of shock; the wound still bled.

Logan knew he had to act fast before she slipped into unconsciousness. He drew Murtagh close. 'Get me a jug of water, ice cold.'

Murtagh slipped back to the kitchenette and returned as requested.

Logan took the vessel from her. 'Natalie. Natalie!'

The woman looked at him, her eyes heavy, listless. The water hit her full on, and she blustered under its harsh, cold onslaught, whooping in gulps of breath as she fought the watery attack. She blinked, and pure evil glared from her eyes. Logan smiled grimly.

'Natalie. I need you to think real clear now. I want you to tell me anything you remember from your meetings that might help us pinpoint where Moshe was holding them.' He paused. No response. 'It isn't right, you know, what you've all done.' The sigh was filled with exasperation. 'Come on!' He shook her hard, and she cried out.

'I don't know. Fuck you! I don't know!'

'What do you know? Else we might as well finish it here.' The menace in his voice made her blanch. 'How did you communicate? Was there anything that stands out?'

Epstein's head sagged, and for a minute, Logan thought she might have fainted. Then she moaned slightly, 'Moshe.' It was as silent as possible while still being a sound.

'What?'

'Moshe, she said Moshe,' Murtagh told him. She shook Epstein. 'What about Moshe?'

Epstein turned her head slowly, heavily towards the American. 'I think he's Mossad.'

'What makes you think that?' Logan allowed Murtagh to work on her. After all he'd been heavy enough.

'Just what he does. Moshe does all the security and ensures David is protected, so we don't figure who he might be.'

Murtagh glanced across at Logan, her eyes wide with knowledge; he nodded. It was time to go. Epstein could tell them no more.

'Thank you, Natalie, for your help. We have to go now,' he told her before taking the jug back to the sink. He looked round for a clean towel, picked one from a drawer and returned. He bathed the wound and wrapped it with a bandage that Murtagh had brought from the bathroom at his request. Then he raised her gently from the chair and helped her to her bedroom, laying her down on the bed.

'Thank you.' Epstein's tone was sarcastic, despite her pain and shock.

Logan grunted. 'You're not dead, Natalie. That's more than more than two million people can say in Damascus.' He gave her one last look and then headed back to her lounge, looking everywhere.

'What'd you want?'

'Phone,' he told Murtagh abruptly, ignoring the Israeli.

'Here you are.'

Quickly, he phoned 101 for an ambulance, telling them the minimal they needed and turned to Murtagh as he ended the call. 'Time to go,' he advised her.

Murtagh rose and followed him. There was a reluctance in her heart. What she had witnessed was something she'd never expected to see, not from Steve.

They made it uninterrupted to the lobby and, after a moment of surveillance, back to the BMW. Sirens could be heard getting closer, but Logan paid them no heed. Key in the ignition, he started the car and drove sedately away from the kerb.

45

The gate closed slowly as the patrol nudged into the road behind the station. The figure that lounged at the junction 200 metres away knew he had thirty seconds before it was shut.

Time to act.

Black walked quickly, counting the seconds and watching the gate. Keeping in close to the high wall, minimising his exposure to the security camera, the American approached the gate, peered through the gap between it and the wall, saw nobody in the yard, and slipped round the leading edge. Entering, he pulled the gun from his belt.

The yard was as small as he'd figured. Two patrol cars were parked near the rear entrance to the station, and there were three civilian vehicles nearer the gate on his right. To his left was a single-storey building with a set of rollover doors raised, revealing a garage, a vehicle on a ramp. A blank wall stretched towards the station house, its expanse only alleviated by a single heavy metal door and small window with thick reinforced glass. Armoury?

Quickly, Black walked across the compound to the garage, gun held low, double grip, ready to fire or threaten as necessary. He slipped into the dark interior, which was obviously empty. Tools hung from brackets on the wall and pristine Snap-on tool chests stood ready. A bench held power tools while drums of oil and fluids rested along the back wall. Black scanned the far side from his entry point. An office with a window onto the mechanic's bay filled the wall that bordered on what he figured was the armoury. A light was on, and Black thought he saw somebody in there.

He moved towards the window, trying to keep his profile small, until he was able to peer through the glass. A figure, in uniform, was engrossed in a phone conversation. Unfortunately, the figure faced the door and so would be able to react if Black came in. The American considered his options and then moved.

Eli Weinberger placed the phone back on the table and turned to his laptop. He enjoyed his job in the garage, preferring working on vehicles, rather than the hustle and bustle of regular police duties. Despite his national service, which was de rigueur for all Israelis, Eli had no desire for fighting and being macho. He was very proud of the fact that he kept the station at 100 per cent readiness to respond. Weinberger scrolled through the spreadsheet, which showed they were down on a few essentials. He began to fill in the blanks; the door clicked open.

'Morning, Peter. You're late today,' he told the newcomer.

'Oh, I don't think I am.'

The mechanic looked up sharply at the unfamiliar voice and found himself staring, literally down the barrel of a gun. The big man behind it had a determined look on his face.

'Don't move a muscle. Keep your hands on the table where I can see them,' warned the intruder. 'Just answer my questions, succinctly and accurately please.'

Weinberger nodded, and the gunman took a seat where he could also pay attention to the door. He was well trained and sure of himself, so probably special ops. Just one question that he couldn't help asking, 'What the hell are you doing?'

'No questions, just answers. How many people in the station house?'

Weinberger stared at the big man opposite him. 'Twelve,' he responded truculently.

Black smiled slowly. 'Now, that isn't true, is it? There are three civilian vehicles in the car park, and I've seen at least one patrol car leave. There were two officers in that; you're in here. I think there are perhaps four, five tops. I'm presuming there are possibly two admin, so three officers.' Black regarded the man, who blanched. Black grinned. 'Good. Three people. Where's the armoury?'

'In the main block.'

Black laughed. 'You really aren't much good at lying, are you? Your eyes tell me that the armoury is the building next door.'

Weinberger slumped visibly.

'So, do you have keys for it?'

The Israeli nodded mutely.

'Show me.'

Weinberger slowly raised the bunch of keys he kept on a chain from his belt. Black noted the man didn't reach for his sidearm. 'Okay. We'll take a trip in a few minutes. We have a couple of other things to do first.'

'What?'

Black nodded towards Weinberger's pistol. 'Put that on the desk please, nice and slow,' he warned as the Israeli jolted it from its holster. 'Okay. Stand up, come around the desk, and advance slowly.'

Weinberger did as he was told and stopped before the American, who waved his own semi-automatic at the door. 'Now, my friend, we're going to walk through the door and head in a purposeful manner towards your blockhouse and pay them a visit. Quickly now,' he encouraged, aware of his time on site.

Weinberger walked as if in a dream to the door of the block. This wasn't really happening, he told himself.

'Code,' demanded his captor. 'Weinberger punched in the code on the door lock and hesitated, before the muzzle hastened his decision. He snapped the handle down.

This was the hairy moment, Black decided, shoving his captive through the door, following fast on his heels. Black was aware of another figure, surprised by their sudden entrance; he piled forward, driving the Israelis down the corridor and into a semi-open doorway on his right. There were loud exclamations of pain as the two collided with the sturdy door and dropped to the floor.

Black swung into the doorway, looking onto an open office area, quickly appraising the situation. Two uniformed women sat at desks, staring back at him in surprise. A door on the other wall presumably led to the front desk.

'Ah-ah,' Black reproached one of the women with a shake of his head. 'No heroics please.' He stepped over the two in the doorway, still coming around from their impact, moving to a position where he could cover everyone and watch the other door. 'Hands where I can see them.'

One of the women glanced briefly towards the closed door.

'How many through there?' he asked.

Seconds later, he was answered as the door swung open and a man stepped into the room.

'What the f—' was all he managed before he saw Black and the semi-automatic held very expertly and pointing at his head. Slowly the man raised his hands.

'Take a seat with the others,' Black advised him, 'hands where I can see them.'

The man did as bid, all the time scowling at his captor. The mechanic and the other man were slowly rising to their feet, and Black backed away from them, ensuring he had a clean line of sight on all the people in the room.

'Okay, you.' Black pointed at the man he'd felled during his entry. 'You take a chair and sit with your back to Mr Angry there.' He motioned to the desk sergeant, still scowling at him. 'You two ladies do the same, back to back.'

When they'd all complied, Black turned to his original captive. 'Okay, Mr Mechanic, please be good enough to handcuff your colleagues together.' Black waved the gun in the general direction of his prisoners. He threw a roll of duct tape to the man. 'And keep them quiet with this please.' He waited as the man did as bid. When he had completed the task, Black beckoned him over.

'What?' The man's tone was sullen but defeated.

Black looked at him kindly and then, in a single swift movement, brought the butt of his gun down on the man's temple, felling him like a log. There were muffled gasps and growls from the others in the room.

Black smiled. 'He'll be okay, just have a headache when he comes around.'

Kneeling, Black quickly and expertly bound the man's hands with restraint ties lying on a desk and used his belt to bind his legs together. He snapped the key ring from the man's belt loop and grinned again at the others. 'Whose is the Land Cruiser out back?'

Eyes turned to the desk sergeant. Black walked over, positioned himself just out of kicking distance and pressed the barrel of his gun against the man's forehead. 'Don't want to do this, bro,' he told him sincerely. 'But I need your wheels.' Black patted down the man and located the keys, extracting them from a pocket and backing up.

'Y'all have a good day,' he said and moved quickly to the back of the block. Warily, in case the patrol was returning, he moved into the back yard—it was clear. He sprinted to the armoury, entered, and smiled.

He felt a whole lot better now.

Moshe was not looking forward to the next few minutes. Whatever David said, he would be justified in being furious at the turn of events. Shit, so was he, and he had left Ariel, in no uncertain terms, aware of that frustration and anger.

The phone rang again, and Moshe was considering calling back when David's gruff voice sounded from the device. Moshe coughed self-consciously. 'There has been an issue at the plant. I can't tell you over the phone. We need to meet.'

David grunted. 'Usual place. One hour.'

They stood under the harsh late-morning sun, looking out at the city, at the sun gleaming off the golden dome. It reminded them, yet again, why they were doing what they were doing. There was no sense of confidence between them this time; a palpable sense of worry cloaked them. Moshe regarded the older man, aware that his concern was not merely borne from their earlier call. He resisted the urge to ask what was wrong, knowing that David would refuse to say until he had advised him of the need to meet.

'Ariel informs me our guest has escaped.'

Moshe waited as his words carried away, across the sandy hills. David continued to regard his city—his city, damn it! The success of only a short time ago seemed to be slipping through his fingers, and now his team was allowing things to go to shit.

'How long ago?'

Moshe cleared his throat. 'Last night, after the mission.'

'Fuck.' David turned and stared at Moshe for the first time, before sighing heavily. 'That's not the only bad news.'

Moshe raised an eyebrow. But for a while, David refused to speak. When he did, there was weariness to his tone. Moshe listened quietly, patiently waiting for the older man to finish.

'So, Golda has been compromised, do you think?'

David nodded, and Moshe saw he was definitely affected by the idea. By contrast, he had no such connection. 'We have to act.'

The older man stared out over Jerusalem for so long Moshe thought he hadn't heard.

'David, we have—'

'I know,' David responded gruffly. 'Golda is of no further use to us. More importantly, Moshe, I want the two who visited her and that soldier found and disposed of.'

'Okay.'

'Get the unit onto it—now.'

He surveyed the road steadily clearing of traffic ahead of him. He wasn't happy with himself or the situation he, they, had left behind. He felt sullied by his own actions, as if somebody else had inhabited him and driven the beast that had shot Epstein in the leg. It wasn't him—whatever such a statement ever meant. Of more concern now was how Brooke viewed him.

The drive from Epstein's apartment had been silent, Murtagh not wishing to break it for fear of bringing back the ghost of the attack on the Israeli presenter. She could still feel the intensity in Logan as he had brutalised the woman. It made her uncomfortable, even though she knew he had done what was operationally expedient.

Even so.

Her idev chimed, and almost instantaneously, she registered the chiming of Logan's. A priority message. She checked the screen of her device—London. 'Pull over,' she advised.

He indicated, taking the first off-ramp and pulling to the verge; he looked at her.

'Black has contacted London and requested we join him. You want to know where?' Murtagh looked across at him, deep in thought, staring, without seeing, through the windscreen.

He turned, saw the eyes, which said what her voice could, would, not. He clenched the steering wheel. 'I'm sorry.'

'She didn't give many options. I know why you did what you did.'

'Doesn't make me feel any better.'

'You need to get that shit out of your head right now, Steve. This may not be war, but it's pretty damn close. There's no time for being introspective and maudlin.' She paused. 'So, are we going to meet John?'

'Patch his location through to the satnav.' He pulled the car back on to the road and headed back to the highway.

Black was waiting on wasteland to the south of the town when Logan and Murtagh caught up with him. He had two large canvas bags, on one of which he sat, a big grin cracking his face as he saw the BMW heading towards him.

As he brought the vehicle to a stop, Logan allowed himself a smile of his own at the sight of his friend. It was good to see the man well. He stopped the car, got out, and walked over to the SEAL, beaten to it by Murtagh but not caring as he saw the two embrace. Murtagh stepped back, and Black nodded at Logan, who returned the gesture.

'How you doing?'

Black grinned. 'Not bad. Thanks, fella. You?'

A moment's consideration. 'I've been better, but it's good seeing your ugly mug. Nice wheels,' he remarked, nodding at the Land Cruiser.

Black grinned but said nothing, asking his own question in response. 'So, what gives?'

Logan and Murtagh glanced at each other. 'Have you heard or seen the news today?'

Black shook his head, staring quizzically at the others in turn.

'There was an attack,' Murtagh's voice was small. 'On Syria, Damascus.'

Black frowned. 'What sort of attack?'

Logan drew a breath. 'Nuclear.'

'Fuck!' Silence, underlined by the distant sound of traffic, descended over them. 'Do we know who did it?'

'Israeli jets dropped the weapon. We … spoke … to a presenter in Tel Aviv who confirmed there is a covert cabal organising action against the accord. This, I think, is just the first attack.'

The SEAL sat back on his bag, drawing a weary hand over his brow. It all seemed too much. 'Fuck. What now?'

Looking round him, Logan recognised the bright day, people still going about their business as if nothing had happened, as if for the first time. Maybe, in a hundred years, who'd care about this moment? No matter; the here and now was the important thing. He sat next to Black.

'What we do now is find the bastards running this show and bring them to justice.'

'Amen to that, bro.'

'First off, we need to find a secure location to contact London.'

'Let's get to it.'

46

Carlisle took the dais at the United Nations. It was a full assembly, the mood grave, the chamber silent for a change—the gravity of the situation not lost on anyone. Almost directly opposite her was the Israeli delegation, still missing the imposing figure of Prime Minister Binyamin Olmet and his entourage. Carlisle wondered if she felt disappointed by his absence. Probably. Certainly not surprised. He would want to keep his exposure to the world's opprobrium to a minimum.

Even so, he was running behind the schedule he had advised her over the phone the previous day, and she felt real pissy with him. She looked over at the secretary general, impassive as he waited for the Israeli prime minister's arrival; he ignored her enquiring glance.

Shit! Are you president of the most powerful country on Earth or not? She resented the delay and swore to get payback on the sonofabitch.

The doors opened, and Secret Service personnel moved in quickly, ensuring the dignitary they were escorting was safe and beyond attack. Appropriate, Carlisle decided, as she took in the bulky frame of Prime Minister Olmet. He and his entourage made their way quickly to the Israeli table and sat, without even a glance at the secretary general. Rikyu Oshikuro was clearly not impressed by the snub.

Olmet and his entourage continued to converse, seemingly oblivious to the room around them.

'Mr Olmet, please.' The secretary general's low measured tone sounded across the auditorium, stopping everyone.

Olmet turned, face stoical.

'Could we have your attention please?' Oshikuro raised an eyebrow to reinforce his point.

Olmet nodded silently.

'Thank you,' Oshikuro told him, before signalling to Carlisle.

The president of the United States of America nodded her thanks and stood to address the audience. 'Secretary General, ladies and gentlemen, two nights ago, an aerial attack unleashed a horror on the world we thought had been buried along with the memories of Hiroshima and Nagasaki. Never before, even at the height of the Cold War, has such a wanton disregard been shown for life.'

Carlisle looked around the hall at the silent assembly. With a start, she noticed everyone was transfixed on her. A lesser person might have faltered, but she had grown in stature since her own brush with danger. She cleared her throat professionally, aware of the expectation in the room.

'There have been many statements, both denying responsibility and of condemnation. But, Mr Secretary, there has been nothing from the cowards who delivered this heinous attack.' She couldn't refrain from staring at Olmet, despite every diplomatic muscle straining in anguish. 'This state of affairs cannot be allowed to continue in any civilised world in which we all want to live. Whoever has committed this crime, and it is a crime, one of the worst kind, must have the sense of morality to stand up and admit to it and face whatever sanction and sentence the world may demand.

'This action has brought the world to the brink of world conflict. Russian forces are already mobilising to protect their assets and interests. The United States is moving forces to the area also to protect our interests but also to work with our colleagues from Russia and China to investigate this incident and to identify the perpetrator.'

She paused just for effect, and this time she was able to resist the urge to point her metaphorical gun down Olmet's throat. 'Make no mistake, we will find the state, and it must be a state that has committed this crime, and bring that state to justice with, or without, the endorsement of this assembly. The United States stands ready to deploy and employ any and all resources necessary to bring the perpetrators to justice. But we understand that it is not for us alone; the whole world is threatened by this event, and someone must be held accountable for it. We request the United Nations take the lead in this situation. We shall do all in our power to comply with, enable, and assist the UN in the fulfilment of that duty.'

Carlisle turned and looked at Oshikuro. 'Mr Secretary,' she said as she stepped from the dais and headed back to her delegation.

The secretary general sat silently for a moment, as was his way. The assembly waited patiently for his deliberation. Slowly, he rose and took the microphone. He was motionless as he stood behind the lectern, his face impassive. But tension was building in the room. A small cough emanated from the secretary general; everyone looked expectantly. Carlisle felt like crossing fingers and toes in attempt to get the result she and her administration so desperately needed.

Oshikuro nodded to Carlisle. 'Thank you, Madam President, for your words.' He coughed again, almost self-consciously, and she felt her heart sink. 'My colleagues, this is, indeed, a most dreadful event and one that affects all our lives. As someone whose parents fortunately survived the horrors of Hiroshima, albeit at great cost, I understand only too well the desire to hunt down and bring to justice those who have perpetrated this act.

'The loss of so many people is to be mourned, and no words can express our shock and dismay at this act. That a nation would stoop to such an act, after so many years of self-control, appears unthinkable. Yet so we must believe.'

A ripple of discomfort sounded through the hall. No one liked to see the slight Japanese so upset, though some wondered if it was merely an act to attract such sympathy. Whichever way, Oshikuro knew that his audience awaited his pronouncement.

'We stand at a crossroads, and we must take a decision that will affect the way in which all countries and all peoples live together from now on.' He cleared his throat, a quick spare sound, which nonetheless echoed in the chamber. 'I shall be calling for the Security Council to sit in extraordinary session tomorrow. Before we move to the next business, I open the floor for other contributors.'

No one moved in the assembly. Carlisle watched the Israelis closely, but they presented a close book. Guilt or ignorance? she wondered. It was difficult to say. Olmet, she noted, steadfastly refused to meet her gaze. No matter; she would get him later.

The day's business went through at a lacklustre pace, delegates evidently preoccupied by the events in Syria.

Carlisle understood only too well how everyone felt. But as the day laboured on, she turned to her aide. 'We need to go, Carol. There's too much to do for tomorrow's Security Council.'

Fleischman nodded and turned to the Secret Service detail, catching the eye of the nearest agent. Fleischman gave the prearranged signal, and instantly the perfectly oiled machine went into action, even before Carlisle was away from her seat. In beautifully choreographed movements, the agents established a phalanx around the president and moved towards the exit.

Outside the building, Carlisle was moved effortlessly towards the Beast. A sound caused her to turn, and her heart sank. The small figure, incongruously wrapped in long black coat, with a firmly planted black homburg signing off the odd garb, was heading towards her. The sound resolved itself into her name and title. With a little sigh, she nodded to her sergeant at arms and came to stop, fixing a smile on her face.

'President Carlisle.' The voice wheezed, masquerading the lilting tone as the figure paused before passing through the cordon.

'Joel, to what do I owe this pleasure?' Of course, Carlisle knew only too well why Joel Wiesenthal was looking to speak to her.

'We need to talk.' The little man appeared pained by Carlisle's feigned naivety. 'You know why.'

Carlisle nodded towards a secluded part of the UN's garden. While her entourage stationed itself on the perimeter, she sat on a bench with Wiesenthal. 'Go on,' she encouraged her companion.

'This situation can't be allowed to carry on. Russia is heading towards the Israeli coast with their biggest warships and plenty of reasons to see Israel fail.'

Carlisle stared at the little Israeli. 'Are … you asking for American help?' Her tone was incredulous, and the man remained silent. Carlisle shook her head. 'You really are something else, you know that, Joel?' When the silence extended, Carlisle continued. 'Somebody,' she checked herself, '*Israel*, has just detonated a nuclear device over the capital city of a sovereign state—'

'There is no evidence it was Israel.' But his tone spoke of defeat.

'Our intelligence shows that three Israeli jets suffered catastrophic crashes on the same night with the loss of all pilots. A little too coincidental, don't you think?'

No response.

'Okay, Joel, so you've been asked by your paymasters back in Israel to apply pressure on the US government to come and strong-arm the Russians into backing away from their interests in the Middle East?'

Looking, Carlisle saw that Wiesenthal appeared waxen, a small man, bereft of emotional content. 'I tell you what we are going to do, Joel. Our ambassador to the UN is going to support a resolution that calls for the Israeli prime minister to be arrested for genocide and crimes against humanity. An international warrant will be issued by the International Court of Justice, so you may want to tell him to get home quickly.' Her tone was hard. 'Good day, Joel. Next time I'll call you.'

With a quick movement of the hand, she called her detail around her again, and they continued onto the Beast, leaving the little Israeli broken.

Timoshenko stared from the bridge of the *Moskva*, barely aware of the orchestrated movements of the crew around him. All his concentration was on the telephone call he had just concluded, with the president of Russia, no less. His orders had been very direct, to the point, with no equivocation. He felt a little sick as he continued to mull over the words that made him responsible for what was to come next.

'Coffee?'

Timoshenko stirred from his reverie and looked up; his executive officer was stood there, two mugs in hand and his usual lopsided smile. The admiral relieved Commander Vassily Antonov of one drink and drew on the dark liquid; it felt good but did little to help him.

'So, you have our orders?'

Timoshenko looked over the rim of the cup at the younger officer. 'I do.'

The other continued to stare. 'Well?'

Timoshenko rose from his chair and made his way back to his ready room, beckoning his XO to follow him.

Antonov sat as his superior went to the room's sideboard and took out a bottle of vodka and two glasses. Timoshenko poured drinks and pushed one to the XO. He hesitated and then took the glass, trying to read the other's face before he downed the clear liquid. He waited as Timoshenko sat on the other side of the desk and savoured his vodka. The admiral filled the glasses again, raising his to his eyes and staring into the clear liquid. Antonov waited patiently.

'Vassily, this vodka looks like water; it tastes like water. And yet it rots the liver, and we Russians love it.'

Be patient, Vassily.

'Our leader spoke carefully and calmly about the situation of Syria and Israel. He expressed concern for the loss of life in Damascus and the graveness of a situation that could leave a huge imbalance in power across the Middle East. He spoke of the abhorrence of nuclear weapons and the need to redress the vacuum the attack on Syria has created.' Timoshenko paused and drained the vodka, licking the last drops from his thick lips.

'Vassily, you might think our immediate task is to wait, assess, and see what plays out in the cauldron. But no. What was most clear was the subtext.' More vodka. 'Our illustrious leader sees the *Moskva* and her retinue as the javelin demonstrating Russia's intent.' When Antonov remained silent, Timoshenko continued. 'It is appropriate, Viktor, for you to respond to the requests of our allies in the region and to ensure that balance is brought to the Middle East.' Timoshenko brooded.

'And we are—'

'Going to war, my friend, going to war.' Another drink found its way between the admiral's lips. 'Vassily, get Andropov from the *Zhukov* on the phone. We have much to prepare.'

The screen didn't lie. That in itself was an issue, Carlisle told herself, for it spoke of a greater game about to be played out. The calling of the Security Council would do absolutely nothing to change the play Russia was now committed to.

What did Glazunov expect from America? Did he expect anything? Who was she kidding? Glazunov always expected something, engineered the situation. But as she looked at the satellite image of the Russian missile cruiser *Zhukov* with two of its forward silos open, she had to wonder what game he was playing.

She passed the idev to Warren Mitchell, who stared impassively at the image. 'What do you think he's doing, Warren?'

Mitchell placed the device on the Resolution desk and leaned back in a mahogany armchair. 'Glazunov is going to balance the odds in the region. He'll attack Tel Aviv. It holds the real power in the country, a powerful symbol of Israel's sway in the region.'

Carlisle steepled her fingers. 'How?'

'Conventional. For now.'

Swivelling her chair, Carlisle looked across the White House lawn. Sunlight glinted off traffic on Pennsylvania Avenue as people began the commute home. Everything seemed so peaceful to the millions of Americans unconcerned with the political world situation. Yet, here she was, with her advisors, trying to avert an international crisis—everyday work.

She turned back.

'Okay. Warren, I need options before tomorrow—all available ones. If we're going to halt this thing, let's get started.'

Mitchell nodded briefly.

'What do you want to tell the media?'

Carlisle looked at Sharone Caulfield, her press secretary. Sharone was relatively new, previously a section editor on *The Washington Post* and *The New York Times*, who added glamour to the White House team. Anyone who believed the five foot ten leggy blonde with piercing grey eyes was all looks and no brains had been forced to revise his or her view very quickly after her first press conference, where she had excoriated an ex-colleague who had attempted to challenge her credentials for the post. He'd been quickly replaced. Carlisle liked her stance and confided regularly with the thirty-year-old.

'Let's keep things low-key for now, Sharone. Tell them we're looking at all possibilities and keeping all options open.'

'Okay.' Pause. 'It may not be enough.'

'I expect you to make it enough. Don't let me down, Sharone. Okay, let's get moving people.'

The lights of Tel Aviv blazed and winked in the night sky as the three waited quietly in the BMW. Silence wrapped round them. Logan was intent only on the road, which passed them by like a slow-moving river of late-night traffic. On the back seat, Black snored quietly and shuffled. Murtagh tried to relax, but the loitering dragged on her nerves.

She glanced at Logan, opened her mouth, closed it, opened it again, and sighed.

'You gonna keep doing that?' He continued to stare out the window.

'Sorry.'

Quiet descended once more, broken only by the low susurration from behind them. She took in the view from the windscreen—still dark and still full of twinkling lights, still empty of meaning.

'If you're going to keep sighing and fidgeting, it's gonna be a really long night.' Logan's hand rested briefly on her leg, and she smiled.

'I'm sorry. I can't help it. This waiting game is killing me. It seems so futile.'

He didn't look, didn't remove his hand. 'You know as well as I that sometimes you have to be patient. This is one of those times.'

'Which wouldn't be so bad if a couple million people hadn't just been obliterated.'

'I know. Just a little longer.'

As if his words had cued the event, a car slowed to a silent halt. Electric cars—Logan smiled—every spy's dream vehicle. Its occupant rolled the window down. He could make out the vague outline of a woman in the dark, confirmed by the slim hand and forearm that emerged from the shadows. The hand held an A4 envelope, which appeared to contain very little. Lowering his window, he reached out and took the envelope. 'All here?' The question seemed loud and intrusive in the night air.

Penny Lane held the envelope a little longer. 'Yes, everything you asked for,' she confirmed.

Passing it to Murtagh, he returned his attention to Lane. 'Anything else?'

Lane considered the request, for a moment deliberately, silently, misinterpreting the officer and then, 'There is some talk of a police station being attacked by unknown assailants. It's been linked to the Palestinian attack on Perez.'

Logan grunted. 'I'm sure Mr Black won't be too worried for the moment about that conflation.'

'No. However, it does muddy the waters for us.'

Yes, it does, he concurred silently. 'What about our Shin Bet colleagues?'

There was a moment of silence in the dark. 'Nothing official.'

'Cover-up?'

'Possibly.'

'Unofficially?'

'Shin Bet is furious with the situation. The Mossad keeps denying it had anything to do with the death of the two officers. but Avi Brun,, head of Shin Bet, is having nothing of it.'

'So, what do you think he'll do?'

Another dark pause.

'We believe he's sanctioned a covert operation against Mossad. There's nothing firm at the moment, but we've noted significant movements by Shin Bet assets across Tel Aviv and reports from Jerusalem.'

Logan considered Lane's words. If that was the case, was it a situation they could prosper from?

'Possibly,' she replied after a moment's consideration of is question. 'How were you thinking?'

The MI6 officer chewed his lip a moment. 'We need allies who know the landscape, ones who are capable of seeing where this madness is leading. If Shin Bet is going up against Mossad, let's give them something that makes it worth their while.' He paused. 'Do any of your contacts profess any support for the accord?'

Lane nodded.

Logan continued. 'This is what you do then.'

Moshe waited, as it seemed he was increasingly required to do, as the old man processed the information he had presented. This was getting embarrassing and dangerous, and it seemed, inevitably, was only going to get worse. He coughed.

David seemed to start at the interruption to his reverie. 'What?' he demanded testily.

'I'm sorry. We need to make a decision.'

'I'm very well aware of that,' came the abrupt response. 'What do you think I'm doing?'

Good question. 'If Shin Bet is allowed to investigate what Mossad assets have been engaged in, we're as good as dead.'

'We dealt with them before; we'll deal with them again.'

'That is why we have this problem now. We need a different approach.'

'And what do you suggest?' David obviously found it difficult to keep the sneer from his tone.

Moshe kept his cool. Now wasn't the time to challenge. 'You need to speak with Brun, threaten to make his unilateral action public if he doesn't back off. You know the public will be against Mossad being investigated. We still have momentum.'

David grunted. Moshe was right. Brun would, probably, back off in a straight fight over this situation. And yet … and yet there was the matter of Damascus. The global backlash was more violent than he had supposed possible. Their next move would intensify, solidify that. Israel would stand alone once more. He straightened and, for the first time this night, turned to address his lieutenant. 'I will speak with Brun, help him see the error of his ways. You will accelerate our programme. Our next package must be ready for delivery in forty-eight hours.'

Moshe arched an eyebrow. 'What if we're not ready?'

David merely glared at his subordinate. 'Make us ready.'

Carlisle considered the message scrolling up the screen of her idev. The intelligence it imparted disturbed her deeply. Her ambassador to the UN Security Council reported that Russia had trumped the United States by stating publicly they would respond aggressively to any further Israeli hostilities in the area. China had merely abstained from the proceedings, but NSA surveillance indicated the Chinese were building up a presence near the Strait of Hormuz. Links with Iran were well known, and if anywhere was to be struck by the Israelis, there was as likely a target as any.

As if all that news were not bad enough, humint from Tel Aviv and Jerusalem was indicating splits and confusion within both the Jewish and Palestinian camps. There was a genuine fear and bewilderment on the part of the Israeli administration at the attack on Damascus, though officially they refused to comment. That would require a resolution.

And then there were the Palestinians. Her opposite number, al-Umari was suffering physically and psychologically from attacks launched by the vociferous mayor of Jerusalem. Intel indicated that he was about to enter negotiations with Iran. That would only exacerbate the situation, providing the Israeli administration the fuel to pour on a fire they may, or may not, have started. It was all a complete shitstorm.

Her device chimed. 'Hello?'

'NSA Director Eissenegger to see you, ma'am'

'Send him in please.'

Moments later, Chas Eissenegger strode urgently into the Oval Office.

'Morning, Chas, to what do I owe this pleasure?'

The director spread his device before the president. 'We're back in touch with Black.'

Carlisle resisted the urge to grin stupidly. It was, after all, only something very small—but it gave her hope. 'Is he alone?'

'No.' Eissenegger had no such reserve as he allowed a big smile to dominate his visage. 'Murtagh and the Brit are with him.'

Carlisle relaxed back into her chair, a weight lifted from her shoulders seemingly. 'Do we know what they're up to?'

He shook his head. 'They're maintaining radio silence. We know only through our Joint Intelligence Unit in Tel Aviv. An MI6 officer from there made contact with them in the early hours.'

Carlisle nodded. 'Good! About time we had some positive news. How does that sit us with the Russians?'

'Not good. The Russians are developing a firing solution on Tel Aviv as their response to Damascus. We believe they will commit in the morning.'

'How much time do we have?'

'Hours, at most.'

Carlisle slumped. 'Okay. Are the chiefs of staff at the Pentagon?'

Eissenegger nodded.

'Let's get over there. Make sure Admiral Shenley is on the line and tell him he has to match the Russians. If they threaten to launch against Israel, I want an immediate response against the vessel that initiates the attack.'

'Of course, Madam President.' Her director headed for the door.

'And, Chas?'

The NSA director turned.

'We need to get this right. Let's not fuck up.'

47

Dawn's half-light stained the sky as the world marched resolutely on its course, oblivious to the stupidity of humanity. Logan wondered what it would be like if it didn't as he pulled the car off the road just before the brow of the hill and killed the engine.

Beside him, Murtagh dozed fitfully, as she had for the last half hour. As the silence encroached, she stirred and stretched.

'Welcome back to the land of the living,' he told her.

In the back, Black had risen from his slumbers, his face appearing between the seats. 'Where are we?' he asked blearily.

'At our destination,' Logan told him.

'Nice.' Black sat back and glanced from side to side at the half-lit landscape. 'Where is it?'

'Over the hill is the farm owned by the mother and father of Judith Olsen. They think their daughter's dead, as does Olsen himself. We've some news for them.'

'Good news, I hope.'

'Better than it was, for sure.'

'But we have to watch out for the old man,' Murtagh warned. 'He likes his guns.'

'Uh-huh. What are we expecting to happen when we've told them this "better" news?'

The pause threatened pregnancy. 'Good question. Perhaps to start asking some difficult ones.'

'Risky strategy,' opined Black.

'That's what I told him,' Murtagh advised the SEAL.

'So, it's not all that we're doing out here then?'

Logan stared through the windscreen, unresponsive but mulling over Black's question in his mind. What did he tell them about what he'd discovered? Nothing. After all, all he had were rumours. They could be nothing.

'It's enough for now. We have to start somewhere.'

Black shrugged in the darkness. 'Okay. No time like the present. Let's get on with this.'

Binyamin Olmet gripped the coffee cup as though his life depended on it. Perhaps it did. He couldn't tell anymore what was important or not. His mind still reeled with the shock of the attack on Damascus. As a hard-line Israeli, he did not view Arabs as friends. But even he recoiled at the vicious apocalyptic terror that had been released across the northern border.

His eyes scanned the report on his idev. Thankfully, his advisers were able to tell him that the fallout from the attack was likely to be driven east on the prevailing winds, sparing the Lebanon, Jordan, Israeli, and the wider Mediterranean coast. Small comfort to the millions dead or dying in the Syrian capital, now left rudderless for the second time in a decade. Turkey, too, was incandescent with rage as it struggled to assess the damage along its eastern border.

Colonel Joshua Moran, his military aide, cast a new flash signal to Olmet, this one apprising him of the situation with the Russians, whose navy had taken up station off the Israeli coast. Indications were they were about to attack, and all forces were on standby to retaliate. Olmet drew a hand wearily across his face. This wasn't going to be like Yom Kippur or '76 he told himself. No, defeating the Russians in their ships in a lightning strike was not an option, lest he brought the full brunt of the Russian military down on him.

What he needed right now was someone, a scapegoat, to string up by the balls for all the world to see. Olmet continued reading the report, stopped, and then continued reading, more slowly. What was this?

He pulled up the dialler on his idev and dropped the ID for the head of Mossad into it. Halfin's face appeared on the screen.

'Yes, Mr Prime Minister.'

'The report from your operatives. It says that there was some sort of isotope leaching off the device that was dropped—that it was salted with a material to prevent access to the area of the detonation. It effectively makes it an area denial weapon.'

Halfin considered the words. 'I'm only just reading the report, Mr Prime Minister. Our teams only just filed it. Let me go away and do some digging.'

'Make it quick, Peter. We don't have much time before the Russians decide to act. I need to know who sanctioned this attack and bring them before the world.'

'Yes, Mr Prime Minister.'

The screen went blank, and Olmet stared at it for a little while before activating the dialler again. This time he called Daniel Brun, head of Shin Bet.

Something wasn't right, and he was determined to sort it before Israel got wiped from the face of the earth.

Admiral Timoshenko folded his idev, placing it on the table before him. Today was a day of action; President Glazunov had decreed it. No more prevarication, no more bullshit, just honest to goodness action, like the leader was fond of. This, he had been assured, was a glorious time for Russia, a time of ascendancy, when the Motherland would be revered, and feared, anew.

Political rhetoric but dangerous all the same. Glazunov loved his reputation as a man of action, loved posing for the cameras for the world to see his muscles. He'd even threatened to fly out to the *Moskva* and celebrate. Timoshenko had dissuaded him of such a move in a conflict zone.

But this?

The sigh soothed his troubled emotions. He allowed another one before he picked up his idev again and looked through the orders of the day. *Zhukov* was in position, four missiles targeting Tel Aviv, Haifa, Dimona, and Bethlehem. They were what Glazunov wanted, to make an example of the Israelis. Timoshenko disagreed, with the exception of Dimona; that was the only legitimate target on the list.

What to do?

He called his XO. 'Antonov, bring me a listing of all known Israeli airbases.'

'At once, Admiral.'

Antonov was a good man, questioning when it was appropriate, doing when it was necessary. But what would he make of his request? He was, after all, a party man, and what Timoshenko had asked for clearly pointed to a betrayal of orders. It was a chance he would have to take, to put the brakes on this madness.

Carl Shenley, Timoshenko's US opposite number, regarded the surreal calmness of the Mediterranean with his counterpart's same reverie. The world was heading for disaster, and someone hadn't checked the brakes. Fortunately, Carlisle was proving to be of stern stuff, and he was quietly optimistic of her responses. A career sailor, Shenley had risen through the ranks, spending a tour with the Marines on his way to the top. Respected for his hard but fair approach, Shenley would have been followed into the jaws of hell by his men, if need be.

It wasn't hell they were facing today, but close enough, he figured as the latest intel came in over his idev. In the Med, several hundred miles away, the Russians were preparing to blitz the Israelis while, to the south, in the Red Sea, the Chinese were just biding their time. Time to sort some shit out.

'XO, my cabin. Call CAG too please.'

Lieutenant Commander William Nelson, looked round and nodded, leaving orders with the lieutenant by his shoulder.

In Shenley's cabin, the admiral poured coffee for both of them, passing a cup to Nelson. The other sat and drew on the liquid, waiting for Shenley to speak.

'What's the latest on the Russians?'

'The *Zhukov* has firing resolutions on four number targets in Israel. They can launch at any time.'

Shenley had a habit of slurping his coffee, which he did now, much to Nelson's annoyance. He clunked the mug on his desk, coffee sloshing down the sides. 'Do we have a bead on the *Zhukov*?'

Before Nelson could answer, there was a rap of knuckles on the cabin door.

'Come.' The door groaned open, revealing Commander Air Group Lisa Crudhoe. Young, she was twenty-seven, and one of the best CAGs he'd worked with, Crudhoe was a faultless pilot and a good crew manager. Shenley trusted her implicitly.

'Admiral. What gives?'

'We're discussing the *Zhukov*. Can you provide a sitrep?'

'Okay. The *Bradley* has two cruise missiles locked on the Russian. Should she look to launch, we can take her out. We have the other assets in the fleet under surveillance, with two AWACS patrolling a hundred miles out.'

Shenley grunted. 'What about electronics? Are we secure? I'm always nervous when we have Russians on one side and the Chinese on the other.'

Nelson nodded. 'Everything is battened down.' He glanced at Crudhoe. 'We got two Growlers cruising above the group, running interference. Our electronics team on the *Greenleigh* are running countermeasures and surveillance. No way anyone can jump us.'

'Don't say things like that,' Shenley warned Nelson. 'It's too easy to think it's okay to bend over. Before you know it, somebody has given you a good hard shafting.' He leaned forward. 'We can't afford to fuck up. Go get me intel on the *Zhukov* and find me a way of getting in touch with Timoshenko. Mebbe I can talk some sense into the guy.'

'Sure thing, sir.'

Shenley watched his exec leave the cabin, yawned, and relaxed in the chair. Fuck, but everything was fucked up right now! Time to sort out the men from the boys. He turned to Crudhoe 'CAG, we need to step up our CAPs and I want two Lightnings on Quick Alert Five. It's looking more like the Russians will try to launch against Israel.'

'We can do that. Boomer and Stingray will be returning as soon as Chaser and Luckyman are on station. We can get Avenger and Starman up too. They were due to be on the Alert Five, but I can push Happy and Bullet into that post if you want? We have UAVs linked with the CAP at two hundred miles separation, forming our outer cordon.'

'Sounds good. Do it. What about our air-sea options?'

'Everything is ready to support the *Bradley* and *Bonhomie* if necessary. We're coordinating with Marine Corps Squadron VMCA-251.'

Shenley nodded. 'Good. Get to it.'

Crudhoe thought it through. 'Are you giving an order to shoot down any Russian plane that tries to penetrate our airspace?'

'Yes I am. And not just Russian. Anything that compromises the security of the battle group is to be denied the opportunity. I trust it won't come to that. But in case it does, you are cleared to engage.' Shenley caught the look on Crudhoe's face. 'This is a presidential directive.'

'Let me see the directive.'

Shenley pushed it to her idev, and Crudhoe read through it, nodding. 'Okay. I'll get on it.'

After she'd left, Shenley stood and peered through the porthole at the blue Mediterranean across which his flotilla of ships was now pushing. He really did hope it wouldn't come to a fist fight, but the signs were increasing that it would. He rang up to the bridge.

'Aye, sir,' came the response.

'Inform the group we're increasing to flank. I want us within fifty miles of the Russians as soon as practical.'

'Aye, sir. Flank speed, the group.'

Trouble was coming, and Shenley was determined his group would be ready for the fight.

Driving down Chaim Levanon Street, one could be forgiven for thinking the buildings between it and the Ayalon Freeway were business or government infrastructure park. That the Israeli Security Agency, or Shin Bet as it was more widely known, was housed in a half mile of offices near the bus station was a well-kept secret, one Avi Brun, its current head, maintained scrupulously in the face of liberal demands for open government. Knowing where your enemy was one thing; taking advantage of a freedom of information-derived 'open day', was another. Not without reason was the agency's motto 'the unseen shield'.

Yet, now, it seemed, the enemy was much closer to home, if the tip-off was to be believed. Brun struggled to understand what Mossad was up to, where the conflict was coming from. True, relations between Peter Halfin and he had been … strained. Even so, to have killed two active officers? Halfin was unusually silent for such a self-interested arse.

The call he had just concluded with Prime Minister Olmet served merely to add to the rising feeling of disquiet in his soul. What was the game in play? It was a question Olmet wanted answering as much as he, and Brun felt the power of a constitutional crisis looming over his shoulder. Returning from his reverie of the early-morning traffic on the freeway, the head of Shin Bet placed his index finger on the desk's intercom icon. The virtual app thrummed as he called his PA.

'Gina, contact officers Markov and Rosenberg. Ask them to come to my office as soon as possible, please.'

'Certainly, Mr Brun.'

The line went dead, leaving Brun with his thoughts once more. He harboured a deep sense of foreboding about the whole sorry situation.

'I have a bad feeling about this.'

The three of them stared out the windscreen at the farm stretching out along the hill before them. Black was unhappy; Logan was silent, staring at the farmhouse where he had confronted the parents of Judith Olsen just a few short days ago. Her father, in particular, had been decidedly unmoved by their plea, though the MI6 officer hoped the two of them had mulled over his words. Maybe he was pissing in the wind? There was only one way to find out.

Logan turned and levelled his gaze at his colleague. Black's countenance was moody and grim, but there was no going back. Murtagh kept her counsel. 'I appreciate what you're saying, John, but we must try. We have to see if we can reason with them about their daughter and grandchildren.'

'What if they're in the loop, Steve? What if they know what happened at Tel Etz, where their daughter is? What we supposed to do? Shoot them? Firefight with the military, intelligence teams is one thing. Killing civilians, another.'

He was right. But they had to gamble, before Olsen committed a further crime. Turning to stare through the windscreen again, Logan turned the ignition key. 'It's a risk we have to take.'

In silence, they headed towards an uncertain meeting and an even more uncertain future.

Olsen rolled over in his bed, the pounding headache no better for the fitful sleep he'd endured in the last ten hours. Damascus had been annihilated by his hand, the area contaminated for another few hours by the gold isotope he'd seeded the device with. Anyone entering the blast area would be affected, would die of cancers and leukaemia, brought on by the deadly environment.

His options were few, diminishing by the minute. Was it a measured response to the death of his wife and children? Was it an eye for an eye, a tooth for a tooth? Or had he committed a crime so horrific, so elemental that he would forever be spoken of in the same breath as Hitler, Stalin, and a dozen other dictators who had ravaged the earth's population with their ideology?

He shuddered and felt the bile rise from his stomach in a series of wet heaves. Halfway to his bathroom, the retch deposited the contents of his stomach down his shirt and across the carpet. Acid burned in his throat and mouth but not nearly enough.

This was it. Stop! He'd done playing the general's game. Now he'd proven what could be done, they were on their own. He just wanted to disappear Be gone, like his family was.

A rap on the door to his … cell disturbed his reverie. He ignored it. It came again. It was a false courtesy; 'they' controlled entry and exit.

'Hello,' he responded in a desultory tone.

The door opened, and a familiar face peered around the jamb. 'Can I come in?'

Olsen shrugged. 'Sure.'

Sharon Horowitz eased, self-consciously, into the room. She pointed at a chair. 'May I?'

Olsen shrugged. 'Why are you asking me?'

'Because it's polite.'

Olsen let out a bark. 'Yes, in the current situation, it's very definitely appropriate to be fucking polite!' His voice rose in crescendo, delirium scratching its surface.

Horowitz perched herself on the seat, and an awkward silence descended over them. Eventually, she let out a quiet cough. Olsen regarded her, an expression somewhere between hatred and hurt.

'What you did, Jo, was a blow for Israel, against her enemies. You should be prou—'

'Really?! Really. I should be proud, you say? I've helped Israel kill millions of Syrians in a cowardly attack, and I should be proud?!' Again, hysteria crackled in his tone.

'Johannes, you helped us do what is necessary. Israel's enemies are on all sides. The world will not help protect us. We do what we can to shield our state.'

Olsen stared incredulously at the young woman who had tricked him into coming here, to this place. 'Can you hear yourself? Do you know what this sounds like?'

Horowitz returned the look. 'What do you mean?'

Olsen stared at the Israeli and then shook his head. 'Forget it. Right now, I don't want to be helpful. I want to get out of here.'

'You can't.'

A harsh bark of laughter. 'No. You're right. I can't. Where would I go, where I wouldn't be arrested for genocide? I've helped the State of Israel do that act. It was me, you understand, me!'

'No, I didn't mean that. You can't leave because the general has one more task for you to complete.'

Olsen stopped. 'Another task? Topol has what he wants. I'm giving him nothing more. He has a bomb.'

'He needs something more from you.'

'He can't have it.'

'If you give him what he wants, there is something in it for you.'

'I'm sure. And what could Topol possibly give me that would make me change my mind?'

'Your family.'

Markov turned the Ford onto Ayalon Highway, heading south. Beside him, Rosenberg was silent, as she had been since their meeting with their boss. Truth be told, they were both in shock. To think that Mossad and Shin Bet were at each other's throat at a time like this.

'This is shit.'

Silence.

'Well? Isn't it?' Her fist punched his arm in that way he was used to now, to the extent he wouldn't know what to do if it never happened again. He nodded, slowly, hesitantly, unsure of vocalising his concern.

'What do we do? Do you think Brun is telling the truth?' Her rat-tat words tailed off, lost in the hum of the car's air conditioning. The road and the traffic spread before them, people busy getting to the office, oblivious to the machinations filling the ether.

Markov gripped the wheel. 'We have a mission,' he ground out.

'Are you comfortable with it? It means betraying everything we're told to protect.'

'Goddamn it! I don't know! Yes, yes, you're right, it does. But those are our orders.'

Rosenberg scowled at her partner as he continued the drive south. She had a bad feeling about this assignment,. Going up against Mossad was not a master plan in anybody's book, even when that tome had been written by Shin Bet.

The farm was dark as Logan rolled the idling BMW to a halt. He took a moment to survey the surroundings, careful to note anything seemingly out of place. Nothing, he decided, sure of his memory from their last visit. And that in itself was out of place. His sixth sense bristled. Things were most definitely not right. No farmhands, no lights, no machines waiting to be used—just a pristine farm, like a child would lay out for playtime. He glanced at his companions; his unease mirrored theirs.

Logan nodded once. Murtagh reached for the Beretta in her lap and checked the chamber, satisfied there was a round ready to fire. Behind came the sound of Black preparing the weapons he'd gathered from the police station. The Brit retrieved his Glock from the door pocket, did his checks, and turned to the others. 'Ready?'

As they gave their affirmation, Logan climbed out and, slipping the pistol in his waistband, marched resolutely to the door, Murtagh just behind him. He caught the movement of Black, a shadow in the twilight, moving to the side of the building, MP5 held in the ready position. The man disappeared, leaving a sense of his reassuring presence.

343

Mounting the steps, Logan came to the door, so recently the scene of an altercation. He played it through his mind once more, seeing the old man and woman defiant, a shotgun between him and them, menacing and yet not so. It was something he had not challenged at the time. Something in the quiet of the night here told him things might be otherwise this time.

His knuckles played a familiar tattoo against the hard wood.

Silence answered from the interior.

With a measured pause, he repeated the pattern, the only answer coming from within his breast. He looked at Murtagh, who shrugged. Both peered through the windows; nothing stirred inside the farmhouse. Logan returned to the door and, on a reflex, grasped the handle. It moved, and the door opened silently. The merest of pauses, and he slipped in, ensuring his silhouette was fleeting in the brief light that must have strobed across the hallway. Behind, he felt his partner following him quickly through the opening.

He moved slowly, silently farther in, Glock at the ready, finger resting on the trigger guard. The quiet was cloying. A door to his right; he checked into the slowly receding gloom of the lounge—no people. But he indicated Murtagh to check more thoroughly as he headed towards the back of the building and the kitchen.

The kitchen table was set for breakfast, but nothing had been touched. A large bowl of cereal sat next to milk, warm now, he could tell from touching the jug. By the hob, bacon waited to be fried, a fly feeding from the glistening pink surface. Coffee was cold in a pot. Logan made a slow traverse of the room. It was perfect, save for the lack of life—in that moment, perhaps, too perfect.

A movement out back made him look sharply, bringing up the Glock before stopping. Black signalled for him from the yard.

'What you got?'

Black pointed towards a hut, a kennel, where Logan saw a shape lying in the shadows caused by the high wall against the hut. He walked over and bent down. The dog had been dead a while, a single shot that had entered just above the left shoulder, travelling downwards.

'Looks like somebody came and paid a visit to your pals,' Black observed fatalistically.

The dog filled his vision, foreboding. 'Yes. But where are they?'

'We got company.'

They both turned as Murtagh attracted them from the kitchen, and they raced to the house.

Markov slowed the car and killed the lights. But inwardly, he cursed, knowing that the people in the farmhouse would have seen them approach.

'Who do you think they are?'

Markov shook his head. 'Not clear. That isn't a Mossad vehicle. Can you run the plates?'

Rosenberg swiped her idev and called up the Shin Bet mainframe, tapping in the number plate of the BMW ahead of them. After a moment, she tapped Markov's arm.

He glanced over, eyebrow raised.

'It's registered to the British embassy. And ... Mossad is searching for it in connection to an attack on Natalie Epstein.'

'What?'

'Dunno,' Rosenberg responded, equally bemused.

Markov tapped the steering wheel. 'Why?'

'Why what?'

'Why is only Mossad looking for this car? And why hasn't there been anything on the police radio about it? If something's happened to Epstein, how come nobody's heard about it?'

Rosenberg snorted. 'Keep up. There was a thing on the news last night that Epstein was going to be off air for some weeks.'

'But why? You don't know. Neither do I.'

Rosenberg pointed at the car. 'Let's go ask them.'

Markov slipped the car into reverse and pulled it back down the hill and out of sight of the farmhouse.

'What are they doing?'

Murtagh peered through the window. 'The car is pulling back down the track.'

'John.'

'I'm on it.' Black headed for the kitchen, stepped into the backyard and, ducking, ran behind a fence that headed to the outbuildings. Keeping low, he slipped into the first shed and came up short with the stench and buzzing. As his eyes grew accustomed to the dark, he resisted the urge to vomit. The hesitation was momentary; this was something for later. Right now, there were more important things to contend with.

Quietly, efficiently, Markov and Rosenberg slipped on bulletproof vests and selected their weapons. Markov reached for a trusted MP5 with collapsing stock, while Rosenberg picked a Benelli M4 semi-automatic shotgun. Both chambered a round and then ascended the track to the farmhouse.

Rosenberg advanced quickly on the house, Markov keeping in step, circling to make sure no one was coming up behind them. As one, they mounted the veranda and took up position on either side of the door. Markov's eyes swept the open ground behind them as Rosenberg rapped on the door.

'Hey! You inside! Come to the door. Slowly!'

No movement in the building. Markov glanced across at his partner and dipped his head at the door again. Rosenberg obliged, banging the stock of her shotgun against the wood. A noise came from within, resolving into slow footsteps. Both Shin Bet agents raised their weapons, focussed entirely on the sounds from within.

'You need to drop your weapons,' came a woman's muffled voice, American, Markov figured.

'No can do,' he responded. 'You come to the door, nice and slowly, hands where we can see them.'

A slight pause greeted his words, and he swore that he could hear a sigh from the other side of the door. He looked quizzically at Rosenberg, who shrugged. Whoever these jokers were, the laughs were wearing thin.

Markov stepped back for space. 'Okay, enough stupidity! Come out now!'

Slowly the door handle moved, and the Israelis braced themselves.

'Do you want to drop those weapons? Everybody's getting a bit tense, and it makes me very nervous.'

They both whirled, to be confronted by a large dark foreboding figure in a combat stance, an MP5 trained on Markov. The barrel bobbed, to signify that Markov should drop his weapon. The Israeli hesitated for a moment, but any thoughts of heroics were brought to an abrupt end as he caught Rosenberg stiffen in the corner of his eye.

A semi-automatic Beretta was brushing the back of her head, held in the unwavering hand of a very pretty American.

Steve Logan appeared in the doorway and smiled. 'Would you guys like a cup of tea?'

Markov regarded the strong tea sat, half-drunk, on the table before him. He was aware of his colleague waiting for him to make a move. Before him stood the three … Three what? Enemies of the state. He shook his head and saw the resignation in the eyes of the Brit and two Americans. But what could he do? What they were proposing was fantastical. Yes, their boss had told them there was some sort of issue with Mossad, but a high-level political action to subvert legal government and to crush Arab opposition in favour of Israel and at the expense of the Palestinians?

'It's a big leap. You're telling us of a cabal plotting to destabilise the Middle-East, which will result in Israel assuming control of the whole region.' He paused. 'I can't …'

'What?' enquired Logan. 'Quite believe it?' The Brit laughed, a short harsh sound. 'Nor us. But'—he paused again—'your boss clearly believes something really wrong is going down, which is why he sent you down here.'

Markov considered Logan. He made to speak, but the American man coughed. Everyone turned to him.

'Before y'all go any further, there's something else you might want to factor in.' Black indicated the outbuildings.

'What did you find?'

Black smiled grimly. 'Shall we go take a look?'

The bodies were abandoned like mannequins across the floor of the building, as if dropped by a careless child. The gunshot wounds suggested it was a really vindictive child, Murtagh figured, stepping gingerly between the corpses. There were twelve in total, all men save one, who was probably the housemaid, cook, or something. The others ranged in age from late teens through to the oldest who was probably in his sixties.

'This is fucked up.' Rosenberg just looked at the devastation, her eyes wide in disbelief.

Murtagh stooped to the floor and rose again in one fluid movement. 'You got that right,' she opined, holding something up for everyone to see.

'What you got?'

'What do you think, Steve?' She tossed something to her partner, who caught it and inspected it.

'Five, five-six casing, NATO issue, so not Palestinians. From a Galil or a Tavor maybe?'

'And the only one in here. Everything else has been cleaned up.' Murtagh straightened from a corpse. 'Everyone was killed in the same way—two to the chest, one to the temple, classic assassination.'

Logan tossed the casing to Markov, who caught it deftly in one hand. 'Still think this is a spat between Mossad and you people?'

Markov slowly shook his head. 'I don't know what to think.'

Black sighed. 'Okay, well, let's take it from the top shall we, while we're contemplating our dead friends and wondering what the shit happened to the farm owner and his wife. It goes something like this.'

48

They marched briskly along corridors at a speed just a little too uncomfortable for Olsen's legs, who struggled to keep in step with his guards. Eventually they arrived at the door of a conference room, one he was familiar with from past meetings. One of the guards swung the door open, ushering the Norwegian through. Four figures waited there, three he recognised, one unfamiliar. All sat across the table from the chair he was directed to.

Olsen sat slowly, regarding Topol, Klein, and the agent called Sharon, who smiled quietly at him. The last person in the room stared at the scientist, stony-faced, ascetic, and piercing, a man whose bland features menaced. He unsettled Olsen, who fidgeted in his seat, waiting for whatever was to come. The silence stretched away.

Clearing his throat, the Norwegian turned eventually to Topol. 'General, why have you brought me here?'

Topol's glance at the stranger didn't go unnoticed by the scientist. The general cleared his throat. 'Johannes, we want to thank you for the work you've done for this country. You have struck a blow seen the world over, but there is more to accomplish.'

Olsen remained silent. What could he say? Wait for the others to speak.

'Johannes, what is the thing you want most in the world?'

Clenching his fists under the lip of the table, Olsen stared at the new face, seeing a smirk hiding in the eyes. 'To be away from here.'

A snatched glance at Sharon and then the man fixed him again. 'Or to see your family.' Statement, bald and teasing in one.

349

'Nice. Think that's going to work?'

The man checked his fingernails, smiling at the table. 'Johannes, Israel sees great potential in you. There is much to be done in the new world. Wouldn't you like to do that with your wife and your children next to you?'

Olsen cast his mind back to a café in Geneva, a stained table in a dark corner. In his hand, a picture of a time past. A woman and two smiling children. The image faded from his mind. It was past. Judith was not coming back, whatever the promises of this individual. It was time to move on—from her, from this place, from everything.

'That isn't going to happen.' He was surprised how calm he sounded. 'My *ex*-wife won't be coming back to me, and nor would I want her to. You cannot bribe me to commit anymore war crimes for you.'

The other sighed. 'You're probably right,' he concluded, rising from his chair. And Olsen saw he was just another businessman, whose profession was death. He stifled the shudder as the man continued. 'Your wife isn't coming back to you. She wouldn't want a worthless piece of shit like you,' he observed flatly, as if deciding on a cappuccino or an Americano. He walked behind his colleagues and picked up a remote from the end of the table, pointing it at a flat screen on the end wall. It flickered into life.

'But you know, there are times when we find we'll do anything for those we love.' The screen flickered into life, showing a window, ceiling, and part of a bare dank wall. The camera panned round and focussed in on a group of people seated at a table—people with hoods over their heads, some trembling, another whimpering. Armed masked men stood around the room. At an unseen signal, one of the figures stepped forward and lifted a hood from one of the smaller captives. Olsen felt his heart dropping, an unfathomable weight dragging him down, down to some doom he had not yet envisaged.

The man stared at him. 'What will you do for the life of your son, Johannes?'

Carlisle sat at the Resolution desk in the Oval Office, reading the report Fletcher had just pushed to her idev. She paused in her perusal to peer at the director of National Intelligence. 'You sure of this?'

Bill Foreman nodded his balding head, the liver spots highlighted in the sunlight cascading through the tall windows. He was sure he could feel himself ageing with each passing moment of this fiasco with Israel. 'Yes, Madam President,' he continued, as if words were required to cement the already known facts, making them real and overpowering. 'We have an air force Constant Phoenix over the area now, and they confirmed the initial report.'

'What does it mean?' Carlisle asked without looking up from the report.

'It means the area of the blast can't be entered safely until the day after tomorrow, so casualties will rise.'

'And what is this process—"salting"?'

Bill Foreman looked round for support, but none of the president's entourage was prepared to help him out. Oh well, he figured, this would have to do. He cleared his throat. 'Salting is a technique for intensifying the lethality of the fallout of a nuclear weapon. What isotope you use determines how lethal. Gold is the least deadly, if you will, lasting around a couple of days.'

'There are worse?'

'Much worse. Cobalt is the doomsday option, many believe. It's thought to be able to extend the lethality by over a year and a half.'

'The effect of which would be?'

How did he say this without causing maximum fear in the room? There was no easy way. 'A nuclear device salted with cobalt is thought to have the ability to wipe out all life on earth.'

Carlisle grasped her idev harder, as if she might squeeze the threat Foreman had pierced her with out of existence. When she considered the congregation around her, the tears in her eyes stung. But so did her resolve. 'Carol, get me the Israeli ambassador immediately, no delay. Bill, I need more detail on the developing threat. Formulate our response and what we need to do in the area to thwart the Israeli mission and any Russian or Chinese threats. Admiral Burke, place our forces at DEFCON 2, effective immediately.'

Burke paused a fraction too long, and Carlisle pounced on his indecision. 'You have a problem with the order?'

A career naval officer, Burke had seen presidents come and go. Given he'd already suggested this, when it might have stopped shit from happening, he wondered if this one had what it took to be one of the greats. *Keep it simple.* 'No, Madam President.'

Carlisle said nothing, an ominous silence falling across the Oval Office.

When she finally spoke, her tone was hard, her words for everybody. 'In case anyone here is in any doubt, a nuclear device has been detonated over the capital of a sovereign state, in an act of genocide. While we need to be sure how, why, and by whom this attack was made, I will protect the United States and its allies from all aggressors. Before anybody draws similarities with Cuba, this is a situation where we are in the aftermath of an aggressive use of nuclear power.

'I want to be able to control the situation. Sharone, give me a piece for the media. I want it to accentuate we are responding to a fluid environment. It needs to stress we are increasing our readiness, but it shouldn't let anyone believe we are panicking. I want a draft in an hour.

'Now, what is the situation in the Med?'

Foreman's eyes turned to his idev and his fingers swiped across the screen, pushing something to the big screen over the fireplace. 'This is the displacement of all forces in the Eastern Med. Admiral Shenley is closely monitoring his opposite number, Timoshenko, and has reported that the missile cruiser *Zhukov* has resolved firing solutions on Tel Aviv and three other targets. As soon as it looks like a launch, he will barricade the Israeli seaboard and attempt to take down the *Zhukov*.'

'And the Chinese?'

Foreman shrugged. 'Still nothing.'

'Do we have overwatch?'

Fletcher affirmed, and Carlisle nodded approvingly. 'I want continuous updates, regardless of the information. Do not leave me blindsided. And, finally, something more sensitive.' Pausing, she rose from her desk and headed round to the sofas. 'The rest of this meeting is for Warren, Bill, Admiral Burke, and myself. Can everyone else excuse us please?'

As the last person filed out, leaving President Carlisle with her top advisers, the sombre mood of the room deepened. Carlisle settled in a wingback Queen Anne, her favourite chair, between the two sofas. Mitchell and Burke sat to her right, Foreman the left.

'Gentlemen, can you advise me what's happening with our people in Israel?'

Foreman leaned back on the sky-blue sofa and scratched his forehead almost dismissively. The director of National Intelligence had been concerned about the unsanctioned action since he'd heard of it, and his view hadn't changed. As good as they were, he wished Black, Murtagh, and Logan had kept their noses clean. He said as much to Carlisle, knowing well how she held, particularly the two men, in high regard. His words clearly irritated the president, but it was what he was paid for.

'That doesn't tell me where they are though, Bill. They are our eyes and ears on the ground, and we need to understand what's happened to them. Has London heard anything?'

Foreman shook his head.

In clear exasperation, Carlisle turned to the other two men. 'Do you have anything to say about this?'

Mitchell cleared his throat, clearly enjoying the discomfort of the DNI. 'Madam President, we need a military solution to this situation. We have enough firepower in the area. I suggest we use it to eliminate the threat Dimona poses. It would have the advantage of heading off threats from the Russians and Chinese.'

'But could just as easily escalate things by causing indiscriminate death and destruction,' countered Burke.

'Gentlemen! When you've all done posturing, I'm expecting proper responses. Warren, a strike on Dimona, without hard evidence that the Syrian strike originated from there, is out of the question. We need hard facts before we commit to that sort of action. Bill, what do we have in terms of cyber or satellite facilities that can be directed to surveillance of Israel?'

Foreman checked on his idev. 'As much of our capability is focussed on Israel as is possible at the moment. But the traffic is really restricted, and they're able to shut us out quite comprehensively.'

'That's disappointing. What you're telling me is that the only hope we seem to have is three assets on the ground, who aren't even supposed to be there.'

'Affirmative.'

'Well, I guess you'd better get in contact with them damned fast, else we are gonna have a world war on our hands.'

353

'Yes, Madam President. I'll see to it right away.'

'See you do. I want the three of you back here in two hours, and bring Markham along with you. I don't know why she should duck out of the action and let you take all the flak.'

With a chorus of yes, ma'am's, the three chastened officials trooped disconsolately from the Oval Office. Carlisle watched them go and wondered just what the hell was going to happen next. She didn't have long to wait, as another knock came on the door. With a sense of uncharacteristic dread, she invited the unknown visitor in.

Again, Fleischman opened the door and ushered a figure in. Robert Weiss hesitated, almost apologetic.

'Hi, Bob. Don't hang round. Come in and tell me what's troubling you.' Carlisle gestured to a sofa.

Weiss sidled over and sat, stiff-backed.

'Well?'

'Madam President.' Weiss shuffled a manila folder in his hands.

Carlisle regarded it, and his behaviour, quizzically. Paper was an unusual method of communication. So she figured it had to be sensitive. Weiss and she had a wary relationship since he had acted up to secretary of state, especially given his pro-Israeli leanings. But he'd proved proficient, if unexciting. His demeanour suggested something threatened his usually calm, steady manner. Carlisle rose, skirted her desk, and sat before the agitated aide. 'Do you want to share that with me?' she indicated the file.

Weiss regarded it as though it had not existed until that moment. He nodded.

'Go on.'

Weiss coughed, opened the folder, and passed the top sheet of paper to the president.

Carlisle cast her eyes over the words on the white surface and then at Weiss, raising an eyebrow.

'This is a police report into the death of Sarah Anderson.'

'You're not making this easy, Bob.'

'No. There isn't an easy way of saying this. DC Metro says that Sarah Anderson was not shot by John. His alibi is rock solid. They've called in the FBI.'

Carlisle caught the sigh of relief before it escaped her lips. John was many things; she was glad he wasn't a murderer. She couldn't show that. 'Do they have any ideas who it might be?'

'Not at this time.'

The look on Weiss's face, though, told a different story. Carlisle could see the first seeds of doubt forming in the young man's face.

It was time to up the stakes. She reached for her idev. 'Carol, get me FBI Director Ed Schwarz on the line. I don't care what the time is.'

49

Was it the rising morning sun pouring through the window or the last half hour that made him feel hot and uncomfortable? Markov wondered as the big American finished speaking. 'That's some story, John. You expect us to believe it?'

Black returned the gaze, causing Markov to avert his eyes. 'Man.' Black snarled. 'I don't give a shit if you believe what I've just spent good air telling you. But believe this. With or without you guys, me and my buddies are going to sort this shit out.'

'Can we have a minute?' Rosenberg appealed to the three foreigners.

Logan beckoned the others and they exited the lounge and into the hall. He pulled the door behind but didn't close it.

Rosenberg turned to her colleague. 'Do you remember when we found that Russian operative who was trying to smuggle nuclear plans out of the country?'

Markov nodded.

'Remember what you said about not trusting the establishment?'

Another perfunctory dipping of the head.

'Well, now is the time to fuck the establishment, Avi. It's time to deal with the problem and hang the consequences.'

Markov leaped from the chair he'd occupied and paced to the window, stood looking across the landscape. What did he believe? Where might this might stop? What was it they were supposed to do? To protect the state against all enemies—foreign and domestic. Now it seemed, more than ever, that meant domestic. Brun understood something was wrong; two agents were already dead, one who'd helped the American. Why would he have helped if there wasn't a conspiracy to drop Israel into a nuclear shitstorm?

He headed for the hallway, pulled the door open, and looked at the three congregated there.

'So, what do we do?'

'*Zhukov* is preparing to launch. Target Tel Aviv. Deploying ordnance, four Kalibr cruise missiles, warheads unknown.'

'She's coming about to take a firing position.'

'Preparing to resolve in ten minutes.'

The reports came thick and fast on the bridge of the *Roosevelt* as Shenley calmly took in all the shouts and alarms that reverberated around it. Captain of the ship, Bob Pritchard was equally calm and monitoring the activity.

Shenley hunkered forward. 'Well, Bob. What do you think?'

'Guess we need to respond, Admiral.'

'Me too. Let's do it.'

Pritchard smiled grimly, picking up his idev. 'Exec,' he called out, 'bring the group about and take a firing resolution on the *Zhukov*, three tomahawks. What's our CAP?'

Nelson consulted his idev and then swiped the information to Pritchard. 'Call signs Omaha and Brightspark are maintaining barrier. Sputnik is on Alert 5. Their opposite numbers are matching them for manoeuvres.'

'Okay, patch me through to *Bradley*.'

'Sure.'

Seconds later, Pritchard was speaking with the captain of the Bradley. '*Bradley*, this is *Roosevelt*. Do you copy?'

'*Roosevelt*, this is *Bradley*,' came a disembodied voice over the intercom.

'*Bradley*, we are in a firing situation with Red forces. They are preparing to launch on Blue asset. You will engage four plus enemy cruise missiles and defend the fleet from attack should one materialise. Copy?'

'*Roosevelt*, copy.'

'We're sending Alert Five, to provide support. Monitor this frequency. Respond as you see the situation, Commander.'

'Confirm, *Roosevelt*.'

'God be with you, *Bradley*.'

'You too, *Roosevelt*. Over and out.'

Pritchard looked over at Shenley, who settled back in his chair at the back of the bridge.

The admiral turned. 'Comms, signal the *Moskva*. Advise we have their targeting resolutions. Advise them we will engage if they commence a launch against Tel Aviv.'

'Aye, sir.'

The response was not long in coming but from a source other than the comms.

'Bridge, this is Tactical. *Zhukov* is opening its silos.'

Pritchard called out. 'Sound the alarm.'

'Battle stations! This is not a drill. Repeat, this is not a drill. All crew to battle stations.'

Shenley leaned forward. 'Communications, raise me Admiral Timoshenko on the *Moskva*.'

'Aye, aye, sir! Link with *Moskva* established on channel four.'

Shenley picked up the receiver from his chair's arm. 'Admiral Timoshenko.'

The voice was slightly crackly, as befitted this crazy fucking Cold War shit of a situation, Shenley told himself with a wry smile.

'Admiral Shenley. It is good to hear from you.'

Indeed. 'Wish I could say the same damn thing, Viktor. What the hell are we going to do here? You want to bomb the shit out of the Israelis, and I have orders not to let you do it.'

There was silence on the other end of the line. Ruminating, Shenley figured.

'So, Viktor. What the hell do we do?'

'Carl, we have our orders also. Israel committed an act of genocide against the Syrian people, for which it cannot go unpunished.'

Shenley absorbed the words, felt each one of them in his heart, knowing them to be real in a way not understood in many a generation. 'That's not in doubt, Viktor, but what you're doing here isn't the answer. You launch on Tel Aviv, we're gonna have to respond.'

'I have my orders, Carl.' The heavy Russian accent was deliberate, almost laboured. But his determination was clear.

Shenley sighed, a long sigh that reached into his gut and turned a knife. He twirled a stylus between his fingers, ruminating on the situation. 'Okay, Viktor. This is how I want the play to be. Will you indulge me?'

There was a long pause on the other end of the phone. It stretched out into the ether. 'Go ahead.'

'So, Viktor, what I propose is this. A forty-eight hour stand to arms. Now, I know that's irregular, but we need to ensure we don't commit to anything that might mean we are on charges for war crimes ourselves. The Israelis can fuck themselves for sure.'

There was a low chuckle on the other end of the line.

'But until we can confirm what actually happened, I'm asking you, as a friend, not to commit Russia to this course of action.'

Shenley was aware of the tension on the bridge, all eyes on him as he faced down his counterpart. It was a high-stakes poker game with no reserve. What would Timoshenko do? How would he respond to the concept? Timoshenko was a pragmatist; he was also a patriot. Shenley breathed in short and let the air exhale long.

'I can give you twenty-four hours, Carl. After that, Israel will pay a heavy price for its indiscretion.'

He held the piece of paper in both hands, wound it round, watching the light from the window behind him play across the surface.

Twirl.

Twirl.

Twirl.

The words stood out, even though they were in pencil, their surface speckled in the sunshine—light, dark, light, dark, in little blinking changes that burned into his eyes.

Robert Weiss ran forefinger and thumb the length of his aquiline nose, rubbing the skin and gently ruminating on the three words that crawled across the white surface in a lazy urgent style.

We need cobalt.

The words vexed him, and he turned the paper once more, revealing the scrawl on the reverse—a cell number. It was an odd request, one he needed more information on. It was a necessary, given his new situation.

He picked up the burner, which had come in the envelope with the note, switched it on, and made the call.

'Thank you for calling.' The voice on the other end sounded at once pleased and a little surprised. But what could he have done otherwise? 'You have our request?'

Weiss nodded, gulped at his stupidity—they couldn't see him—and spoke. 'Yes, I have it. It's … weird.' Silence. 'I mean, what the hell do you need cobalt for?'

Silence emanated from the cell.

Robert waited—he could play a waiting game too. The seconds stretched out, and he was aware of them and of the heat in the room. Or was that just in him? Probably.

He scratched the itch above his eye. Come on, you fucker, stop keeping me hanging on. I got a job to do.

'Cancer treatment.'

Weiss shook his head. 'Get it from a supplier.'

A sigh emanated from the cell's speaker. 'The quantity required isn't possible in the time frame we have. We need it today. We're reliably informed you would be able to provide.'

What the fuck?! No pressure. Weiss sucked in air and leaned back in his chair, tapping his lip. He knew what the questions would be from his supplier. That wasn't the issue. When they inventoried for the regulator, that would be the shitstorm. He would have to pay for this and said as much.

'We can pay whatever is required for anonymity.'

Weiss shrugged his shoulders. 'Okay then. Let's get this gig on the road.'

Carlisle was surrounded by her top advisors, but one place was conspicuously empty. She let it go for the time being. There were more pressing issues—such as what they hell they were going to do with the

Russians? It was a clusterfuck, and the room was generating a whole load of hot air. She took in the faces, the worry, and the words.

'Bill.' Her voice cut through the fog of conversation. 'Give us the sitrep, please.'

'Madam President.' Foreman stood and motioned for the others to sit. 'We know the Russians planned a strike against Tel Aviv. Timoshenko has agreed to stand down for twenty-four hours. That was'—he glanced at his watch—'five hours ago. We have until eleven thirty tomorrow morning.'

'What are our options? Anybody?'

An uneasy silence settled on everyone, each unwilling to be the first to offer an answer.

Almost apologetically, a hand rose. It was Sarah Markham. Carlisle was pleased to see her there—finally. It seemed to have taken a while for the CIA director to actually turn up on site. But she was here now. And right now, that was all that mattered. 'Yes, Sarah?'

'It seems we have two immediate options here. We can either let the Russians attack and work the aftermath, or we pre-emptively strike the Russians and risk triggering a major conflict beyond the current sphere of operations.'

'Huh, not great options,' opined Mitchell. His feelings were plain.

'No,' Markham agreed, 'which is why we need another strategy. We have a few hours before Timoshenko's deadline expires, right?'

There were nods around the room.

'Well then, we may be able to move on the information from our British counterparts.'

Mitchell leaned forward, eyes narrowing, scenting a potential weakness. 'What've you found Sarah?' The gravel-filled tones rumbled in the atmosphere.

Markham regarded the secretary; he was like a crocodile, seemingly idle, lazy, but the eyes were always watching, calculating, ready to strike as soon as the prey got within easy distance. She cleared her throat. 'Our colleagues in London and Cheltenham passed information relating to telecommunications made the night of the attack to and from a location in Tel Aviv. We have one device that had received one previous call, from somewhere in southern Israel. That was triangulated with the second call, which was somewhere in the area just south of Jerusalem.'

'So what does that mean?' Mitchell's crocodile gaze never wavered.

Markham coughed self-consciously. 'Well, Mr Secretary, we were able to mark a three-kilometre diameter circle centred on Chaim Levanon Street.'

'That's some radius,' Foreman opined glumly.

'It is, but NSA and GCHQ are confident that any further such communication will be readily pinpointed.'

'What about the person, persons talking?'

'Madam President, their conversation was predictably cryptic. There is discussion concerning a product and how well it worked. Also, some content relating to competition being resolved.'

Mitchell snorted. 'All very cryptic, Director. But what are you doing about it? From here, it feels like you're just blowing air up the president.'

Markham coloured. 'We will have a profile of the three people involved in the calls in the next twenty-four hours.'

'Not soon enough. We need to accelerate this. I want actionable intel.'

'Yes, ma'am. We have everybody working on this —'

Carlisle's face was deadpan as she delivered her rebuke. 'Sarah, you don't have enough people or enough time. You need to provide us with information and quickly, if we're to stop the Russians.'

Markham bit back a retort, limiting her words to, 'Yes, ma'am. I'll get on to it.'

'Make sure you do.'

Smarting, Markham rose, flicking her idev closed. 'If you'll excuse me.'

'Thank you, Sarah.' Carlisle didn't look up.

When the door had closed behind the CIA director, Carlisle looked at the two men. They were keeping quiet for the sake of their departed colleague, but it was unusual for Carlisle to be so harsh on her employees. Where might it all end? 'Gentlemen, we need to get in contact with John Black as quickly as possible.'

'We're trying our best, Madam President. But it is difficult, given the conditions.'

'Bill, we have a Russian fleet poised to launch an attack in the next few hours. We could be at war very soon. A huge humanitarian effort is required, but nobody wants to enter Syria while we and the Russians are poised to fight.'

Foreman considered his boss. 'Have you been able to speak with Glazunov?'

Carlisle's brow furrowed. 'No. His chief of staff tells me he is unable to take my call,' she informed Foreman with undisguised rancour. 'Busy with affairs of state. Because this shit's apparently not important enough to stop playing war games and start talking.'

Foreman cast a glance at Mitchell, seemingly oblivious to the president's little outburst—probably because Mitchell was spoiling for a fight as much as the Russians. *Shit, all this dick swinging*, Foreman thought. He'd hoped to have a quiet few years, perhaps retire next. Instead of which, everything was about to plummet off the edge of a cliff, and everyone was trying to see how fast they could beat the other to it.

'Ma'am, can I suggest that we re-task satellites to attempt contact with Black and the others?'

Carlisle looked up. 'Yes, Bill. Good idea. I want to know what they know, as fast as possible.'

50

It had been a robust conversation, the two Israelis shaking their heads continuously, interrupting in disbelief for the first hour every time Black made an assertion that cut across the collective cultural psyche. Logan chomped at the bit. Talking was all well and good, but he had an increasing sense of foreboding. They were running out of time. Finally, he could stand it no longer.

'This is great, getting to know each other and everything, but a couple of things.'

The others stopped their discussion and looked.

'We have the aftermath of a bomb to resolve, the possibility of another attack, by party or parties unknown, and we're stuck in the middle of nowhere.'

The observation settled uncomfortably over the little group. Markov drew a circle in the dirt with his finger. 'What do you suggest?'

'You're the local asset,' Logan rebuked him. 'What are you guys hearing? Why did your boss send you out here? There must be a reason.' He paused. 'But you're not telling.'

Markov refused to meet the gaze of the Brit. Instead Rosenberg spoke, hesitant at first and then with growing conviction. 'You're correct in your supposition. There is a reason. For sure, Mossad are of some concern. But of greater worry to Shin Bet is the work of three, apparently unaccountable, foreign agents, with a conspiracy story and a trail of injured people and stolen property behind them.'

'You sure ain't been listening, lady.'

Rosenberg regarded the big American. 'Oh, I've been listening. But you're going to have to do more than you have this morning to shift us.'

'Is that right? Because,' opined Murtagh, 'from where I'm sitting, if you were that unconvinced, you wouldn't still be here.'

Markov's mouth opened to retort, but he was interrupted by an increasingly frustrated Logan, who held his hand up, shutting down further discussion. 'Enough! This has gone on long enough. You,' he informed the two Israelis, 'are, either in or not. Decision time.'

'And if we're not?'

'You won't be leaving here,' Black informed him grimly. Not that they would kill them, but it didn't harm in exigent circumstances for people to believe you would do what was necessary.

'Not much of an incentive. You know how Israelis are when boxed into a corner.'

'For God's sake!' Logan's thunderous explosion cut the heavy atmosphere lowering over the group. 'Can you guys, for one moment, stop this fucking posturing? It's time to stop fannying around and move forward.' With that, he stalked out the font door of the farmhouse and stood in the morning sun, his back to the others.

Markov beckoned Rosenberg to one side, aware of the watchful glances of the two Americans. He turned his partner away. 'Well?'

Rosenberg looked into his face. 'What do you mean?'

Markov bit back the sigh and patiently explained his thoughts, Rosenberg listening attentively if not with good grace. "It's what Brun wanted us to do,' he concluded.

Rosenberg considered this last point. It was a good one, but how could they change anything? Even with these three ragtag foreigners? It seemed a tall order, and she said so.

'I think we have to try—for the sake of Yakin and Goldstein.'

And there was the real reason, for both of them. She nodded. 'Okay, you're right.'

Markov smiled, a watery affair, devoid of both emotion and conviction. He turned back to the Americans, noting that the Brit had also returned but was standing removed, as if he found the whole situation distasteful. 'What do we need to do?'

Tension and concern bled from the Brit's frame, washing away the grime of extortion to get what you wanted. 'Okay! There are three things we need to get straight immediately,' he told them all.

'One, we need to understand what happened here and where Olsen's family are. Two, we need to flash London, find out what is happening in the world. Three, a weapons check, make sure we aren't going to get any surprises in a tight situation.'

Markov's fingers curled round a hard object in his pocket—the bullet casing. He retrieved it and looked it over, before addressing the Englishman. 'I can figure out the first one, if we're okay to go?'

A brief nod.

'Good,' Markov said. 'In which case, we'll be off. Shall we meet here again, say midday?'

Logan paused, mulling over the request. 'This is rally point one. If, for any reason, it becomes compromised, do you have access to an alternative?'

'Yes. We'll flash you the GPS for it should it be necessary.'

'Good. Let's get to it, people. We have a lot to do and little time to do it in.'

'Is it a good idea to let them go?'

The concern in Murtagh's eyes, burrowed deep into Logan's insecurities. She was right to question his decision, and he intuited that Black almost certainly felt the same. After all, he was considering the veracity of it himself. What if the Shin Bet officers were going to betray them? Would they point them to a second rally point and an ambush? He dismissed that with a little shake of the head. Why go to all the bother, when they could despatch them here, away from prying eyes.

'We don't have an option.' He drew a weary hand over his face. 'Let's get real. We need their help. Otherwise, what we're doing is absolutely doomed to failure.'

Probably already had been, Murtagh thought silently. Still, no use complaining and wishing for what could have been. There was a big frightened (probably) world out there that needed contacting, if only to verify that the gut-wrenching fear she felt wasn't unique.

So … 'We gonna get on the blower to Washington, London, or whoever?'

A weathered smile. 'Guess we better had.' He shook out his idev, placing it on the kitchen table. Cueing up its secure comms, he started the search for a satellite he could bounce off.

Murtagh, conscious of time, did the same with hers, figuring she could access NSA, or a milsat, faster than Logan could reach London.

Thus, it transpired. Moments after beginning the hunt, a female voice requested her security clearance. Soon after, a familiar voice filled the space around the two agents.

'Hello, Brooke,'

'Hello, Director.'

'We've missed you,' Sarah Markham continued, without the slightest trace of irony. 'What have you been up to?'

Don't be flippant, Murtagh's mind screamed; Markham wasn't known for her sense of humour, good or otherwise. 'It's been eventful,' she rejoined, giving a brief outline of their time in Israel, omitting for now the recent discussions with Shin Bet officers. 'How are things back home?'

'Oh, you know, nuclear strikes tend to focus everyone's attention—Russian, European, United States. And all the time, the Chinese are circling. Palestinian groups, the Iranians—you name it—they're all coming out of the woodwork to claim a piece of the cadaver.'

'Director Markham, it's Steve Logan, ma'am.'

'Hi, Steve, how's it going?' She sounded weary, he mused, though that was no wonder. 'Is John with you?'

'Yes he is, safe and sound.'

'Good!' There was evident relief in the other's voice. 'What's been going down?'

Both officers recounted their time in country, their interrogation of Natalie Epstein, and the grim discovery at the farm.

'Did Epstein give you anything actionable?'

'We're still working on it.' His response was bound in the international language of obfuscation.

It wasn't lost on Markham, but she chose instead to focus on the farm.

The Brit recounted what had happened.

Markham's silence spoke volumes and it was during the quiet Logan took the plunge. 'We've made contact with sympathetic elements in Shin Bet.'

Silence extended across the ether. 'Shin Bet?'

Logan coughed. 'Yes.'

'At what level?'

What should he say? Should he say at leadership level, though there was no way of knowing if the people had been telling the truth? Or should he tell what he knew? *Tell what you know*, a little voice told him. 'It's two officers. They have orders to investigate Mossad activities … and us.'

'Gee, great. And what did they find out when they investigated you three?'

'Ma'am, nothing we didn't want them to know.'

'You're sure about that then, Brooke?'

Despite distance and audio only, Murtagh coloured up but stood her ground. 'Yes, ma'am. They appear to be on board with us.'

There was audible distress from her superior. When she had collected herself, Markham's response was restrained, something both officers silently congratulated the hard-bitten director on. 'Brooke, I'm sure I don't really need to tell you that appearance can be deceptive. Having said that, the situation is what it is. Be careful.'

'We will,' Logan assured her. 'What we need to know is what you want of us now.'

'We understand from initial surveys of the blast site that the weapon was potentially salted with isotope of gold, extending the period of radioactivity and making the ground response too dangerous in the short term. It should be good to send in relief agencies in the next month.'

'What's the thinking on reasons why?'

'Unclear, Steve. Potentially a test weapon? We don't know. But we suspect the next weapon will be similar, except perhaps using a different isotope.'

'Do we know what types?'

'There are a number of options. We believe that tantalum will be a "go-to" for them. It sends a clear message to their enemies, but it doesn't last beyond a few months.'

'And the others?'

A pause on the other end. 'If they really wanted to fuck things up, cobalt would do it. It's colloquially termed the "doomsday option". If a bomb salted with cobalt were to be detonated, it would contaminate the whole world within five years, effectively wiping out all life on the planet.'

Hence the pause, Logan figured laconically. *That is some heavy shit.* Even the Israelis wouldn't be that careless. But what about a man who had lost everything, had been duped and used by a cynical system? What might he do? 'You're sure about tantalum then?'

The mark of sarcasm was heavy in her reply. 'Steven, do you really think Israel would use cobalt?'

'No,' he assured her. 'I don't. But Olsen might. He's a man who's been fucked around a hell of a lot.'

For the second time in their concise communication, Markham went quiet. 'Shit. You're right. Okay. I'll get all available resources tracking consignments of both isotopes, wherever they are in the world. I'll speak with DNS and Joint Chiefs of Staff to mobilise a strike response should we get any activity out of Dimona. That is your priority—monitor the plant and inform us immediately if there is any move to launch an aircraft from the facility.'

Wow, exciting. He caught the sour look in Murtagh's eyes and grinned at her, launching his eyebrows heavenward in a pique of impatience.

'Ma'am, Murtagh here. Isn't that something that drone surveillance could be better tasked with? We have this covert organisation to uncover.'

'Usually, I'd agree. However, on this occasion, two things override that argument. First, the Israelis are taking out any remote surveillance we can put in the air. And second a doomsday weapon trumps any cabal. Hopefully, if we defeat this weapon, then we can take out their secret society out afterwards.'

'Okay, ma'am. In that case, do we know what will happen if the aircraft carrying the weapon is brought down? Will that trigger the payload?'

'We believe that the weapon will be inert if it isn't armed prior to us taking it out. But there are no certainties in this. We need to act quickly.'

'I agree. That consignment mustn't make the facility. Director Markham, I think there are two priorities then—take out the consignment and take out any weapon that leaves Dimona. Do you agree? I think they'll try and deliver something else, regardless of whether it is salted or not.'

'I'd agree with that assessment, Mr Logan.'

'Very well. We'll get on planning and update you this afternoon.'

'Thanks. Logan, can you give me a moment with Murtagh?'

'Sure.' He rose from the table and made his way towards the living room where Black was going through their arsenal.

Murtagh watched him leave and when he'd closed the door behind him spoke to the idev. 'Yes, ma'am?'

'Regardless of Logan's agenda, this is a US mission, end of discussion. Make sure you communicate that to him and take control if you need to. Understood?'

Understood? Oh yeah, for sure she knew what the director meant. It wasn't comfortable listening, and she briefly wondered why Markham hadn't just come out with the directive herself. But, of course, it was better getting her to do it to her lover—a little twist of the knife, easing open a little separation between them. Nasty bitch. 'Yes, ma'am. I understand.'

'Good. I'll wait to hear from you later. The clock is ticking.'

With that, the line went dead.

Murtagh walked into the living room where the two men were intent on checking over their arms, each engrossed in the methodical process. For a moment she hesitated and then, 'Logan we need t—'

'Markham wants you to take the lead and to tell me in no uncertain terms this is a US operation.' He smiled, his open easy smile.

Murtagh bit back the automatic response. 'Yes. How did you figure?'

The laugh held no malice or frustration. 'She asked to speak with you directly, without me there. And she's right. This is a US mission, predominantly. So, what do we do?'

Murtagh's eyes flitted from her lover to Black, who'd looked round and was watching the exchange with interest. He grinned at the indecision in her gaze, and it suddenly solidified her thoughts.

'What we always do. Figure it out collectively. After all, we are the A-team, aren't we?'

51

Brun smoothed a hand over his still bald pate, seeking to keep the words Markov had passed him in his head. His heart lurched constantly as each letter, construct, and phrase circled around his mind. They were vicious, nervous names, threatening his normally controlled demeanour but, worse, the safety of everything he stood for, that his organisation stood for, that Israel stood for.

Or so he had thought.

Now, there was change.

The chair creaked as he swivelled to take in the late-morning traffic racing obliviously towards a destination that, since yesterday, had become immeasurably more unknown. He was aware of both Markov and Rosenberg waiting on the other side of the desk for his deliberation, the one patient as ever, the other punctuating the atmosphere with little sighs of exasperation.

At last she could curtail her frustration no longer. 'We need to be careful of what the foreigners are saying. After all, it is only their word we have to go on.'

Is it? The words formed silently, not for fear of the response but from a sense of ennui, a feeling that he was operating above the capacity of his people. 'Expand.'

'They are spinning tails of conspiracy, when we have evidence of a series of unconnected attacks. You taught us always to be careful of relying too much on the evidence of the eyes—that we should always search underneath for the truth of the situation.'

It was true; he had always advocated that. Things were often not as they seemed. But that could work both ways. He was fairly sure that the Western agents were on to something. The electronic chatter indicated something was—how did they say—afoot. The farmhouse was evidence of that, of Rosenberg's naivety … or something else.

He turned the chair back to face his two operatives, regarding the woman longer than was perhaps polite. At this moment, he didn't care. 'The situation at the farm is unnerving. I don't like riddles,' he informed them both as he picked the shell casing from the table where Markov had placed it. 'We have a major industrialist, important to this country, dead; a news anchor in hospital, seriously wounded; a nuclear scientist brought into the country clandestinely; and a major nuclear attack carried out days later. You think,' he asked, concentrating on Rosenberg, 'we need any foreigners to spin tails of political intrigue for us?'

Rosenberg hung her head to hide her embarrassment, slowly shaking it to affirm her agreement with her boss.

'Then bring me the evidence, the truth that will bring an end to this lie. Speak to Epstein. Find out what she knows. And then I want this thing shut down.'

The building they pulled up alongside was unassuming and of indeterminate age. A faded blue door, flanked by shuttered windows, the blinded eyes of conformity, let into its dun-coloured fascia, denying its identity as a CIA safe house. With a quick all-encompassing, glance around the vehicle and the surrounding environment, Logan signalled for them to exit.

Murtagh swiped the face of her idev, sending the code to the house's door; it clicked, and they pushed inside.

By the time they'd reached the kitchen, scanners in the hallway had surveilled them and confirmed their identities from the active field officer database held at Langley. The two officers inhabiting the inner sanctum still eyed them suspiciously, as if it were the right thing to do.

After they had exchanged protocols and confirmed who they were, the three were offered coffee and food. Logan realised he hadn't eaten since lunchtime the day before, and hunger washed over him in a wave.

Even so, training and pride prevented him from devouring the food placed before him.

'So, you understand the situation?' He addressed the slightly built agent, who nodded. 'And you know what information we need?'

'We do,' answered the other, a bigger steroid-enhanced individual whose features were shaped by a healthy contempt of others. 'How long do you plan on being here?'

'No longer than necessary.' Black stared down the man, who looked away momentarily.

It was enough. The female officer smiled, a barely warm effort, but it was enough to change the mood.

'We need a change of clothes, some gear, and then we'll be on our way.'

Big guy nodded to Logan. 'Sure thing. Let us have your list, and we'll get on it.' He jerked a big thumb at the door and then to his right. 'Shower's down thataway.'

Twenty minutes later, Logan was standing beneath a stream of relaxing, refreshing water, letting the grime of the last few days be flushed from his skin. This was a good feeling. Long may it last.

The car across the road from the safe house pulled away from the kerb, its passenger deep in conversation on her cell. From the opposite direction, a battered Range Rover Vogue turned into the street and pulled alongside the house, stopping. The four people in it sat, waiting.

Towelling himself slowly, Logan allowed himself the luxury of standing naked in the silence of the shower room. He'd be glad when all this shit was over. It was beginning to take its toll on him, and he was sure Murtagh was feeling the same. What Black's position was was unclear, but he'd been through a lot.

A bang on the door, rapid and urgent, drove him from his reverie. He poked his head out. Black was there, looking thunderous. 'We got company. Front and back. Tool up, Stevie.'

Logan ducked back in the room and quickly shrugged himself into the jeans and T-shirt he'd grabbed from a drawer, followed by socks and boots. He joined Black, Murtagh, and the others in the situation room. All turned from their concentration on the monitors as he walked in.

'What gives?'

'Four front, green Range Rover. Six rear, black Toyota Hi-Lux. No evident weapons, but they look tasty.' Steroid guy never took his eyes from the screen. 'Been there for the last ten minutes.'

'What's the protocol?'

The other shrugged. 'Don't know. Never been here before. These guys're supposed to be friends.'

Logan understood. Things had changed somewhat. 'Weapons locker?'

The merest of hesitations then, a finger beckoning, steroid guy left the room. The three followed, the Brit noting the woman was already packing a sidearm. Being prepared.

The CIA officer passed him a H416 assault rifle then a big, brutish Beretta and thigh holster. 'Know how to use this?'

Logan thought back to the moment on the firing range when Murtagh had demonstrated her skill with it, versus his Glock. 'I'll manage,' he replied, with a knowing smile to Murtagh.

She flashed one back.

Steroid guy flipped out his idev and slapped it on the wall, double-tapped a vid-link app. The device showed a split screen of front and back. Both cameras showed individuals congregating, hands in jackets, readying for … something. A takedown.

Logan glanced at Black, who returned the look knowingly. 'Okay, listen up,' said the SEAL. 'Steve and I will take the back door. You two'—he indicated the safe house operatives—'go with Brooke and cover the front. As soon as they blow it, pour as much fire into the smoke as you can. Everything has to come through that breach point.' He glanced at the screen and then addressed steroid guy. 'Is there any other way in?'

The other paused, unsure.

'Hurry,' Black exhorted.

'No!"

'Yes,' retorted his colleague. 'There's a skylight. I'll cover it.' She turned and headed up the stairs.

'Same process,' Black called after her. 'When they breach, concentrate your fire where the skylight was.'

She nodded once and was gone.

Black looked at the others. 'Okay! Let's do this.'

The operator finished affixing the shaped charge device to the door's face. Designed to concentrate the blast centrally and through the structure, the resulting explosion could cut through most security devices, hurling metal and debris into the building and disorienting the defenders.

He nodded to the commander who double-clicked his radio, indicating to his second team that he was ready to go. A double-click back affirmed they were too.

Fingers held up prominently to his people on either side of the door, he counted down.

Let the breathing shallow; empty extraneous thoughts; focus. Years of training kicked in as the adrenaline sharpened his nerves, tensed his muscles. Every sound seemed heightened. Any moment now. It had to be. He settled acoustic ear defenders in place, his whole attention concentrated on the door at the other end of the room.

The bang, when it came, rippled through his skin, pushing into him like a giant hand threatening to force him over on his back. Without thinking, his finger squeezed the trigger, sending short bursts of shells into the daylight shimmering in the curtain of dust that roiled where the door had once been. From somewhere behind him, gunfire could be heard for what seemed like eternity but was seconds.

Silence.

What now? He caught a look from Black, just before a shape hurtled into the space between them and the door. It hit the floor, rolling awkwardly towards him. Instinctively he scooped at it, grasped it, and threw it back the way it had come.

Not a moment too soon. The explosion filled their senses once more, showering the room with plaster, wood, and more debris. This time, concussion battered their minds and shuddered through fingers and muscles, jellifying them. Logan was aware of a shape moving into the room, but it was a dream, and his hands wouldn't respond to the thoughts screaming, *Fire! Fire!*

Then a short bark of semi-automatic fire and flame spurted vividly in his vision; he wasn't sure from where. Before him, the figure seemed to dance a marionette's crazy dance, before falling backwards to the floor, as if to sleep. Before he could register what was going on, more fire towards the door, and then a tumult behind him, towards the front of the house. Now, gunfire was being returned from outside, though it felt like less was happening where Brooke was.

Shaking his head to clear it, Logan raised his 416 and began firing. A figure appeared in the doorway, only to crumple as it was caught in crossfire. The smell of cordite hung in the small space, stinging. The cacophony of sound felt to him as if it would bring the whole of Tel Aviv down upon them, and still it raged.

The hit, when it came, was biting, even though it was a glancing blow. The cry of pain was involuntary, a shouted expletive that bounced from the walls and gave rise to a berserker in him, who went fully automatic, emptying a clip into the space framed by the shattered door. To his side, Black laughed and joined in.

Their moment of abandonment drew a silence across the battle lines. Cautiously, he checked himself over—a nick and burn to his right cheek, seeping and bloodied, but he'd live. Even as he thought it, Black was calling out to their comrades, seeking assurance everyone was in one piece.

Logan breathed again as he heard Brooke's voice sing back, breathless and excited as child with its favourite toy. Steroid guy sounded exhausted. Possibly this was his first intense action. From the woman, there was nothing. Maybe she hadn't heard.

It didn't bode well when she didn't answer at the second asking.

'Hey. Americans!'

The voice captured their attention, an assured sound, one that knew it was in charge, prepared to offer a deal that no one believed would be honoured. They ignored it.

'We know you are hearing us. You might as well surrender yourself. We have another unit on its way; we can always pull in more people. Where will yours come from, huh? Let's sort this out. Come out of the building without your weapons, with your arms raised, and we can sort this out.'

Black glanced at Logan and grinned. 'Fuck you!' His big voice boomed across the space to the other. His hand ejected the empty magazine from his rifle and picked another from the floor beside him and slammed it into place, cocking it in one slick movement.

The other let out a very audible sigh. 'Really? That is your answer? Okay, that's okay. We wait for our people to get here, and we finish it, once and for a—'

The cough of a suppressed weapon, quickly followed by several more shots, abruptly punctuated the disembodied words.

'In the house!'

Black shot a glance. Logan returned the look. Yes, the voice sounded familiar. 'Yeah?'

'It's Markov. With Rosenberg. We okay to come in?'

'Carefully, yeah.'

Boots crunching over the debris of shattered plaster and spent casings, the diminutive Israeli stepped gingerly into the damaged room, followed by his taller compatriot. He stood and surveyed the scene briefly. 'This is a shitstorm,' he said, shaking his head in disbelief and frustration.

'You don't got that wrong,' Black retorted with some feeling. 'But we're mighty grateful you came along when you did.'

Markov acknowledged the thanks with a short dip of his head. 'We were monitoring the airwaves. These guys were a bit, shall we say, overconfident. It was relatively easy to find you. Is everybody okay?'

Logan rose from his position behind the doorjamb and gingerly touched the burning crease on his cheek. 'We are,' he responded, indicating Black and himself. He turned to the front of the not-so-safe house. "Brooke, you two okay out there?'

By way of reply, two dishevelled characters walked wearily into the back room. They were tired but grimly satisfied. 'We're okay. Jesse here'— Murtagh indicated her big colleague—'has a nick on his arm.'

'What about your partner?'

Jesse stared at Logan. 'I-I'll go check.'

'Be quick,' Markov advised him and then turned to Black. 'Good job we were in the neighbourhood,' he observed laconically.

'No shit.'

'What were you doing in the area?'

Markov looked at Murtagh. For a moment, it appeared he was affronted, bordering on, embarrassed, and then his face broke into a broad smile. 'Short band radio is very entertaining at times. We heard communications about something happening at this address and advising the police to maintain their distance.' He shrugged. 'Rosenberg and I rarely do what we're told.'

'Lucky for us.'

'Indeed, Steve.' Markov made to continue, but at that moment Jesse returned. His eyes were misted up.

'She's … dead.'

Everyone turned to the young man. He appeared on the verge of collapsing. Logan caught his arm and steered him to a chair. Jesse slumped into the rubble-strewn seat and shivered. 'I've never had a colleague die before.' His voice was small, broken.

Markov steered Black and Logan away from the man. 'We have no time for this. Other units will be on their way as soon as they understand it went wrong for these guys.'

Black nodded. 'We'll get him to the American embassy.'

'It will be better if we do that. You are wanted. But you also have another mission to complete. We will be better placed to get him there.'

Black considered Markov's words and then nodded. 'Sure thing.'

While Markov went for his vehicle, Black and Logan helped the unsteady Jesse to his feet.

Murtagh, though, was regarding the silent Rosenberg. 'You appear to have a lot on your mind,' she observed.

'What happens here'—the Israeli let her hand traverse the scene—'hurts everyone. Not just you. Or Mossad—'

'So, it was Mossad?'

Rosenberg ignored the question, but Murtagh saw she was correct.

'Everyone hurts, Brooke Murtagh, everyone.' Rosenberg stared out a window at passing traffic, its occupants apparently oblivious, maybe inured to the activity that left bloodied people strewn on the ground, like so many destroyed shop mannequins. 'And now, we have to clear this up. Come, let's get you and your *friends* out of here.' She hustled Murtagh to the back door.

The mood in the car was sombre as they drove from the 'safe house'. A multitude of thoughts fought their internal battle for dominance in Logan's head as he followed the traffic out of the city. He discarded most of the theories rattling around as inconsequential and irrelevant to the moment. What mattered now was distance—and in the right direction. Leave Markov and Rosenberg to clear up the mess.

They had work to do.

The clear-up team arrived twenty minutes after they'd left. Interestingly, Markov noted, no Mossad or police units appeared. Complicity? Embarrassment? Whatever, it made their job easier and ensured Brun had one less headache to confront his arch-nemesis, Halfin, over.

As the team completed its tasks, Markov wondered what the fuck was going to happen next? What were they going to find when they questioned Epstein?

'Torture is the least of your worries, right now, Miss Epstein,' Markov warned her as he and his colleague took in her whining about the way in which she had been made to talk about her involvement in recent events. 'If what we believe is true, you are looking at treason and complicity in genocide.'

Epstein blanched, but kept her silence in front of the two Shin Bet officers. Markov sighed and rose, indicating for Rosenberg to stay with their recalcitrant ward.

As he went searching for a doctor to find out when the journalist would be released, his colleague leaned in towards the anchorwoman. 'You know you can't continue this, don't you?'

Epstein looked blankly at the woman.

Rosenberg heaved a sigh. 'Come on. You know as well as I that you've burned your bridges with your friends. You are expendable, Natalie.' The operator was pleased to see fear stalk the eyes of the anchorwoman. 'What are you going to do about it, Natalie?'

'W-what do you mean?' Epstein made clutching motions with her hands on the bedcovers.

'I mean, how are you going to rectify this situation, this monumental screw-up you have put your friends in?'

There was that phrase again—*your friends*. The way the woman pronounced the words sent a chill down Natalie's spine. She decided to bluff it. 'My friends will be fine with what I've done. They will stick by me.'

Rosenberg glanced at the door, turned, and laughed. 'You really believe that bullshit, do you? Or is it some kind of bravado? Your "friends" don't know who you are Natalie. They would be appalled by what you are a part of. Your partners, however, are less than impressed with your ability to keep your mouth shut.'

'I was shot in the leg,' the anchorwoman hissed. 'It hurt like fuck.'

'I'm sure, Natalie, but sometimes you have to take a hit for the group.'

'Easy for you to say. You weren't there. They were very efficient and ruthless.'

'Get a drink, Natalie,' Rosenberg indicated the water jug on the table across the bed from her. 'You're getting excited.'

Epstein snorted but reached for the jug and beaker all the same. Having filled it, she turned back to her interrogator. She was getting pissed off with this and was going to tell this bitch so. 'Who the f—'

The suppressor deadened the sound of the bullet piercing one of Epstein's eyeballs. The popping sound of the skull expelling the bullet was accompanied by the sudden satisfying corona of blood that, for a moment, framed the shocked expression on Epstein's shattered face. The slack lifeless body dropped back to the bed. Rosenberg quickly bagged her gun and rose to leave.

'How's our— Fuck!'

She glanced up as Markov entered the room, the two coffee cups falling in slow motion to the floor, coffee spurting from the lids in a grotesque ejaculation. Ah well, she figured, never liked the shit anyway. Reaching into her bag, finger curling round the trigger, she fired through the leather, even as Markov was attempting to draw his weapon. Her first shot shattered his windpipe. The second entered the temple, just right of centre. And for the second time in minutes, a shattered body slumped lifeless.

Rosenberg pulled the body into the room, thankful that this part of the hospital was quiet. Normally, she would wipe down where she had touched things, but it would be kind of obvious who had killed Markov and Epstein. No. What was more important was to get the hell out of there. Although it was messy, her job was done.

As nonchalantly as possible, she walked down the corridor of the hospital, breathing more easily with each unchallenged step away from the anchorwoman's room. In the reception area, among the people gathered there, she texted a quick message—'It's done'—to the number she'd been given.

Moshe nodded, though David couldn't see him. 'Yes I understand.' He killed the call, dialled a number, and waited.

'Yes?'

'The job is yours.'

'Thank you.'

The line went dead, and Moshe tapped the palm of one hand thoughtfully with the device. He was about to undertake the ritual of burning of the phone before deciding to make one last, quick, call. He worried momentarily about making two calls on one device, then dismissed it. Who would be listening to a call such as that?

'We have a trace!'

The operator's voice over the idev connection matched the broad grin on his face.

Okri smiled back. 'Tell me what you have.'

Rosenberg walked through the hospital doors and dropped the pieces of the cell phone in the litter bin, keeping the SIM card—best to discard that elsewhere. Crossing the drop-off zone, she looked for Markov's car in the parking area. There it was. Quickly, she walked over and bleeped the central locking, fingers curled round the handle.

The force of the shell, slicing through her skull and exploding out her forehead, pushed her body against the car. Even as she slumped, the second shell burst through her body ensuring that Rosenberg couldn't speak about the events in the hospital ever again.

 52

'**M**adam President, you're gonna want to see this.'

Carlisle registered the alarm in the expression of her chief of staff, who placed an idev on the desktop and synced it to the screen on the wall. A news report appeared, a grim-faced anchorman with three familiar faces on the screen behind, capturing her attention in a gut-wrenching way.

'Here's what we know so far,' the anchorman was saying. 'Three Western operatives, two American and one from the UK, are said to be involved in an attempt to overthrow the Israeli government. They are being linked to the bombing of Damascus, working with elements in Israel determined to upset the peace protest and foment unrest in the Middle East. The Israeli government has vowed to hunt them down and bring them to justice—'

'Turn it off.'

Fleischmann did as she was bid and waited for Carlisle to continue. The president, in turn, swung her chair to stare out over the West Lawn. Seconds dragged into minutes, and just as Fleischmann made to speak, Carlisle turned.

'Carol, assemble the cabinet, emergency briefing please. Then get me the Israeli ambassador. And after that, get London on the line.'

'Do you want to speak to the Israeli ambassador—'

'In person, yes, please, Carol.'

'Very well, Madam President.'

'Joel, thanks for coming at short notice.'

'It is my pleasure, Madam President.'

'You know why I've summonsed you?'

Joel Wiesenthal, remembering his recent humiliation at the United Nations, suppressed the smile. 'Yes, I do. It is most unfortunate what your people do in our country.'

Carlisle bit back a caustic comment. 'If indeed, they have committed the atrocity they're being blamed for.'

Wiesenthal sank, unbidden, into a sofa and leaned back. After all, he was in control of this situation. 'Madam President, you're right. It is merely speculation at this time, but it is strong nonetheless. Your people were involved in an action at a CIA safe house in Tel Aviv, which saw an eight-person Mossad team taken out. Two of them had already been identified by Natalie Epstein as having tortured her to extract information. You wish to question the facts?'

Carlisle sat opposite the little Israeli, hoping her poker face was on. His interpretation of the facts had a compelling quality to it, but she knew it was wrong. Was that gut? Possibly, hopefully, it was more than that. To think Black, Murtagh and Logan would do what they were being accused of was counter to who she believed them to be.

'Mr Wiesenthal, I asked you here to discuss what is being done to find these three. These are difficult times, and allies should stick together.'

Wiesenthal's lips curled in a satirical smile. 'Ah! Allies? Last week it was not so, I think.' He rose and smoothed his jacket. 'You wish to stick together? Ask your people to give themselves up. Then we can stick together. Good day, Madam President.'

It was a sombre mood that infected the cabinet room, a virus of depression and anxiety falling on each person, threatening to devour them. Fletcher was deep in conversation with Eissenegger and Markham. Mitchell merely brooded over his third coffee, the caffeine showing in his eyes and the slight tremor in his hand as he gripped the cup tightly.

By a window, on his own, Robert Weiss was shrouded in thoughts of treason and intrigue. It wasn't that it had been his intention to commit such acts but, rather, that he had owed a debt to the mother country, had felt compelled to pay and to continue paying. Would it return to haunt him?

Carol Fleischmann entered, a precursor to the appearance of the president. She had been the perfect administrator to a senator and was now gatekeeper to the most powerful leader in the Western world. All eyes turned to her.

'Good morning, ladies and gentlemen.' Her voice was authoritarian, demanding immediate attention from everyone in the room. Even Mitchell was able to raise his eyes from their reverie of the brown liquid cooling in the White House cup.

'You have your briefs on your devices?'

Heads nodded in assent.

'Good. The president wants to move quickly on this. She will be here momentarily.'

A secret glance passed between the three intelligence individuals, while Mitchell merely raised the cup to his lips and drained it. He considered another and decided against; he was buzzing already.

Behind the chief of staff, the door opened, and Angela Carlisle strode into the room, sitting at the head of the table. She sat in silence, syncing her idev to the table before raising her head and addressing the assembly.

'Good morning, everyone. We have a situation in Israel, I think it's fair to say. I had a … robust and frank exchange with the Israeli ambassador.'

'How did that go?' Mitchell growled the words out.

'Just peachy, Warren. He suggested that we give up Black and Murtagh. And Logan,' she concluded almost as an afterthought. 'If we did that, he thought we could work together.' The anger was plain to all as her voice tailed off. The silence was palpable, everyone waiting for her next words. As always, Carlisle figured sourly. Just once, could someone else say something profound in this situation?

'I think we should do it.'

The small words filled the space in the room, inconsequential on their own but together imparting grave consequences to the listeners, causing exclamations from some.

'Are you out of your mind? Jesus, Robert, that's tantamount to surrender to a foreign power.' Even through his caffeine, Mitchell's attention was still concentrated on the cup before him, but he echoed the minds of everyone else, including Carlisle.

She drew breath. 'Robert, I have to say, I agree with Warren. That would be an unusual move for us to commit to.'

'Undoubtedly. But we are on the brink of a conflict in the Middle East, the likes of which the world has not seen, with untold destruction on all sides. What Black and Murtagh have committed out there is small compared to what happened in Syria. Two things.' He raised a digit. 'One, the Israelis will keep our people on ice. Two'—a second finger pricked the air—'we can let the Brits take the fall. Talk to their prime minister. Get him to agree that it was their operator who convinced us to do what we did.'

'And then what?' Distaste dripped venomously from Sarah Markham's lips, her dislike for Weiss evident, uncaged. 'Drop the peace talks? Consign the Palestinians to more decades of abuse by an uncaring foreign power?'

Weiss inclined his head, listening for the first rustling indications of his prey moving towards his jaws. 'Perhaps we do need to drop the talks, Sarah, because, of course, we need to do something about the whole situation out there. It can't go on as it is.' The stand-in secretary of state warmed to his thoughts, knowing there was never a better time than this to ensure the end of the accord and to avert a potential catastrophe. If only he could—

'I think a little something is lacking in your approach to this, Robert.' The voice of the waspish director of Homeland Security, Rose Cundy, crackled over the mahogany table, stabbing at Weiss's conscience, demanding he come clean. *Of what?* the more brazen part of his id questioned him. The cobalt shipment passed through his mind momentarily, and he felt he blanched before recovering and questioning his antagonist. 'Expand, director.' There was just enough inflection to infer a slight but no more. Cundy refused to acknowledge it, as he knew she would. She could be thick-skinned when it suited.

'Naivety, Secretary. This isn't going away just because we pull some pieces of paper from the table. Too much water, to borrow a tired metaphor, has gone under the bridge; too many people have been slighted and left with little response. And now, Israel has, or has allowed some among them to, detonate a fucking nuclear weapon over a sovereign state. The accord has to stand. If not, everything this presidency stands for'—Cundy looked pointedly at Carlisle—'goes down the shitter. You can bet Fox News will love that!'

Carlisle remained impassive, despite her colleague's rant. After all, both were right, to a greater or lesser degree. For a moment, which seemed an age, the president allowed the noise to carry over her. It was such moments that tested her most—the thing she hated and why she was not looking forward to the remainder of her term. So much posturing, testosterone (even from the women). People were cunts, she decided. Around her the chatter rose and fell, without end, without resolution.

'Enough!'

All heads turned.

'What is wrong with you all. Can we have an adult conversation about the situation instead of this incessant racket?'

No response. *Tell me something new*, she informed herself. *Goddamned fools.*

'Robert. We are not abandoning the Jerusalem Accord. I'm sure I made that abundantly clear previously. As such, you are to inform our friends in the Eastern Mediterranean that we will expect a signed document before the week is over. Warren, you will tell Israel to get a handle on whoever is to blame for this Syrian debacle.'

'What about Black and Murtagh?'

What about them? 'We are not handing anyone over. I want intel on what was happening at that safe house—every available record. Get a team in from the embassy, and don't brook any nonsense from anyone on-site. Robert, you will assist Warren. Now.' She turned to Sarah Markham and Rose Cundy. 'Ladies, please tell me that we are getting somewhere with identifying this cabal that may be behind the attack?'

Markham cleared her throat, aware that what she was about to divulge was flimsy at best. 'Ma'am, we have some intelligence out of London, received just a couple of hours ago.'

'Well?'

Looking at her notes Markham ran through what Amanda Galbraith had passed her. GCHQ had been lucky basically, listening at the right moment and scanning the right networks and had picked up the same ident twice in minutes from a mobile, which then went dead. In the time given, and working with NSA operatives, they'd been able to place the phone within a half-mile-wide circle of Tel Aviv. 'Within that area are two organisations. First is the Ministry of Defence.' Markham allowed a moment to pass, aware of faces waiting impatiently for her to name the second.

'And?' Eventually Carlisle couldn't resist pushing her CIA Director.

'Mossad.'

Silence fell over the room, punctuated by a quick, almost nervous laugh.

'Are you seriously contending that Mossad is involved in a conspiracy to unleash a nuclear holocaust on the planet?'

Markham fixed the stand-in secretary of state with a withering look. 'As if Mossad hasn't been involved in clandestine operations before. But,' she cut off the reply being framed by his opening lips, 'no, that's not what we're saying. We believe that the source of the call was someone high up in Mossad, possibly this man.' Markham cued up a photograph that she pushed to everyone's device. A bearded face, with clear open nondescript eyes and a swarthy complexion stared back at them.

'This is Peter Halfin, director of Mossad.'

Carlisle glanced from the picture to Markham. 'Wh-What are you saying? That Halfin is implicated in this ... somehow?'

'We're seeking confirmation, Madam President. Our British counterparts believe that he is, as were Natalie Epstein and David Perez.'

Carlisle's head nodded slowly. Sometimes things did come together. 'Keep digging, Sarah. Rose, I want you to continue working up contingencies with FEMA and FBI on a possible attack on the US. Warren, coordinate with Admiral Shenley. His deadline with the Russians has to be approaching fast. I have a plan. Get to it, everybody!'

Chairs scraped, and papers rustled as people rose to leave. 'Chas and Sarah, Bob, wait please.'

When the door had closed behind the other, Fletcher, Eissenegger, and Markham dutifully remained seated.

Carlisle leaned forward. 'Okay, how credible is this intel from the Brits?'

It was Foreman who spoke up. 'Very credible. In fact, we think we can identify the other members of the cabal.'

Carlisle sat back, wide-eyed. 'Pray, expand.'

Foreman and Eissenegger looked at Markham, who flushed slightly. 'Ma'am, we couldn't give more information in the meeting. We believe there is a compromised individual in the senior team, someone who is sympathetic to current Israeli objection to the Jerusalem Accord—.'

'Spare the blushes please, Sarah. You're talking about Robert Weiss, aren't you?' When Markham nodded mutely, Carlisle slapped the table. 'God dammit! For two pins I'd— What do we do with the shit?'

'Nothing, yet, Madam President. We want him to think his cover is still intact. The Secret Service has been appraised and is keeping a watching brief on him. We think he's in contact with another of the cabal and may have been responsible for a recent shipment diversion of cobalt to Israel.'

Slumping in her chair, Carlisle looked into the faces of the three intelligences community heads. 'Je-sus, you sure know how to spoil a party. How credible is intelligence on this?'

'Until four hours ago, not. However, a shipment of cobalt was landed at Haifa in the early hours of yesterday morning and immediately overlanded to Dimona.'

'What are we doing about it?'

'We have our people tracking it. And Black and Murtagh have been tasked with infiltration and making safe—'

'Really?' Carlisle stared at Markham, who flushed at the tart rebuke. 'Not enough, Sarah.' Carlisle paused, deep in thought. After a while, she leaned forward, decision writ large in her eyes. 'Okay, this accelerates the situation. We have to move fast to stop them from launching another weapon. Do we have any idea where they'll attack next?'

'The most likely target is Fordow. There has been activity recently in the vicinity of the plant.'

'Shit! Everybody wants a nuke these days. Right. The Israelis will want to strike fast, given everything ranged against them. I want solutions in the next two hours.' She tapped an icon on her idev. 'Carol, alert the Joint Chiefs of Staff that I want to speak to them by video, in the next twenty minutes. Tell them I want solutions for taking down Dimona in the next two hours and a backup if these people manage to launch an aircraft with a bomb on it.'

'Certainly, Madam President. Anything else?'

'Not for now. Thanks, Carol.' She turned to the occupants of the room. 'Okay, get to it! We have no time to spare.'

Four thousand miles across the Atlantic, Amanda Galbraith was smarting from an equally bruising encounter with Prime Minister Adams. The call she had just concluded with Markham had merely ramped up the pressure, and now she had to return to COBRA and request special forces for an incursion onto sovereign territory of an erstwhile ally. It was fast turning into a shitstorm, but she understood America's thinking. Israel was a state without control, an accusation it had levelled at so many of its Arab neighbours and enemies for so long.

And here we are, her thoughts continued, *at a crossroads*—not just for the Near and Middle East but for the whole world. Take the wrong decision, make the wrong move, and the whole of humanity could be wiped out in the blink of an eye. She had assured her counterpart that she would do all she could to convince COBRA that the SAS should be deployed. But shit, the timing was short; so much could go wrong. Galbraith glanced at her watch, willing the fingers to slow down so that she could have one more moment before having to ring and activate COBRA.

One more minute.

Cabinet Briefing Room A was a sombre affair as Galbraith rationalised activating a detachment of 22 Squadron, SAS. On a screen behind her, Sarah Markham and Bill Foreman had dialled in from the States to lend their support to the appeal. As Adams listened, Galbraith sensed him working up for one of his legendary tirades. She tensed.

Instead, as Foreman drew to a close, Adams nodded, paused, and then turned to the head of the Chiefs of Staff Committee. 'General Hurley, I want the detachment available in two hours. Director Foreman, I presume they will come under American command?' When the director nodded, Adams turned again to the general. 'Get it done. Exigent circumstances.' Adams looked at the figures on the screen. 'Director, please pass to the president my good wishes for the operations you are about to embark on and tell her that she can count on the United Kingdom to walk in step with the United States.'

Foreman seemed a little nonplussed by the prime minister's words, merely responding with, 'Thank you.'

The screen went blank, and for a short moment there was a silence in the room.

Then Adams skewered the other attendees. 'Let's get moving, people! No time like the present. We have a war to prosecute.'

Logan shuffled in the BMW's driver's seat. He was beginning to be sick of the sight of the bloody car, and the seat just felt unyielding and worn beneath his bottom. The others, he knew, were just as irritable and desperate for action, as if the CIA safe house hadn't been enough. Talking with London and Washington again, it felt things were happening around them, despite them being at the epicentre. It was frustrating, like nobody believed they could do what was required of them. He knew that wasn't the case. Even so.

He glanced over at John Black, the big man tapping his foot on the footwell. Pent-up aggression needing some outlet. Logan shook his head and smiled, before checking his watch. The Breitling showed seventeen forty-five. Soon, the Russian armistice would be over. What would happen then? What were they going to do?

'Flash message!'

Black and Logan swivelled.

Murtagh was tapping on the face of her idev, alternately keying in words and then swiping.

'What does it say?'

'Just a minute.'

Her face screwed in concentration, bringing the faintest of smiles to Logan's face. *Can it. No time for sentiment—you're on a mission.*

'Okay.' She spoke as she scanned. 'We're to rendezvous with special forces, consisting of SEALs and SAS. Coordinates to be sent separately. Negotiations have begun with Russians to target ... Israeli defence establishments and communications hubs, early hours of tomorrow morning, depending on the outcome of discussions between POTUS and the Israeli prime minister.' The pause extended briefly as she took in the next words. 'Okay. An international arrest warrant has been issued for Olsen and an executive order has been released to "seek and destroy" remaining elements of the cabal. Prime target is currently Peter Halfin, director of Mossad.'

Murtagh looked up from her device. 'This is it,' she opined, slightly breathlessly. 'Endgame.'

It gave the three occupants of the car pause for thought, each shackled to his or her own feelings for the next hours. Adrenaline coursed through them, almost binding them in that small confined space, making them one, a team.

Eventually, Logan broke the silence. 'When do we rendezvous with special forces?'

Murtagh checked. 'We have four hours.'

'Okay. What say we get some shut-eye and then find somewhere to eat before shoving off for the rendezvous?'

Nods accompanied the suggestion.

He checked the surroundings. They were parked in an innocuous enough place that shouldn't attract attention. Hunkering down in the seat, he set the alarm on his watch.

'See you all in two hours,' he told them and, without another word, fell into a deep sleep.

53

Not for the first time, Olsen found himself railing internally at injustice. But this time, things were different. This time, he had all the cards. Walking the corridor, from weapons lab to site restaurant, he considered the work being completed behind him by robots and technicians, a process dramatically speeded up by technology. But there was one thing the Israelis' systems couldn't account for. He smiled.

The restaurant was almost empty when he entered, which suited him fine as he picked food from the displays. Did he want to eat? Probably not; it was just a means of passing time. He took a table by the windows that looked out over the busy airfield. Various military types he didn't recognise sat waiting on the apron. One was receiving special attention, a sleek fighter, its spine enlarged as if something abnormal grew there. Beneath the slim pointed nose, a gaping mouth snarled at him. The smile returned. Yes, you had a shark, but he had developed the hammer—one that would crush all before it, in a maelstrom of destruction.

'You look happy. It's good to see.'

Olsen glanced up from his reverie. The Israeli agent, Sharon? Natalie? What did it concern him now? But he had to play his game for a while longer. 'Thanks. I do feel better for getting things finished.'

Sharon slipped into a seat opposite him, examining him as she made small talk. There was a glow about him, as if he'd had some experience, something that sat ill with her. Paranoia? Anything she couldn't put a finger on was subject to scrutiny. Olsen continued to eat. Sharon maintained her watch.

Eventually, Olsen could stand it no longer. 'What?'

His waspish tone drew a little internal comfort for Sharon. 'I'm intrigued. How do you feel now you've completed your task? Are you looking forward to seeing your family?'

Olsen regarded her as if he were seeing a strange animal for the first time. He picked at the remaining chicken on his plate and then pointed at it. 'Do you think this chicken knew what was about to happen to it when they came to slaughter it?'

'Doubtful,' Sharon responded truthfully. 'I mean, how would it understand?'

Olsen chuckled and popped the meat in his mouth, chewing satisfyingly for a moment. He swallowed. 'Precisely.'

Sharon swallowed. 'What do you mean?'

'Oh, nothing!' Olsen responded blithely before tucking into his dessert. 'Are we meeting with the general?'

'Yes, in half an hour.'

'Good. And when do they arm the aircraft there?' Olsen jerked a thumb at the machine he'd watched being worked on earlier.

'Shortly.'

'Good. I've got some last-minute things to see to, so I'm going back to my room. Will you come for me there?'

Sharon nodded mutely as Olsen rose and carried his tray to the returns area. A sense of foreboding settled over her. Why did this look like it was going to shit?

Weiss grimaced at the reflection in the restroom mirror. He didn't look his best and for good reason, he decided. Diverting medical supplies of cobalt to Israel, whatever the reason, was something he was increasingly regretting. What if it was useful in some sort of weapon, something that made Damascus look like a walk in the park?

Stop it, he scolded himself. How could that be the case? Why would his contacts want to increase the opprobrium being heaped upon the country by the international community? Didn't make any sense. He shook his hands of water and smiled grimly to himself. Yes, it would be all right; he'd done the right thing.

As he headed back to his office, he could hear his aide talking with others. Something in the tone made him pause.

'Secretary Weiss is unavailable at the moment,' came the strident tone of his aide.

'When will he be available?' The other was hard, deep, a voice that did not accept no for an answer.

'Where is he?' Another voice, exasperated with the messing about.

Weiss continued to vacillate in the corridor. As he did so, a head popped out of the doorway to his outer office. Eyes touched momentarily, a spark of recognition in the other, and then a voice raised in authority. 'Secretary Weiss, a moment please.'

The head was joined by a body and then more people coming out of the office and heading down the corridor towards him. An urge to run rose in him, which he fought against his better judgement. After all, what did he have to hide? He stood his ground as the three Secret Service agents advanced towards him.

Agent One looked the secretary of state up and down, his face grave. The other two positioned themselves to intercept Weiss should he have second thoughts. 'Secretary Weiss, you need to come with us.'

'What for?' Even though he knew, he couldn't resist asking.

'Not here, Secretary.' The hand beckoned, threatened to manhandle him towards his destiny. His feet dragged against the tiled floor of the hallway. 'I demand to know, agent, before you take me anywhere.'

Agent One glanced at his colleagues and shrugged, in an 'okay, you asked' kind of way. 'Treason and genocide.'

Even though his voice never rose in pitch or intensity, there were audible gasps as the words cut the air. This time, the hand made contact with his upper arm, as though Weiss had crossed a line, and by some form of agreement, it changed the dynamic, gave permission for him to be arrested. He felt all the fight drain from him and allowed the agent to propel him down the corridor towards whatever fate awaited him.

Shenley gazed out at the Mediterranean as it began to greet the dawn. Timoshenko's deadline was fast approaching. What was he going to say when he relayed the president's proposal? Would it prevent the Russians from attacking unilaterally? Did even he believe what his commander in chief was offering?

Glancing at the bridge clocks, he saw it was late in the capitol. Diplomacy and war waited for no one though. He knew Washington would be awaiting his call in a few short minutes. It was time to get this over with.

'Comms, call the *Moskva* please.'

A few seconds later the face of Admiral Viktor Timoshenko appeared on his idev. The smile on the Russian's face was contained to his lips; the eyes, grey and suddenly old showed no degree of levity.

'Good morning, Viktor. How goes things on the *Moskva*?'

Timoshenko regarded his counterpart with something approaching suspicion. 'Good morning, Carl. Things are as good as can be expected— how do you Americans say?—under the circumstances.'

Shenley grinned. 'That's a Brit thing, Viktor. We prefer "situation normal, all fucked up".'

'Ah yes, from the Great Patriotic War.'

Shenley could see where this was going so elected to change the tack. 'Well, with such a bright beautiful morning, where are we going, my friend?'

Timoshenko rubbed his swarthy chin, ruminating, more for effect than to determine his next words. The die had been cast, so to speak. Nothing further to discuss. 'As I informed you, Carl, President Glazunov has given his orders. *Zhukov* will launch in the next two hours. Our ambassador is delivering the ultimatum to the Israeli government as we speak.'

Shenley allowed a little laugh of derision to fall from his half-open lips, mocking his adversary and reprimanding his people's complacency. 'You did tell me that we had twenty-four hours left before you would act. I have a proposal to put to you, before you act, from our president.'

Timoshenko had foreseen this move. Did it make a difference to Russia's position? Let's see. 'Very well.'

Shenley shucked down in his chair, considering his words carefully. There was no reason to suppose the Russians would go with this, he warned himself. Still, only one way to find out. 'President Carlisle asks that you join us in targeting Israeli bases, denying their ability to launch another attack.'

Timoshenko couldn't prevent his eyebrows rising in astonishment. Quickly he composed himself. 'An interesting proposal.' He paused, still assimilating the information. 'What brings about this change of heart? Don't you want to continue to protect your friends?'

'Sometimes friends need a reality check,' Shenley offered by way of explanation. 'We believe this will provide the quickest resolution, rather than attacking the civilian population. Those things, as we know, only lead to entrenched positions.'

'They wiped out Damascus.'

'I know, but let's not get into any "eye for an eye" shit. It won't help. Taking out their ability to launch against another target will.'

Timoshenko pulled away from the camera. It was an interesting proposition and certainly felt better than obliterating Tel Aviv. But he had his orders. He told Shenley as much.

'I agree, Viktor, but please consider it. Our ambassador to Moscow is with your president as we speak.' God, he hoped that was so. 'Call Moscow. Speak with your people. And let's do something definitive, something that can change this thing positively. Can you give us another hour?'

Timoshenko regarded his opposite number. He was a good man, in another situation perhaps a good friend, to have a vodka or a whisky with. 'Carl, I shall contact Moscow and give you a response within the hour. Don't trust too much in the abilities of the ambassador though. President Glazunov was quite clear.'

Shenley smiled. "Let's see. Thank you, my friend.'

The call was taking longer to connect than usual, Carlisle decided as she continued to look at the blank screen before her, and that irked her. Who the hell did Olmet think he was, to keep her waiting like this? It was unacce—

'Madam President.'

Carlisle instantly rebuked herself for calling out the Israeli premier. He looked shattered, half the man he had been, despite his bulk. Grey sacks of worry hung beneath his grey eyes, and he had a visible tremor. 'Angela please, Benjamin.'

Olmet dipped his head in acquiescence.

'Apologies for the early hour of this call.'

'No apologies necessary. It is, after all, getting later where you are. And these are difficult times. What is it you wish?'

Now she had him, Carlisle confessed to herself that she felt a little trepidation at what she was about to say. It did, after all, amount to a declaration of war on a friendly state. *Can it*, she admonished herself. 'Benjamin. What are we to do with this situation?' Perhaps appeal first was the best policy.

'Angela, you have to realise the Israeli government has no knowledge of the people perpetrating this outrage. We wish to find them as much as you.'

'Benjamin, I appreciate that. But you're not moving fast enough. We have credible intelligence that forces in your country are preparing a much more lethal weapon, one with the capacity to destroy life on earth.'

Olmet's face sank further, and there was a dread in his eyes Carlisle hadn't seen before. 'Benjamin? Are you okay? Do you know anything you haven't told us before?'

The Israeli prime minister seemed to see her for the first time. 'N-no. It is all good, Madam President,' he advised, sinking back into formality. 'I have to go. I have to speak with my chiefs of staff.'

Carlisle wondered if he'd grown another head during their conversation. 'Benjamin, this is serious.'

'Yes, it is. I must—' His eyes darted, unwilling to be caught in the net of Carlisle, who was becoming increasingly cold.

'Prime Minister Olmet, I understand that you must go and attend to this matter. I shall be blunt. You have given me no assurance that you are in control of the situation. Consequently, I am informing my carrier group to launch a force denial operation, targeting your military bases. We will supply you a list of those bases I have sanctioned for assault. That assault will begin within the hour. If you can't control your people, we will.'

Logan pulled the car off the deserted road, well, track, his eyes getting accustomed to the predawn that would soon disappear. The mountains that reared beyond the Jordan kept deep shadows in the intervening territory from which a team of operators would soon be appearing.

He strained his eyes to pick up the first signs, but it was Black who nudged him and pointed. Following the finger, shadows moved, coalescing into the bulky shapes of six people—four men, two women. *Not many*, he thought. But then Black pointed again. Another six came out of the shadows to stand before the BMW.

Logan turned to Black. 'We're never gonna fit them all in here,' he advised the American, who grinned in return.

'What gives?'

The Brit turned to where his partner was rising from her slumbers in the back. Hair stuck out at odd angles from her head, and her eyes looked glued together and puffy. She'd never looked more beautiful, he told himself as he smiled at her vulnerability.

'What you smiling at? You laughing at me?'

'Would I?'

The arched eyebrow told Logan what she thought about that.

'When you lovebirds have finished, we have an international incident to avert.' Black reached for the door handle and stepped into the gathering light, the Brit joining him in the fresh Jordanian air.

Lieutenant Tylon Hale snapped an easy salute to Black. The hand he offered Logan was firm and confident, a grip that told the Brit he was assured but not an egoist. He returned the compliment.

Pleasantries and quick introductions out of the way Hale flicked a look between the two men. 'What's the sitrep?'

Without preamble, the American spoke quickly, telling his compatriot all that had happened that was pertinent to the here and now. Hale listened impassively, making no notes but taking everything in.

When Black came to a halt, Hale was straight there with questions. 'Do you have intel where we can nail this Halfin? We need him; he's the lever. And what about this Olsen character? Do you think we can extract him? His family are nearby to him?'

Logan grinned at the quick-fire nature of the inquiry. 'Halfin is being traced as we speak. We should have intel on that in the next couple of hours. Our other targets are Olsen, his family, and Dimona.'

'Expand.'

With Black and Murtagh's support, he told the story, leaving nothing out of the narrative, knowing that the people in front of him needed every last detail, however insignificant it might seem, to be able to complete their mission. When the story was told, he waited for Hale's response. It wasn't long coming.

'First, don't concern yourself about Dimona. That's scheduled to be flattened in, about'—the SEAL checked his watch—'two hours' time. As for Olsen, we need him out of the country as quickly as possible. Where is he?' Hale punched details into his idev as he spoke.

The reply was succinct. 'Dimona.'

Hale looked up sharply. 'Dimona?' When Logan nodded, Hale shook his head. 'You guys sure are the deal, aren't you?' The tone was laced with exasperation, which the MI6 officer chose to ignore. 'Okay, what's your extraction plan?'

Logan glanced at Black, who shrugged. After all, what could he say? 'Our plan?' The Brit grinned loosely. 'It sorta depended on you not blowing up the whole site he was working on.'

'Do you know his location on-site?'

'No, not yet. NSA is working on that as we speak.'

Hale flashed a look at one of his operatives and then addressed Black. 'Well, sir, extract may not be a consideration in the circumstances.'

'It'd be useful to get him out if we could. He has a lot of intel that we could use.'

'What about his family? Do we know where they are?'

'Possibly at a Mossad safe house in the south of Tel Aviv. One of our local assets has said there had been increased activity there in the last couple of days, mostly at night.'

'Then that's our missions resolved—Halfin and the Olsen family.'

'We need Olsen.' Logan reached out impulsively, against his training, to Hale, hand resting on forearm.

The American regarded the hand much the same way he would've regarded a turd he'd stood in. 'Sir, remove your hand—now. Our mission parameters are quite clear. Dimona is off limits. A cruise missile strike is scheduled for 0800 Zulu. Now, we have to move before we get caught in the open. Olsen will have to make his own way.'

54

It was unexpected; that much Topol had to concede. The Olsen who stood before him now was subtly different to the one who had stepped from the aircraft a few short weeks before at Ben Gurion Airport. What did that mean? Topol regarded the younger man closely, searching for better clues in his demeanour than just surprises.

Olsen sat on the other side of the desk, hands resting on his knees, returning the general's gaze with a surety that even he figured bordered on the zealous. Unlike his scrutineer, he knew what this all meant. It felt … delicious; yes, that was the right word! He allowed the warm glow to flood his stomach, suffuse through his whole being. He wondered if this was how the Muslim felt, at the moment he knew he was to sacrifice his life for his beliefs. They had no idea what was coming, of that he was sure, though his mentor, Sharon, was uneasy in his presence.

Jee-sus, they were going to be more than uneasy. He couldn't help the smile that burst on his face, threatening to vocalise into laughter.

'Tell me, Johannes, what is so funny?'

'You,' replied the Norwegian pointedly. 'And you,' he remarked, glancing at Sharon, who shuffled uncomfortably in her seat.

The scientist was suddenly irritating, Topol decided, and he entertained the prospect of putting a bullet through the smug bastard's face. Instead, 'And why am I so funny?'

'Because you have no idea, you and your little band of conspirators, what it is that you have unleashed on the world.'

'Don't presume to understand what it is we are trying to achieve here, Mr Olsen.'

Olsen gave a derisive bark. 'Oh, but you see, I understand only too well what it is you're trying to bring about. You think that by showing the world how strong you are, how you have access to the most powerful weapons, and that you're unafraid of using them, that you hold the world to ransom, that you can dictate the way the lives of others will play out.'

'We are protecting Israel—something neither the government nor the world will do.'

'From who? Who are you protecting Israel from? The Arabs? The Palestinians? All the Palestinians want is the right to the same opportunities as everybody else, not to be imprisoned in a short slither of land or to be dispossessed of what is theirs.'

'This is the State of Israel, given to the Jew by the world.'

'Which resulted in the Palestinian nation being raped in the process, stripped of what was theirs, and forced into ghettos.'

'It isn't that simple.'

Olsen snorted. 'It never is! This isn't a messy divorce that's "complicated".' He punctured the air with sarcastic fingers. 'This is about people, people's lives, their fears, their hopes, and their peace. And you'— he pointed his finger at Topol—'you have taken that from them.'

Topol returned the bright-eyed stare levelly. 'You are in this with us, Olsen. Your hands are just as dirty. Get off your high horse and smell the coffee.'

'Fuck you, General.' Olsen laughed at the astounded Topol. 'Yes, my hands are dirty, as anyone else's in the world. But, you see, I can resolve it. I have the means to ensure this never happens again.'

Oh fuck. He's become a nut. Sharon stared at the once mild-mannered Norwegian and wondered what proclamation would spurt from his lips. The silence became a cage—if no more words were spoken, no more exhortation from his captors, Olsen would be controlled.

Olsen had other thoughts.

'When Richard Oppenheimer witnessed the detonation of his first experimental atomic bomb, he's often quoted as saying, "I am become death."' Olsen nodded at the window and the airfield beyond. 'When you got me to upgrade your weapons for you, you gave me the very ability to do what Oppenheimer only surmised he was.'

'I don't follow you.'

'Johannes, what have you done?' Sharon's voice was small and frightened, almost lost in the cage of quiet.

'Oh, it's quite simple. I intend to cure the world of humanity. I've created the ultimate doomsday weapon.'

Topol blinked. What was his ward saying? It made no sense. Worse, it sounded like the ravings of a delusional from some sort of B-movie. 'You, you've done what? Stop talking rubbish. Don't forget we have your family. Whatever happens to humanity happens to them also.'

Olsen, settled back into his chair, allowing a smile to suffuse his expression. 'You're labouring under a misapprehension that I care anymore, General. I don't. You've taken my freedom, abused me, worked me like a dog.' He ignored the slur in the snort from Topol. 'You kidnapped my family, terrorised my wife and children. She'd terrorised me already by taking them from me.' He leaned forward again. 'So, I'm hollowed out, General. I don't care. I have nothing left, and'—he spread his hand out in the air, an encompassing gesture—'I'm happy to take everything with me.'

Topol flicked a glance at Sharon, who shrugged. 'Tell me what you've done to create this doomsday machine?'

Olsen stared into the general's eyes, saw the disbelief that lurked behind their surface, cat's eyes watching for any move, any tell that would expose the lie they believed came from their captive scientist. 'It's really simple. As you know, what we salted the first weapon with was gold. Gave the radiation a little extra kick, made it more difficult to survive in the local area—just for a short while. Yes?'

Topol gave a short nod and, for the first time, felt his mouth go dry.

'Well, then you wanted more, and I said I could give you more; just give me the right chemicals, and I can make sure nobody will fuck with Israel again.'

Another quick dip of the head.

'So, after our last little talk with your friends, and you showed me the video of my family and kids, I figured that I needed to give you something with a bit more of a kick.'

'What have you done, Johannes?'

Olsen turned to Sharon. 'You sound scared, Sharon.'

No response, from either of them—that was good, decided the scientist.

'Well, I guess you should be. The material, the isotope I asked for?' He looked from Topol to Sharon. 'Cobalt. You see, the great thing about cobalt is its long half-life. This isotope will make the radioactivity last a long time, contaminating many, many things.'

'How long?' Sharon felt her voice disappear into the ether, until she wasn't sure if he'd heard what she'd said.

'Five years. Enough time for it to circle the globe from wherever the bomb is detonated and contaminate the whole planet. Nothing will be untouched. Nothing.'

The air was driven from Sharon's lungs, and for a moment, it seemed her last meal would decide to join the discussion. She just about managed to hang on to it, but the sting of bile burned in her throat. 'What do you mean?' Her voice hid from the enormity of the atmosphere in the room.

Olsen turned to her and smiled, the smile of a beatified acolyte. 'I mean it will wipe out all life on earth. You, you'—he pointed at Topol—'Israel, and everyone else will perish. And there will be no more petty infighting or war.'

Topol blanched. What had they created? The man was obviously mad, but how to deal with it? Topol addressed it the only way he knew how. 'What you're saying is preposterous. You will kill your wife, children, and family in the process—'

"They're dead anyway. You will not let any of us survive your stupid plan, because then we can tell the world about the monsters you have truly become.'

Drawing his gun, Topol aimed it at Olsen. 'You will disarm the weapon now. Sharon.' He turned to the Mossad agent. 'Call flight control. Tell them to abort.' Even as he gave the order, the sound of an aircraft taking off suggested he was too late. 'Fuck!'

Olsen laughed harshly. 'So, they take off and into history—what's left of it.' He inspected his nails and then, 'What are you going to do, General? If your pilot hadn't taken off, there might have been an option to trade with me. I could have disarmed the bomb, with the right conditions, but … ' He tailed off.

Topol glared at the Norwegian, but his heart had lost the fight. What the hell could they do now? The pilot had strict orders not to break radio silence, and he'd taken off as planned, exactly as planned. What a time to be on mission. Fuck! He flexed his pistol at Olsen. There was only one thing to do now.

'Take this bastard back to his cell, while I think what needs to be done,' he spat at Sharon.

As the two left the room, he pulled a cell phone from his drawer and dialled a stored number. Time to tell Moshe how their plans had been fucked up.

55

David looked visibly more shaken than Moshe had ever seen him. The older man's skin was the pallor of death, loose and in danger of falling from the frame, as if the news of Olsen's treachery presaged the fate he'd brought upon humanity. David's hands clung to the balcony rail as his eyes swept Jerusalem's skyline, without seeing.

Moshe coughed, self-consciously, almost hating himself for interrupting the man's reverie. 'What do you want to do, David?'

I want to shoot the cunt myself, thought the older man. 'Find out what our scientist wants and move to give it to him. As soon as we get the result we want, terminate him.'

The NSA operator stared at the picture on the screen and checked again. Having the Fifth Fleet in the Mediterranean had proven a godsend on top of the re-tasking of surveillance platforms. It meant that long-range reconnaissance drones could be deployed relatively easily, and with their better optics and scanning devices, operators such as she could see and hear things that even a couple of decades ago would have seemed impossible to achieve.

And now, she had tasked a drone from an Arleigh Burke class destroyer to take photos in the early morning of two men stood at the balcony of a Jerusalem hotel. The image was pin sharp, despite being taken from a range of seventy kilometres. It was clear who the two men were; one was who they had expected him to be. The other …

406

The operator reached for the secure phone on her desk and punched in a number. Anachronistic, but safe. She waited, and then a voice answered.

'Operator two-six-three-Adam-five-Mary-seven. I need to speak with the director of National Intelligence right now.'

A silence came from the other end of the line. Seconds later, Bill Foreman's gruff voice barked over the line.

'Director, apologies for the late hour. I'm on surveillance of Jerusalem in accordance with orders. I have intel that is of grave importance.'

Foreman detected the concern, almost anxiety in the young woman's voice. 'Okay, what do you have?'

'I'm sending to your secure device now, sir,' she told him.

Foreman caught the flash of an incoming message icon on his wrapped idev. Quickly he flicked the device into shape and opened the secure file. The photograph was undeniable, and he felt his stomach heave with the shock. Halfin they had identified, but the other. 'Thanks for your work,' he told the operator. 'Maintain your watch and inform me immediately of any developments.' He gave her a direct line number. 'Use this, any time to catch me. It's secure.'

With the call terminated, Foreman pondered only briefly. He had to tell the president, and soonest. Determined fingers punched at the number icons on his device. 'Dan? Bring the car around immediately.'

As he awaited his driver, he dialled a second number, to Carol Fleischmann, chief of staff. A fatigued voice responded to his hello. 'What do you want, Bill?'

He drew a breath. 'I need to see the president, Carol. We have the identity of the leader of the cabal.'

The bastard. It was all she could think as she stared at the image on her idev. Always smiling, seemingly calculating at every point of their conversations together, seeking to blindside, to control. *How often has it been like that?*

Carlisle dropped her idev onto the desk and swung her chair to look out over the West Lawn. Dawn was just dusting the sky over the capital with its pink fingers, but the harsh LED lights bathed the pavements and roads won for now. In the political highway, would the light now shining on the Israelis also bathe her mistakes with harsh relief?

'Bill, you still there?' Carlisle had kept video off for the call.

'Yes, Madam President.'

'What's your prognosis?'

The pause. 'We always knew it would be difficult with a new government in Tel Aviv, but this puts a whole new cut on it. At least we know there won't be the sort of negotiation that John was expecting.'

Carlisle reflected on her former secretary of State, Kemble, who had placed such store on the ability to move the man they were both looking at, as the winning formula. 'You got that right.' She gave a short bark of a laugh. 'Everyone thought it would be Iran or North Korea that would go stir-crazy with nukes.'

'What are you considering?'

'I'm trusting Shenley to convince the Russians to work with us and fast.'

'Any news?'

'Not yet. If I hear nothing soon, we need to just get the hell on with it. I have the order on my device.'

'What's stopping you?'

'Being the president who fucks over the Jews, because that's how this will play out.'

Foreman sighed; he understood her dilemma. Right now, that seemed the least of her problems. He said so.

The sigh was deep and heartfelt. After all, what was most important? Upsetting the Israelis or saving the world? Maybe this was the catalyst, she told herself. Perhaps this time, with a strong arm against the wheel, things could change. Carlisle nodded slowly, silently to herself.

First, she had to stop the Israeli ex-prime minister from blowing the world to shit.

'Admiral?'

Shenley rose from his reverie and peered at his orderly with one bleary eye, the price for taking a power nap when there wasn't time.

'Admiral Timoshenko is on the line, sir.'

That woke him. Brushing his shirt straight and jamming his cap on his head, he passed the orderly and practically sprang to the bridge. *Give it a minute*, he advised himself as he settled into his chair. Comfortable, he called over to the communications officer. 'Give me Timoshenko.' The statement made him smile spontaneously, at the ludicrous nature of the comment—like a Cold War novel.

'You seem happy, Carl.' It was a statement, but a quizzical air inhabited the Russian's eyes.

Shenley waved it away. 'Just thinking on something. Do you have an answer?' Change the subject.

Timoshenko nodded. 'The president is not …'

Here it comes.

'Unsympathetic to your request. He has given me full authority to work with you.'

Yes! Shenley kept his face straight. 'That's very good news, Viktor.'

'Yes, it is, my friend. I should not have rejoiced in putting you at the bottom of the sea.'

Shenley laughed. 'Nor I you, Viktor. Now, we have targets that our intelligence people believe are the best options for ending this thing quickly. Shall we set up a conference with senior officers?'

'Indeed. We have little time. Our intelligence suggests another attack is imminent.'

'Let's do it. Send us your codes, and we'll set up the links. Ten minutes?'

With the merest of hesitations, Viktor Timoshenko nodded his head.

Shit, Carl told himself, detente was alive and well in the middle of nuclear holocaust.

'Flashfire Main, this is Flashfire Actual. We are boots on ground, in contact with friendlies. Securing position and awaiting instruction.' Hale refused to acknowledge the raised eyebrow of his second in command. After all, it wasn't a strict lie. They were in contact with the friendlies, just not at the moment.

After a heated discussion, lasting only minutes, Black, Murtagh, and Logan had agreed to follow a separate plan than that of the SEALs, much to Hale's annoyance. The one thing he had been promised was that those already on the ground would join them in action to retrieve the Olsen family. After all, Olsen was as good as dead. What they were proposing was foolhardy at best, catastrophic probably. Without hesitation, he'd blamed the Brit, hoping to get his compatriots to see sense—to no avail. Their funeral, he figured as he played his binoculars over the house sitting lonely in the fold of land below him.

It was a good position, he confessed. No cover to an approach from any angle, so no chance of creeping up. It would require some shock and awe. The transport, two black Mercedes M-class SUVs were the primary targets for the first strike. That would have to come from the Avenger ready to launch from the deck of the *Roosevelt*. Everything had to be carefully orchestrated for the attack and the exfil. An Osprey would follow in the Avenger, covered by Lightning IIs, while an E-3C would launch the operation with a controlled denial-of-service attack on Israel's command and control network. Once he sent the order, everything would drop into place. They expected the whole thing to last no more than forty-five minutes.

Hale's finger hovered over the transmit icon on his idev. Now or never.

'Flashfire Main, are you receiving?' His voice was small in the early-morning quietness.

'Flashfire Actual, this is Flashfire Main. Receiving. What is your situation?'

'We are in position. Eyes on target. Ready to engage. How is Main Force proceeding?'

'Main Force engaging at 0550. DoS, five minutes after. You are cleared to assault at 0600.'

'Copy that.' Hale checked his chronometer—fourteen minutes. All he had to do was say one short six-letter word. The merest of hesitations. 'Commit.'

'Understood. Sudden Sunrise is active.'

And that was it. Shortly, the US Fifth Fleet, together with elements of Russia's Black Sea Fleet, would commence bombardment of select targets. The confusion generated by that and the denial of service attack would provide his team the cover they required to liberate Olsen's family and, hopefully, capture Peter Halfin, head of Mossad and second in command of the cabal that threatened the world.

Hale scoped the building, outhouses, and vehicles below him one more time and nudged the SEAL next to him, pointing out the vehicles in front of the house. 'We take out the back two vehicles with Javelins. I want the Sprinter. Can you hack the EMU?'

The SEAL stared back in mock rebuke. 'There ain't an engine management unit I can't breach. It'll take seconds, and the vehicle's yours.'

Hale nodded. 'Good man. Stand by. The fireworks are about to start.'

Silence descended on the band of operatives, carefully positioned to take advantage of the ground around the target. Hale shuffled to his left and stared over the shoulder of his drone operator at the hooded screen receiving low-light television back from the miniature flying machine. All was quiet on the display. Hale nudged him. The man looked up. 'Go thermal,' the lieutenant instructed him.

The screen turned monochrome, an array of greys, forming shapes and blocks.

'How many?'

A pause. 'Thirteen tangos in the building. A group, second floor, three adults, two children. Looks like the hostages. There's one tango on the ground floor, appears to be unharmed.'

'Halfin?'

'Unknown.'

Hale stared at the screen and then at his chronometer. Any moment now.

As if his words were a cue, a flurry of activity in the house bloomed. Hale smiled grimly and turned to his waiting operatives. He held his fingers high—five digits—preparing the attack.

The sky to the north of him erupted in colour and smoke. Rolling towards them was the shock wave, pushing sound before it, the aftermath of the explosion. A quick glance at the screen. Mayhem.

'Move.'

Pushing down the slope, night vision turning all around him monotone but clear as day, instinctively understanding his people were in train, he approached the house. A whoosh, followed closely by another, streaked over them. Quickly he and his team raised their night vision. Seconds later, crashing light and sound erupted before them, the vehicles he had identified for destruction. Figures erupted from the house, startled and then ducking into the remaining shadows. A dark figure came from the back of the house, heading towards the SEALs. Hale brought up his supressed HK416 and fired two shots, centre mass. The body dropped quickly to the ground.

As he smiled, three shots whizzed passed him. Behind him a grunt, Simmons; that he chose to ignore. The mission came first. Grundy would pick up the fallen operative. Time to light it up. He sprinted, crouching, knowing that two of his team were either side of him. Figures appeared in the scope of his rifle. He picked off two as he rounded the bonfire of automobiles, aware of the sound of his own breath, still easy, his heart rate barely elevated. The door was close now. He slammed into the wall. Taylor passed him, crouching low and checking the doorway. He glanced at his boss, nodded, and pointed to the door. Hale moved past him, followed by the third SEAL. The house had gone dark, though he hesitated to use n-vis. What if the enemy switched on lights? He remembered the story of pirates who wore eyepatches not because they'd lost eyes but because they wanted an eye that could see at night.

He wished that could work in reverse.

A movement. Close. A flash. The knife creased his cheek, but already he was reacting, pushing the arm up and away against the door jamb, even as he stepped forward into his attack, his other hand thrusting the assailant's chin back. His boot stood on the other man's foot, unbalancing him. With a cry, the man fell to the floor. Hale brought his foot round into the man's groin, before stepping over him into the room. Another movement.

Hale brought his weapon up, his finger depressed the trigger—three shots in quick succession; the person in the shadows dropped to the ground.

Move, check, move, stop, fire—one more down. He sidestepped a table, aware of the SEAL behind him. Another door ahead closed. He hesitated, hand hovering over the handle. Around him, he could hear the sounds of battle. It was difficult to decide who was winning, as though he had any doubt. He pulled his hand away, turned to his colleague, and mimed pulling a grenade and throwing it. The other nodded and took a flash bang from his belt, pulling the pin.

Hale grabbed the door handle, twisted, and threw it open. The grenade sailed through a gap into the room. A voice shouted in Hebrew, and then there was an almighty flash and bang. Cries of pain came from the room. With a bound, Hale was in, sweeping the space for enemies.

Two men were on their knees, hands covering bleeding ears.

Pulling one of the men to a standing position, Hale turned them and looked into the weeping eyes of the suited figure. 'Good evening, Mr Halfin. Our president would like a word with you.'

A hole would've been nice, Logan considered as he finished scanning the perimeter fence to the Dimona facility. No such luck. What else? Olsen to be standing there ready to walk away with them? He shook his head at his own naivety. He scoped the facility again. The aircraft was on the runway, pilot and weapons officer strapped in and ready to launch.

Come on.

'They need to hurry up if we're going to stop this shit.'

He felt Black's anxiety. If the aircraft got off the ground, they would struggle to prevent a second catastrophe. Where was that strike?

As if disdainful of his thoughts, a screaming rose out of the desert air. He watched the aircraft lurch off its brakes as the pilot made a full military power take-off, surging along the runway, attempting to rise on its mission of Armageddon before it met its own destructive demise.

Come on!

The aircraft was beginning to rotate, its nose wheel unsticking as aerodynamics took hold to lift it into the air. It's banshee engine note competed with the incoming missile. And then there was the moment of coterminous as the two notes merged into one ululation of impending doom. The shape of the incoming cruise missile glinted briefly as the early sun caught its fuselage.

The fireball erupted from the facility, a huge pall of black smoke vomiting from the flames and billowing into the bright sky. Where was the aircraft? Had it cleared the airstrip? He could see nothing, but most of his vision was obscured by the still rising column of flame and smoke.

Perhaps.

Then came gut-wrenching knowledge and despair as a shape caught the rays of the sun, winking a Morse signal of destruction. He watched as the aircraft settled into an easterly course, climbing away from Dimona.

'We missed the aircraft at Dimona.'

Shenley refused to look at his XO, as if that would cement the failure and disable any option to change the outcome. 'What are our options?' He stared at the sea through the porthole of his ready room.

'We have an Avenger airborne over Iraq. It can be on an intercept within minutes. There is an AWACS providing real-time tracking of the target. We know exactly where it is and have a number of plots to potential targets.'

'Don't tell me—Iran?'

Nelson remained silent.

Shenley returned to his regard of the sea. In years from now, would there be anyone to care what happened this morning? It was his job to ensure it was so. He considered, briefly, requesting the president's permission but discarded the thought. He was here; she wasn't. What could she do, or say, that would be different to the course of action to which he knew he was committed? He drew a hand over his tired brow and allowed a deep sigh to push through his lips.

'Give the order, Mr Nelson. Shoot the sonofabitch down.'

The dust hadn't even settled as Logan, Black and Murtagh, accompanied by the two SEALs left by Hale, insinuated themselves into the devastated Dimona nuclear site. Fortunately, the main reactor building was undamaged, the blast having targeted the runway and hangars, to try and deny the Israelis the ability to launch an attack. That had worked, was the Brit's laconic assessment as they ran through the dust settling around them

As the attack had unfolded, one of the SEALs had discussed with them the layout of the buildings and where they figured Olsen was holed up. It was that three-storey block that they now approached.

A figure loomed out of the gritty fog, what looked like a rod extended before him. Logan hesitated, but a gentle *pop, pop, pop* indicated the SEAL had no such qualms. The figure crumpled, and they moved on hurriedly. Reaching the corner of the building, they oriented and moved towards the position of the main doors. Rifles at the ready, they waited as one of the SEALs moulded a CME, conformable miniature explosive, to each of the hinge positions and then pressed a shaped igniter into each patty. Pressing the centre of each ignite, he shouted out, 'Fire in the hole!'

With scarcely any noise, the explosives detonated, the blast being forced inward to the hinges by the shape of the explosive. The door rocked for a moment and then toppled forwards to the ground inside. The SEALs stepped forward, training ensuring they assumed command. People stood in the space, in shock and bemused by the commotion. The SEALs took full advantage.

General Topol shook himself and rose unsteadily from the floor, grasping for the desk that was no longer as it had been. Across from him, Olsen was similarly staggering and, from within the building, the sound of small-arm fire reverberated.

Who?

Why?

The second question was easier to answer, the reason currently trying to brush the brick dust from his jacket, the first less so. Topol settled for Americans. They had issued ultimatum after ultimatum through the night. It was hardly surprising, as the Israeli government could do nothing to accede to their demands, that they would launch an attack with cruise missiles.

It also made sense that they'd launch a raid to seize the scientist. That thought told him Olsen must die, now. Topol picked up the gun that had been flung from his grasp and levelled it at the Norwegian. 'Well, nothing more left for you, my friend,' he told the other. 'Now that you've fucked the world, I'm going to fuck you. Just so you know, we'll make sure your wife and children suffer.'

The shot rang out and Olsen flinched and then opened his eyes, in time to see Topol toppling to the floor.

'Nice shot.'

The words came from behind him.

'Shit, I was aiming for his leg, not his head.' A female voice, filled with sarcasm.

Olsen cautiously turned, to be confronted by two men and a woman who looked sardonically at him.

'Mr Olsen, hi. I think you have some explaining to do.'

'Wh-who are you?'

The taller of the two men spoke first, a frown inhabiting his broad forehead. 'We are both your saviours and your worst nightmare.' Unlike the others, this guy wasn't smiling. Olsen blanched.

'Don't listen to our colleague here. He likes to be melodramatic.' The final figure, British by the accent, advanced towards Olsen, who still found himself stepping back. His foot caught an obstruction behind, and he started to tumble back. A hand caught him, the Brit smiling in a disarming way. 'However, you do have to answer some questions for us.'

Olsen brushed the hand away and glared in what he hoped was an intimidating way. The looks of the others suggested this wasn't so. 'I don't have anything to say to you, or anybody else for that matter.' He turned away, righteous indignation coming across as sulking.

'Unfortunately, your demands in this aren't important,' the Brit told him.

The man opened his mouth to speak, but he was beaten to it by the woman. 'Mr Olsen, I'm Brooke Murtagh, CIA. Before you get all righteous on us, there's a little matter of genocide.'

That knocked the bluster from the Norwegian, who dropped to his haunches, holding his head in his hands. A sobbing noise came from behind the hands. The others watched as Olsen rocked slightly and let all the emotion he'd pent up inside all these weeks flood, in big drops of salt water to the dusty floor. He drew his hands over his face, massaging the weariness and sudden exhaustion from his cheeks in vain. 'I didn't mean to.'

'Well that's good to know. Thanks.' Black stared contemptuously at the shuddering Olsen. 'It'll be a great comfort to any family remaining to all those millions killed in Damascus. Where are you headed next? Oh wait! You want us all to pay for your fucking hardship.'

'They told me they had my children. They were going to kill them.'

Black was over in a single bound, grabbing the scientist and hauling him up so that his toes just touched the floor. 'You fucking shit!' The words spat across the other's face, lashing him. Olsen turned away. 'I got kids; millions have kids. Sometimes we suffer for them. We don't do your shit!'

'Easy there, John.' Logan touched his friend on the arm.

Black stiffened, and then his hand opened, and Olsen dropped to the floor. 'He's all yours.' And then he was gone.

'Luckily for you, Mr Olsen, it's probably best we do this somewhere else. Before we go, though, where is your next bomb to be deployed?'

Olsen shrugged. 'You think they told me?'

'Maybe. You ne—'

The SEAL who entered the room whispered into Logan's ear. He turned and regarded the tall Norwegian quizzically.

'What?'

'You may or may not be pleased to learn that we've rescued your family. They are on their way to safety. Hopefully we can catch this aircraft with your new bomb before it reaches its target. Otherwise, you'll have some serious explaining to do to those children you say you love so much.'

Shenley read the report handed to him by Nelson, with grim satisfaction. The joint Russo-American strike had wrought havoc with Israeli command and control. Civilian casualties had been minimised. The only fly in the ointment now was the aircraft carrying the nuke.

That was being addressed, and he trusted that there would be more good news for the president.

The Avenger operator, in air-conditioned comfort seven thousand plus miles away, scanned the skies projected to her screens as the UAV pulled round in a sweeping arc in the crystal-clear air on the Jordanian-Iranian border at 25,000 feet. Transmissions from the Boeing E-3C orbiting some two hundred miles east, kept updating the position of the Israeli Air Force jet.

This was a waiting game for now. Any action had to be completed cleanly and efficiently and on the right side of the Iraq-Iran border. Still better to let things fall on the Iraqi side; at least they still supported the Americans in this area.

Whatever happened, this was the first air-to-air action for Avenger—taking out the aircraft of an erstwhile ally, to save the world. No pressure then.

'Madam President, the Israeli ambassador is here to see you.'

'Thanks, Carol. Send him in.'

Carlisle kept her attention on her idev as Joel Wiesenthal was ushered in and shown a seat before the Oval Office desk. She continued reading a report, always conscious of Wiesenthal's increasing impatience; she allowed herself an inward smile. The report made some good reading, she had to admit. Four targets had been hit in Israel—two air force bases, the naval station at Haifa, and the nonnuclear facilities at Dimona. Working with the Black Sea Fleet had been interesting, a masterful move by Shenley, she admitted. *Let's see what the Israelis have to say.*

Carlisle rose from the desk and strode over to the ambassador. 'Good morning, Ambassador. How are you?' She extended a hand to the Israeli.

The lightest of touches from the diplomat showed this would be a difficult meeting. 'Well, Madam President, all things considered.' The tone was clipped, almost strained, and the face set.

Carlisle settled on a sofa and waited for her adversary.

Wiesenthal drew himself up and looked straight into the president's eyes. 'I have been asked to remonstrate in the most strenuous way the manner of the attacks on the sovereign State of Israel.'

'Your complaint is noted, Ambassador. Was there any loss of life?'

'There has been some,' Wiesenthal confessed. 'It is an odd place for us to be in, Madam President. Our prime minister cannot understand why our friends would wish to attack us in such a manner.'

Truculence and naivety all at once, Carlisle observed. 'I'm sure, Madam Ambassador, that you've not forgotten the devastation of Damascus.'

Wiesenthal's face darkened. 'Our government resolutely denies the charge that we had anything to do with the attack on the Syrian capital.'

'Nonetheless, there's no doubt that the weapon used in the attack was of Israeli manufacture. We have the bomb's signature, and we know this is the case.'

It was clear Carlisle's words caught the Israeli ambassador off guard. He recovered quickly. 'That is something we refute. We would need to see the evidence.'

'Be assured, you will see that evidence, Ambassador. But now there's a much more important matter. And time is against us—we need decisive action.'

'The matter is?'

Carlisle placed her idev on the table between them, activating its small projector. A picture blinked into view, and both could see the interior of an aircraft, with people staring at screens, moving about. Before all of that was a stern-looking officer.

'Commander Ryder, good morning. Is it still morning where you are?'

A brief smile kissed the lips of the commander. 'Just about, Madam President. Apologies for the early time back home, but we need your approval.'

'How come, commander?' Carlisle flicked a glance at the Israeli ambassador.

Before the commander could continue, there was a knock on the door. Carlisle bid the knocker enter, and the door opened to allow in a flow of senior officials to come stand with the president—the defence secretary, along with the directors of homeland security, CIA, and NSA. The one office not represented was the one recently vacated by the disgraced Weiss. At least the post was not necessary for this phase of the battle. Carlisle caught the distraught look on Wiesenthal's face.

'Carry on, Commander Ryder.'

'Ma'am. We have a jet headed east towards the Iranian border. We've tracked it since it became airborne from the Dimona facility, shortly before the *Roosevelt's* attack. It's our assessment of the flight plan trajectory that it's headed towards the Iranian nuclear facility at Fordow.'

'Commander, this is Sarah Markham, director of the CIA. How confident are you that the aircraft is headed for Fordow?'

'Director. The aircraft has crossed into Iraqi airspace, with its IFF switched off. The last waypoint calculation placed its flight path across the position of the Fordow nuclear facility.'

'Wait one.'

'Aye.'

Carlisle paused the transmission. 'Ambassador, your call. Whether this is a government-sanctioned attack, which we think unlikely, or an attack by some cabal over which the Israeli government has no control, there is a world at stake, and that takes precedence over anything else. We cannot let that aircraft attack the Iranians.'

'I have no authority to order the downing of an Israeli aircraft.'

'You don't have to, Ambassador. But you are a witness for your government as to what will happen next.'

'What do you mean, Madam President? You must know that you cannot shoot down our aircraft without the sanction of my government?'

Carlisle smiled. 'Oh, Joel, we're not seeking the sanction of your government, and we most certainly are not waiting to let you do it.' She unpaused the transmission to Ryder. 'Commander Ryder.'

'Yes, ma'am?'

'You are clear to engage the target at your discretion.'

The F-16 pilot checked his instruments, scanned again the dormant threat warning panel, and began his descent towards the 'deck'. Still over Iraqi territory, he was sure that neither the US nor the Iraqi Air Force would interfere with him. His trajectory took him towards the enemy— Iran. No, he would be safe from attack, this side of the border.

At 250 feet, he levelled off, engaged terrain following, and set the final waypoint. He thought of the weapon hanging below the belly of his mount. Unleashing nuclear hell on the sworn enemy of Israel was something he had dreamt of from time to time. Every soldier, sailor, or airman knew the threat posed by Iran, despite the promises of the United States. Now it was up to him to deliver Israel's response. Grim purpose inhabited his features as he settled down for the bumpy, low-level ride.

The Avenger pilot took over the tracking of the Israeli fighter from the AWACS when there was 150 miles separation. The target dot moved slowly to the centre of her screen as she pulled in behind the target. Her hand hovered over the launch button for one of the aircraft's air-to-air missiles. Launch one, not targeted. Explode it, and the Israeli would be alerted; she would have to abort the mission.

The fingers flexed over the buttons. Save one man and lose the world; that was the antithesis of her mission. Eight billion people relied on her scratching this one Israeli. Yet he was the one she could see, the one who, at this moment, inhabited her universe, thousands of feet above the planet—a planet this person was on a mission to doom with his one weapon.

Her finger rested on a button.

'To be or not to be.'

And depressed it.

'Missile armed, passive tracking available.'

'Designated target, bearing one-three-eight degrees at 102 miles.'

'Target acquired. Query command decision. Target is Isra—'

'Override query. Lock target, launch at optimal envelope.'

'Optimal envelope achieved.

'Launch.'

The Avenger bucked as the missile dropped from its bay, falling through the stratosphere, away from the UAV. The operator brought her craft round in a steady turn, intent not to present any signature to the unsuspecting Israeli.

One life for many.

The Israeli thought for a moment that his scopes registered a flash, and then it was gone. Soon he would be on the final approach to his target— Fordow. A nuclear message for a nuclear threat. His fingers tapped in the launch sequence.

Soon.

A series of green lights on his weapons panel, and the target was coming into the launch window. He felt proud to be doing what he was, for the greater good of the Israeli nation. He knew that he would be vilified, but every Israeli was prepared for the world's opprobrium if that was what it took to keep the country safe.

Routine determined he go through checks again. Nothing unusual happening. He scanned the horizon. Mountains rose in the south-west, parallel to his path. Momentarily, they hid him at this altitude from the attentions of the Iranian radar. A few more klicks, and all hell would break loose.

The operator looked at the two spots on the scope before her, converging. Two more minutes, and the target would be in Iranian airspace. Just under a minute, and the hypersonic missile would hit it; the kinetic energy would destroy the aircraft and the nuclear weapon hanging beneath it. Even as she thought the words, the two points of light became one.

'Madam President, the aircraft has been downed. The threat has been averted.'

'Commander Ryder, thank you for your diligence in this matter, and well done.'

'Ma'am.'

The line was dead, and Carlisle turned to the Israeli ambassador. 'Ambassador.'

Joel Wiesenthal looked up.

'We have neutralised the threat posed by your jet. Now your government needs to do something to resolve this goddamned situation with President al-Umari and fast. Or so help me God, I'll resolve it for you.'

Wiesenthal rose slowly, unsteadily, drawing up his diminutive frame as best he could. 'You will be hearing from our government before the day is out.'

Carlisle rose from her place and stepped towards the Israeli ambassador. 'No. You will take this message back to your prime minister.'

'I can't.'

'Ambassador, the Jerusalem Accord will be signed within the month, or I will personally march you to The Hague for war crimes and give al-Umari the keys to the Knesset myself.'

O n the *Roosevelt*, Olsen had been placed under armed guard in the XO's cabin. Halfin's fate was far more prosaic; he was cooling off in the brig after an eventful flight, where he had shouted and railed at everybody on the plane. On deck, he had remonstrated, shoved, and spat at the SEALs. They had taken it in their stride and handed him to marines, who were less kind.

Two marines guarding him took a step back as they presented him to Shenley, but not too far that they couldn't restrain the dishevelled Mossad director should it be necessary.

Shenley's cabin was crowded; Logan and Murtagh, Black, and Nelson were all there to see what, if anything, Halfin would say. The admiral relaxed behind his desk, a large tumbler of whisky swirling in his large hand. It was, Logan felt, smiling inwardly, a Mexican stand-off—Shenley being inscrutable, Halfin glowering. This continued for an interminable time, so it seemed to the observers. The marines remained as inscrutable as Shenley.

Eventually, Halfin broke the silence. 'What is the meaning of this?'

Shenley regarded the Israeli quietly and took a sip of whisky. The moment stretched again, seeming to compress the walls of the cabin. He placed the tumbler on his desk.

'I asked you what the meaning of this is.'

'Mr Halfin.' Shenley leaned forward. 'You're under arrest, on suspicion of conspiring to commit genocide.' He sighed. 'Or some such shit. Peter, this is a real cluster fuck. What the hell are you thinking?' Another shake of the head. 'What's happening at Dimona? What is The Seven?'

Halfin played it cool. Logan was impressed, but then the man was head of Mossad. The man leaned back in his chair. 'I don't have any idea what this talk of … Seven is. As for Dimona? Would you tell me what was happening at your famed Skunk Works?'

'Not long since, we would've.' Shenley chuckled and looked over to the intelligence officers.

Murtagh took up the cudgel. 'Mr Halfin, we have records of you in conversation with unknown others.'

Halfin chuckled and shrugged. So what?

'Calls made from a burner phone to another who went by the name of David.' Inwardly she smiled as she noted the slight tick.

Halfin remained still. 'So?' The stillness in the cabin threatened to become stifling. Halfin regarded his accuser levelly. 'You have no evidence for your accusations.'

'No? How about this?' Murtagh placed her idev on the desk before Halfin and tapped an icon. A voice inhabited the space between the CIA officer and her quarry, soon joined by another:

'Well, Moshe, well. It seems the product works.'

'Indeed.'

'What of the deliverers?'

'They've been paid off.'

'That's good news. So, we move to the next product.'

'Yes. Ariel confirms that it won't be a problem to go to that stage.'

Murtagh paused the recording and looked squarely at Halfin.

He returned the gaze. 'What of it? That could be anyone talking. And who is it talking? You have nothing.'

'Perhaps not in that single recording. But, you see, the person who was using that phone had made a call only moments before, speaking with someone called Ariel. Now, Mr Halfin, we believe that the names Ariel, David, and Moshe are covers, for people who are part of the cabal we seek. We know that David Perez was a member of such an undercover group, as was Natalie Epstein.' She caught herself momentarily remembering the encounter she'd shared with Logan.

'We think that second call was a break of protocol. Maybe the individual who was involved, thought, *What the fuck? We're close to victory. What could possibly go wrong?* Whatever your reasoning, we were able to pinpoint your calls and put you in the same place as "Moshe". Unsurprising that your code name would be Moshe really. Don't you think? After all, you would want to model yourself on one of Israel's greatest generals, wouldn't you?'

'Speculation.'

'We don't think so, Mr Halfin. The look on your face, suggests you're concerned how much we know.'

'And you are?'

'Logan, Secret Intelligence Service.'

'Ah, British. Still hanging on to the belief that you are of any relevance to the world.'

'At least we're not trying to blow it to kingdom come.'

Halfin's eyes narrowed. 'How—'

'Cobalt.'

'I'm sorry?'

Logan approached the director of Mossad, smelling the smoke in the man's hair, the slight smudging of dust on the cheeks belying the calm demeanour. He knew there was turmoil, disruption beneath the surface. It was just a matter of picking at the scab.

'Cobalt is an isotope that can be used to salt nuclear warheads. But of course you know that, don't you, Peter?'

Halfin glanced up, self-consciously. 'What do you mean? Salt?'

'Okay, rudimentary physics. A nuclear warhead's radioactive fallout can be intensified and extended by using a variety of isotopes. That ensures that the radioactivity is more lethal for an extended period of time. Gold, which has been identified in readings from the Damascus blast site, has a half-life of two days.

'There are other isotopes, with increasing lethality—right up to … cobalt.'

Halfin didn't move, didn't flinch in his regard of Logan, who continued. 'Cobalt has the longest half-life and, thus, the greatest lethality. The radioactive fallout from a nuclear weapon salted with cobalt is approximately five and a half years. We're talking enough to contaminate the whole planet, wipe out all life—families, lovers, everything.'

A moment of terror inhabited Halfin's gaze fleetingly, and Logan felt a satisfaction in his gut. They'd gotten to the man.

'You'll be pleased to know then that the aircraft carrying the bomb your little cabal put together was shot down ten minutes from its target, Fordow.'

That got Halfin's attention. His shoulders visibly slumped. 'I know nothing of what you speak.'

'What you also *don't know* about is that you employed a nuclear physicist with extensive knowledge of how to build, configure, and modify a nuclear weapon.'

'You then decided to kidnap his kids, to make him feel there was no hope.' Murtagh approached the Israeli.

Logan saw she was spoiling for a fight; what he didn't know was whether it was real or a play act. Interesting.

She closed. 'You say you know nothing of this. We can place you on the calls, you were at the weapons enrichment site, and you are the head of Mossad. Your operatives were involved in the kidnapping of a Norwegian scientist from Geneva, using an airplane owned by a company whose CEO was David Perez. Perez's shipping company was used to deliver material to Dimona, which had been transferred from a shipment to a US chemicals company. That product was cobalt. Ring any bells?'

Halfin remained silent, merely staring at the CIA officer.

'How about we fill in some gaps?'

'Whatever you want.' His tone was sullen. But was that a brokenness Logan detected? Possibly. Wait to see his reaction to Brooke's next words.

'So, because you didn't want to be involved in a historic settlement for the Palestinians, you decided, along with a number of others—seven in total—to derail the agreement. You thought you'd do that by trying to assassinate President al-Umari, which didn't work. At the same time, you thought that the best way to ensure that everyone did what Israel wanted was to launch a series of attacks designed to ensure Arab nations would be hobbled by the fallout, literally.

'How'd we do so far?'

Halfin glared at her but said nothing.

'But who to attack? Who would give the biggest bang for the buck? Well, Iran has always been a thorn in the Israeli side, hasn't it? What with its support for Hezbollah and all. Then, there was the thorny problem of testing the weapon's technology, and you couldn't bomb the same country twice—unless you had to.

'So, what better way to resolve issues with Syria than to use them as a test site for a salted weapon, which your friend from Geneva was only too happy to build for you when he found out that his family had been killed in a terrorist attack on their settlement.

'Test one proves the theory—job done. Now it's time for the big one, the one where Iran would pay for all the times they'd affronted the State of Israel. Which gets us to today.'

'But who had the most to gain from such an attack, such a move?' Logan regarded his captive, looking for the slightest twitch. 'It had to be somebody high up in the hierarchy of Israeli politics, somebody who had the most to lose from such an agreement.'

Halfin refused to match Logan's stare, contemplating the surface of the table between them, stoic in his silence. This was getting nowhere.

He turned to Shenley. 'Admiral. I have a new target for you.'

Shenley's eyes narrowed, an eyebrow raised in query.

Logan consulted his idev and then pushed a note to Shenley's device.

'What's this, Commander?' Shenley addressed the Brit by his MI6 rank.

'Be'er Sheva is home to Mossad's cyber-intelligence gathering operation, a number of aerospace operations, and IDF facilities. I think a judicious deployment of Tomahawk missiles would be appropriate, given the exigencies of the current situation.' He cast a glance at Halfin. The Mossad director's face was set, drained of colour.

Shenley had noticed also. "It seems our guest is less than enamoured by your choice of target. How come?'

Halfin stared ahead, determined not to make any eye contact with his captors. Logan slid a photograph to Shenley's device.

'Ah, I see. Mr Halfin, you have a beautiful family. I'd hate to see them share the same fate as so many in Damascus.'

'You wouldn't dare. We are allies, Admiral.'

'Just watch me, Mr Halfin.' Shenley swiped his device, bringing up his command console. 'Mr Nelson, contact the *Bradley*. I want a firing solution on Be'er Sheva. A salvo of Tomahawk cruise missiles is to be patterned across the city.'

'Any specific target, Admiral?'

'At this time, we've no option but to target the whole city, due to the nature of the threat. You might want to contact our Russian colleagues for assistance.' Shenley turned to Halfin. 'Mister, you have about a half hour before that strike goes in and consigns your family to dust. Do you have the balls to face us out on this, given the extent of your crimes on humanity?'

'You're not saving Israel with your actions, Halfin.' Logan changed tack. 'You and your colleagues are doing it the worst possible damage. If you help us, we can help protect what's left. If you don't, then we'll have to stand aside while the courts and world opinion rage against your country and demand retribution. That demand will be extremely high for Israel.'

'The demand of you will be your family, as well as your country.'

Halfin looked at Murtagh but didn't respond. She thought she saw the turmoil in his eyes, but he remained inscrutable for the main part.

Shenley rose and went to a cabinet on one side of his cabin, where he poured himself a large whisky before returning to his desk. 'You know, Peter. My granddad had an Alsatian one time. Big brute of a dog but with a temperament that was protective and loving. We kids loved the goddamned animal and would play with it in the fields behind the ranch. It kept us safe out in the wilds and was always there, a constant friend and protector. As it got older though, it got damned crotchety and would snap and snarl at people, even us kids as we grew bigger. Maybe it had dementia or some such.

'Anyway, one day a neighbour was with my gramma, with her grandkids. Ole Buster came in from the back yard, ambling in in his old way and saw the kids. In a flash, he lunged at them and bit one so hard we had to take the poor lad to hospital for stitches to his arm. When my granddad got home, he took Buster into the fields and had his last moments with him. Then he put a two-two calibre slug between his eyes.'

Shenley took a slug of whisky and looked hard at Halfin. 'Where I'm sitting, Israel is Buster, and I'm putting a round in the chamber. The clock is ticking.' He sat back and finished his drink, ignoring the Israeli.

The silence in the room grew in intensity. No one moved. Nobody felt they could; the atmosphere was so charged.

After what seemed an age, Shenley let out a tired sigh and checked his watch. He reached for his idev. 'Mr Nelson, how are we with that strike?'

'*Bradley* and *Zhukov* have a strike element of forty cruise missiles targeted on Be'er Sheva. We calculate a 95 per cent target destruction.'

'Well, calculate 100 per cent. Launch on m—'

'Wait!'

All eyes turned to Halfin. The man looked suddenly drawn and tired, resigned. 'I will give you what you want.'

Shenley nodded to the marine guard. 'Take him back to the brig and get those goddamned answers.'

As the door closed behind the Israeli, Logan turned to Shenley. 'Thanks for sharing the story about Buster, Admiral. Shame about the dog, but it did the trick.'

Shenley eyed him, with a glint. 'Hell, there was no fucking dog, Mr Logan.' He laughed out loud and reached for the whisky once more.

58

It was with a certain amount of satisfaction that Carlisle regarded the haggard face of the Israeli prime minister. Telling him that his Mossad director was incarcerated on the *Roosevelt* and that he was making a fine example of saving his own ass gave her a much-needed feeling of power and righteousness, even as she realised she had to temper it.

'This is most irregular, Madam President. I cannot emphasise the damage this is doing to the relationship between our two countries.'

Carlisle laughed, a short staccato bark that brought the Israeli to a sudden stop. 'Mr Olmet, please. Your inability to understand the writing on the wall is perplexing and worrying. We have Peter Halfin in custody, and he is implicating senior individuals in Israel in a conspiracy to derail the Jerusalem Accord.'

Olmet tried his hardest to maintain his indignation, but Carlisle thought she saw the chink opening slightly, the consideration that things might be out of his control, that he may need help.

Carlisle pressed on. 'You need to understand the predicament you and Israel are in now. Work with us, Binyamin. Help us to bring down this cabal.'

The Israeli shook his head slowly at first and then vigorously. 'No, no. You are wrong. There is no cabal, no conspiracy.'

'We have evidence this cabal existed. And if it didn't, that doesn't work out well for Israel. You need to help us take out the leader of the cabal and close this down, once and for all.' She paused, considering the Israeli, who said nothing. 'Do you understand what will happen if we don't take down this group, this leader?'

'Only too well, Madam President.' Olmet sighed, a deep heavy sound that dragged with it the weariness of all the years of Jewish oppression. 'Let me consider what you have. The information.'

Carlisle shook her head. 'We don't have the time to let you go away and decide whether to help. I don't have to remind you, Binyamin, that this cabal has put your country in a very difficult position in the international community. We need to shut it down. She stared at his face in the device, saw the indecision.

'Now, David.'

'All right, all right. Tell me what you have.'

Carlisle said a private prayer of thanksgiving. 'Thank you, Binyamin. This is going to come as a shock, Binyamin, but we believe that the leader of the cabal is your predecessor.'

Olmet's gaze hardened. 'Ehud? You believe Ehud is behind this? It's unbelievable.' He shook his head. 'No. I won't believe it.'

Carlisle pushed closer to the camera on her idev. 'Believe it, Binyamin. Your predecessor was fronting a cabal that threatened to obliterate the world.'

Olmet pulled a hand over his face. 'Can you leave it for us to deal with this?'

'It's gone beyond that, Binyamin. You need to keep out of the way. We have an arrest warrant, signed by the chief justice to the International Court of Justice. Just give us the okay to go get him.'

Silence was an almost visible presence, increasing Olmet's bulk but still diminishing the man in Carlisle's eyes. He nodded briefly.

'Is that a yes?'

'Yes.'

'Thank you, Binyamin. Israel won't regret this. I assure you.'

'We are good to go.'

Lieutenant Hale regarded the people in the ready room. There was the usual calm, despite Black; Murtagh; and the Brit, Logan, being there. Black he respected, SEAL commander himself. Murtagh he had seen could handle herself. The Brit, not so sure, though he'd heard tales of SAS and the Company. Time would tell, he reckoned. He indicated the big screen behind him, on which a satellite image showed. In the centre was a farmhouse, surrounded by trees, in front of which were several SUVs.

'This, ladies and gentlemen, is our target. We have constant satellite and drone surveillance on it. Our main target has been identified at the site. He has a guard of up to twenty individuals with armaments believed to be personal sidearms and CQB weapons.'

'LT?'

'Yes, Alvarez?'

'Do we know if the security has surface-to-air capability?'

Hale shook his head briefly. 'Not at this time. We must assume that such is the case and be prepared accordingly.'

'What's our profile?'

'Good question, Hussein. We are point and protection for these three,' Hale indicated Logan, Murtagh, and Black, before bringing up a schematic on the screen. 'We launch in thirty, three-zero, minutes, on-board an Osprey with two F-35s on escort. We secure the site, and they will identify the primary. On their signal, we exfil to the Osprey and back to the *Roosevelt*.'

'Who are we extracting?'

'That's need to know, Hussein, and you don't need to know. Just aim at the guys with guns, and we'll be okay. There is no indication the target of this operation will be armed. For this mission, Taylor and Steinberg will provide overwatch from this position.' Hale indicated a position marked X on the displayed map. 'You'll be dropped first, picked up last. Any further questions?'

'Just one, LT.'

'Yes, Alvarez?'

'Given Taylor can't shoot for shit, is there a necessity to take extra body armour on this mission—specifically, to protect the ass region?'

Hollers and laughs accompanied Alvarez's query. Taylor stuck a digit in the air and good-humouredly mocked his colleague. 'Hell, Alvarez, it's fucking difficult trying to miss your ass.'

'Wouldn't mind, but you're supposed to be protecting us, not the enemy.'

'Okay, pipe down guys. Wheels up in twenty. Let's do this.' Hale ushered his people from the room.

Black caught him just as he was about to leave and pulled him to one side. 'You good with us leading you guys in?'

'You? Yeah. Some of the others—not so much. But, hey, it is what it is, Lieutenant. Let's get the job done.'

Hale shrugged off Black's hand, who watched him head to the hangar deck.

'Everything okay, John?'

Black glanced at his friend and nodded. "Yeah. Just making sure we don't get stuck in the ass ourselves.'

Logan smiled. 'At least we'll have someone to blame.'

The Osprey hit the coast south of Tel Aviv, headed at speed across the dunes just north of Ashdod, before turning slightly left and north towards their target. Hale pumped the noisy air in the Osprey three times with his fist, to indicate fifteen minutes to target. The SEALs got down to prepping their equipment. This phase would see them head behind their target to drop off their overwatch, before sweeping over and descending on their quarry. The men and women worked in quiet determination, checking weapons, magazines, helmets, strapping, and anything they had that might get in the way if it wasn't stowed properly.

All was silent again, save for the whine of the turbines and chopping of the huge blades, scything holes in the Israeli sky. The droning was the wrong side of soporific, but Logan felt his mind wander as time dragged on. Then, suddenly, the green light blinked on and a klaxon sounded on the cargo deck. To the rear of the ship, the quartermaster was dropping the ramp. Taylor and Steinberg assumed position for the drop-off.

With the merest of touches, the Osprey kissed the back of the hill, and the two SEALS jumped off and headed up the hill. Swinging the big aircraft round, the pilot headed away from their target before turning and heading back round. They hurtled round the hill, keeping trees between them and the farmhouse. Even so, Logan could see the Mossad agents running to the wooded area, weapons ready, some beginning to fire at the huge aircraft. The marine on the closest door turned his pintle-mounted 7.62mm machine gun on them, triggering a concentrated stream of white-hot fire on the vehicles, ensuring the Israelis kept their heads down.

Still behind the trees, the pilot brought the Osprey to a hover, and the SEALs disembarked, splitting in a predetermined pattern to pincer move on the farm. Black followed Hale's team, with Logan and Murtagh in train. Crouching, they all moved quickly into the trees. Bullets still scythed the air around them, but this time they knew it was from Mossad. The Osprey had stopped raining down destruction and was pulling out of the area. The sound of its mighty motors subsided, and only the hiss and whoosh of live rounds could be heard. Logan crouched and surveyed all round him. To his left was Black, a dark figure slinking from tree to tree, stopping briefly to target someone ahead of them, arms raised, HK416 barking roughly, clinically, to despatch another defender. On his right, Murtagh was equally effective, dropping individuals with surety and without remorse.

He moved forward, aware of every little sound as they approached the short treeline. Ahead of him, a Mossad operative dressed in black levelled his weapon at Logan. The Brit raised his Glock 17, drew the bead, and let two shots off in quick succession, grim satisfaction lining his face as the man went down in a corona of blood.

The action was over quickly as the SEALs overwhelmed the more lightly armed Mossad teams. Quickly they began securing those who still might offer resistance, collecting and making safe the firearms that littered the ground. Satisfied, they moved to phase two. Cautiously the SEAL team converged on the house from front and back. Hale beckoned Black and Murtagh forward.

'Taylor says there are vehicles headed this way at speed. Could be Unit. I don't want to be here if it is. I can vouch for my people; can't do the same for you guys and your hostage. Let's get this done.'

Black nodded briefly. 'Breach it.'

Hale nodded back and turned to his team, waving forward an operator wielding a Remington shotgun and another to cover him. Everyone else fell into train behind them, eyes alert, heads swivelling for any movement.

Quickly, the operator lined up the heavy shotgun and blew out where the door hinges were and then the latch, pulling back quickly as the door fell forward. The woman on point quickly moved forward and dropped two flash bangs in quick succession. 'Fire in the hole!'

Everyone fell back as the two grenades went off, light and sound bouncing around in the confined space of the hallway of the farmhouse and the room off to one side. As the noise subsided, the SEAL team surged into the house, breaking in doors and loosing off more flash bangs into tight spaces where people might be hiding. With easy precision, the operators leapfrogged each other, working through the rooms and clearing each one.

Hale led four members, Black, Murtagh, and Logan up the stairs to the second floor. The first shots cracked over their heads, smashing the glass in the window that looked out over the hill behind the farm.

'Taylor? Eyes on, second floor, middle window.' Hale's urgent whisper, barely heard by those around him, was answered shortly afterwards by two shots that ripped the window apart. The thud of a body slumping on the floorboards was followed by the clatter of a weapon being thrown down and kicked across the floor.

'Come forward slowly, hands clasped behind the head. Let's see you.'

The young Israeli woman advanced to the top of the stairs, hands interlocked behind the lustrous black hair tied in a ponytail. She looked too young for this shit, Logan figured as she stopped in full view of them, defiant and proud nonetheless.

'Turn around and drop to your knees.'

As she complied, Hale waved forward one of the team, who secured the woman's hands with zip ties. Carefully, she led her captor down the stairs and outside.

Black continued up the stairs and along the corridor to the door, outside which the body of another woman lay, a congealing pool of blood forming a halo round her broken head. What a fucking waste, figured the SEAL as he stood outside the door and heaved a breath into his lungs.

'In the room, my name is John Black. I am here at the behest of the United Nations and the International Court of Justice to serve an international arrest warrant. Please step away from the door, turn away, and place your hands interlocked behind your head. Anyone in the room with a weapon, place it on the ground and kick it towards the door. Then place your hands interlocked behind your heads and face the opposite wall.'

Black waited, briefly acknowledging Logan and Murtagh, who had joined him. They listened as there were clattering sounds on bare floorboards, followed by shuffling. All three raised pistols as Black gingerly closed his hand around the doorknob and turned.

Carlisle took in the Palestinian leader and couldn't quite understand why he was so resigned. His whole demeanour actually annoyed her. She kept her emotions controlled, hoping her disappointment hadn't leaked out.

For his part, Jamal al-Umari stared at his American counterpart, wondering exactly what she had hoped to elicit from him. Yes, it was good news that the countries of the world had faced down Israel to prevent them turning everything to a dust more dangerous than Chernobyl, but Palestinians were still without a home, and Israel hadn't made any overture to signing yet. It was good that this cabal was about to be stopped for good, and yet.

Situation normal. 'How do you say? "All fucked up."'

Carlisle flushed at the crudity, but it was clear that al-Umari wasn't in a giving mood. 'Jamal, I completely understand your position. But we now have an opportunity to reset the agreement for the benefit of your people.'

'You like to let me think that you do all this for the benefit of Palestine and the West Bank. Do not insult my intelligence, Madam President—'

'Angela, please.'

'Madam President,' al-Umari emphasised. 'You all did this to save your own skins, not for any sense of moral duty to the Palestinian Arab.'

Carlisle was silent, taking in the indignant Palestinian. Then she drew a breath and leaned into the camera. 'You're absolutely right, Mr President,' she replied, adopting his grim politeness. 'I make a promise, here and now, that we will deliver a signed Jerusalem Accord within the month. We have the support of the Chinese and Russian administrations in this.'

'Let me think about it. I will confer with my colleagues and with Mayor Qureshi.'

And with that, he was gone.

Carlisle stared at the screen. All she had to do now was to convince the Russians and Chinese of the necessity to get Israel to sign.

The door swung open quietly to reveal a strange tableau. Two Mossad agents stood beside a large man sat on a single chair in an otherwise bare room. They were both expressionless and yet defeated in their blankness.

The man, dressed in a crumpled white shirt, tie hanging limply from the neck and encased in a battered linen suit that had fit properly once upon a time, sat listlessly on a chair that was too small for his big frame. His fingers tapped restively on his fat thighs.

Black flicked his hand at the two Israelis, indicating they should move aside. A slight hesitation as they inclined their heads at their boss. He gave a short, impatient nod, as if he needed this all to be over as quickly as possible. Black considered this thought. His had reached to a zipper and opened the breast pocket of his body armour, pulling out an envelope that was as rumpled as the man's suit. He held it out to his quarry and drew him up to deliver the words he had been rehearsing, even in the heat of battle.

'Sir. Are you Ehud Malbert, ex-prime minister of Israel?'

The man merely nodded, and Black carried on. 'Ehud Malbert, on the authority of the International Court of Justice and the United Nations Security Council, I am arresting you for the crimes of conspiracy to genocide and the illegal development of a weapon or weapons of mass destruction. You do not have to say anything, but it may harm your defence if you omit to say something that you later rely on in a court of law. Do you have anything to say at this time?'

'I did what I did for the State of Israel. And generations to come.'

'Good for you.' Black turned to two of the SEALs. 'He's all yours. Let's get out of here.'

Epilogue

'It's a historic day for Palestinians and Jews everywhere, though both parties may be seeing the momentous occasion in very different lights as the parties come forward, here at Camp David. First forward is the president of the United States of America, Angela Carlisle, flanked by the presidents of Russia and China, who together have brokered this final chapter in the Jerusalem Accord. Does this usher in a new era of realpolitik? Time will tell.

'But now, we await the emergence of the two protagonists of this long drawn-out affair. And here they come! Almost hand in hand, an occasion few of us thought we would witness in our lifetimes, President Jamal al-Umari and Israeli Prime Minister Binyamin Olmet walk towards the great mahogany desk to sign the agreement that will mark the formal end of centuries of conflict between Jew and Palestinian and the creation of a single entity of Israel, open to all.

'Just behind them is the newly elected mayor of Jerusalem, Mohammed Qureshi, equally beaming in the sunlight that streams through the windows to highlight the auspicious moment in world history. Let's think o—'

'Another beer?'

Black held up his glass to his partners. Logan considered the dregs in his glass and nodded. Murtagh too gave the nod on the offer. 'Bartender!' He waved his glass, and the refilling began.

As they waited, Murtagh indicated the unfolding ceremony on the screen. 'Who'd've thought?'

Logan smiled, a little wearily. 'It is crazy to think only a month ago we were staring down the barrel of nuclear destruction.'

'Strange shit indeed.' Black served up the beers. 'But we can say that it was down to us that (a) there will be a place for the Palestinians in the world for the first time and (b) we're not all gonna die in five years' time. Which would be a shitter.'

'Drink to that.' Murtagh clinked glasses and drank deeply. 'You okay?'

'Tired is all.' Logan smiled weakly.

Black laughed. "Getting old, man. You'll be hanging up your spurs next.'

Logan's eyes narrowed. 'We did save the world from nuclear destruction, and that's a big claim nobody can dispute. Olsen, Malbert, and the others will have their day in court, and the world will get justice. But somebody else will come along. Not sure I want to go through all that again.'

Black's eyebrows rose, and he glanced at Murtagh. 'You listening to this?'

Murtagh smiled. 'Yes I am, and I agree with him. We've done our bit. Now's the time to kick back and enjoy life.'

Their friend regarded them suspiciously. 'What you gonna do ?'

The smile returned. 'Get a boat.'

'A boat!? Neither of you can sail.'

Logan laughed. 'Canal boat. We're going to drift along the canals of England and just chill, maybe write our memoirs. But for now, we'll just take time out to enjoy what we have.'

Black's face cracked into a broad grin. 'Amen to that friend. Well, we saved the world. And that's as much as anyone can ask. Here's to canals.'

'What will you do?'

Black considered. "Hey, man, I'm too young to sit back and do nothing. My commander is talking about an operation. Figure I've still got some world to save.'

'There'll always be some world to save.'

The three paused on that moment, and then, with a clink of glasses, they downed their drinks.

The courtroom of the International Court of Justice was austere, clinical, and packed. News reporters and camera crews filled the public gallery, the eyes of the world facing those behind the glass screen. Ehud Malbert, Peter Halfin, Benjamin Kompert, and Miranda Klein sat quietly in the dock, staring impassively ahead, not acknowledging the steady intonation of the senior judge reading he list of indictments.

Finally, she stopped reading and looked at the four defendants. 'To the charges as they have been read out, how do you plead?'

Malbert returned her scrutiny and, without flinching, intoned, 'Not guilty, your honour.'

Johannes Olsen stared at the photograph, his children beaming at him from behind the creases. He missed them. All he had agreed to do had been for them; all he had been forced to do, to consider, had been for them.

He blanched when he considered how close he had come to a final act of annihilation, an apocalypse. Not exactly the best way to woo your ex, Olsen considered ruefully. That was past now; there would be no reconciliation, no path back. As those who had cajoled and coerced his actions were to have their day in court, so he, Johannes Thor Olsen, would have his, both as witness and defendant. But before he defended himself, there was the matter of bringing down the hammer of justice on those who would ruin everything. And bring it down he intended.

About the Author

C live was born in Sheffield, England, in 1960 and adopted the same year. One of two children, he grew up in a family where reading was encouraged, and he developed a penchant for the science fiction of Asimov, Simak, Dick, and Silverberg, among others. By the late seventies, an interest in aircraft had morphed into an attraction to the Cold War and espionage and, in particular, the works of Craig Thomas and Tom Clancy.

Trained as a chartered surveyor, Clive has worked in a number of different environments, from sales to IT through to his current role as strategy manager for a drug and alcohol action team in the Midlands, where he develops strategies for communities and individuals blighted by drugs and alcohol misuse. He has always been fascinated by people and what motivates them to do certain things and take specific decisions.

Writing started in 1992 as a means of relaxing and getting away from the stress and hassle of everyday work. He has written a number of short stories. He has published two novels previously: *Operation Thunderhead* and The Convert.

Clive lives in Birmingham with his partner. He has four children— Daniel; Laura; Lucy; and Emily.

Lightning Source UK Ltd.
Milton Keynes UK
UKHW041909130519
342583UK00001B/35/P